green 1

green *Eros*

DHIVAN
THOMAS
JONES

Apus Press · Cambridge
2008

First published in 2008
by Apus Press
25 Newmarket Rd
Cambridge CB5 8EG

Designed by Dhivan
Printed by Lulu.com

ISBN 978-0-9558-5540-5

Front cover photograph by Andrew Okey
Back cover author photograph by Advayasiddhi

The front cover figure is from Henri Breuil's drawing of 'The Sorcerer' cave painting in Trois Frères, Ariège, France (13,000 BCE)

May all herein find strength
against inconstancy and despite
and loss and pain
and all the bitterness of loving.
      – *The Romance of Tristan and Iseult* [1]

Tell me, what is it you plan to do
with your one wild and precious life?
      – *Mary Oliver* [2]

[1] from that of Beroul, as retold by Joseph Bédier, trans. Hilaire Belloc,
George Allen and Co.: London 1913, p.184.
[2] from 'The Summer Day' *House of Light*, Beacon Press: Boston 1990.

the flames

DO WE LIVE in order to love, or do we love for our lives?

I think that if you love like Tristan and Iseult – passionately, sacrificially, amorally, for your life – you end up sliding into love's dark night. But they'd drunk a love potion and didn't have a choice. Do any of us, really, when the moment comes? If you say 'no' to *eros*, are you really alive?

But people impale themselves on love's arrows. I knew a man, Barry, who set his heart on a woman, then bent his life to attain her. Two years later she left him, saying she couldn't stand his jealousy and possessiveness. He'd built his life around love but treated his lover like a thing he owned. Or take my cousin, Beth. She used to feel awful walking down Greyston High Street because she didn't have a man. My girlfriend Ros told me this, not Beth. Beth thought she must be missing out on the most important thing in life, but I know for a fact that most men would find her expectations scary. She's not so much like that now.

'Remember the teaching of Professor Bosch: falling in love is mostly an illusion!' my friend Tim says, when he gets the chance.

'You're one to talk,' I tell him.

'The point is,' he reminds me, 'to remember friendship.'

What he means is that if you value friendship – kind, steady, brotherly love – you stay warmed by love's sun; you get to keep your own life. But for most of us, there's a madness we crave a happy hour with. Everyone has to find their own way through love's stories. Where you come out might be the place you call home.

MY PARENTS HAD A FARM outside Silverthwaite. Nothing special, sheep and hay and in the summer, caravans. I'd always lived there; my dad had been there his whole life too. After leaving school, I worked the summer on the farm, which meant mowing the grass and emptying the bins in the camping fields. That was in 1984. I'd half moved out of the family home, into an empty farm worker's cottage that had just a water pipe into a clay basin. Since I was sixteen, I'd been turning it into my own place, taking my friends there and dreaming green dreams. I took my girlfriend, Kate, there, the summer we went out.

Then I moved to London in September, a volunteer with a city environmental project. The local council fixed me up with a flat. The lift to the eighth floor smelt of piss, and the concrete walls on the ground floor were paint sprayed. The flat had an old gas fire, brown lino tiles and cream paint. I shared it with Tim Curtis, a volunteer at a community mental health project. He came from Brixton.

On our second evening in the flat we went out for a drink, and when we got home he tried to seduce me. I didn't know what was going on; I thought it might be what city people were like, perhaps being less physically reserved. But when his hand touched my dick, I guessed the truth. Being bigger, I could hold him down and tickle him. We both laughed until we cried. He admitted that he'd never managed to seduce anyone. That evening got us through the barriers that men usually have, and we became good friends.

The next summer, we tagged along to a pop festival with Mark, one of the full-timers at the project, who drove over with his partner, Carol. They were veterans of the festival scene, while Tim and I were aspirants. We pitched our tents in the throng, more leaves on the wood floor. On the Saturday night, after Aswad had played their set and while the laser show laced the buxom Somerset sky, we sat around a campfire, passing joints.

Carbon dioxide, locked up in organic molecules in the ripple of wood, then burning in the oxygen rush, released again; a chemical reaction like a living thing, possessed. On the other side of the fire, Carol sat cross-legged, wearing torn jeans and a hand-knitted woollen jumper. She was talking to a woman with red hair that tumbled out and everywhere. She wore patched purple dungarees and many-coloured boots. There was a sort of festival dress-sense that I longed to acquire. I had no fashion but my thick, three-year-long black hair.

Through the flames blistering from pine off-cuts, I glanced at the redhead. Her face and arms were pale and full.

'Hi,' she said. Flecked blue eyes, freckled face. She came near. 'I'm Renata. Do you want me to put a braid in your hair?'

'All right,' I said. The tapestry of the world was bright and fresh, the weave still loose and open.

'What's your name?' she said.

'Roger,' I said, the name I went by then. 'I like your hair.'

She wound coloured threads into my hair and talked. Her voice had a gay, fruity steadiness, with a distant Dublin lilt. At three in the morning, we daubed each other's faces with poster paints, and under the touch of her fingers I felt a stirring of desire. We kissed next to the embers in the salmon dawn.

It was two years since I'd spent the summer with my first girlfriend. I did not suspect guile in the workings of desire, and simply opened the door of my heart as to a summer's day. I spent the rest of the festival with her, and the next weekend we met at her shared flat in Chalk Farm. She was twenty-five. She worked as a temp, but her love was music; she composed and recorded using keyboards and technology, and we listened to her fragmentary explorations lying on the floor. The next weekend she came round to Tim's and my flat. I cooked; she was full of impressive ideas.

A week later we dressed up and went out clubbing. I felt nervously cool; she told me to feel like we were in disguise, a pact of intelligence in the crazy night. We met friends of hers; we danced; the night was hot. In the neon exhaustion of three AM, Renata whispered, 'Come home.' I gave myself to spinning together, to the plunge into love, like my first easy, country passion.

She pulled me into her life like a hooked fish. We went dancing, we stayed at home, always what she wanted. I was so young. I saw a lot of her but lost the sense of being centred in my own natural self. We'd listen to her music, then we'd have sex, her limbs shaking as she had big orgasms. She'd lie motionless for minutes, listening to her body's blissful reverberations. We'd spend Sunday afternoons walking in London parks. From the hideout of irony, we looked at people, families, strangers, telling their stories for them as if we were original and elect. For weeks I had no words to say I was unhappy. Then one night some words came, pushed out by a man in my belly.

'You're using me.'

She was running her hands over my white, long chest. She stopped and looked up, shocked.

'Well, if that's how you feel –' She moved away, then lay down on her side, her back to me. The browny-pink freckles across the flesh of her shoulders were suddenly strange. A coldness in her voice sent a shudder through me. I was naked and unprotected. There was silence for minutes as I lay on my back. The feeling in the room was horrible, sick and green. What had I done? I reached across the bed.

'I mean, we don't talk –' I wanted to say 'about sex,' about the way it was a hole into which we threw all of our feelings and fears. But I felt afraid to say anything, and started stroking her side. That night I dreamt I was David Attenborough, sitting among the gorillas as they groomed each other. I told Tim what I felt.

'Get out of it, mate, dump her,' he said, but I didn't know how.

I thought I loved Renata's creativity, the intensity that she worked so hard to express. She'd spend days locked away, or so she said. One day there was a postcard half-hidden on her desk, a reproduction of a Vermeer, just the front of a house. *Ms Renata Twomey. Dear Renata, you'll remember this one I'm sure. Will you come with me again next week? Love, Gerald.* Renata snatched the card from me.

'How dare you read my private mail!'

3

I felt embarrassed. 'I'm sorry. I just wanted to know who the artist was. Who's Gerald?'

'It doesn't matter who Gerald is.'

'Why not?'

She threw her hands in the air, turned and stomped around the room. The story came out gradually, between fits of rage. A man she'd been seeing for years, married, with children. He took her on his business trips to Europe; they stayed in hotels and visited art galleries. She loved him, or had done, but he wouldn't commit. She had thought it was over, but then the postcard had arrived. She didn't mean to hurt me. I went home at a loss.

She rang up next day. She had thought about it and wanted to stay with me. She would finish with Gerald; it was a dead end anyway. I was pleased. I went over and we had a mature evening together, though our lovemaking had a quality of mournful sensitivity. But a few days later I got a postcard from Barcelona.

It wasn't the dishonesty that hurt, so much as the false reconciliation. That was evil.

Bleak, silent days passed, as summer wore itself out. Tim cheered me up with lasagne and psychiatric tales.

A MONTH LATER she rang up.

I couldn't really concentrate on what she said, but we managed to arrange to meet in Covent Garden. It was late September, and quick, grey clouds skimmed over streets mottled with puddles. We found a small café and sat on plastic chairs outside. She looked much the same, but wore a duffel coat and had her hair tied back. I was glad to see her, but wondered what 'being in love' had meant. She told me about her music and I said I was moving to Devon. We spent an hour together; then I felt glad to say goodbye. Innocence is easily lost and never regained; I wondered when she had lost hers. I could see she was a self-enclosed and rigid feat of will; a calculus of needs and damaged instruments. We didn't stay in touch.

Albion Cottage

LIFE IN THE CITY is mostly in the mind. You don't need to know where you are on the earth, because you only have to be able to read the signs. I wanted to leave London once my year at the project was up. I heard an old spirit calling, an animal presence that broke through and ran off into the light. The people at the project gave me a tent. Tim saw me off from Paddington. We hugged under the sooty arches, small sparks of life; then I swung my rucksack up and boarded the train. West London rolled by in wet autumn light. The light broadened; the green brightened; the train headed towards Devon. I had never been so far south. Around a bend after Exeter, the sea suddenly lapped up against the track, frothing grey waves, and then we were plunged in and out of tunnels in the red shale cliffs; I felt I was cleansed of the last bits of London grime. Ten minutes later the train eased into the station at Totnes.

As I walked up the hill into the town, my nerve began to fail. Grey clouds spat bits of rain through cool air, shaking the leaves on the trees, and my belly clenched. At the festival I'd met some friends of Mark's, and they'd told me that Totnes had a good alternative scene. They'd said, come and stay sometime. So I'd come, free as a bird, letting destiny guide me along my life's path. But in Totnes, walking up that hill, the elation of freedom turned into a rat's cellar of worry, and when there was no one at Mark's friends' house, I felt horribly alone.

It was a Saturday afternoon in the small town. I walked among people, feeling separated from them by my lack of somewhere to go home to. I looked around the Norman castle that dominates the town. From the battlements I saw rooftops, snapshot between the ancient crenelations, spread out within medieval walls, and past them the wider sprawl of the modern town. Beyond that were the surrounding hills and, in the distance, Dartmoor. The brown, yellow and green patchwork fields were part of a rolling, historical landscape, in which the human presence was an interwoven sharing, not like London's massively unnatural street map. My belly-clench broke open as I felt the relief of being back in a landscape. I was young and free, and I had my own tent; I could live where I pleased.

I strode back down into town with a smile. I was a wanderer, an explorer, a tramp. I didn't care if Bill and Sarah weren't at home. But they were, and seemed happy to see me again. There was an awkward moment when I told them I wasn't just visiting, that I'd left London for good. Bill was so laid back he just said, cool, stay as long as you like; but Sarah looked alarmed. She needn't have worried. On the Monday following, I found myself a room through an advert in a local wholefoods shop, where I got a part-time job, packing muesli and unloading the vans. Within a week I felt at home.

I barely spoke to Bill and Sarah again; they moved down to Plymouth once she got a teaching job. I moved in with a woman called Jude and her daughter, Ragweed; she may have had another name, but I never heard what it was. Jude lived in a clutter of potted herbs, coloured pencils, dirty mugs and rucked rugs, but amidst the shambles of the house she taught me to bake bread, to knit and sew, and I helped on her allotment, planting leeks and digging over the potato beds.

The animal presence burrowed and roamed, and I followed. I took evening classes in organic gardening, and read books on smallholding and self-sufficiency. Pictures of homes with goats and solar panels slaked a thirst in me, stoked a vision that blazed into a fire. I was deciding who I was and what kind of life to make.

At the winter solstice, there was a ceilidh in a church hall. Dancing in the circle, long-limbed, in dungarees, I wondered who I would befriend. I found myself sitting next to a girl I recognised from the wholefoods shop. We leant back against the wall on adjoining old chairs, sweating deliciously in mid-winter.

'Do you want a swig?' I asked her, offering my can of lemonade.

'Ta,' she said, reaching for it.

A flame swayed slightly, on a candle stuck in a green wine bottle. The can had left a circle of cool water on the table, and she placed it down carefully in the same place.

We sat out a square dance. She looked away from me towards the scratch ceilidh band, who were all long hair and concentration. She was wearing a long, gathered cotton skirt and an old white shirt without a collar. She turned and caught me looking at her. She smiled, her long chin full of beaming.

'What's your name?' I asked, laughing.

'People still call me Goose,' she said, her green eyes fresh, brows and lashes thin and pale. 'But my name's Rosaline, and you can call me Ros.'

'Well, Ros, I'm Roger,' I said, and we shook hands. Her long straight hair was tied back; a girlishness hung about her, in her soft, open face and the way she swung her feet as she leant against the wall. She was pale, but not in a fragile way; she looked like a Viking.

'It's my eyes,' she said; 'my dad said they were like gooseberries, so I got called Goose. Where do you come from, then?'

We talked so naturally that it seemed normal to share another can of pop. We partnered for the next dance, and her tall, strong body moved like an ash tree in wind, her hair swinging as she span. I danced better near her.

She worked at her father's nursery, not far out of town. She was local, born and bred, a couple of months older than me. She had recently moved out of her parents' house to live with friends in town, and cycled the couple of miles to work each day. I wanted to visit the nursery, and she offered to show me round. We struck up an easy friendship, and found we shared a vision of how we'd like to live. I met her dad, Mr Trevelyan; he had a big heart, a lined face and tough hands you'd feel safe in. He was at home on his land like Tom Bombadil, an ancient presence on the earth.

IN A LIBRARY BOOK, I found out about plant succession: cleared land left to revert is first colonised by grasses, then shrubs, then trees, and if left will develop into the climax community: deciduous woodland in temperate England. Ten thousand years ago, at the end of the ice age, behind the dripping snouts of retreating glaciers, most of England had been a waste of gravelly moraine, milky-cold streams and broken rocks. Then had come tundra: heather, moss and small flowers, scraping a living in the short summers and rocky soil. Then scrub birch and juniper came to pioneer the wildwood creeping back. After the pioneers came rowan, willow and pine, trees that still live high in the mountains. The richness of the deciduous forests gradually appeared: lime, oak, hazel, alder and elm.

Birch is short lived, its light tresses of leaves leaning over the ferns of the hills and flashing in the sunny breeze. Rowan has the solitude of the hills, rich autumn colours of leaves and berries, its bark that peculiar grey-blue. Juniper is a pioneer on the moss-clad scree. I loved the sense of the wind in its thorns, the way it clutched at the sun and defended its land. I changed my name to Juniper. Of course, my mother still calls me Roger, but everyone else soon took to my new earth-name; and for all the strangeness of the change, the name stuck and became something I believed in.

ROS AND I would hug when we met, and I'd massage her feet and finely curved ankles. I liked her but was in no rush to get into anything. In the summer we decided to go camping one weekend. In our sleeping bags on the first night, in the wilderness of a grassy hollow on the moor, we wrestled until she lay panting on top of me. With her face so close, I could feel the heat of her breath. I had a sinking feeling in my stomach at the thought of sex, as if I'd gorged on rotten fruit with Renata. She sensed my reluctance, rubbed her nose on mine, and rolled off.

She lay sideways close by and looked at me. She slowly placed her hand on my face and cupped my ear, stroked my cheek.

'I like you,' she said. 'I keep thinking we're going to get together, you know; but we don't go past a certain point.'

'No,' I said, laughing, not looking at her.

'Do you actually *want* a girlfriend?'

'Girlfriend,' I said, suddenly aware of the assumptions behind an apparently simple idea, how conventional they all are.

'You make "girlfriend" sound like *dog shit*,' she said.

'Something like that,' I said.

'Why's that?' she asked, leaning up on her elbow, pulling impatiently at my ear.

I told her what had happened with Renata. It poured out, as if Ros were conducting it away. I lay on my back, looking out the open tent-door at the clear night. Ros kept her arm around me. It felt I'd got something off my chest.

'Why didn't you tell me about her before?'

'Didn't want to think about it.'

'So you're *scared* of having a girlfriend,' she said. 'Well, don't worry. I like you as a friend.' I felt relieved. I turned my head and kissed my friend, on her wide, harmless Devonian lips.

Next day we walked in sunshine, dipping down to a river that plunged to a granite pool. We raced each other to strip to underwear and plunge into the rocky, chill water.

'I love Devon,' she shouted, splashing. 'I love living near the moors.' We climbed out of the pool and sat, towel-wrapped in sunshine, warming up. She reached for my hand, and a painful burning feeling rose through me. We stood, and I shook, looking at her smooth, young body, her full breasts, all her curves. She looked at the knotty angles of my young man's form, my bony shoulders and chest, my thicker arms. Still slightly shivering, we made love in the sun beneath a sycamore tree, laughing. Then she lay and basked in womanly ease, her hands behind her head, plucking spears of grass, while I leapt, naked, from high rocks into the pool.

We woke up late next day. Ros's tangled head rested on her crumpled clothes. I smiled, soft with physical affection. Outside, the smooth undersides of grey clouds moved slowly to the east. I looked north, over the rolling moorland, hill after hill. The clouds hung low, as if listening for some secret ancient message, then drifted on. I got up and lit the camping stove to heat water. Naked, I set off at a run towards sheep grazing in the hollow. They panicked as I approached. As soon as

I stopped chasing they returned to their chomping, looking sideways at me. I walked back panting to the tent. The kettle was boiling. Ros was watching me without stirring.

'Tea,' I said, passing her a steaming orange plastic mug.

'Mmm.' She was unwilling yet to uncurl into the day.

I rolled a cigarette slowly, a habit I'd acquired living with Jude. I sat on a granite outcrop, watching the quiet breeze in the grass, drinking tea from a blue mug, with Ros still watching. That day we walked to a summit and looked out across the moors. The clouds had blown off, and the landscape shone with a spacious beauty. Back in Totnes we became a couple, staying at my place with Jude and Ragweed, or at the house she shared with three other girls. We settled into Totnes life like well-kneaded dough rising into plump loaves.

IN THE AUTUMN I took her to visit the family at the farm. My sister Erica Louise came home from nursing college for the weekend. I showed Ros my old cottage. It was still watertight, though the inside was more peeled and flaky than ever. She ran through the rooms in wide-eyed excitement. I caught up with her in the big bedroom, where an old mattress still lay on bare boards, and the pear tree rubbed its yellowing leaves on the glass.

'Is it really yours?' she called excitedly as she opened old doors, raising dust and breaking spiders' webs.

'I just used to use it, and they still call it mine.' Father had never quite got round to doing it up for rent. It would have cost a lot because there was so much to do.

She rushed back to me, grabbed my hands; her eyes were bright, her cheeks flushed.

'Juniper, we could live here! We could convert it from scratch, put in passive solar heating for water, a wind-powered generator; we could stay off-grid, with composting toilets, water-recycling; and look out there!' – her gaze rushed out the back window – 'Room for a vegetable garden right next to the back door!'

I had been plodding on steadily on my allotment in Devon, supposing that Totnes was my new home. Ros's excitement broke in on me like a wave and carried me along. I asked my father what he thought of Ros and me living in the cottage and renovating it according to radical environmental principles.

'fine with me,' he said. 'Plenty of work for you both to do on the farm as well, if you need jobs. Your mother would love to have you around a bit more too.'

'We'd need more land than the little garden out the back.'

'How about the orchard that adjoins the place? Hardly been used since you kids grew up. Farming these days is all machines and subsidies. Have the corner of the pasture there, too, if you like – better than renting it out to some other bugger to stick his sheep on.'

I told Ros what he'd said, and at tea she rushed up and kissed him, which he liked. Ros and I spent the rest of our stay talking over ideas for the cottage, whilst walking the footpaths that wound through the local meadows and woods. A clear day slowed autumn to a gallery of still colours and small, sweet odours of decay. The air was sharper, leaner, cooler than Devon, and I appreciated my home country more for living away. Before leaving, we crunched through dried pear leaves to the cottage door, walked round in silence, and then stood on the back step. Beyond the garden were meadows, sloping down on one side to the sands of the Bay. The colours of low tide on the wide expanse sang with the cries of oystercatchers and redshanks.

'Albion Cottage,' I said. 'That's what its name should be.'

'Sounds nice.'

In my mind, Albion was England before industrial decrepitude, and maybe also the future, when the long dream of glory had finally faded away.

'Do you really want to leave Devon, your family, all your friends, to live here?'

'You know, it feels like a *destiny* or something. Part of me doesn't want to leave Devon at all; it's my home, everything I know. But there's something here I *want*.'

I smiled. This was a new side of Ros, something more ambitious than a local girl. I wasn't at all sure about moving back home.

'But if we come here, that's making a big commitment to each other, isn't it? Do you want that?'

'I hadn't really thought of it. I just think of you and me together now.' She laughed.

'Fancy it?'

'I suppose I do,' I said. I hadn't really thought of it either. 'I feel a bit afraid,' I said.

'So do I,' she said. We looked into the old kitchen's dusty dark, into our future.

love without illusions

WE MOVED UP TO SILVERTHWAITE in the spring of 1987. Ros became a woman of considerable focus and purpose. She made friends with my cousin Beth, and worked with mother serving cream teas in the summer. I went back to helping my father, and when we could Ros and I worked on Albion Cottage. One weekend in late summer Tim came up from London. He was halfway through training as a psychiatric nurse.

Our lifestyle was considerably less convenient than his. He was appalled by the outdoor composting loo, with its pit under the raised seat and its decomposing smell; but he loved digging up new potatoes, like finding treasures in the ground. We'd planted just potatoes, courgettes and beans that first season, to start off the vegetable garden where there had been tall grass and docks. One evening we sat around a fire in the lounge. It wasn't cold, which was as well because the old fireplace was useless.

'Juniper, something I like,' said Tim, 'is that the only thing about you that has changed in three years is your name. You're your own man. I mean, you're much the same here, among the sheep, as you were in London with all those trendies we used to hang out with.'

I smiled. Tim could be very sincere. I poured elderflower wine into three glasses. It was rough but drinkable. We toasted basic country life.

'Who was that girl you went out with?' Tim went on, with a smile. 'The one who got you dressed up in leather and took you out clubbing? You wore make-up as I recall.'

'Leather!' exclaimed Ros. 'You never told me about that.'

'It was Renata's idea.'

'You seemed pretty keen about it yourself at the time,' said Tim.

'I must have been in love,' I said, ironically. Ros was looking with interest between us.

'Did he tell you about Renata?' Tim said to Ros. 'The older woman who messed him around?'

'Once, briefly,' said Ros. 'You know what he's like.'

'She wasn't his sort. I tried to tell him,' Tim added. 'Too complicated.'

'All right,' I said. 'I learned my lesson.' I lit the joint I had rolled some time before, made with our first small crop of homegrown grass.

'So, Juniper,' said Ros, passing the joint to Tim, 'you admit that you were in love with her?' I shrugged. 'But you won't say that you're in love with me. You don't much like talking about *love* at all.'

'That's because you've been hurt,' said Tim, blowing smoke up towards the yet-to-be-repainted ceiling. He gave me one of his psychotherapist looks, fingers bridged.

'Is that true?' asked Ros.

'So, what's falling in love?' I said. 'You think you've met someone who's fantastic and interesting and who thinks the same about you, but it turns out it was all in your mind. What a joke.'

'Maybe you went into it too naïvely with Renata,' said Tim, 'but that doesn't mean falling in love is always like that. I mean, isn't Ros just more your sort?'

'Ros is much more my sort, but I think the reason you fall in love with someone is because they are in some way or other opposite to you. Isn't that why you fall in love with all those totally unsuitable guys?'

'That's a different issue. Anyway, it doesn't mean I won't find someone.'

'You're a hopeless romantic,' I said. 'Why not just find someone you get on with and stick with them? That's what Ros and I have done. If you base your life on falling in love, it can only be disastrous. Falling in love is like a walrus and a leopard trying to cook dinner together. It's a mess and doesn't taste good to either of them.'

'But that's because you've been hurt, mate!' said Tim. 'What do you think, Ros? Don't you want a bit of romance?'

'Not really,' she said. 'Of course, it's *natural* for men and women to get together and all that. But the kind of love that works has to be down to earth, not based on loads of incompatible expectations.' She smiled at me.

'Don't you think there's any use in falling in love, then?'

'Not for *women*. Men have these huge fantasies about the perfect woman, but women are much more practical. I love you,' she said to me, 'but I don't think you're my other half or anything.'

'Fair enough,' I said. 'But, Ros, does that mean you've never fallen in love? – I mean, let go into that passion that says this person is the best thing in the universe –'

'Well, of course not,' she said. 'That's silly. I'm not that unrealistic about men.'

'You just haven't met the right one yet,' said Tim, laughing.

'You can have him if you like,' said Ros.

'Yeah, all right,' said Tim, pulling on my arm.

'When I was at school,' said Ros, 'I used to get *soppy* about certain boys, you know, cute ones; but that was a kind of experiment that all the girls tried, a kind of play-acting of emotions so we'd know what it felt like when we met the real thing.' She paused, grinning. 'Only later, we discovered that boys weren't really all that interesting. They do their boy-things and they can't much talk about their feelings.' She paused, then, looking at me, added, 'They're good for *some* things though.'

I laughed. Tim danced about the room. Ros pushed me onto the floor, to make sure I knew she wasn't getting sentimental. We finished off the wine and rolled another joint. It was one of the happiest times of my life. Afterwards Tim sent me a letter and a book. He wrote:

I found this and thought it would interest you. It made me think that maybe you were right about love. Anyway, it was fantastic visiting you. We always talk about things that matter, and that's a lot of what friendship's about.

The book was *Love Without Illusions* by Professor Hans Bosch, and he'd put into different words what I'd been trying to say. Falling in love is a con trick pulled by nature to get people together to reproduce. It's not real. What you really need is a mature human love, based on respect and a sense of the other person as they are. That's what Ros and I had. Or so I thought.

FOCUSED AND PURPOSIVE, Ros in some ways was not much like me. Mature human love is a good idea, but the reality is that you don't always get along. One day, in the autumn of our first year at Albion Cottage, we were walking across meadows a mile away when we came across a row of dead moles hung on barbed wire. A steel barb was pushed through soft pink nostril flesh. We counted twelve. The farmer and his son were on the other side of the meadow; people I'd known all my life, who from time to time had come round to talk of sheep and fences.

They wore cloth caps. The father held a shotgun in both hands at his hip while the younger man dug into the black, thin soil. They were digging out moles to stop them crossing into their meadows. But Ros asked them what *the hell* they were doing. The men became agitated and told her to leave off. I said nothing. For days after, she was furious with me for not backing her up. I wasn't that I didn't care; I'd gone back in the evening and unhooked the moles. But at the time I hadn't thought it worthwhile to argue with the farmers; they were at war with the pasture-ruiners, and that was the world they knew. Ros couldn't make me out at all.

And then her dad died. He'd been reaching up to pick a cucumber and had a massive heart attack. Ros spent a lot of time in Devon, and when she came back she was crabby and small. I did my best to look after her, but it wasn't much fun being around all day. In the end I applied to study Environmental Science at Greyston University.

'What's the *point* of that?' said my grumpy girlfriend.

'I want to get the bigger picture on things. And I'll get a student grant. That's better than signing on for income support.'

We had a good talk about it. It turned out that she was resentful about the idea of my doing a degree, because it would have meant her doing more work about the house. We talked some more and she said she'd like to take up pottery. So before I even started my course, she was doing courses over in Kendal, and we were soon eating off her wobbly plates.

When eventually I started my first year, I studied philosophy as well as the natural environment. But then my friendship with Jim Fletcher really pissed Ros off. I'd met Jim in Professor Rampton's philosophical ethics class. Jim used to argue with everything in his Yorkshire-gravy voice, and one day we met for coffee after class. He was in his late twenties, a working lad from Leeds, who'd climbed out of life as a garage mechanic to study. He had the cynicism of someone who'd survived on his wits, but the determination of someone who'd read Plato in his breaks. I went out to the pub with him one evening, and got back home about six hours late. Ros wasn't happy.

Two weeks later, I met Jim again after our class.

'How's about going out for a drink tonight?'

'I ought to get back to see my girlfriend,' I said.

'And what's the worst that could happen if you didn't?' he said. 'You know I don't go along with utilitarian thinking, but I reckon there'd be more happiness in the world if you and I drank a beer or two.'

I rolled into Albion Cottage some hours later.

'Were you out with Jim again?' said Ros.

'Yeah,' I said. 'What's wrong with that?'

'I was *worried*, that's what. I thought you'd be home around four, like you said, and now it's ten.'

'I'm sorry,' I said, meaning, never mind.

'That's not good enough. You should have known I'd worry. That's what I'm like.'

'What's the point?' I said. 'I should be able to stay out if I want.'

'Like I don't *exist*,' she said.

The following weekend we were out walking through an autumn mist that kept the leaves on the trees, despite the rot and failing sun.

'I'm not trying to control you or stop you doing what you want,' she said. 'We're both doing our own things but I still want to feel like we're *sharing* our lives; I want you to trust me to tell me what you do.'

I had to admit there was some logic in this.

'Phew,' she said. We squeezed through a gap in a limestone wall and entered a wood.

'But it's like —' I said, the words sticking as if they were locked in a tree. 'Like, who am I, if you know everything about me?'

'I don't want to know *everything* about you, just when you're going to stay out late.'

'But it's like you're my mother or something.' We'd been crunching through horse chestnut leaves curled on the path, but we stopped walking and stood facing each other. She stretched up to a hazel bough leaning over us and shook it. A sudden cold rain drenched my head and shoulders.

'I am not your mother,' she said. I laughed. She put her hands on my chest. 'I am not your mother!' She pushed me until my back was against a beech tree.

'Get off,' I said.

'You're just scared,' she said.

'What do you mean?'

'Scared of women.'

'Don't be stupid.'

'You don't *know* you're scared. But it's why you hide your feelings so much.' She was pushing my head back into the tree trunk, which hurt.

'Get off,' I said. She pushed harder. I pushed her away. She picked up a piece of rotting wood from the wood-floor and threw it at me.

'What are you doing?' I said, brushing the soft white pulp from my coat.

'I don't know. What are you doing?' She threw more wood at me, harder this time. Suddenly a livid white anger spread through my chest. I picked up a thick length of rotting beech and swung it hard against the tree. It snapped, and pieces flew through the air, some towards Ros, who turned away, flinching.

'OK, you're not my mother,' I said.

'So tell me what you *feel!*' she shouted.

'Pissed off!' I said, and walked away.

home life

ROS WALKED INTO MY ROOM at Albion cottage, flushed from her bike ride from Silverthwaite station. It was late September 1991, and outside my open window the light was fading over the bay. The tide was in and the grey water seemed full of life, crabs and mussels wrestling over the sands.

'Juniper, we need to talk,' she said.

Ros had been in Greyston visiting Beth. She sat down on my bed with her hands between her knees. That was her something's-up gesture: the first time I'd noticed it was when we'd just set up the wind turbine in the corner of the garden, hooked into twenty batteries in the old outside loo, and she'd come into the kitchen to say she'd broken it. But it was all right; she'd only blown a fuse.

'I'm pregnant.'

We'd talked about babies, years before, after Ros's dad had died. But we hadn't since, so her words left me groping for sense.

'But −'

'But we haven't had sex for about two *years*, were you going to say?'

'No, I remember it, at your mum's place; but nothing went wrong −'

'Oh you actually *remember*, then?'

'How pregnant are you? I mean −'

'Well it couldn't be less than a month then, could it, because that's when we were down in Plymouth.'

'So how did you find out? Doesn't it take longer to know?'

Ros sighed. She was staring at me, her squeezed mouth puckered at the corners. She had the knack of very fierce disapproving stares.

'I'm not pregnant really. I just wanted to make a point.'

My heart sank. Ros was pissed off again. We'd spent the last year arguing. From outside the window came the hooting of a tawny owl. We sat listening, but trapped in the tension between us.

'Well, that's good, because I wasn't thrilled by the idea of a baby,' I said.

'Were you not?' she said, stony faced. My thoughts skidded off: it occurred to me that Ros had been living in Lancashire for four and a half years, and had taken on some local speech characteristics, like ending a question with 'not.' Back in Devon, she would have said 'Weren't you?'

'If there's a problem, let's talk about it. But that was a stupid way to make a point, especially when I don't even know what the point is supposed to be.'

She started to cry. This was how it went. I sat by her on the bed and put my arm around her. She leant into me.

'Sorry,' she said, through tears. 'I'm being horrible.'

'Something must have happened,' I said.

'Beth's pregnant. She found out today.'

'So you don't want to be left out!'

'Oh, *don't*, Juniper,' Ros said. 'At least she's got a boyfriend who *wants* to have sex.' Beth lived in Greyston, and a guy called Peter had moved in with her about six months before. I'd gone off sex with Ros; or at least, I wasn't always interested. I thought maybe that was what happened if you lived together for five years. You get bored.

'Let's go down and talk by the fire,' I said. We usually had our serious conversations sitting by the fire.

We sat in two old armchairs that Ros had spotted in a skip in Silverthwaite. I'd brought them home with my father's tractor and trailer. They were pulled in around a cast-iron stove with windows now lit by a kindling-fire, a present from my parents the Christmas after we moved in. I poured some home-made rhubarb wine into stoneware mugs and passed one over to Ros.

'Ta,' she said. 'I'm *glad* we can sit and talk like this.'

'Do you remember the Recycled Paper Issue?'

Ros laughed. 'You were on such shaky ground.' She'd completely lost her cool because I'd bought a thick pad of paper to write my lecture notes on. I'd just started at Greyston University, nearly two years before. She'd come up to my room, brandishing sheets of paper still blank on one side, and accusing me of wastage by buying more. It wasn't the end of the Amazon Rain Forest, I'd retorted, but she hadn't liked that and had stomped out in a huff; and it hadn't stopped there.

'And then the Tea Leaves Crisis?'

'Oh, stop it,' she said, wincing. She'd shouted at me for dumping used tea leaves on the compost heap, because she said they made it go anaerobic and turn to stinking slime.

'So, do you want to start having babies?' I said.

'Well, yes, but not right away. It's not that really.'

'But there's a problem, right?'

'It's – Juniper, I want to have babies *sometime*, but we don't seem to be getting on so well. I mean, there's not much sex anymore.'

'Right,' I said. My heart sank. It was a problem, I knew.

'Do *you* think there's a problem?'

'I thought it was mutual.'

'Well, I can't *force* you, can I?'

'No, I didn't mean that –'

'Juniper, are you still interested in *me*, you know, the whole thing we've got here?'

'Yes, of course,' I said.

'Are you seeing someone else, some student?'

'You can't be serious,' I said. 'Absolutely not; put it out of your mind.'

'But you're much more interested in your *books* than in me. It's more and more like that. I hate it; something's changed.'

'It so happens that, yes, I am very interested in my studies.'

'You've got your head so far into it all that you can't even see what's happening,' she broke out. 'You're *obsessed* with it.'

'That's because I'm about to start my final year and I have a lot of work to do.'

'See? You won't even admit what's happened. Well, I don't know if I can *stand* another year of this; I *hate* it.'

'Are you serious? I mean, this year is going to be a lot of work.'

'But what about the Cottage? And getting an organic veg business going? And –' she hesitated a little; 'I need to know if you want to have children with me *sometime*.'

All this stung. Ignoring the babies thing, she was accusing me of forgetting the things we'd based our lives together on.

'I've got one more year to do, that's all. Let's not go into all this again, Ros. You're just jealous of –'

'I am not *jealous*,' she shouted. 'Why should I be jealous of those stinky male assholes you spend your time staring into?'

'Just calm down, will you? After –'

'I don't want to know about after,' she retorted. 'That's just talk.'

'No it's not –' I started, but the phone rang out in the kitchen, and Ros got up to answer it. I heard short low tones, no conversation. I stared into the fire, my heart jangling. Ros stood in the door.

'It was Beth. Peter's left her. He took his stuff away in his car and he's moved in with a girl he met at the pub.'

'Shit. How's Beth.'

'How do you think? I'm going back over. If I leave now I'll catch the eight-thirty train. I'll ring you in the morning.'

I sat by the fire, thinking, until the glow behind the glass doors dulled. The phone rang. It was Ros, saying she was at Beth's, and that she was sorry she'd left while we were in the middle of a talk. I sat and thought some more. When you first start living with someone, there's no way that you could ever predict how the two of you will settle into the gritty quality of particular resentments, like the dust patterns under the front door mat; no way you could foresee how you will both develop the slightly stupefying habits that keep you from noticing what you've both become. And then there comes a moment when those habits don't suffice, when the resentments come into the light.

AT THE BEGINNING of October I made the fifteen-mile trip from Albion Cottage to Greyston University. It was a perfect autumn morning, with almost a frost, a mist along the meadows below the cottage, and the bay vague, half a mile away. I left home at eight-thirty, and the only sound was the rushing of my bike tyres over the tarmac of the slightly wet lane. Cows stood huddled by an old ash dripping its blackened keys; ivy flowers hung on along the dry stone wall that bordered woods full of the exhalations of decay. The wheels bumped over conkers and husks scattered on the road; the sun rose weakly through a cool, wet gauze. I locked my bike to the railings at the station and caught the train with schoolchildren and people in suits.

The two-carriage train rattled across salt marsh then through undulating meadowland. It was the first day of my final year. Environmental Science had been interesting, but hydrology and laboratories weren't what I'd been looking for, whereas the first-year philosophy that I'd taken for fun had become what made the daily journeys worthwhile. Through my second year, everything had fallen into place, ideas and books unfolding the big picture of life, like a spring meadow its thousands of flowers. The one cowpat in the field, however, was the fact that Professor Rampton, who'd suggested I try writing a dissertation, was going to be on sabbatical leave for most of my final year. She'd arranged that a member of the department I didn't know, Dr Paul Corbett, would supervise my work.

Towards eleven I was filling in forms in the departmental secretary's office, when a man walked in, moaning, oh God, oh God, and flicking through a sheaf of papers.

'Brenda,' he said. 'Do you know where the Professor's lecture notes are for the Theory of Mind course? She said she'd leave them for me, but they're not here. I'm teaching her course starting tomorrow.'

'No idea, Dr Corbett,' said Brenda. 'You could look in her room.'

'And – God – she's asked me to supervise a dissertation on the philosophy of love. Do you know this person? Juniper Johnson – is it some sort of new-age tree hugger?'

Brenda was glancing nervously towards me from behind her typewriter, but I didn't say anything. 'He's a young man,' she said. I took a look at Paul Corbett. He was smallish and lean, with a tight mouth but quite boyish eyes. He looked to be in his early thirties, yet sunk into academic middle age.

Wanker, I thought. He glanced at me, then hurried out of the office, leaving Brenda to smile weakly.

'Don't worry,' I said. 'I'll go and see him in his office.'

I knocked on Paul Corbett's door and leant into the room, but he was talking to someone else. She emerged two minutes later, swinging her black leather bag, a girl with amazingly avid eyes. I walked in, and introduced myself. He squirmed in his chair.

'Shit,' he said. 'Look, Mr Johnson – Juniper – I'm terribly sorry if I offended you; I didn't realise –'

'It doesn't matter,' I said. 'Juniper's a name I gave myself. I don't care what you think about it.'

'This isn't a good start, is it?' he said. 'Let me try and explain myself. I've just come back into the department after the break, and discovered that Professor Rampton had overlooked to mention you to me before she left.'

I didn't say anything.

'Or, to be perfectly clear, she overlooked to confirm the contents of a memo last July, which I failed to read, and –'

'OK, OK, never mind,' I said. 'Do you want to supervise my work or not?'

'Ha-ha-ha,' he stammered. 'What exactly are you interested in?'

'Have you heard of a book by Hans Bosch called *Love without Illusions?*'

'I've heard of it; I believe it's a work of popular psychology.'

'Well, the plan was to subject what Bosch says to some philosophical scrutiny. To see if it stands up. That kind of thing.'

'I see. A critical reading.'

'That's it. It's had a big effect on my life, and I want to take my thinking on it further. He has this idea of mature human love which isn't based on the illusions of romance, but I'm beginning to think that there are problems with it.'

Dr Corbett raised his eyebrows a little.

'I've brought you a copy, actually. I lend it to people.' I passed it over, but he didn't look at it.

'You really have taken it seriously,' he said. I nodded. 'Have you by any chance read Aristotle?'

'Only on scientific method.'

'It so happens that I'm engaged in some work on his ideas on friendship in *Nicomachean Ethics*. Why don't you read up, and then we'll have something to discuss. And you'll have what might become part of your critical angle on Professor Bosch.'

'Sounds good,' I said.

'Would you like to get in touch when you've read the Aristotle?'

'OK. And thanks. Shall I call you Dr Corbett?' I said.

'No; please call me Paul.' He stood and reached out his hand. I shook it and left. A truce.

at Lyndhurst

A COUPLE OF WEEKS AFTER the start of term, I met Barry Driscoll in town, one of the lecturers in the Environmental Science department. He was the one who'd first interviewed me and given me a place at university. Although I'd dropped ES, we'd stayed sort of mates. I was on my way to meet Jim, but had some time to spare.

'How are things, Barry?' I asked.

'Feel terrible, Juniper. Christine left, and now she won't even speak. I'm dying.' He looked washed out and miserable, his eyes dark.

What a victory for True Love it had been when young, bright, final-year student Christine had succumbed to Barry's intense and vocal longing. I heard about it all, blow by blow; I was such a polite listener. They had lived together for a year. When we'd gone out for end of year drinks, Barry had clung to, dripped and drooled over his precious piece of flesh. She was quite compliant in this constant canoodling: touching, holding on, even when talking to somebody else; from time to time turning to look into his eyes before they wetly, sweetly kissed. But it turned sour in the end; girls grow up and, once she'd finished her teacher training, she moved to Edinburgh to start a teaching job there.

We went to a café and I bought him a milky coffee.

'I did everything I could to make her happy,' he said.

'Maybe you did too much,' I suggested. 'Maybe she wanted more independence.' He looked down at the mahogany table top, with its flaking varnish. I looked at the walls, decorated with bulging tongues of plaster, painted off-white. A group of schoolchildren laughed on the other side of the room. Two old ladies shuffled through the glass door, wearing macs.

'Maybe,' he said. 'But why didn't she say? I could have been different. And why won't she talk to me now? I went all the way to Edinburgh, but she wouldn't let me in her flat.'

'Sounds like she didn't want you to visit. Maybe she needs some time to herself.'

'I'm going crazy without her,' he went on, still staring at the table. 'We did everything together. We were going to go to New Zealand next year, during my sabbatical. How will she manage without a washing machine?'

I didn't know what else to say. Barry was in a bad state. He went off to ring Christine's parents, to see if they knew why she wasn't speaking to him. Later, I discovered through Brenda, who was friends with Jane, the ES department secretary, that Barry had been ringing up Christine every half-hour or so, until she had to have her number changed.

I went to see Jim. He thought that though Paul Corbett was arrogant and uptight he wasn't half the prick Barry Driscoll seemed. Jim tended towards assessments of men like that. I told him about the sex and babies conversation with Ros. It had been preying on my mind.

'What do you expect?' he said, blowing a plume of smoke up and to the left. He was experimenting with French cigarettes. 'If you choose to live with a – *woman* – then it's a reasonable conclusion on her part that you are open to giving her children. Why else would you want to live with her?'

'Jim,' I replied, 'it's much more complex than that.'

'Is it?' he said rhetorically, his dirty-brown, close-set eyes bearing down upon me, 'or are you making it more complex? Perhaps you're indecisive, because a big commitment is required.'

'But she's not being herself, Jim.'

'Don't change the subject. Tell me, what do you want?' We sat in silence. Jim continued to stare down at me from amidst the rough mosses of hair around his face. We'd already been in the café for two hours, embroiled in disputation over whether coffee objectively had a taste, or whether taste was merely a subjective interpretation made by the mind. I suspected that we agreed, but that Jim didn't like the flaccidity of my arguments.

'I need to go home,' said Jim. 'Paul Corbett's coming round for dinner at eight. Why don't you come back and talk to me while I cook?' Jim saw Paul as his mentor and a friend.

We walked past the railway station to a large terraced house. Carved in an arc in the lintel above the door and picked out in orange paint was 'LYNDHURST'. Two ex-student mates of Jim's owned the place. A thin dog leapt up at us as we stepped through the door.

'Naught but a mangy pet,' Jim said. We walked along a bare hall.

Passing a door left ajar, I could see a man with a woman curled in his lap on an old settee: the other lodgers. The room swirled with smoke and they were watching TV.

'Dog,' the woman said in a very slightly raised voice, not moving.

The dog trotted back in and leapt onto the woman's legs.

'Mind the pipes.' Jim motioned to the floor. In the gloom were mounds of lead and rubble on bare boards. We went down steep, bare stairs to a basement kitchen lit by spotlights that left gaping, dusty shadows. One wall had all the plaster knocked off and heaped on the floor. The bare stones beneath were like sorry peepshow girls.

'Matt and Chris are in the habit of imbibing cannabis before embarking on ambitious and visionary building projects,' said Jim. 'Unfortunately, an evening's inspiration doesn't often take them past the destructive phase of work.'

'Leaving reconstruction for sobriety.' We laughed.

'Fancy a cup of tea?' Jim asked.

Jim began preparing a stew from vegetables and dried field beans. He was presently experimenting with a strictly local produce diet. Transporting food from far away was stupid and irrational, needlessly exacerbating greenhouse gas production and encouraging industrial farming. He'd got some of these ideas from me but had taken them all much further.

While he cooked, I told him about how things had been going between Ros and me. Since our disagreement, she and I hadn't spoken very much. She stayed overnight with Beth quite often, and when we did speak, it was mostly about Beth's situation and state. We'd had one fairly normal weekend together. Our friend Harry and my sister Erica Louise had come, and we'd gathered up apples from the orchard near the house. Then I made apple and blackberry jam, the big preserving pan bubbling burning liquids over the range. Harry would have liked to live as we did, but instead had a flat in Silverthwaite and delivered cleaning supplies for a firm in Kendal. Erica lived in Manchester, where she was nursing. Erica had helped me with the jam while Ros and Harry made a start on the pears. But when Harry went home and Erica left to stay with our parents at the farm, Ros went to bed, tired, while I read by the fire.

'And that's what happens; she goes to bed and I read by the fire. We used to talk.'

Jim shrugged. '*Women,*' he said. The phone rang at the top of the kitchen stairs. Jim answered it. The call was for me.

WHEN PAUL CORBETT descended to the kitchen underworld, he looked wide-eyed from his encounter with dog, rubble and house. Then he saw me, and panicked even as he was taking off his coat.

'Good evening, Paul,' I said, trying to put him at his ease.

'Mr Johnson,' he managed, and formally shook my hand. He sat down at a pine bench next to the table, with his coat at his side. Jim made a pot of tea. I sat opposite Paul, Jim at a chair at the end. Jim offered me his tobacco tin, and I rolled a thin cigarette with the fine-cut moist tan weed. It was less pungent than the French in the small space.

'We're in the midst of a crisis,' said Jim.

I explained to Paul what had happened. Ros had rung me because Beth had rung her in Silverthwaite, from her house in Greyston, in tears and very frightened. Peter had come round for the first time since he'd left three weeks before. She had opened the door, on the chain, and he had said he wanted to make sure she was all right, and could he come in and talk? She had thanked him for his concern but hadn't let him in. When she'd closed the door, he had attempted to open it, and had thus discovered that she'd changed the lock. He had lost his temper and began shouting abuse. He promised to return later to smash windows and break down the door.

It had come out since Peter had left Beth for the new girl that he had been violent before; he'd twice hit her and had often been in some dangerous rage. Previously, he'd always won her around again with promises and repentance, but since he'd walked out Beth felt much happier in herself. Now she was in a quandary. She was scared he'd come back, but also scared to ring the police, in case he would be provoked to some resentful anger. In the light of all this, Jim and I were discussing the concept of natural justice.

'When my mother was a girl in Yorkshire,' Jim said, 'a man stopped his bike as she was walking home from school. Come over and look at this, he said, so she went over, and he showed her his cock, all laid out along the saddle. Just stroke it, he said, so she did, then ran home to tell her dad what had happened. Now, this fellow was known in the village, so my granddad got together some of his local friends, and they went round to the pervert's house and beat him up. It wasn't that he was a violent man by temperament, not at all; but he was angered as a father.'

'But isn't that kind of thing a risky way to determine justice?' I said. 'Where would it end? Neighbourhood vigilante groups might have the right intentions, but what if they pick the wrong culprit or get carried away?'

'There is a story in my family,' said Paul, 'that my great-grandfather, who was a farmer in Gloucestershire, caught a gypsy scrumping apples from his orchard, so shot him out of the tree. Now, whether or not the story is apocryphal, I think it rightly appals us.'

'But in the case we're discussing, the police can't act because Peter hasn't actually done anything unlawful yet —'

'— while Beth is at home, feeling terrified.'

'We have,' concluded Paul, 'reached a perception of the limitation in the practical ability of our judicial executive to prevent dangerous incivility.'

'But also a perception of the need for some sort of non-violent intervention,' mused Jim.

'Though not of any unlawful acts,' I added.

'A man-to-man talk,' Jim continued, 'to let him know that Beth has family and friends who care.'

So, with a righteous swagger, we walked into town. Beth was relieved to see us, but unconvinced by our plan.

'But what if this bravado makes him want to come and take out his resentment on me?'

Jim assured Beth that we had no intention of rousing his anger by some show of macho courage.

The new girlfriend, skinny and young, opened the door at Peter's address. When I said I was a friend of his, she obligingly let us in. Peter was lounging in a frayed armchair, grasping a can, watching TV.

'Hello Peter,' I said. We'd met once or twice over the half-year.

'Hello mate,' he responded with icy cheerfulness.

'Sorry to call round unannounced, but I wanted to have a word. But first, let me introduce my friends, Jim and Paul.'

'Good evening,' said Paul. Jim nodded.

'What can I do for you then, mate?' Peter asked. I sat down on the edge of the plastic-covered sofa, beckoning Jim and Paul to do likewise.

'It's about Beth, Peter. You're frightening her.' Peter's gaze wandered stonily back to the TV.

'What's between Beth and me is nothing to do with you.' My heart was beating hard, and I had no idea what to say next. Jim leaned over and switched the TV off.

'Excuse me,' he said. I took a deep breath and continued.

'I mean it's wrong of you to go to her house and threaten her.'

'You are such a stupid prick, Juniper,' Peter began, his voice pinched and harsh. 'You don't know the first fucking thing about Beth and me, so just keep your big nose out of it.' I wanted to leave it there.

'I'm afraid,' Paul said, 'that my friend here is bound by familial association to keep his nose in it.'

'Get yourself and your fucking smart-arsed friends out of my house,' Peter said quietly, in a tone of casual disbelief.

'Not until you promise that you won't threaten Beth again.'

'A pregnant woman,' added Jim, 'needs support, not threats.'

'She's changed the fucking lock,' said Peter, to no one in particular. 'All I wanted was to see how she was. It's my baby, in't it?'

'We're not here to sort all that out,' I said. 'All we want is for you to promise that you'll leave Beth alone.'

'Or what?' Peter sneered, waving a hand in the air impatiently. There was a crisp, sweaty silence. Jim stood up in front of the TV and crossed his arms. He looked like a raving giant, his wild tangly curls silhouetted against the standard lamp in the corner. Paul rose jerkily and stood in the lounge door.

'You *bastards*,' Peter said.

'You're in the wrong, Peter, that's all,' I said. 'Now will you promise to leave Beth alone?'

'I only wanted to know how she was,' he pleaded to his beer can. 'And I lost my temper a bit.'

'I tell you what,' I said. The guy was not as tough as he'd seemed. A rough bargain might wrap things up. 'You promise that you'll leave Beth alone, and we won't visit again.'

'Yeah,' he said, absorbed inside himself as if looking around for something he'd lost, staring at the stained nylon carpet. 'Yeah, OK.'

'We're going now, then. All right?'

'Yeah, all right,' he said, vaguely. He looked around at Jim and Paul, then back at me, nodding. Jim switched the TV back on.

'See you then, mate,' he said to me at the door.

We walked quite slowly back to Beth's.

'Look,' I said, 'my hands are shaking,' holding them out.

'Excellently done,' said Jim.

'That'll teach him!' said Paul.

Beth was relieved to hear that Peter had promised not to come round.

'And if you need any help around the house,' Jim offered, 'you just need to ask.'

BACK AT LYNDHURST, we were too full of adrenalin to eat. I rang Ros, to tell her what had happened and to say I'd be late back. Jim made more tea and rolled a thick, hairy-ended spliff, which he smoked with a cowboy gusto.

I could see Paul looking at the tobacco tin, the spliff and the smoke, with disdain.

'No thanks, I don't smoke,' he said when Jim passed the joint to him. But I could see that he wasn't sure and, after I'd taken a puff, I passed it back to Paul.

'May I?' he asked Jim.

'Aye!'

Paul grimaced as he inhaled. He had small, well-formed hands that held onto the spliff and mug tightly. I'd been impressed by his courage.

We sat around the kitchen table in silence, slowly calming down.

'Beth seems a sensible lass,' said Jim, with bent brows. 'So why would she have got involved with such a little prick?' Paul and I looked at each other and laughed.

'Jim, it's more complex than that.'

'It can be the case,' said Paul, 'that one becomes involved with someone, but only later does one discover their particular failings. At which point, it is by no means straightforward to disentangle oneself.'

'Sounds daft,' said Jim. 'Are you talking from experience?'

Paul tightened his lips and shook his head. I took that to mean that he wasn't about to share his soul. Another silence.

'Now you're both here, I've a question,' said Jim. 'Why are we studying philosophy?' He liked to get through small talk to what mattered – to him. Sometimes it was relentless.

'You start. Why are *you* studying philosophy?' I asked.

'I wanted to be able to stand my ground.' Jim paused to inhale, hold and breathe out smoke towards the bare-beamed ceiling. 'Wanted to know what I thought and to be able to argue for it. But then, studying with you' – he nodded at Paul, who demurely nodded back – 'I realised that there was a whole tradition to learn, a *discipline* to master.'

'I refuted all the arguments in his first essay and gave him 48%,' said Paul.

'I was humiliated,' said Jim. 'How about you?'

'Curiosity led to interest led to fascination,' I said. 'I suppose I'm following my passion now. I don't really know where to or why.' Paul laughed.

'Why did you become a philosopher?' I asked him.

'Well,' said Paul, raising his shoulders, 'I suppose I could have been an historian, but –'

'No,' said Jim, dismissively. 'What inspired you to take up the love of wisdom – not the academic discipline.' Papery ash dropped onto Paul's navy blue woollen sweater, and he brushed it off and onto the bare concrete floor, then patted at the grey stains that remained till they were gone.

'You chaps,' said Paul, laughing, 'you chaps.' He looked at us, smiling, but Jim and I did not smile back. Paul smoothed his fine brown, balding hair across his head and pulled on his spliff. In silence, Jim poured him some more tea. The bubbling sound filled the closed space of the kitchen, drawing attention to the background hiss of the gas oven. It was warm amid the debris.

'Ten years ago,' he said eventually, shaking his head. 'I don't believe I've ever told anyone this. I was sitting on a bench near the Clifton suspension bridge in Bristol, in my first year, reading Spinoza for the first time. I was sitting in cold spring sunshine, looking up from time to time at the Avon Gorge, wild and wooded on the other side; all that grandeur in the middle of the city. Spinoza explained, as you would share your truth with a lover, how he had turned from the common world to the intellectual quest for perfection, and shivers ran through me. I felt I had found something I had been looking for. I read his *Ethics* like a novel over the next few days and fell in love with philosophy, with his vision of blessedness. It all seems a long time ago, now. The feelings are much rusted in the rain of the years; the gate of words grinding on useless hinges.'

Jim and I stared at Paul. He seemed to be in another world. He came around suddenly.

'Does that answer your question?' he asked Jim.

'Aye'.

'Useless hinges?' I asked.

'Sometimes my life seems bankrupt now,' said Paul, matter-of-factly. Then, reaching for the tobacco tin, he added, 'do you mind if I roll a cigarette?'

'Bankrupt,' I said. Paul looked at me uneasily.

'The feeling of getting older,' he said, in a superficial, bright tone. 'I reached thirty last summer.'

Jim served up the meal as Paul and I smoked and talked.

'What's in this?' asked Paul, spooning the stew down hungrily.

'Mainly Juniper's organic vegetables,' Jim replied. 'And the bread's his recipe too.'

'It all tastes inexplicably delicious,' Paul said, as if confronted with a philosophical conundrum.

'That's called being stoned,' I told him.

'Really?' he said, surprised and almost childishly delighted.

'I propose,' said Jim, after the meal, 'that we form a small men's group of philosophical friends, to re-imbue our studies with the original Greek spirit of philosophy.'

I smiled. Jim had a Principle of Male Association with which, as he put it, he opposed the false egalitarianism of university feminists.

'The ladies can go and do their sewing, I suppose?' said Paul, smiling.

'No,' said Jim, eyebrows knitted. 'I have nothing against women. But men do need good masculine company to sharpen their swords in.'

Paul seemed to take it as a joke and did not reply. He left at eleven, still smiling. I caught the last train back to Silverthwaite. Ros was already in bed.

'Well done, Juniper,' she said, half-asleep. 'Beth is grateful. Shows that you guys aren't completely up your bums.'

the men's weekend

TIM SENT ME A FLYER for a 'mythopoetic men's weekend.' The green sheet pictured a man's head with impressive antlers. To be led by Brendan Wildwood, mystic and shaman, and George Pelham, psychotherapist. Awakening the mature masculine. Ritual. I wasn't very interested, thinking it would be a lot of townies, dressing up. But then Jim saw the flyer.

'I've been reading a book on this,' he said. 'It's important; we should go.'

So, in mid-November, Jim and I took a train down to London, and to Tim's flat in Stepney. By now, Tim had qualified as a psychiatric nurse and was working in a community call-out team. Tim and Jim had not met before. Jim looked rough, with broad chest, hairy hands and belly pudging out. His heavy curls flopped around his bearded cheeks. Tim seemed urban and sophisticated in contrast, his dark hair cut down to a neat carpet, his body slim, handsome and healthy. I opened a bottle of two-year-old sloe gin after we had eaten together. Tim had become a very good cook.

Next morning, we took the Northern line to Clapham and found our way to a Unitarian church hall. A tape was playing: a middle-eastern male voice wailing up high, percussive instruments as dry as a desert, low drones and baritone flutes conjuring dusk among baked-mud houses. We hung around, strangers gathering, waiting for something to happen: Englishmen exquisitely ill at ease. Eventually, we gathered in a circle on red plastic chairs, and Brendan Wildwood introduced himself. He looked quite ordinary for a mystic and shaman, in jeans and woolly jumper in autumnal shades, though he sported an impressive black, slightly greying beard. Small, wiry George Pelham had bright, sky-blue eyes, but otherwise looked passably like a psychotherapist.

Around the circle we went, introducing ourselves. Some married men, some with children, needing a chance to reflect. Buddhists with Sanskrit names, who lived together in a men's community, interested in psychological integration. Professionals, students, artists and men of leisure. George and Brendan nodded inscrutably at everything.

So to the work: like sportsmen preparing for the big match we stretched, limbered and shook out. Wild men in training: Jim puffed, Tim pranced. Then we danced, and I untied my hair. We danced to taped native drumming, and Brendan said over the beat: give expression to how you're feeling right now. Small self-conscious groans and snarls came from various swaying men-shapes; but, after ten minutes and for no apparent reason at all, embarrassment and tension fell away, and the room filled with laughter, shouting, swinging, stamping, hooting, and men generally giving expression to how they felt. Outer garments were flung off, shoes removed, shirts untucked; we renounced the superficialities of garb, and a sense of fellowship welled and flowed, in sweat and rhythm, as we headed on into the unknown.

After lunch in a local pub, we sat back while George gave a talk on mature masculinity, a man's ability to access emotional strength while keeping his boundaries.

'This is all very well,' said the bank manager, 'but if I told my wife about all this, she'd go up the wall.'

A man who had been acting rather nervously through the morning laughed derisively, but George ignored him.

'I'd say that was her problem,' he said. 'This work is not for making women happy, but for enabling us as men to experience wholeness.'

'No, I think our friend has a point,' said another man. 'I mean, most of us have to be in relation to women, and it's been difficult enough for women to gain some sort of equality anyway.'

'Bollocks,' said the nervous guy, sneering.

'What's your problem?' said the questioner. 'I'm not interested in misogyny.'

The nervous guy looked over at George for support.

'This is an important area,' said George. 'Each of us has to consider it for himself.'

'You're not writing off the whole of feminism, are you?' said one of the students.

'Feminism!' said the nervous guy. 'What a load of crap.'

'I'm not interested in all this mature masculinity stuff if it means putting down women,' said the student. The nervous guy rolled his eyes.

'You're acting like an asshole,' said the student, and there were murmurs of assent round the room.

'Heh, let's not start attacking each other, eh?' broke in George. The nervous guy was staring at the student with his fists clenched. 'Look, Terry, if you want to hit something, use this.' He reached behind him for a large stuffed toy and threw it over. Terry caught it, then held it to his chest and rocked it. Now laughter went around the room. 'This is no time for laughing at someone,' said George. An itchy silence followed.

'So,' said Jim slowly, through narrowed eyes, to George, 'you owe us an account of how the mature male relates to women.'

George smiled. 'I'm not going to get bogged down in ideological discussion,' he said. 'We're here as men, to explore masculinity, that's all. You each have to work out for yourselves what you think.'

'But what if you're a raving woman-hater?' said the bank manager. 'I'm willing to listen to what you have to say, but you're not answering the question.'

'I think he's deliberately not answering the question,' said Jim.

'How do we as men relate to the other half of the human race?' asked the student. 'It's an important question.'

'Gentlemen, please,' said George. 'I assure you I'm no woman-hater. At least, my wife says I'm not.'

'So what do you tell her that you're doing, on weekends like these?' asked the bank manager.

'She doesn't particularly want to know,' said George. Brendan was smiling at this point, and making a gesture with his thumb, as if to say George was under it. 'As a matter of fact,' added George, with good grace, 'she thinks that what I'm doing is important work. She tells me that all her women friends agree that it would be a fine thing if men were more emotionally developed and mature.'

The discussion went on for the rest of the afternoon, leading into the theme of 'archetypes of mature masculinity'. Back at Tim's place that evening, Jim began hacking up the epistemological coherence of the theory of the archetypes. Tim retired to the kitchen to prepare 'a manly curry.'

'Have you read any of Jung's horrible neo-Kantian metaphysics?' Jim demanded.

'Jim,' I said; 'you're over-identified with the Warrior. Look.' After the day's workshop I had picked up a book from a table of books that George and Brendan had for sale. I had scanned it briefly on the journey home. I showed Jim a list of the qualities displayed by a man acting through the archetype of the warrior: analysis, incisiveness, determination, discipline, and the capacity to cut off from emotion. I had witnessed Jim argue with cold intensity, until his opponent buckled and fell, over the correct use of the semi-colon. He looked at the page to which I was pointing.

However, the warrior, cut off from the higher power that he should truly serve, becomes a cold and calculating machine interested only in his continuing victory. This dark or shadow form of the warrior is a terrible danger in these modern days in which traditional objects of reverence, such as king and country, and symbols of ultimate reality, such as God, are absent, or debased into mundane and impotent forms.

'What the fuck does it mean, "higher power"?' Jim mumbled, and then snatched the book from me to read on his own. I wandered into the kitchen to see if Tim needed a hand. Brendan and George had recommended we spend the evening quietly, considering whether there might be some ritual we'd like to carry out the next day. Ritual? 'Like making tea?' wondered Jim. He went outside to smoke, then retired to the floor of the lounge, behind a futon and beneath a silk painting of cranes flying past Mount Fuji. He was deep in thought. Tim and I quietly discussed the day's implications.

'I know I can organise psychiatric nurses,' he told me; 'sometimes even under stressful conditions, like when we get called out to someone who's had a breakdown in their home, and the family are panicking. I'm beginning to hold positions of authority, and I feel confident in making decisions that affect people's treatments. I know the textbooks, the drug parameters, the diagnostic indicators, inside out. I'm a successful, capable, professional human being. But can I get my love life together? I see a guy I like, someone completely unsuitable, I turn into a weak, passive idiot who's up for grabs, who gets used and thrown away. I get lost in all the giving and feeling of love, without having strong boundaries, that kind of strength.'

'So maybe you need to do a ritual that gets you in touch with that kind of maturity.'

Tim looked off into space, into a near, bright future. A voice floated over from near Mount Fuji.

'And you, Mr Johnson, need a bit more of the warrior and a bit less of the lover – your woman pulls your strings and you don't even realise it.' I laughed, shocked.

'What do you know?' Tim shouted back.

A muffled roar flew past the unruffled cranes, as if the volcano was coming back to life. Jim's craggy visage stared like a hot bear's over the plump beige of the futon.

'Sorry chaps,' he said. 'I didn't mean to sound offensive, but since you, Juniper, seem to have become the guru of mature masculinity, after nothing more than skimming a book on the underground, I wanted to test your mettle a little.'

'Sounds like something's got your goat.'

'This guy,' he said to Tim, 'has to let her know if he's going to be late home. He's under the thumb, I tell you. He comes to my house and then he gets on the phone. And it's not just because she's neurotic –'

'It's just politeness, you oaf,' I told him. 'If you lived with your girlfriend you'd get pissed off if she made a habit of coming in late without warning, having been out with her mates when you expected her home.'

'Sounds dumb to me,' he said.

'Maybe you're a man's man,' suggested Tim.

'Maybe that was a bad example,' Jim went on. 'Too much of my prejudice in it. But what I mean is, who's wearing the trousers? You're King and Queen in your own little kingdom, all very sweet and self-assured. Your hippie friends come by, and you're Ros-and-Juniper, a living eco-idealistic couple. It's not some bourgeois dungeon of a marriage, I'll grant you that; but sometimes I see you together, and I see Ros getting you to do exactly what she wants you to do; mending the gate, baking the bread; and I think, who's in charge here? I worry about you. You're soft, man, soft.'

'You've never said this before,' I said.

'Well, like you said, you got my goat.'

'What do you think, Tim?' I asked.

'I'm not the guy to ask,' shrugged Tim.

NEXT MORNING, BACK IN CLAPHAM, we had some ridiculous fun, evoking qualities of the mature masculine through gesture and mime. At lunchtime, George invited us to take ourselves off alone, to consider if there was any ritual we might like to carry out in a supportive, safe gathering of men.

When I came back at two, after a walk in a local park, a man wearing the skin of a wolf greeted me at the hall door. Green eyes peered from a shaggy head resting on Brendan's, and claws dangled over his shoulders and down his back. Around him were wrapped pieces of velvet, canvas, leather and wool, in many colours and patterns; an anarchist morris man, he brandished a staff with a carved skull mounted at its head. The staff jangled, glittering with dull brass. He stood across the door with a fierce gaze and inquisitioned me.

'Beyond this door is sacred space and the place of ritual. Do you wish to enter?'

'Well, yes,' I replied. Wolf-head continued to bar my way.

'Will you honour the sacred space and respectfully join the circle of men?' he intoned.

'Yes!' I said, more loudly. Brendan – or whatever he was called – slapped me on the shoulders with the back foot of a wolf, then let me past and into what had been the church hall. Before the door quite closed on its smooth spring, I could hear him ask the same questions, and Jim's voice roaring YES, YES, back.

The curtains were closed, the dimming light of a late autumn afternoon left to sulk outside in the wet car park. In the sacred space, the heavy smell of incense filled the air, billowing from a brass bowl in the centre of the room. Around it were fat candles with thick, smoky yellow tongues waving upwards like panting demons. In a circle around the flames were blankets and cushions; several men already sat there, lit dimly, as if in some ancient cave.

Jim sat heavily beside me. He had smeared mud across his forehead and down his cheeks, his eyes sparkling out of a darkened face. He didn't smile. Tim was on the other side of the circle, with a dark red blanket wrapped around him. He had a blue-glazed clay drum stood on its narrow end in front of him, his hands on the stretched skin. I looked around. There was an array of drums and percussive instruments on the floor below the curtained-off stage. On the narrow lip left revealed of the stage were bags, boxes and pieces of cloth: a pagan sacristy. I took a shaker and a small drum.

No words were spoken.

When the final man had entered and taken his place, the Brendan-creature came in, rattling and stamping. George, still wearing his neatly creased blue trousers and collared shirt, but grinning, lifted a brass bowl on a plump cushion in one hand and struck it hard with a padded mallet with the other. A low, soothing metallic bong grew and then subsided. In the peace of the bong's afterglow, Brendan slammed down his rattling staff and George struck the large drum that was by his side. Boom – rattle – boom – rattle; then George struck a beat on a smaller drum and looked up expectantly. Haltingly, a few of us began eking out some kind of beat. The rhythm strengthened until Brendan, who had been swaying more and more, seemed to fall into a walking trance, arms lifted in some invocation, then rattled and stamped around the circle three times, before swaying over to the stage and picking up a bag. Out of it he pulled a skull. He looked at it for a short while and then took it to George, who also contemplated it, felt it, weighed it in his hand. He then passed it to the man on his right, and so the skull made its way around the circle.

In my hands, it had the weight, the presence and the gravity of the brain that had once lived within it. It suggested the rest of a body, twelve stones of muscle and bone, the ropes of neck muscle holding in place the solid heaviness of what was in my hands – as it might once have lain in the lap of a lover, as Ros had liked to put her head in my lap as I sat on the carpet in front of the fire. I could imagine the hundred billion neurons, each hooked up to five thousand others, synapses sparking across the lit city, the complexity of awareness and thought, hidden in a cave of bone.

And here the cave was empty, and Ros's brain and my brain were fireworks in the earth's long night. The sparks of this one had soaked back into the earth. Here were all the details that this man's fingers would have known: the precise contours of the ridge along the crown, the curve of the forehead, the transition from the thin spars beside the eyes to the cheekbones. It was a large, imposing skull, a man's skull, with no signs of damage or injury. The skull was death, mortality, but also something more: in the circle, we had briefly gone beyond time. We were men together in a way men have gathered for millennia, over the whole earth, to meet as living bodies on the skin of the earth, and the man whose skull I held had been a man just as I was. The joins in the dome of bone wiggled like rivers on a plain seen from orbit, and we were gathered to bathe in that river of enduring life. The austerity of the naked skull reminded me of the luxury of my actuality, the patterns on my skull still, briefly, hidden by rich flesh. A skull is a synoptic, comprehensive, suggestive view of life, the satellite overview. I passed it on.

The shaman next brought a short sword in a brass and wooden scabbard, and this began its round, while the skull took its place in the centre of the circle. The sword, too, was real and strong. It glinted as it was pulled from its sheath, like a rough man's wink. It was not a ceremonial sword, but something old and worn. I felt the nicks along its tired edge. What shields, what rocks, what bones had this chipped? In what cause, in love or hate?

A stone passed around, an inert hunk of the earth's unthinkable prehistory, rounded in the sea's restless violence, weighty in the hand, pitted and marked with freckles of fossils. Then came a lingam, an ebony black shaft of stone, rising from a lipped cup to a rounded head. One of the Buddhist men got up from the circle and retrieved an extravagant pewter and brass Buddha-image from his bag. I saw Brendan and George exchange glances as the metal icon passed into the round; George shrugged and Brendan smiled. I got up and fetched a potted plant from behind a curtain at the back of the hall. I had noticed it soon after we arrived the day before: a Christmas cactus that had come into magnificent, decadent early flower, dark pink blooms against the dusty desert-green of its rubbery leaves. The bank manager brought out an old, hardbound edition of Shakespeare's complete works, which smelt of time, inscribed 'to Archibald, 1907' in blue ink in a fluid, ornate hand.

The drumming maintained a natural, gradually steadying beat through this preparation. As I relaxed into the background pulse, I felt my way into the near-physical sense of timelessness that had gathered. Men seated in a ritual circle; it seemed peculiar, unlike anything I'd experienced, but also somehow familiar, something that had been all the while beckoning; something both ancient and significant. I looked around. None of the men looked different from how they had in the morning of the day before, when I had first seen them. And on the day after they would all go back into the world to be bank managers and fathers, businessmen and students; but for now we had taken ourselves into a bigger, older space, and I supposed that that was what was meant by it being 'sacred'. We had opened a door nearly forgotten in busy, technological, rational life, into a space where we were a miraculous collocation of elements, with a soul hardwired into the earth's rich crust, the sea's tide, the air's freshness, the sun's warmth. We had stepped into a world of myth, a world that had always existed as a homeland in dark corners of our bodies, but one that we had forgotten how to access, and forgotten what healing and wisdom that doing so might serve. Until now. Something seemed to relax its vigilance within me. I felt a sense of trust in being there.

Eventually, the ritual apparatus was all in place on a rucked square blanket of black velvet, as if for some chthonic picnic. Brendan, who seemed to be the celebrant of the ritual proceedings, now sporting antlers towering up point by point to leadened tips, began slowly circumambulating the circle. In one hand he held a large brass bowl by one of its three legs and in the other a brush-whisk. He flicked water onto each of us as he passed behind. All the while he chanted under his breath, a muffled drone hidden beneath the resonance of the drums. I felt a series of cold spats hit my head and cheek, then a sensation of wet run down my neck and back.

Brendan placed the bowl and whisk in the circle, sat down next to George, and spread his hands above his head. Slowly, the sound of the drums died down, but the emotional texture of sacred space remained.

'Gentlemen, the space is yours,' Brendan said, in a tone of complete familiarity and ease, as if all this were the most natural thing in the world, and this vibrant, pulsing circle as ordinary as a cinema trip. He smiled at Terry, sitting next to him, and put his arm around him. I had no idea what was supposed to happen next.

A MAN STOOD UP, one of the men present who, I gathered, had worked with George and Brendan before.

'My partner's had a baby, and he's one month old now,' he said, looking up and around. 'So I'm a father.' He'd said this several times, in the preceding day and a half. 'I'm scared shitless,' he went on. 'I was there at the birth, and it was wonderful, a miracle; and when I hold my son now I'm filled with awe and love. But part of me just wants to run away from the responsibility.'

The man looked about my age. Some of the other men smiled or nodded.

'Why are you bringing this into the ritual circle?' asked George, frowning through his glasses. I was surprised at this question, its apparently hard tone.

'I want you to help me face up to the responsibilities of being a father,' he said.

'Why don't you take this,' said George, seemingly impatient with the lack of direction in the man's request. He passed the man the large teddy bear that had already seen service the day before. 'Sit down and hold your son. Believe that you are holding your son. Hold that small, fragile life in your arms, hold your own son.'

The man sat in a shocked daze. It was as though he had certainly wanted some help in the ritual circle, but the reality of what he now realised he had wanted to happen was overcoming him.

'How do you feel?' asked George. 'Shall we continue?' The man girded himself to answer firmly.

'Yes.'

'Frank would like us to remind him of what responsibilities his child will bring to him, to help him come face to face with being a father, to move fully into this new role.' Frank nodded slowly. A short silence ensued; a candle hissed slightly; the incense had burned out.

'What's your boy's name?' asked one of the two young friends who were on the dole and not particularly ambitious. He spoke slightly, gently.

'He's called Samuel, after his mother's grandfather.'

'When I'm with my little boy, who's eighteen months old now, I feel so much pride and joy in him, something I've not much felt before. Samuel might bring that into your life.'

Frank nodded, smiling.

'But there is also such a fear,' said another man, an engineer; 'Samuel is so small and vulnerable. Every day you will hope that he is still alive and well; every time he goes outside you will hope he hasn't fallen down or run into the road. You have to hold that constant worry and still let him get on with living.' Frank nodded, gravely.

Then various men spoke.

'You have to be able to offer Samuel love and comfort when he's unhappy, and the right kind of firmness when he misbehaves; and no-one can tell you exactly the right thing to do. You will worry whether you're being a good father, but it's the same for all of us.'

'You'll find yourself behaving towards him exactly as your dad did to you, and that'll frighten the shit out of you.'

'And you're not responsible only to Samuel; you have a responsibility to his mother that you can't really escape.' Frank's shoulders were beginning to shake.

'You'll have to help him get through the terrors of school, the pain of being unpopular or bullied, the injustices of his life; and it will bring you back into all sorts of corners of your own childhood that you thought you'd escaped, and yet you will desperately want Samuel to survive better than you did.'

'He will be your son for every day for the rest of your life, and for at least fifteen years so dependent that you won't be able to go outside your door without wondering to yourself whether everything will be all right.'

'And for the rest of your life you will be a father, yet you will never be able to make your boy turn out how you want him to turn out; he will go his own way in his own way, and you will have to accept this and support him through all the crazy things he will do, just as you wanted acceptance through all the crazy things that you did.'

Frank was by now clutching the floppy old bear and weeping, not from sadness, it didn't seem, but from intensity of feeling, from all the knowledge he was now allowing into his heart. Spontaneously, all the men who were fathers, including George, now grinning impishly, got up and formed a smaller circle around Frank. He was still sobbing and shaking. The bank manager offered him a hand and pulled him up. They formed a huddle and Frank wept and hollered in the midst of the big, warm embrace.

Finally, Frank regained his composure and stood, smiling radiantly, and each of the men gave him a blessing: a rub on the head, a touch on the back, some words. I was glad to witness this ritual, I was glad for Samuel. The blessings finished, Frank lifted his arms and yelled 'YES!', and the whole room burst into cheers. The ritual had worked.

After a minute or two, when the room had quietened down, another man stood up, a scout leader, Brian. He'd also worked with George and Brendan before.

'I've just had an operation – a week ago,' he said. He pulled down his trousers and pants and held his penis. The end of it was swollen, an ugly, eye-wateringly plum-coloured mess. A circle of thick black stitches ran around it. 'I've been circumcised. My foreskin was always too tight and didn't retract properly, which made sex painful. So I finally had it off, so to speak.' We looked at his slashed, stitched and bruised penis with terror; I thought, can it ever be worth it? 'It looks terrible, doesn't it?' he continued. He looked over at George. 'I've got something I'd like to do in this circle.' He pulled his trousers back up and took from a pocket a small glass bottle filled with pale yellow liquid. 'Here's my foreskin.' He looked into the murky preservative; indeed there was a little flap of something in there, a little ring of flesh. 'My tight foreskin always symbolised something about me – a tightness, not being able to let go. Well, now it's off, I want to mark the change.'

'How can we help you with this?' asked George. Brian hesitated and then made up his mind.

'I want to eat my foreskin. Ritually. I want you guys to witness this ritual of renewal. OK?' Brian looked around.

'Why do you have to eat it?' asked Tim, his face aghast. 'Couldn't you burn it or something?'

'I could, but I want to eat it. I've been thinking about it since the operation – it's like I want to take and in and digest the old tightness. Not just burn it or get rid of it.'

'All right,' said Tim.

'Ready then?' said George.

'Yeah, think so,' said Brian.

George began a quiet, slow drumbeat, and a variety of small rattles and thuds started around the circle. Slowly the rhythm quickened and the volume increased, and Brian stood, breathing deeply, soaking in the growing force of noise. As he began to unscrew his little bottle, the sounds moved to an anticipatory crescendo. He pulled out the little bit of his own flesh, held it up in the air, then put it into his mouth and swallowed. A mild disgust crossed his face, then he lit up in a smile. He screwed the lid back on the bottle and raised his hands. Again cheers and clapping, and this time also laughter.

The circle again took a few minutes to settle, then Jim stood up. He said:

'I want to put myself at the service of the truth.' His eyes were burning with something that could have been madness, could have been fear. 'I never used to feel that there was a truth I might be able to serve. But that's changing, and I'm fed up with my own cynicism.'

'So what are you going to do?' Jim was quiet for a few seconds.

'If you've got nothing to say, get out of the circle. We can't solve your problems by magic.' Jim flashed a strong look at George.

'OK, here's what I want to do. I'm going to arrange some of this stuff to symbolise a higher truth, then take that sword to symbolise being a warrior, of an intellectual sort. Then I'll make a prostration on the floor, to symbolise putting myself in the service of a higher power.' George threw up his hands, as if to say, well, if that's what you want. I started up a drumbeat once again.

Jim arranged the four candles around the skull resting on the book.

'The Buddha-image is a symbol of wisdom, you know,' said one of the Buddhists. Jim looked at the elaborate cast form, and then put that in the centre, with the skull and book to each side. He put the pot plant in front, with the incense bowl. The Buddhist handed him an incense stick he'd pulled from his bag, and Jim lit that from a candle. Then he took the sword from the scabbard, placed it in front of the little shrine, and lay himself down on the floor, face down.

George suddenly leapt up, walked over to the shrine, and kicked the Buddha, so that the figure fell over. The Buddhist who had offered Jim the incense gasped and was about to get up, but his friend held him back, and I heard him whisper, 'If you meet the Buddha in a church hall, kick him.'

Jim, meanwhile, had lifted his head, surprised, and was looking at George as if hurt.

'You don't really believe in this ritual crap, do you?' said George, speaking down to Jim and beginning to blow out the candles.

'Stop him, Jim, stop him – can't you see what he's doing?' Brendan shouted. I was amazed, looking from Brendan to George to Jim, suddenly understanding what was going on. And so did Jim – he roared, leapt up and grabbed the much smaller, lighter George around the waist, picked him up and carried him backwards, away from the shrine. George was not saving Jim from kicks and blows.

'Put me down, you idiot!' he shouted. 'What do you think you're doing? Have you started believing in God or something? Are you going soft?'

When Jim got him back to the cushions next to Brendan, George dropped onto them and sat, sullen and quiet. Limping, Jim returned to the shrine and righted the Buddha. But as he was relighting the candles, George leapt up again and, with a yell, slammed into Jim, who fell over, twisting to avoid his shrine.

'Amazing grace! How bad the stink!' George shouted, 'of one who's giving up trying to *think*!' He grabbed the sword and started waving it around and leaping about in quite a dangerous way, while moving to blow out the candles again. Jim was altogether confused, and evidently distressed.

'Don't compromise yourself, Jim!' I shouted, and the others shouted support. Jim got up and rather gingerly moved himself between George's waving sword-tip and the shrine.

'Who the hell do you think you are, then?' demanded George. 'The fucking protector of wisdom or something? You arrogant git. Go and sit down.'

'Put the sword down and sit down yourself,' said Jim, pretty firmly. George stopped dancing about. The room became quieter. George stretched out the sword until the tip pushed into Jim's chest.

'Put the sword down and sit down,' said Jim, louder, more firmly. The two locked eyes, George panting, Jim shaking. The battle went on until Jim reached up and took the sword from George's hand. George's hand dropped, though he kept up the vivid eye contact.

'Are we finished?' asked George, his voice almost gentle.

'Think so,' said Jim, sword hanging from his hand, rubbing his chest. 'You were being my ego, quite rightly, but I still definitely feel I want to dedicate myself to the truth.' He put the sword down. George smiled.

'Congratulations.' He reached out his hand, and Jim shook it. Jim began laughing, George and Jim hugged, and the strange, violent tension of the room came apart as sun breaks through mist. Relief and sweetness swept through.

Then I stood up.

'I want to do a ritual to help me make a decision,' I said. My partner wants to have a family and don't know what I want. But I want to make the decision that's right for me, not just go along with what makes her happy.'

Nods of agreement. George looked at me expectantly.

'The ritual Frank did has given me an idea for what I'd like to do. I'll put the teddy bear over there, to symbolise a baby, and I'll sit here. And then I need to get in touch with the real feelings of the situation – maybe all it needs is some drumming and that collected space, I think – and then I'll try to make the journey from here to there; but you guys will shout suggestions about what it will involve, how it might feel, and I'll find out if it's a journey I want to make.'

'Uh-huh,' said George. 'Well, carry on. Be decisive.' He threw me the bear and I set it up on the other side of the circle, and then sat myself just in front of my place. The drumming began again and I closed my eyes, trying to feel my way into the possibility that Ros and I should have a baby.

When I opened my eyes, the bear had gone. The flowering Christmas cactus was in its place, with the sword unsheathed next to it. I looked around, but no one would meet my eyes except Brendan. He had removed his antlers and was holding the brass bowl and whisk. He beckoned me to him, and I went over. He spoke quietly, so that no one else would hear over the drums.

'I don't think we can help you make your decision,' he said, 'but we can help you find your centre so you can do what you need. Let me give you a blessing.' He splashed some water on my head with the whisk. I didn't move; I didn't know what to do – my mind had gone blank. He splashed some more water on my head. Still I didn't move, so he tipped the whole bowl over my head, and the water ran down my back and stomach and down my trousers. That got me moving. I pulled off my wet woollen jumper and t-shirt. I took up the sword and lifted it above my head, taking a bow at Jim's shrine, which was still in place, the stick of incense nearly burned down. It all felt very strange, but I felt I had begun something I needed to complete. I walked out of the circle and around it, with the sword above my head and water running down my legs. The rhythm of the drums became tighter, crisper. I could feel the effect of it on my mind, which steadied and focused. I strode round the circle and back in, to the pot plant.

I realised as I looked down that the cactus consisted of two separate plants growing together in the same pot; two stalks, two systems of leaves, bound together in the brown plastic pot. I knelt to examine the meshed thing. I took the sword and placed the tip in the gravelly soil between the two old flaky brown stems, thick and woody.

'Not the sword, for god's sake, don't use the sword!' Brendan hissed. Feeling stupid, I put the sword down. I spread my big hand over the surface of the soil, stalks between my fingers, and turned the whole thing upside down. The root-bound mass slid out of the pot, and I pulled over my t-shirt to catch the falling gravel and dirt. I put the naked root-ball on the cotton and gently began to pull the two plants apart. Slowly, my fingers discovered ways into the jungle of fat root and wet filament until, with a quiet ripping sensation that I could feel pass through the bones of my chest, as when a tooth's roots rip out of the jaw, the plant split in two. The leaves shook apart more amicably, although four pink flowers fell onto the gritty t-shirt.

I held the two halves of the cactus, one in each hand, and cried. Tears welled as from a spring of sadness, revealed when a tree falls in a gale, the clear water bubbling in the raw wound of the hollow, a kind of blessing on the new. I put the plants down. The dirt on the wet shirt had begun to dissolve. I took two handfuls of mud and smeared them across my face, down my chest, not war paint but mourning, and the tears dribbled down through the ash. I took up the sword again, held it aloft, and walked sombrely around the circle. I bowed at the shrine once more, then sheathed the sword and put the two halves of the plant back in the pot, carefully topping it up with soil from my t-shirt. I hoped the plant would survive.

AT THE END of the afternoon, with darkness outside, we dismantled the ritual space; put skulls back into bags and plants onto windowsills, piled cushions, blew out candles and switched on the lights. The weekend closed with each man saying something in the way of appreciation or encouragement to every other. We were all exhausted. The rituals had gone on for three hours.

Before we each went home, I had a question for Brendan.

'How did you know the plant could symbolize my relationship with Ros?'

'I had no idea,' he said. 'I saw you put it into the circle, so I guessed it was significant for you. More significant than the bear anyway.'

I was sure that I hadn't consciously noticed when I picked it up that the plant had consisted of two plants; I had taken it into the circle, or so I had thought, because it represented nature and life.

'We live in a mysterious, interconnected universe,' added Brendan, 'and properly done ritual is a key to full participation.' He grinned through the thick hair of his face. 'We shamans live in the texture of the universal weave. Take care, Juniper.'

Jim was deep in conversation with George: a hulk of brain leaning down to the wiry little psychotherapist talking up. Tim was laughing with Brian. He had invited Tim to join him, Frank and some others in a men's group that George facilitated.

Outside, the twentieth century was enjoying the early evening of its weekly day off. Most of the constellation Orion was visible between clouds, southeast, over the wet roofs of houses.

'My secret warrior name is Orion,' Jim whispered to me. 'George says.'

the tearing of roots

I RANG ROS from Jim's place when he and I arrived back in Greyston. She was glad I'd rung. Beth had miscarried on the previous Saturday night.

'I'll come as well,' Jim said. 'She might need some help.' We walked over to the hospital together. Beth's normally rosy cheeks were pallid, her lips thin.

'Could you go and see Peter?' she asked.

He seemed scared and baffled by our news. But next afternoon he met us outside Beth's house, and Ros let us all in. Beth's house was among the small terraced workers' dwellings in a gardenless grid near the centre of Greyston. She was wrapped up in her double bed, looking small and sad. She had a large *le baiser de l'hotel de ville* hung on the wall. Images create expectations, I thought.

After Peter and Jim had gone, and while Ros was doing some washing-up, I sat on the edge of Beth's bed. I held her hand and she cried.

'Don't leave her,' Beth said to me through tears.

'Why should I?' I said, confused, supposing Beth to be comparing me to Peter, which I hardly found flattering. When I told this to Ros, she wouldn't look at me.

'I've something to tell you, when we're both home.' The air seemed clogged with a sooty emotion, but I didn't dwell on it, not knowing what it might mean. I was thinking more of Beth, and Peter, and love: the way people live their lives in an emotional mess until they no longer see what they're putting up with. Some people live such long emergency lives.

I STAYED WITH JIM that night at Lyndhurst. Next morning I went home on my own to Albion Cottage. Ros had asked mother to come down from the farm to let out the chickens. As I toured the garden I spotted a little owl, day-roosting on the window ledge of Ros's room. It peered at me intensely through its wide spectacles, then launched and turned around the corner of the house. I brought in a basket of split logs from the woodshed to get the range burning. The water in the tank was barely warm from the solar panels, so I left the range grill full open, and went off for a walk while bath water heated. In the messy, nearly bare woods, the trees and leaves seemed to want to let me through into that same timeless life that had come into our men's circle in Clapham. A couple of roe deer browsed among holly trees and trotted off on their points when I crunched on leaves. I felt at home in my world. That night, alone, I dreamt of following an owl as it looped through trees, until I came upon a man with antlers, laughing, but pinned against the wall of a female giant's cave.

Ros came back next evening. We sat to drink tea.

'Why might I want to leave you, then?' I said, half in jest.

'It's Harry,' she said. Harry was our friend in the village. He'd always been keen on Ros. We'd laughed about it.

'What about Harry? Did he propose to you?'

'No, we slept together.'

That was a shock, totally unexpected. My heart felt a shatter of whatever strength and sense the men's weekend had made. Ros suddenly threw her mug, tea not yet poured, one of her own, a stoneware half-pinter with a silvery-blue glaze, across the room. It shattered against the chimney breast, spraying shards over the room and sending another shock through me.

'Damn Beth for saying anything!' she shouted. I fetched another mug and poured the tea. Ros laughed bitterly.

'Beth doesn't like secrets,' I said.

'I wish I hadn't *told* her.'

'You know she speaks her mind.'

'I didn't want it to be like this.'

'Harry's nothing, he's a barnacle.'

'I'm in *love* with him, Juniper.'

'Bollocks, you just wanted to have sex.'

'And what's wrong with that?'

'You tell me.'

'I really enjoyed it.'

'And how do you feel now?'

She burst into tears.

'Do you remember that day when Erica Louise was visiting?' she said. 'He and I were picking pears, and I knew from things he said he was going to tell me he loved me.'

'How romantic,' I said.

'I liked it,' she said.

'So what happened?'

'He came round on Saturday, and I showed him my new kiln, and then he was admiring my pottery. Then he was talking about how much he wanted children, and how he and I −'

'You told him about our argument?'

'I have to talk to people. I bet you talked to Jim.'

'He's a bloke, it's different.'

'I talked to *Beth* as well.'

'And to bloody Harry!'

'He just wants me to be *happy*, Juniper! He helps me, he cares for me, he wants to be a father for my children, he –'

Ros broke off suddenly and there was nothing to say. A crunching feeling began in my heart, like the back shovel on a JCB pulling through rooty gravel.

'We were drinking some wine by the fire, and he *touched* me, and then we were kissing and then –'

I was feeling close to tears.

'On Sunday morning I felt *crap* and sent him away.'

'Good,' I said. I couldn't have said anything else because my throat was blocked. I got up and took hold of the compost bucket that was piled high with sprout peelings and headed for the back door. The metal bucket clanked in the tense kitchen. Ros was looking down at the table. Our mugs sat on the elm boards about a foot apart, handles facing opposite directions.

Outside, a three-quarter moon was already quite high in the sky. The evening was still. I heard a sheep cough over the back wall, then the hoot of a tawny owl, away over the woods. My heart welled a red despair and I started to cry. I sat on the limestone step from yard to garden and my tears fell on the sprout peelings. Why crying? The same tearing of roots that I'd felt in the transmogrified church hall. Everything seemed ruined between my country wife and me.

Ros came out into the garden and sat next to me.

Ros, my accomplice in plotting an adult life. Ros, the partner I'd not looked for, but now couldn't imagine being without. I remembered that first winter we'd made friends, her pony tail. Now her hair was shoulder length, her eyes and mouth harder, much less vague. We were looking down over the garden we'd created, but the spell was broken and it was wilderness. She was sitting next to me but we were apart.

'It was really *stupid* of me, Juniper, I know, but –'

'This weekend something happened for me as well,' I said. We went inside and lit the stove. I told her what had happened in cold detail. We ended by sitting in silence together. The fire ached and pulsed, and starlight brushed the windows. Ros started to cry and leant her head on my shoulder. The tears rolled down my cheeks and into her hair. It was late, so we went to bed. Grit dripping from the torn roots of that Christmas cactus ground in my heart. I fell into a haunted sleep.

In the morning, I just felt angry.

'Maybe I should have just kept it *secret*,' she spat back. Then Harry turned up mid-morning and stood like a dangled dishcloth in the kitchen while I leant against the window ledge with my arms folded and Ros stirred a cauldron at the range.

'I love Ros, I couldn't help myself,' he said. 'Juniper, you don't appreciate her, you don't treat her with the respect and love she deserves.'

I looked over at Ros, who was stirring furiously.

'Well, well,' I said. 'So maybe you deserve each other.'

'You haven't listened to her,' added Harry.

'Don't say another word, Harry,' said Ros. 'What happened was a big *mistake*.'

'Speak for yourself,' he said.

'I am,' said Ros. He laughed.

'Can you go away, please?' I told him.

'What do you say, Ros?' he said.

'Go away,' she said quietly.

'I mean it, I love you, and it's not a secret now.' He turned and left.

Quiet closed in on the low-ceilinged kitchen, the wooden spoon scraping around the iron pan. The winter day thinned into light grey overcast. The tide was out of the Bay, and the sand looked almost black. Ros and I talked after bread and soup. I expected her to say sorry, for adulterous lust, that kind of thing, but she wouldn't.

'I only did it because you've become such a brain-on-legs frigid student. I don't feel like I should have to practise *chastity* for a year.'

'A few weeks ago you were wanting my babies,' I said through clenched teeth; but she just screamed in exasperation. Bosch says mature human love means open honesty; but it felt like we had ripped claws through each other. The wounds were too deep, too different, to be bound. It was physically difficult to be in the same house, so I moved over to Jim's. The couple who had been living there with a dog had moved out.

After a week, Ros and I met at the cottage and went for a walk. I couldn't see her as that girl in Totnes now at all. She was a stranger. We didn't talk about what had happened. There was a politeness, a reserve, and a determination in the distance. I didn't know what I wanted; only that something irreversible had happened.

There is a ring of beeches in an ancient wood a mile from Albion Cottage, seeming to spring from an ancient world. A light rain began as we walked into that ring. A sick ache had opened between us as we tried to talk of spring planting at the cottage, but without any idea of how we could come back together there. We stood under the ragged circle of dulling afternoon light that was cut into grey pieces by the bare branches above. The sky spat cold drizzle. We stood there, on the soggy ground, on wet leaves, and I smiled miserably, thinking that we could have been medieval lovers, peasants bogged in the same drab emotions. Ros broke the strain of silence.

'You don't want to have children with me, do you?' She turned into the circle towards me, hands in her Barbour, hair under the collar. 'That's what your ritual means. But you're too scared to say it.'

I opened my mouth to say, no, no, that's jumping to conclusions, wanting to appease her, keep the afternoon from its bitter dusk. But I couldn't bring myself to say that sort of quarter-truth; the spindly words crammed in my throat.

'No I don't,' I said, the words coming from an animal place deeper in me, a voice goaded by the hurt felt at her infidelity.

I too turned into the circle. Her face was full of mangling emotions.

'Ever?' she said. 'Even in a year or so, when maybe we've got over all this?' In a flash I saw her tough, female logic: no apology for infidelity, unless she knew that saying sorry would be worth it, would lead to what she wanted. And the obverse calculation: if she allowed her will to crumble, allowed the healing feelings and words to spill out and bind us together again, then it would become more difficult to address her child-desire. Hence, she kept up the momentum of separateness, so that she could move on if she needed.

'No!' the animal voice cried into the damp trees. Two jackdaws flapped off down the slope. 'I can't say never but I can say now, no.' In the cold silence, the drizzle turned to icy rain.

'Well, go home, then; leave me alone.' Ros unstifled her anger into these words, the bitterness shocking me, the mix of feelings. A raw compassion welled, and I moved to hug her, mark the moment somehow. She stiffly acquiesced, then threw me off.

'Go on, go away,' the anger shouted; so I went.

In the following weeks, we saw each other quite often, at home and in town, but only because we couldn't be resolute. On the winter solstice, I collected some things from the cottage. Before I left, she said:

'Let's not meet for a while. To let things settle out. So I can let you drip out of my heart a bit.'

I cried, but agreed. Six months apart. And then? There was nothing we could say about that.

Tim's visit

IT WAS FEBRUARY. Snowdrops banged their numb heads against each other in the freezing, brightening days. I cut my hair off, an act of renunciation, and bought a black woollen hat from the market. Jim and I talked a lot and smoked too much. I worked hard and re-read Bosch's *Love Without Illusions*. He says that falling in love is just a way for people to get together, but to find lasting satisfaction you need a realistic human love. But what happens when that human love sours, and you've already made sure that you're not in the grip of foolish illusion? It seemed inevitable that a couple would come apart, but Bosch didn't say what to do about that. I read Aristotle on friendship, about how intellectual friendship between men is the highest form of love. But sexual love didn't seem to feature at all, so that didn't help much either.

I felt bitter about Ros, but didn't want to see her. She'd sent me a letter.

Dear Juniper,

I am writing to say that Harry has moved in, at least for a while. To be honest, I don't think he is Mr Right or anything, but he has been very kind and helpful, and I was finding it difficult living here on my own. I have told him that I am not thinking of him as a long-term partner, but he still wants to stay, so that's how things are for the moment. I thought I should tell you. I think it is right that we spend some time apart, for you after your ritual and for me to think about what I want, but I still think we should meet up in June.

Hope you are getting on OK with Jim,
R.

I'd gone over to Albion Cottage on Christmas day. After dinner at the farm, mother and father were snoozing in front of the TV; Erica was doing a nursing shift. Ros had gone down to her mum's. I sat in her room, in the weak sunshine that crept over the back wall and poured timidly through the upper windows of the house and across her bed, the double bed I'd made myself when we first moved into the cottage, of timber from the old pear tree in the front garden. Then, six weeks before, I'd thought that things would work out somehow. Now, even that hope curled in the cold and damp. Winter eats away at your memory until you can hardly remember the feeling of the sun.

One day, up at the university, I met Barry Driscoll and told him why I looked miserable.

'Join the broken-hearts club,' he said, and took me off to a quiet coffee bar.

'Are you still single, then?' I asked him.

'Actually,' he replied, 'I've got this amazing thing going now with a Danish postgrad, on a more casual basis.'

'I'm sure,' I said, not believing him.

'These Scandinavians are so horny,' he said. 'Last week, she came to my office, locked the door, and said, I want to do it with you right now, so I –'

'Yes, thank you Barry,' I said. I didn't want to put fantasies from Barry's head into mine. I wanted to be able to think clearly about love. I left him waiting there for his hot new date, and went back to the library. I was looking into social psychology books. Before I could work out the problem with Hans Bosch's opinions and advice, I wanted to know more about what the experts thought love was. I read:

Romantic love has been found to have three basic behavioural components: (i) thinking constantly about the beloved, (ii) longing for the beloved's presence and for love to be returned, and (iii) idealisation (unrealistic evaluation) of the imperfections of the beloved.

I couldn't help but think that these social psychologists were playing a game, pretending to be dull-witted beings from outer space, looking at the humans through Martian eyes.

Within the love relationship, it has been found that there are 'rules' for couples which, when associated with the skills relevant to such a relationship, yield criteria for measuring its success (or "rewardingness").

Two examples of the 'rules':
    1. *touch the other person intentionally*, and
    2. *be faithful to one another.*
Good luck, earthlings!

I left the library and sat in the Nelson Mandela coffee bar, to drink tea and smoke. Two students I knew from a philosophy course joined me. We got talking about love, after Phil had asked me about my project. Rachel said that she was in a relationship with a guy who didn't talk to her very much; they slept together after he'd been out with his mates.

'Do you like that?' I asked her.

'Of course not,' she replied.

'So why do you stick with him?'

'Well, you live in hope,' she said, and a whole world suddenly broke open in front of me, like a cloud splitting and, inside, an aerial city full of streets and towers – the city of those who long for love. Rachel looked up at me from the cigarette butt she was stubbing out in the little foil ashtray that slid about on the red Formica tabletop, a mixture of apology and petulance in her face. I nodded back at her, having nothing to say. It struck me that, even if a psychologist thought up the best idea of love in the world, still it wouldn't mean that Rachel would dump her bloke. It wasn't far from the question of why I had got involved with Renata. The truth is: you live in hope; you learn – or not – through disappointment. It's not a very rational thing.

Living in hope. People get stuck in loops of endless giving to husbands, wives, lovers; hoping for a reward, then giving more. There are yawning splits in the floor of that city of those who long for love, and they threaten to let people through to the long, empty drop to a dusty, lonely earth. It's hard to want to be dignified when you're desperate, and it's painful whether you hang on to a love you don't like or wait for a love you can't make happen. By the conventional standards of attractiveness, Rachel was not going to be striking poses in Cosmo. But that's just another convention – that pretty people get loved. Anyone can be reduced to a desperate lover; it's a matter of self-confidence, not looks.

Rachel and Phil went off to a lecture, and I went back to thinking. Another problem with Bosch is that he doesn't go into how people invest their hopes in romance; even if you don't believe in falling in love, you might stay with someone for all the wrong reasons. At least social psychology put words on what's needed for love to work. Rachel just wanted to be loved.

'I know the rules!' some egghead might tell her, touching her intentionally, and making a mental note to be faithful.

'But do you fancy me?' might come her reply.

'I have idealised your imperfections, if that's what you mean,' he replies, honest empiricist that he is. 'And I long for you to return my love.'

And she might think he was weird, but decide to give it a go. What was there to lose? She finishes with her old boyfriend, who then, of course, decides she is the love of his life, and begs her to come back to him.

'No way,' she tells him. 'I've found a guy who knows the rules!' So he staggers off in dismay, and pours his heart out to his mates in the college bar.

'Forget her!' they counsel him. 'And have another beer. You'll find a new girl.' And sure enough, in a couple of weeks, he does. Meanwhile, Rachel and her cognitive lover discover a mutual interest in travel and, when she has finished her degree, he gives up his lecturing to go off around the world with her.

In South America, they stay with Yanomani people in the depths of the jungle. The Yanomani wear no clothes except a single string around the waist. One day, he is hanging out with a group of youths, when he notices that a girl's string has slipped its knot and fallen off. Then she also notices, and he realises that she is acutely embarrassed and that her friends are giggling at her indiscretion.

'Conventions!' he thinks, and politely turns his head away.

As the girl re-ties her string, he begins to understand that social conventions are a means to an end, and that the end is the endlessly fascinating business of human beings managing to live together, with dignity and culture. As ends in themselves, conventions are either laborious or absurd.

From that day on he eschews all cognitivist views and begins to write love poems of passionate intensity, comparing Rachel to the Amazon and its untamed ardours. All the while, within a love that is private and unique, she blossoms into a woman of great intuitive empathy. Eventually they settle as aid workers in a remote part of sub-Saharan Africa, where she is recognised as the reincarnation of an ancient tribal priestess, who used to heal the social wounds that sometimes festered within the closed structures of their lives. As such a woman's husband, the man is permitted to take three extra wives, despite his being thin and pale and by no means a warrior. He refuses, explaining haltingly in the local language, which utilises forty-eight sorts of clicks, that he is a poet, and therefore a strange and unconventional man.

But Ros and I hadn't stuck to the rules.

I WROTE TO TIM to tell him what had happened, having left it some time because I knew he'd be upset. He rang me the day he got my letter.

'I feel responsible for your splitting up,' he said, 'because I invited you on the men's weekend.'

I told him I was glad I'd been on the men's weekend, and that he couldn't take responsibility for anything that had happened between Ros and me. But I didn't deny that I was feeling miserable. He came up to visit me the very next weekend, arriving late on the Friday evening. He gave me flowers. We caught the train up to the familiar

Silverthwaite woods on Saturday, and he extracted the story of what had happened. Then I went home while he visited Ros.

He arrived back at seven. Jim had cooked a wholesome pie, with chestnuts I'd picked and dried the previous autumn.

'She's mad that you ritually tore the relationship apart,' said Tim.

'What the hell −' I began but, looking at Tim, I knew there was no need to say more.

'What did she say about her unfaithfulness, eh?' asked Jim, saying more, raising his eyebrows, looking stern.

'She didn't mention it,' said Tim, 'and I didn't know how to bring it up.'

'Sexual ethics become a matter of personal taste, has it?' said Jim. 'If it was me, I'd −'

'You'd bash her over the head with a club and drag her back to your cave by the hair,' said Tim. Jim continued stirring the thickening sauce, unperturbed.

'No,' he said. 'I was going to say that I'd point out the very basic breach of trust engendered by screwing someone −'

'Enough!' I said. 'This is personal stuff.'

'Sorry,' said Tim.

'I don't agree,' said Jim. 'We're discussing the universal nature of sexual ethics. You'd be a right prick not to admit that when your girlfriend fucked with −'

'Jim!' I said. 'Be sensitive!' He creased his brow awhile.

'Sorry,' he said.

'She's changed, though, Juniper,' said Tim. 'You know how she can be so forceful about what she wants? Well, it wasn't there.'

'Harry around?' It was what I most wanted to know.

'Yeah, he was around,' said Tim. He paused. 'Now that I can't understand. She doesn't seem to, you know, *love* him; I mean, he's not like a substitute for you − or maybe that's all he is; but, anyway, yes, he's around, a bit like a dog.'

Jim laughed. 'She likes her men on leads,' he said. 'Sit, beg, lie − good boy!' He started lolling his tongue, panting and whining, still stirring.

I wanted to tip the sauce over his head. Tim had his lip curled in distaste. But Jim kept on, and we both found ourselves laughing, and Jim started barking, his wooden spoon wagging. Then Tim started howling and I joined in too.

'I don't want to sound critical,' said Tim later, to an apple-crumble-serving Jim, 'but I do wonder why you don't seem very bothered by Juniper and Ros's splitting up. It's like you don't care.'

'I don't think I have much sympathy for the supposed traumas of divorce,' he said, handing out heaped bowlfuls of gold and green crumble. 'It always sounds like self-absorbed bourgeois individualism to me. As for Juniper and his woman, there were weaknesses in their relationship, and now there aren't.'

'True enough,' I said.

'Have you never been in a relationship?' asked Tim.

'Course I have,' said Jim.

'Who with?' I asked, unable to recall.

'When I was seventeen, eighteen, nineteen, when I was doing the apprenticeship, my cousin and me used to get together —'

'Your cousin!' exclaimed Tim.

'Aye,' said Jim. 'Naught wrong with that.'

'Were you in love?' I asked.

'In love? Piss off!' he said. 'We just liked fucking.'

'Ah,' I said. Tim shook his head.

'What are you shaking your bloody head for?' said Jim. 'As I recall, you've bemoaned your own proclivities at length.'

'I've never been proud of them, though,' said Tim. 'And anyway, I've got a boyfriend now.'

'Really?' I said, grasping his arm. 'Who?'

'You remember Brian?' said Tim, grinning. 'We've been going out ever since that weekend. Three months and one week. Going steady!'

'Congratulations!' said Jim. 'You can have the skin of the custard for that.' He passed a steaming glass jug.

'Are you in love then?' I asked Tim.

Tim shrugged. 'It's early days. We're not infatuated though. After we started going out, we sat down and talked about what we each wanted from it, so that we would be able to have realistic expectations.'

'Did you find any differences?' I asked.

'He doesn't have many expectations around sex, but that might change now that —' Tim waved his hand up and down vaguely, until we remembered Brian's ritual on the men's weekend. 'And I would like one day to live with a lover, though he's done that in the past and is less keen about it himself.'

'So there's no sex and he wants to live on his own,' said Jim. 'I'm having half the skin back.' He reached his spoon over the table, but Tim clonked his on Jim's knuckle.

'You'll make someone a good cook but a useless boyfriend,' said Tim. Jim humphed and mumbled into his crumble.

'Jim,' Tim asked him later, 'do you think you might be gay? I mean, you're consistently negative about relationships with women, you don't seem to fall in love with them or have much regard for them, and you seem altogether more interested in men.'

'Not in their dicks, though,' said Jim.

'But how do you know?' Tim persisted. 'You might be suppressing your attraction to the stronger sex because of conventional morality.'

'Might be,' Jim shrugged. 'It's a daft argument though. I say I'm not gay, you say it's because I'm suppressing my attraction to men, therefore I can't know if I'm gay, therefore I might be gay. You could just as easily wonder if I'm really a transvestite stamp-collector because I read my mail while I'm wearing a bathrobe.'

'I've got an idea,' said Tim. 'Why don't we go to the gay pub in town and see if we can fix you up with a man? Then you'll find out for sure.' This sounded absurd.

'OK,' Jim shrugged.

THE HORN OF THE Hare was a big, open pub with yellowy lighting and a rowdy feel. On a Saturday night it was pretty crowded, but we three stood by the bar and looked around. Jim had put on his big black donkey jacket. Tim looked as ever the elegant townie. He stood between us, his neat head just above Jim's and my shoulder levels. Jim rolled a fat smoke.

'Do you go to places like this in London?' he asked.

'Sometimes,' said Tim. 'But not clubs anymore. My tastes in music have changed.'

'So what do you do to find a man?'

'Put your hand up,' said Tim.

'You're going to do it?' I asked.

'Don't see why not,' said Jim.

It took about fifteen minutes. A large, leather-capped German took a shine to Jim's big face and took him off to his flat. Tim and I removed to another pub for a quieter drink. We talked over in closer detail his observations of Ros. Tim thought that she was miserable, but didn't want to admit it. I told Tim I was finding it a bit of a relief to be more independent; at least, that's how I'd been feeling that weekend, in his and Jim's warm company. We walked home at eleven, through streets brushed with the steel wool of winter wind.

'I hope Jim's all right,' said Tim.

'He can look after himself.'

'But he doesn't know what can happen.'

'I wouldn't be so sure,' I said. 'Jim doesn't always tell you what he knows.'

Jim came home at ten-thirty next morning.

'I'm not gay,' he said calmly. He had sat in Wolfgang's flat drinking coffee and smoking joints until the German had attempted to seduce him. Not much had happened, however, so they lapsed into conversation. Wolfgang, it turned out, was well read in philosophy, so they discussed the French philosopher Foucault's ideas on sexuality. A further attempt at seduction had proved slightly more successful, but Wolfgang had pronounced Jim officially 'not gay.' He slept over on his sofa and came home after breakfast. 'It was all good natured, and I think we might meet to talk again.'

Tim was relieved to see him home.

'I didn't think you were gay really,' he said, rubbing Jim's unbrushed head.

Tim left at five on the train back to London. The weekend marked the beginning of a new life for me. I could mope and think about what had been lost, regretting choices or rehearsing old conversations. Or I could turn my life resolutely to work and friends. It was a choice between stagnation and the bracing pain of free-flow.

in the Red Cow

THE RED COW stood opposite the cinema on the one-way system, part of a stone terrace of shop fronts, its door aggrandised by two half-pillars and a stone portico, beckoning into a soft, quiet space with the bar to the right and seating left. Old red leather chairs and wall seating gleamed in the light flickering from the coal fire and from dim lamps on chandeliers; jazz music nattered and sang among the mirrors and shining tables. A cocker spaniel lay to one side of the bar, making occasional forays among the table-legs and chairs, nosing for nuts and crisps and ignoring patting hands, completing its route by collapsing into a curly heap.

When Jim and I walked in, out of the tangy March air, the pub was almost empty, except for a couple in one corner and Paul Corbett in another.

'Drinks, gentlemen?' he asked. He brought back three pints of beer. He looked over at the couple in the other corner. 'I think of that couple as "the married socialists",' he said, under the music. 'I see them selling revolutionary newspapers together every Saturday at the centre of town.'

There had been a poster on the campus once – *Kick Out the Tories and Keep on Kicking!* – and since then I had always thought of revolutionary socialism as a sort of bad-tempered donkey. The young couple looked so normal, a man and a woman drinking beer in a free house. What apocalyptic visions, what courageous faith flowed in people's hidden inner worlds: I felt I would like to sit down with them and discover the inner force and feeling of their beliefs, feel their energetic certainty, if only by association.

'I used to be a socialist, until I started to think,' said Jim. 'It's obvious that if you've got less, you want everyone to be equal, and if you've got more, you want things to stay that way. Socialism isn't about truth or goodness; it's about believing that you've a right to get what you want.'

'Surely that wouldn't be true of someone like a union shop-steward, who was working for the good of his or her comrades?' said Paul.

'Camaraderie is a strategy,' said Jim. 'Give them some power, some money, then see whose interests they want to represent.'

'But, when you were working in the garage,' I said, 'didn't you think that it was rather arbitrary and unfair that this man had a Jaguar and you were changing his oil?'

'It *is* arbitrary and unfair,' said Jim. 'That's life. But it takes true strength to face the fact and not take refuge in comforting beliefs.'

'But one might at least say that Marx was optimistic about the human condition,' said Paul, 'in regarding social progress as possible.'

Jim was about to say something else, but instead he looked over the socialist couple. They were talking quietly in their corner, absorbed in each other's company. Jim shook his head. He lifted his glass.

'Here's to the truth: its own reward.' We laughed and drank deep.

Paul produced a packet of tobacco and some papers and offered them around. We rolled up in silence.

'So,' said Jim, waving out a match, cigarette in his mouth, 'have you come round to the idea of a philosophical men's group after all?'

Paul coughed and looked at the table. 'It is true that our discussions,' he said, looking at me, 'of Aristotle's *Ethics* – the chapters on friendship – have reminded me of the importance of good companions in one's life.'

Jim nodded. 'And?'

Paul paused. He looked up with some fear in his eyes. He sighed. 'Gentlemen, I have become dissatisfied with my relationship to Jackie.' Neither Jim nor I knew anything of Paul's private life. 'And I have no one to talk to about the situation. If you could bear to hear me out, I would appreciate your advice.'

'This doesn't sound very philosophical,' said Jim, frowning.

'No,' said Paul; 'no, it isn't very philosophical.'

'first tell us who Jackie is,' I said.

Paul took a deep breath, clenched a fist, and then exhaled.

'Jackie is what you might call the woman in my life. But I'm not in her life I'm afraid, as she made it abundantly clear to me last evening. So something has to change. The situation is intolerable.'

'No, no, no,' said Jim. 'Tell us *properly*.'

'Is she beautiful?' I said.

Paul's face crinkled up as if he might cry. He pulled on his cigarette.

'Yes, she is beautiful,' he said. 'Let me elucidate.' He thought for a few moments. 'She has thick blonde hair that tumbles past her shoulders, apparently spontaneously, but in fact as a result of the most precise artistic methods; and framed by the idealised naturalism of this hair is her wonderful mouth: large and lively and strong, with fascinating lips; and above her mouth are eyes on the grey side of blue, with a bright seriousness like a high lake under storm clouds. Away from her strong nose in every direction flows a smooth creamy-beige elastic, like skin on rice pudding, that holds in the liquid play of her face.'

'And did you meet on a boat or a plane?' I asked.

'Yes,' said Jim, nodding. 'Tell it like a story.'

'We met here in Greyston, at the end of our first year of postgraduate study, at an academic's garden party. We became friends –'

'Describe the party,' I said. Paul looked at me, warily, but Jim was nodding.

'The garden looked west and down over the spires, the clock towers and the castle, over the river and out towards the sea – is this OK?'

'Aye.'

'Jackie and I stood and drank punch and watched the sun stoop beneath the clouds, spreading bold light over the town and the bay, before setting behind the hills of the Lake District, visible along the horizon. We were both ambitious, with our sights set on academic careers, but also a little new and awkward with it all. I could describe the party more, the antics of drunken historians and so on, but I don't think it's relevant.'

'Fine. Tell it how you want.'

'We became friends, and began going for country walks at weekends as a healthy balance to the intellectual work; soon we became lovers. We moved into a flat together at the beginning of our second year, partly for convenience, so we no longer had to live in shared houses made up of odd postgraduate assortments. We supported each other through the whole PhD thing, and hardly interacted with people outside the academic world.'

Jim shook his head. 'Sounds right cosy.' Paul looked up half-gratefully.

'So what happened?' I asked.

'Our quiet life together; it was what I wanted at the time. After we'd gained our doctorates, I started teaching here at Greyston, and she got some part-time work, teaching sociology, over at the university in Leeds. She stayed there three nights a week, for a couple of years. Once she was offered full-time work, she decided to move to Leeds permanently. She said she wanted to be more independent. Then, after six months of us living apart, she said she wanted to end the relationship.'

Jim looked perplexed. 'But how can you be feeling dissatisfied with your relationship if you don't have one?'

'We must infer,' I said to Jim, 'that the relationship is not yet really over.'

Paul looked pleased. 'Exactly.'

'Last evening,' I said.

'I returned to my flat at four-thirty, feeling like my neck had been nailed straight. I don't know why, but I quite often feel like that these days, coming back from work. So I took a shower and then made tea and listened to a CD of a baroque concerto in my study.' Paul looked at me and smiled. 'You should ask why.'

'I shouldn't need to ask why.' We laughed.

'The precise constructions of the music, the consistent shifts in texture and tempo, are images of a higher life that remind me of contentment. So I relaxed, permeated by tangy Assam. My thoughts found their way behind a tedious departmental meeting to a lovely tutorial in the morning with my favourite student; she seems to light something up in me, an intellectual emotion. And then I started cooking. I enjoyed the way the clean, sharp knife slid through the carrots on the oiled end-grain beech of the chopping board; I became absorbed in the wet, ligneous granularity of resistance as the knife pulled through the dense texture; the sprung grain, the elasticity, when the two halves of a carrot bend apart with an orange gleam.'

'This is good,' said Jim.

THEN THE PHONE RANG. Paul let his machine take the call. *Hi Paul, this is Jackie. I'm over in Greyston today – some meetings in the Women's Studies department. Mind if I come round this evening? And would it be OK if I stayed over with you tonight? See you around six. Bye.* He played the message again, standing in the hallway, with the familiar half-sinking half-thrilling feeling she provoked in him. This was the third time she had wanted to stay overnight with him since they had split up. He felt used, but he also felt a little flutter of excitement; despite himself, he liked her vivacity and laughter. She was very definite that the relationship had finished, but for him each of these visits was a numbed and stretched extension of the old tie; sexless, without commitment, but still weighted with the shared past and the intimacy; and with a spark of hope that they might get back together again.

He cooked a chilli sauce, waiting until Jackie arrived before putting the spaghetti on, since she was invariably late. He made more tea and sat out on the galvanized balcony of the flat. An early spring evening light spread across the view, and an easeful, muted sorrow rose through him. He rolled a cigarette and smoked it with a gritted relish. He'd started smoking, very lightly, after the remarkable evening with Jim and Juniper some months before; the act of rolling and inhaling connected him with something that had happened that night which he did not want to forget. For a while, a cool peace hovered over the car park, the garages and the cast-iron fence, the trees around the playing field, the gas-tower, the back gardens and rooftops. He liked this view. He used to dream of a room in a college in Cambridge, or a study with stained glass windows, richly decorated with pre-Raphaelite prints; but that was in the days when he had dreamed of a brilliant academic career. Now he quite liked the reality of a renewable-contract lectureship at a new university, and the ordinary details in the view from his balcony.

At six-thirty the bell rang. Jackie bounced into the flat, kissed him on the cheek, then threw her mac and bag on the sofa.

'Present,' she said, producing a bottle of wine. 'Sorry to give you so little notice, Paul, as usual, but it was a last-minute thing. You didn't have anything booked for this evening did you?'

'As it happens, no,' he replied. 'So I've cooked you some food. Would you like a cup of tea?'

'Oh yes please, love one.' She started wandering around. 'flat doesn't look much different from last time – I thought you were going to repaint the hall?'

'Well –'

'I had to meet with Fiona and Alison today – we're co-editing a collection of papers on "images of feminism in media and society", just started commissioning and selection, still need to sort out the details of the publishing contract, make sure we agree on our basic aims. Fiona wants a general non-specialist approach, but I can't see the point. If there isn't a clear focus we aren't going to get the best papers. Paul! You've taken down the Chinese lampshade in the kitchen! The room looks so bright and bare!'

'I prefer the bare bulb.' She didn't pursue the topic.

While the spaghetti was cooking, they drank tea and talked of respective academic projects. She had been researching the nature and condition of the female body-subject, but had reached an impasse.

'I suspect you are still making unclarified suppositions regarding the primal equivalence of male and female bodies,' he suggested.

'Bollocks, Paul,' she retorted with her usual gusto. 'There's a difference between a presupposition and a strategic, not to say political, assertion of equality – at the formative level of theorising.'

He hated this sociological tendency to call thinking 'theorising' and to bend logic to fit ideological needs. It seemed to make an implicit assumption that truth was relative, and that there was no point in trying to establish thought on firm foundations. Meanwhile, Paul was working away on his project of delineating the differences between Spinoza and Descartes, aiming to be able to outline clearly the universal originality of his old philosophical hero.

'You're turning into a monster, Paul,' Jackie told him. 'Stuck in your dark cupboard, you're going mouldy and blind.'

'That's a bit extreme,' he replied, feeling weakly hurt. 'After all, this research feeds into the ethics classes I teach. It maintains my attention on the fundamental questions, which leads to some very good

discussions on contemporary issues. Just the other week, for example —'
but she yawned wide and loud. He served dinner.

'Paul, shall we go out for a drink?' Jackie asked brightly. 'I fancy a trip
to the Red Cow, you know, the place with the dog. I'll buy you a pint.'

The crocuses were starting to wilt in the municipal flowerbeds. But
there was the naked pleasure of hyacinth perfume as they walked past a
particular bank, and in gardens the tall blades of daffodils stood bulging
dangerously under the yellow streetlights. The town was quiet. There
were no other customers in the Red Cow. Betty, the white-haired
landlady, stood drying glasses behind the bar. The spaniel cocked an eye.

'Quiet tonight,' Paul said, taking off his coat.

'Aye,' she agreed. 'film's just started over at cinema.' He ordered
two pints of lager, not even checking with Jackie to ask what she wanted.

'I'll buy the next round,' Jackie offered from the deep red seat into
which she had sunk, her legs crossed elegantly and her hair pushed
forward and heaped around her shoulders. This usually happened; she
would offer to buy the drinks, then he would do so from habit or duty,
and she wouldn't stop him. And he always felt this slight pride in being
with her, a kind of vicarious attractiveness. He pulled tobacco and
papers from his pocket nervously.

'Paul, you're not smoking are you?'

He had been expecting this. 'Yes, I am.'

Jackie shook her head with pity, but said nothing, perhaps
recognising certain limits in the area of legitimate criticism. Paul
enjoyed the doleful despond that welled satisfyingly from the suck and
plume, blocking a vague unease and hanging an ashy anchor into the
moment's shallow bay. The smoke separated him from Jackie by a veil
of judgement and preference, and that was a relief.

'Paul,' said Jackie, some time later, 'there was something I wanted
to tell you.' Jackie fingered her empty glass, some strands of golden hair
almost sweeping the sticky table as she leaned forward, looking down.
She looked up. 'I'm going out with someone. It's been a while now,
actually, but I didn't want to tell you until I felt confident about it. Say
you don't mind.'

He felt a bland shock of surprise, then irritation. Always that
packaged delivery, pre-insured against an adverse response. He tried to
say something sensible and mature; he sat back in his chair, opened his
mouth but nothing happened. Tears welled up suddenly; a pain in his
chest bloomed. He fought it all back furiously. Jackie looked through
that lovely flowing fringe, from those bright, lively eyes, with slight
distaste as well as a certain concern.

'Don't be so melodramatic, Paul. I thought you might be happy
for me, actually.'

'So, who is it?' he managed.

'The professor in the department, Ken Evans.'

He snorted involuntarily and was immediately ashamed. It was hard to distinguish jealous hurt from anything else he was feeling. Tears rolled down his face, hot and red. Then he felt a sense of pride, like a hurt boy standing tall. He sat back in his chair, looking towards the red velvet curtains. The folds were deep burgundy, and the forward curves caught the dim light of the wall lamps. The lights of a passing double-decker bus flashed yellow on the worn edge of the slightly parted centre. A saxophone extemporised rather gaily over a cautious rhythm and bass. He was vaguely aware of a large number of noisy people entering the room; the film must have ended; he could feel billows of cold air as the door opened and was pressed shut. It was a relief to feel the presence of others behind, around him. Jackie was telling him a long story about how she and Ken had got together, all the boring details about his ex-wife and how careful they had had to be to avoid the jealous woman's crazy accusations, as well as to allay the typical prudish disapproval of fellow members of staff, but actually they hadn't rushed into anything, she hadn't wanted to after such a long time with him, Paul. Her two hands were placed on the table, and she occasionally lifted one or the other to make a gesture, turning her fine, long hands over, the pale fine skin shining against the old varnished pine.

'Would you get me another drink?' he asked, interrupting the flow of her story. She looked up. The way that the saga flowed suggested much telling, which increased his bitterness. 'Uh? Oh, yes, of course.' She moved off towards the crowded bar, steady and composed. He enjoyed a respite from her words, a chance to collect his wits. Did he hate her? Had she let him down? Probably not. He was ashamed to realise that part of his identity had become bound up with the possibility that they might get together again; with that illusion destroyed, he was unable to control his grief. Feeling broken and absurd, he shed more of those racking, satisfying hot tears, his head tucked in a corner. He rolled another cigarette with indulgent precision, thankful for a friend in tobacco, a glorious kind of refuge from the world. Jackie came back with two more pints and two packets of crisps.

'Look, green flavour, your favourite.' She smiled, a little anxiously. He didn't respond, a bitter sense of control coming over him with the drink and cigarette.

'So, when did you first sleep with him?' It was too intimate a question, but he felt reckless.

'Uh, I don't quite remember –'

'Oh, really,' he retorted; 'you usually remember such details exactly.'

'Last summer. He invited me round to a dinner party with some visiting academics. We'd gone out a few times before that.'

'While we were still having a relationship?'

'Uh, was it?'

'Oh, come on, just be straight with me.' He hated this conversation. He hated his own suspicion, wanting to find grounds for blame. He hated the disillusioning that was implied, the possibility of his own stupidity.

'Yes, we went out a few times. I don't think there's anything wrong with that, do you? Just going out with a colleague for a drink.' The beginnings of a frost crackled slightly in her voice. He found himself contracting with fear.

'I feel upset and I'm trying to piece together what happened. I admit I suspect you left me for him, and that is a hurtful thought.'

'Paul, I've told you before: the reason I wanted to end our relationship was because it seemed unworkable with me in Leeds. You didn't want to move over with me, did you?' That old grenade. 'And anyway, it felt stale and too much like settling down.' He didn't want to move into this landscape of conversation again.

'Yes, yes, all right. But you've very much kept your new relationship to yourself, and that arouses suspicions, in me at least.'

'So? What was I supposed to do? Tell you everything in my life, just so you feel secure? Anyway, I knew you'd make a fuss if I went out with anyone else, so I didn't want to say.'

Her cat eyes: blue, pale, smoky: warning lights. Her mouth was a living door, rippling with emotion, shut tight against him. And still he felt a twinge of love for all that energy, and felt angry and stupid with himself for that. This rebellion became a force wanting to push past those feline eyes, those lips, and speak something of his strength; but in a flash this force collapsed under its own weight, an imploding anger, and again he was not able to stand up for himself against her. He cried some more, his heart a smoking ruin. Her smouldering eyes continued to burn over him. She shook her head and looked away. Briefly, he wanted to smash a glass over her head, over that high broad forehead, but that feeling also quickly died. A dull headache began to pound.

'Where exactly do you live now?' he asked her, continuing to probe suspiciously.

'Still with Molly, the place I've lived in for three and a half years.' Her tone was exasperated.

'Oh.' He had completely expected her to say, in a bland or cheery tone, that she'd moved in with Ken Evans. He knew that she knew that he had expected that; further evidence to her of his stupidity and preconceptions. 'It's just that I've never seen the place; I tried to visit –

do you remember? – but you never wanted me over there. I've never had much idea what your living situation is like.'

'I've told you often enough, Paul. It used to be pretty horrid, because Molly was unhappy, the kids were messy, and I really didn't want to have to spend a weekend there with you as well. Now the kids have moved out, I have a bigger room, and it's all much better.'

They sat in silence for a while.

'So, do you want to stay in touch?' he said. She sighed, as if tired with having to explain everything to his confused dull mind.

'Yes, of course, Paul. I just wanted to tell you about Ken so that we can continue to be friends. You are one of my closest friends, you know. Who else would cook me spaghetti and chilli at two hours' notice?' Her grateful smile irritated him.

'I want to go home now,' he said. As they picked their way through the crowded seats and tables, a young woman at a table smiled and waved. It was Charlotte, his favourite student, and he was both glad and ashamed to see her.

'She looked pleased to see you,' said Jackie, as they zipped their coats out on the chilly street. 'Tell me, Paul, are you interested in anyone?' Jackie was grinning.

'I'm sure you'd be the first to find out if I was,' said Paul. They walked back to his flat saying little else. Jackie seemed unperturbed by the evening's conversation, and chattered away as she prepared for bed. In the morning, she left early for her meeting on campus.

IN THE RED COW, Betty had placed her hand-knitted 'Time Please' socks over the wooden pump handles. The spaniel had gone home with the barman.

'So now, gentlemen,' Paul said, 'you may perhaps understand why I seek your advice. I am, you might say, pissed off with Jackie, and with myself for being so dependent upon her.'

'So you should be,' said Jim, after downing the last of his beer.

We walked back to Lyndhurst together and sat round the kitchen table with a pot of tea.

'You two have got something in common, then,' said Jim. 'I mean, being under the control of women. But Juniper hasn't told you about his ritual, has he?'

'His ritual?' said Paul.

I felt reluctant to talk about the men's weekend, but Paul quietly demanded to know about it, and Jim explained. Paul took it in, pulling on a thin cigarette and making difficult faces.

'Mythopoetic, mythopoetic,' he said. 'It sounds like an appalling excuse for indulgent vagueness; but on the other hand reminds me how

Plato uses myth to illustrate what he describes as those things which cannot be explained through rational discourse – like wisdom, of course, or love.'

'I see my work as that of renovating the fixed assumptions of modern philosophical discourse,' said Jim, 'by returning to a wiser understanding of the human situation, as rooted in myth and tradition, enabling us to depose this false god, reason.'

'To get back to the truth of the *id*,' I said.

'You always want to reduce things to psychology,' said Jim. I threw up my hands.

'I was just trying to help Paul along.'

'I have no need of reductive walking-sticks,' said Paul with good-natured confidence.

'I suggest you need a ritual to bring to life the spirit of the warrior within you,' said Jim.

'Yes,' he said immediately. 'So what is it that I should do?'

'The matter at hand,' I suggested, 'is the establishment of clearer personal boundaries, a stronger sense of how, practically, you are prepared to relate to Jackie while maintaining integrity and self-respect.'

'OK,' said Paul.

'But the ritual has to come from you,' said Jim.

We picked our way along the hallway through the debris and ascended to Jim's spacious attic bedroom, the refurbishment of which was complete. The stonework of one wall had been revealed, cleaned and sealed, and spotlights picked out sanded beams. It was furnished simply, with varnished floorboards and an old rug in the centre of the room. A big ginger cat turned its sleepy head from a duvet stretched over a mattress on the floor in a corner.

'All right, I think – I'm not sure, but I think – I'd like to ritually invoke that warrior-aspect of myself,' Paul said.

'You think –' I said, putting my hands on his chest – 'you'd like to perhaps' – and shoved him, like boys in a playground shove – 'invoke the warrior, huh?' He nearly fell over, and then seemed almost to cry, like a boy, and looked at me, upset. With effort, Paul stood up to me.

'Yes, warrior,' he said, shoving me back a little. 'Though I was never in fights at school and I despise violence.' I shrugged. I could have said the same about myself.

'I've got an idea,' said Jim. He brought out a kukri, a curved Ghurkha knife in a black leather sheath. He placed it in front of a bookcase full of philosophy books – his shrine. He suggested that he and I stand between Paul and that knife, and that Paul fight his way through us to ritually reclaim his lost weapon.

'I thought the idea was supposed to come from me,' he said, laughing.

'It's just a suggestion,' said Jim.

'I'll do it,' Paul said. But I was three, Jim five, inches taller than him; and I a stone or two, Jim three or four, heavier. He stood looking at us, weighing up his chances, which seemed remote, until his face bloomed into a reckless joy.

Jim and I stood firm. I flashed my eyes and teeth at the little man before me. He stepped towards us and tried to pass between our bodies. Jim and I pushed him forcefully away.

He threw himself at us with a mild roar, managing to push us back about a foot, until Jim, energy stirred, lifted him up and threw him back onto the bed. He landed with a thump of back and head, the mattress letting his weight through to the hard floor. The cat bounced in the air, hissed, and clawed Paul's face before trotting haughtily to the hatch-door and down the stairs. He sat up, looking shocked, four scratch-lines down one cheek. He pulled his palm over it and looked. The blood, now wiped across his cheek, was a shock. He leapt up and returned with a short run-up, and quite winded me with his shoulder. But the adrenaline flowed; I brought him down heavily, twisting his arm until he cried out. Blood was smeared across his whole face, my hands and Jim's t-shirt. The big man pulled it off and growled. Paul growled too and unbuttoned his shirt, and wiped his blood on his forehead and chest. Jim growled louder, and Paul made something of a half-hearted roar, then managed better, and better still. I stamped my feet, leaping up and down. Paul's body was slim but lean and taut.

Then something strange happened. Paul closed his eyes and seemed to disappear into himself briefly, gently pushing up and down on his feet. He looked completely relaxed. Then, swiftly, boldly, he swung his arms, approached me, and I found myself falling onto the floor. Jim's bulk joined me before I'd managed to turn over. By the time Jim and I had sat up, Paul was standing between us and the bookshelves, holding the kukri above his head.

'Would anyone like to dispute the *cogito*?' he enquired of the two men sitting at his feet.

Jim and I looked up, shocked, then laughed. He resheathed the knife.

'I've practised Tai Chi for ten years, but have never had cause to use it before now. I suspect neither of you is trained in the martial arts.' We shook our heads.

Two days later we received a card in the post. It showed African warrior tribesmen, naked and strong; Paul had written: *I haven't felt so good since I defended my doctoral thesis four years ago. And that was just academic! Love to you both.*

spring beauty

THE LIGHT GREW LOUDER every day, freshness tingling through the late March air. I was feeling stronger than I had for months. I knocked on Paul Corbett's door one Thursday for another discussion session; I walked in, but he was talking with a student, the young woman with avid eyes I'd met coming out of his room the previous October.

'Come in, Juniper,' he called as I stepped out of the room again. 'I was just telling Charlotte about you.' She was smiling as I walked in.

'Hello,' I said.

'Paul says you're doing some work in the philosophy of love,' said Charlotte.

'With his good assistance,' I said, glancing at Paul, surprised at her informality.

'Have you convinced him yet of the chaste delights of intellectual love?' Charlotte said to Paul, with a blithe quickness. 'That's his friend Spinoza's take on passion,' she said to me.

'Hang on there,' said Paul; 'I think you're overemphasising the cerebral connotation of intellectual –'

Charlotte put her hand up.

'A joke,' said Paul, looking at me. 'She baits me, Juniper. It isn't dignified. Get along with you,' he said to Charlotte. She left, swinging her black bag over her shoulder, moving with a precise, fluid motion.

'She's my favourite student,' Paul said to me, once the door had closed.

'Likes you,' I said.

'If I was eight – even five – years younger –' he began.

'But you're only thirty! And she's – what? Twenty-two? Three?' Paul laughed, then looked somewhere past my left shoulder.

'Twenty-three in June. Somehow I feel that I belong to a different generation. Odd, isn't it? I don't suppose you'd have such a perception, although you're only four years younger than me. Anyway, I believe she has a boyfriend named Toby; though he seems to be a little strange.'

'But might you be interested in Charlotte if you felt younger and she didn't have a strange boyfriend? You don't have to be honest with me of course.'

Paul laughed. 'I suspect that you are attempting to establish whether I am receptive to the thought of a new romantic relationship. Well, in this particular case, Charlotte seems already to have taken me on as a sort of confidante, in the sense of sharing with me certain personal issues and questions that she presumably feels I have some notion about. So Charlotte and I seem already to have gone beyond the point at which we might act on some spark of mutual attraction; and I now have to take into account the duties of friendship. Indeed, it is rather a relief to eschew the indulgence of romantic fantasy. Although it is not illegal for an academic to have a relationship with one of his students, it is certainly unprofessional. And I wouldn't want to imagine the anxiety such an involvement would provoke in me.'

'Does that mean that in fact you fancy her, but that you've somehow sublimated it?'

Paul smiled. 'Juniper, when one is teaching, because of the nature of the dynamic between older male and younger female, it is extraordinarily easy to fall in love with these pretty, vivacious young women. There is often one or two in one's tutorial groups who have open faces, unspoiled hearts, slim bodies and quick wit; over and again, I've found myself brimming with a sweet joy and a yearning desire to tell them they are the most perfect young things; only to find that the next month brings along a new beauty to distract me from the melancholy into which I'd fallen over the first. It's a working risk. The adrenaline of putting oneself into a position of authority, to which students naturally defer, leads directly to this welling of benign tenderness from a position of superiority.'

'But – Charlotte?' I asked.

'Charlotte, yes. She is different in that, as a postgraduate, she has already lost some of the innocence of –' he paused.

'You mean that with her you have less power?'

'Something like that,' he grinned. 'But I still fell for her; she has a confidence and a naturally sparkling intelligence. But curiously, my sense of wonder did not last very long, certainly not since we became more personally acquainted. Perhaps she reminds me just a little too much of Jackie.'

'How so?' I said, dismayed.

'Not in any negative sense,' he said quickly. 'Simply that I can hardly help associating the emotions produced by association with ambitious, capable, independent yet highly feminine women with my experience of Jackie, at least in some degree.'

'That sounds superficial,' I said. 'It could be taken to mean that you're scared of independent women.'

'You think so?' said Paul, frowning. 'All I meant to imply was that my experience with Jackie has had a determining effect on my perception. But then again, I must confess that, despite years of being a good liberal feminist, I am beginning to realise that there are certain qualities essential for philosophy – a robust self-confidence and a honed intellectual rigour – that seem to me to be peculiarly masculine.' He smiled. 'And then Charlotte comes along, certainly feminine, with the usual justifiable complaints against men in general, and I can fault neither her mind nor her confidence.'

The guileless conservatism of his outlook made me laugh.

'Don't you feel frightened by some of these women?' he asked me.

'I don't feel frightened of anything,' I replied.

'Oh,' he said.

There was a knock at the door. Charlotte put her head into the room.

'Sorry,' she said. 'I left a book.' It was on the black plastic seat beside me. I passed it over, looking more closely at her in the light of Paul's praises. The smallness of her, being a woman, the small curves of her nose; the brown-ness of her, the way the skin was darker in the creases of her skin; her otherness, the way she was not-me and not like me; the way all this difference was in a mysterious way superficial yet absolute. The avidity of her eyes now seemed diffused through her whole body, as an intensity of presence. She smiled at me and glanced at Paul. He did not look up, lost in thought.

'Thanks,' she whispered, and moved from the room with the same precise actions as before. The door closed silently.

'So you regularly fall for your women students; but have you ever really fallen in love with one?' I asked.

'When I was a student myself,' Paul said, not meeting my eyes; 'but that was a long time ago. Whilst Jackie and I lived together, there was no real temptation to fall in love. These days I occasionally trip up, as it were, over the feelings of attraction that have arisen, but it is always rather painful,' Paul said finally. 'One has moral qualms. She often leaves things here,' he added, looking towards the door. Then he reached for his copy of Aristotle's *Ethics*.

By a happy coincidence, I met Charlotte again at the bus stop. My bike had a puncture that I hadn't yet repaired, so I was travelling to and from town by bus. I joined her in the queue.

'Do you live in town then?' she asked.

I nodded. 'Salt Marsh Road. And you?'

'Sort of halfway. But I'm going into town now to do some shopping.' The common ground we'd acquired through meeting in Paul's office ran out. An awkward silence ensued as we stood in the quietly humming queue.

'So you're doing an MA,' I said.

'It's great,' she replied, bursting into life with a smile.

'Paul says you're his favourite student.'

Charlotte smiled, gratified. 'He's such a sweet man, but he can be so square. Did he say I tease him too much?'

'No,' I said. 'I don't think he minds.' Another small silence ensued. 'So, what are you studying?'

'Who,' she said, 'not what.'

'Who?'

She leaned towards me, looking up directly, intensely.

'Kant,' she said in a lowered, reverent tone.

'Ah,' I said. She continued looking at me, as if expecting some sort of pious response to the passion of her philosophical commitment.

You are rather pretty, I decided. She looked Indian, with the fine facial bones and large dark brown eyes of the race. Her shoulder-length hair was made of hundreds of dark, thick, long curves. But her accent was English, not to say upper class. There was a faint smile around her mouth, belying her piety.

'Immanuel Kant,' I added, nodding, not wishing to break the eye contact, the very interesting bond. But at that moment, the bus appeared over the edge of the hill that led up from the main road from Greyston to the campus. The queue woke to life and arranged itself like an orderly giant millipede, clinking change in all of its hands, then gradually climbed, foot by foot, into the bus. Soon Charlotte and I were seated together in the comfortable, warm bus, top deck front row.

'There are some nice things about this campus,' I said, pointing at the daffodils that blazed out in unbroken lines on each side of the road, as the bus swayed down the hill.

'Look,' said Charlotte, pointing to a flatbed trailer standing on the tarmac in front of the groundsmen's barns. A peacock stood right in the centre, tail raised and spread, gradually turning its halo of metallic starbursts. Two peahens sat calmly on the edge of the trailer, completely ignoring their impressive suitor. 'As far as I can make out, he's the only peacock up here. But despite that, the peahens don't seem to fancy him at all. Have you ever seen any peachicks? He spends most of his time hanging out with a goose.'

'The cruelty of women,' I said. 'You would have thought that the peahens might feel an obligation at least to pretend to like him, given that he has to carry around that piece of environmental art to impress them.'

'The irony of environmental ethics,' added Charlotte, with mock pathos. 'Nature herself isn't ethical or kind.'

'Do you think nature can be thought of as a whole like that?'

'No, no,' she said quickly. 'It's just a figure of speech that represents our perception of an interconnected and united world of appearances. In reality, of course, the source of this perception is the unity of the mind, not the world.'

'I bet you got a first.'

'Yes. Cambridge. Look! That's where I live,' she said, turning in her seat and pointing to a large house next to the road on the outskirts of town. Her excitement at showing me made me smile.

'Paradise Hill,' I read off the street sign. 'Nice place?'

'Huge house, a bit run down. Four other postgrads, all Christians. It's a sort of Christian community.'

'Are you a Christian, then?' I asked.

'I'm a bit of a spanner in the works, to tell the truth.'

'Didn't Kant's philosophy hope to let science make room for faith?'

'Very good,' she said. 'But Kant's Christianity is a long way from Roman Catholicism. I'm not a Christian at all; I just happened to end up living there. Who do you live with?'

'Jim Fletcher, in a house owned by a couple of his mates. Do you know Jim?'

'Yes,' she said. 'We've argued a couple of times in the postgrad study room. He has a typical post-modern line on Kantian philosophy, though he doesn't seem to have grasped the main arguments at all.'

'Ah,' I said.

'Do you talk philosophy at home?'

I laughed. 'Would you like to come round for tea to find out?'

'You mean dinner?' she said. I nodded. 'When?'

I hadn't seriously thought Charlotte would take up the offer, though I had meant it.

'Tomorrow?' I said.

'OK,' she said. 'Eight o'clock?'

I remembered the existence of Toby, but decided against inviting him as well. After all, she would have mentioned him if she'd wanted him to come.

'Kant's pretty useless on love,' she burst out suddenly, as if admitting something but having thought about it carefully first. It was time to get off the bus.

'See you tomorrow then,' I said.

'I'm looking forward to it,' she said, smiling. She turned and walked away, with that quick, light step.

I walked up the hill in the centre of Greyston, past the castle and down the other side, towards Lyndhurst. The evening light held out, the season eating into the night. The blue of almost-summer sky beckoned in the distance, a band over the sea between harmless low clouds. I felt almost happy, despite living in a city. It was a surprise.

At home, Jim was hunched over a mug of tea and a newspaper in the dark basement kitchen. I told him I'd invited Charlotte for dinner the next day.

'You know she's a neo-Kantian?' he muttered, with a frown.

AFTER JIM AND I had eaten, we walked to a wholefood café in town for a meeting organised by the Green Party. The local council had announced plans for a new bypass for the town, to reduce congestion around the busy one-way system. There seemed to me to be a thousand better ways to reduce congestion than to build more roads. The glass-fronted cake shelves in the restaurant were empty, the coffee machine stood with its round glass jug full of clear water, and the refrigerated salad bar gleamed stainless instead of with shredded vegetable colours. The tables were pushed back against the walls, and thirty or forty activists sat in rough curves on the in-turned chairs.

A man sporting a thick black beard stood and looked around the meeting. He was Professor Horrocks, a figure locally famous for his proactive campaigning for a bicycle route between the campus and the town.

'Here's a map of the route,' he said, lifting a large map onto an easel. 'From the motorway near the university, it cuts through the fields, down to the salt marsh. It skirts the edge of the Site of Special Scientific Interest and then spans the river at its narrowest point, to join the Heycombe road here.'

Jim and I looked at each other. Just the weekend before, we had walked past the spot where the bridge was planned; it was a pleasant twenty-minute walk from Lyndhurst, a wild, empty flatness along the estuary that led into the Bay, full of the impatient calls of oystercatchers and mournful curlew cries.

'As I've told the DoT,' the professor continued, 'my studies, based on careful research over three years, indicate that the bypass can at best relieve only twenty per cent of the town centre traffic. Unfortunately, estimates suggest that traffic will increase by that same amount within five years. Net congestion relief afforded by the bypass: nil. What we really need is an integrated public transport system, not a new four-lane highway that will ruin the salt marsh.'

There was some clapping and mumbling. The business of delegating tasks began. I had joined the Green Party a couple of years before, but this was the first time I had been involved in anything active. The planned bypass had thrown me into a new and uncomfortable position of resistance, and I was having to learn how to act.

'Face it, Juniper,' Jim had said; 'you've lived in your own private Eden for years, and now you're waking up to the ugliness the bastards

74

are making out here.' Jim was new to Green concerns, but an old hand at opposition.

My attention was suddenly diverted to a face that appeared between the shoulders in the row in front. It was Monica Macdonald, with whom I had been painfully, hopelessly in love for almost two weeks in the first summer term of my degree. I'd never told Ros. She had seemed to me astonishingly, radiantly beautiful; I had hardly been able to believe how beautiful she was. I had seen her in philosophy lectures, but one day we sat opposite each other in the library. The sun was streaming in onto her bare arms, was shining in her curly black hair; she was wearing a white sleeveless dress and I had felt a dumbstruck love, a devotion and awe, that was almost impersonal, but that had made my body shake. She had smiled at me from the midst of her sunshine, and we had talked a little about the forthcoming exams – a hurried, furtive, thrilling whispering, leaning towards each other over the flat expanse of the tabletop. Now, years later and in well-wrapped March, her large brown eyes met mine but didn't recognise them. But my heart fluttered a little.

I thought of what Paul had told me that morning, of how he fell in love with his students. Now I remembered something of what that feeling was like; how such passions amuse our minds, while playing with our hearts. Monica was still good-looking, though she didn't have the same effect on me. I thought of Charlotte, then of Paul; then laughed to myself. Jim looked at me, and poked me to raise my arm. Yes, I would be walking the route of the planned road on Sunday. And again, yes, I would be prepared to do some door knocking to encourage people to oppose the plan. I would be active.

over dinner

CHARLOTTE ARRIVED AT EIGHT o'clock exactly, with a bottle of wine.

'Welcome to Lyndhurst,' I said, and led her down to the kitchen. The rubble in the hall had disappeared, as had the old lead piping, but some cowboy-rewiring had created new obstacles: coils of solid-core ring main cabling nestling in corners, raw copper tongues pricking from plastic mouths. The walls were lined with the scar tissue of new plastering over implanted wires. Down in the kitchen, a dividing wall had been taken out, leaving stone stumps baring surfaces unseen for a century and new piles of rubble.

Despite the squalor of its raw stonework and the half-finished electrical surgery, the kitchen had an enjoyable basic charm. The big old porcelain sink, set beneath the grimy window that looked up a thin chute towards the daylight of the front yard, had a smooth beauty that spoke of older, tougher days. Chris and Matt, Jim's mates who owned the place, had acquired masses of solid beech from a refitted clothes shop, and a friend of theirs had transformed it into simple but strong furniture: table, benches, worktops and shelves. The latest demolition had created a wide basement space, at the back of which was a sitting area with a pot-bellied woodstove on a flagstone plinth. Recently installed spotlights lent a contemplative air, despite the handfuls of wires looped between the rafters, tumbling like vines down the cracked plaster walls. Jim was at the kitchen table, reading. He stood up when I entered with Charlotte.

'Good evening,' he said, offering his hand. 'Welcome to our subhuman abode. Can I interest you in a mug of tea?'

'Yes please,' Charlotte replied. 'Can I have a look around? I love old houses.' Jim made tea and I laid the table, while Charlotte explored. She opened the stove and shoved in another log, then tried the hanging basket chair that Matt had found in a skip, tucking her legs beneath her and wriggling into the creaking enclosed space. She found her way out of the back door and into the long, dark back garden, and came back in holding a large ginger cat, which suffered its carriage with a dull feline patience.

'Is he yours?' she asked me, scratching behind the chipped ears on its heavy head.

'Archie? No, he came with the house.'

We sat at the table to drink tea. Jim removed the hand-knitted woollen tea cosy his mum had given him for Christmas to reveal a large

76

stoneware teapot that glowed with blue and green glazes, like the colour of lichens on mountain rocks. He poured into matching, fat-bellied mugs.

'Lovely pottery!' said Charlotte. 'It must be hand-made.'

'By Juniper's ex,' said Jim.

'Is she a professional, then?' Charlotte asked me, one hand grasping the handle of her mug, the other with elbow on table and chin in hand.

'She's heading that way,' I said. 'At least, she was.'

'May I smoke?' she asked, producing a packet of cigarettes.

'If you don't mind us joining you,' said Jim. We drank tea and smoked Charlotte's cigarettes, the swirling grey haze gathering in the weak spotlights. I served a thick macaroni cheese enriched with sweetcorn, mushrooms and peppers, Jim poured the wine Charlotte had brought, and we ate and drank and talked, the banter of academics unwinding their minds.

'That was great,' said Charlotte, pushing her hand-glazed plate away, although she'd left quite a bit uneaten, mainly pieces of pepper and carrot.

'Did you not like it?' I asked.

'It was lovely, thanks, but too much for me.'

'She wouldn't want to dull her powers of thought,' added Jim. 'I'll finish off what she's left. What does life offer us but consumption now that we've woken from the long dream of Reason? More wine!' He laughed to himself.

Charlotte smiled as she poured him another glass, but could not help commenting, almost casually, that the post-modern denial of the task of pure reason was mere nihilistic recidivism. Jim's face contracted into a sharp look, and I tensed out of my complacent relaxation.

You could almost hear the discrete slipping of steel, with a swishing slide, from scabbards hung beneath loose cloaks; see the blades, held behind tensed legs, glint mischievously in the slant light.

'Only those who have not actually understood the task could be so naive as to sweep aside its significance for the destiny of humankind,' she continued, swinging a piece of wool from side to side in front of Archie, sitting on the bench beside her. He followed its swing twice and then ignored it.

Jim coolly flipped his zippo and relit the stub of a roll-up, exhaling up into the dim recesses of the ceiling with an intimidatory flourish. Charlotte did not flinch, indeed, took no notice.

'The deflation,' began Jim, 'of the vast arrogance of the transcendental ego is so painful to contemplate that the emasculated modern mind holds on to the old myth of progress, unwilling to abandon the comforting old certainties.'

Charlotte appeared to blanch slightly, but she bluffed with extraordinary precision, reaching a hand down to stroke the cat, then, with a fluid motion, pulling her thick black knitted jersey over her head and tossing it behind her onto a Workmate. She turned to face Jim, shaking her hair straight.

'The rejection of reason – reason as a task, I mean, not an achievement – in favour of the easier, so-called 'truth', of instinct is in truth symptomatic of a failure of nerve. This weakened post-modern mind manages to use its remnant power of thought, but merely to defend its failure.' One hand lay palm down along the table; the other returned, cool as a snake, to the cat's head.

Jim's eyes filled with a smoke of burning oil. He swung his cigarette from his right side over to the ashtray on his left with fencing accuracy, and knocked his ash with a single perfect blow into the bull's eye of the turned, ash-patched bowl. I knew Jim believed in a tactical violence, never a pacifistic withdrawal. A pause meant not that he had stalled, but that he was assessing the quantum of force required. I felt the decision snap and the motion of his retaliation begin.

'What could be less reasonable than a faith in the power of reason for the further progress of humankind? Reason was only ever the puppet king of imperialist powers that marched from Europe – true home of reason – across the whole benighted globe, spreading the fruits of rational progress, which so happened also to make Europe very rich.'

He reached for the wine bottle and swung it across the table towards Charlotte in a motion stripped of crass politeness. Red liquid, gift of the vine-god, spilled violently into her empty glass. He dropped the bottle heavily on the table between them. She pushed the glass away, met his look with hers.

'In the matter of imperialist ambition, whose bastard child I might claim to be, I do not doubt the powerful influence of the instinct to dominate in the European mind; but to what end therefore do we abandon the goal of rationality, abandon European culture itself to the jackals and madmen who use truth to barbaric ends? Nihilism is understandable after what has happened, but does not deserve praise.'

Holding his smoking gaze with her deep, dark Asian eyes, she flipped the lid of her cigarette box over the slumped head of the cat and thrust it towards Jim. The little yellow butts hovered in the air. He grasped one with his huge, thick fingers and pulled it slowly from the gripping box. It slid free like a torpedo, aimed directly at his mouth. With his other hand, he flipped and lit his lighter; thrust it towards Charlotte's chin. She sucked alight her cigarette without acknowledgement. He lit his, sucked in, exhaled, inhaled.

'In real life we call people mad who live as though what they dreamed were their truth. The dream of reason, the perfect revelation of the mind of God, the benign reign of beneficent clear universalizable principles – all this is madness when made the only guiding light, and the clearest sign that someone, perhaps a whole culture, has lost touch with what is real. The power that spins the stars, drives the sap in the trees, the speech of philosophers – all this is unknown, indescribable, absolutely beyond the puny power of the rational mind. To bear the truth – to feel into the terrifying abyss of life and instinct – this is the way towards real self-knowledge.'

Charlotte suddenly looked small; Jim's onslaught seemed to have crushed her. Her hand seemed to tremble as it clutched the thin stem of her wine glass. But her voice rose in an arc, high and free; it soared in the darkness and came down with the spotlight glare onto Jim's unbrushed hair.

'And every star follows its course, and every tree has its spring, and every true leader is in harmony with the light of reason that guides her. Faith, so close to madness, so close to dream, faith in the rationality of existence, is a self-augmenting light that cannot be quenched. The mind of God – if we must use that culture-bound, limited expression – does not speak loudly, but everywhere whispers in the midst of anarchy and willpower; speaks in voices hard to understand; and only slowly, over centuries, come geniuses – Descartes, Newton, Kant – who can render into human speech something of the majesty of truth, in a progress that few can even follow, let alone add to. It is the most precious, difficult achievement there can be.'

I had sat, passively transfixed, as battle raged. A sweet odour from the oven roused me. I staggered to my feet, back and away from the table. The cat looked up sharply. The combatants did not look, horns still locked; on my left, the dark force of femininity and perceptive reason, a Saracen with laser-fine scimitar, slighter than I had imagined in her black t-shirt; on my right this livid hulk of masculinity and intelligent instinct, a huge Englishman with his broadsword and heart of oak; twin powers facing off across the turmoil of Europe. I snatched up the tea cosy that had lain limp on the table next to the cool, empty teapot and threw it down between the foes.

'Does anyone fancy some pudding?'

Jim and Charlotte looked up.

'Is there pudding, then?' asked Jim, shifting attention with a nearly audible clanking of armour. Charlotte's eyes slid up blandly from the cat.

'Dessert? How splendid!'

We ate treacle tart and custard in near silence, then, over coffee, talked over the politics of the planned bypass.

'Would you like to walk the route on Sunday?' I asked her.

'Yes!' she said. 'As much as anything I'd like to get out and see the local countryside. I've lived in Greyston for nearly six months but I've hardly got out of town.'

'Excuse me, I must leave,' said Jim. 'I told Beth I'd be there about now.' Beth had begun to have anxiety attacks on Friday and Saturday evenings around the time that the pubs closed. Peter had been as good as his word and left her alone, but he had left a deeper wound that was far from healed. Jim had taken to visiting her to keep her company.

As he reached the foot of the stairs, Jim turned.

'Madame, I salute your courage,' he said. Charlotte nodded. He left.

It was ten o'clock. Charlotte, Archie and I shifted to the sitting area, and Charlotte climbed into the hanging chair. I passed her a glass of my rhubarb wine once the chair had stopped swinging, and then settled with Archie into an enormous, ugly armchair. Red warmth flickered from the curved open door of the stove.

'So, tell me about your place out in the countryside,' she asked. Charlotte sipped her wine and looked interested, as I told her about myself.

'It's as if you've been thrown out of the Garden of Eden, into – this,' she said, looking around.

'I quite like it at the moment,' I said.

'I bet you won't for long.'

It was time for another cup of tea. The cat left for his nocturnals, and the woodstove required poking and tweaking.

'How did you end up in Greyston?' I asked. 'A woman with a Cambridge first might have stayed there, I think.'

'I was thrown out for being too clever,' she said.

'Begin at the beginning,' I advised.

CHARLOTTE HAD BEEN BORN in London. Her parents were doctors, from middle-class Indian families. They had trained in medicine in Britain, met each other and stayed. They now lived in Surrey, successful specialists in different medical fields. Charlotte had been sent to public school, and on leaving had spent a year working with the homeless in London before she went up to Cambridge to read English; then she discovered philosophy, then Hegel, then Kant.

She had applied to stay on at Cambridge to continue her studies, then, once her finals were over, had flown to India for a long summer break. She had been several times before as a child, but this was her first visit alone. Her parents owned a house in New Delhi, which was mostly left empty, though tended by an old 'boy' who kept it clean; she based herself there in spacious ex-colonial style and began to explore the ancient city as her confidence increased. Despite her native looks, she was of course a tourist, without a word of Hindi or any of the special skills of patience, humour, passive tolerance of inconvenience and ability to survive in a crowd that the chaos of India demanded. But she had learned quickly, donned semi-native garb, and ventured out on the train down the Ganges plain towards the holy city of Varanasi.

There, in the Yogi Lodge Hotel, while eating chocolate fudge cake and drinking coke, she had met Toby. He was a Westerner who had come to India to immerse himself in the religious life of the ancient culture. He wore a white lungi, white Indian shirt and blue flip-flops, and he ate curry with his hands; with his blond hair and pale face, he shone like a ghostly sadhu among the sweaty Western travellers and pious Hindu pilgrims. He had come up from the south, where he had been staying at an ashram. Toby was intending to travel on up the holy Ganges to the town of Rishikesh, in the mountains.

So it was Toby Simmons who introduced Charlotte to the history and practices of her own ancestral religious culture. He showed her the temples of Shiva and Durga, and explained the activities of the brahmins and devotees, waving smoky flames and banging drums. He introduced her to the orange-skirted, dreadlocked ascetics and sadhus he'd met on the riverbanks, their foreheads crusted with horizontal stripes of paint, with wooden rosary-beads around their necks, some carrying iron tridents, symbols of Shiva. Ancient Varanasi was Shiva's city, the god of both asceticism and passionate love, of yogic power and of jealous possessiveness of his consort. They smoked a chillum, an inverted ceramic cone stuffed with cannabis resin, with two old sadhus, who laughed as Toby choked on the sweet, acrid smoke; Charlotte inhaled gently and then nearly passed out. Another day, she paid for a boat and rowers to take them out into the river, and when they reached the town limits upstream, they jumped overboard with the rower-boys into the muddy monsoon-swollen water, to drift down and gain the blessing of that holy river. Which was a distinct health risk: dead lepers and brahmins were weighted and dumped off boats to decompose in the holy stream. To die in Varanasi was to go straight to heaven, and many Hindus made the pilgrimage especially. Toby showed her the burning ghats, where oily black smoke billowed from the fierce, dark pyres; where stony-faced families gathered around shrouded bodies, and filthy, black-skinned low-caste people organised the firewood and cleared up, shouting in the midst of all the death and grief.

They practised yoga and meditation with an old Indian who taught on a flat rooftop in the evening. For Toby, Charlotte was a grounding influence, an earth, and she took him to the house in Delhi for a week. He met her grandparents, uncles, aunts and cousins, and for the first time she heard them talking of their religious beliefs and views; her uncle visited a Ganesh temple every day. Her parents had shielded her from this whole side of India, which they regarded as superstitious and un-Western. She herself couldn't take seriously the idol-worship and quaintness of her relatives' faith, but she was drawn to keep exploring her background.

By the time Charlotte and Toby had left for Rishikesh, a bond had formed between them, which they could no longer undo, and they had to turn their minds to what would happen when they returned to England. Toby had a year more to complete of a religious studies degree at Greyston, so she decided to ask to transfer to a Master's course there. She wrote letters, and made swift arrangements when she reached home; most of her Cambridge friends had left town, so she moved up north with no sense of loss. Toby had contacts in the chaplaincy on the campus, and it was through these that Charlotte had found the room in the house on Paradise Hill. Toby, meanwhile, lived in a house in town. However, things could not be said to be going well between them. The spontaneity, engagement and joy that Toby found in India did not seem to be transferable; back in England he was rather awkward and solitary, unable in his home environment to combine his spiritual concerns with the lifestyle of a modern student. Although he remained Charlotte's closest friend in town, and she remained for him possibly his only source of natural ease, the pleasure had ebbed from their bond. There were difficulties.

'For instance,' she said, allowing herself to express some frustration, 'he has a spiritual routine, as he calls it. He does his meditation in the mornings and some yoga before dinner in the evenings; which is all very laudable, but he can be so rigid about doing it, and sometimes blames me if he's been with me overnight and in the morning doesn't feel like meditating. And then on Monday, he fasts – no food, just water. He gets in a tight mood, but keeps on forcing himself to do the whole day, saying he's training his mind to loosen its habitual appetite. Does this sound extreme? Or am I just an indulgent hedonist, undisciplined, a spiritual backslider?' She looked at me hotly.

'It's a bit strange,' I said. 'Monastic, you could say.'

'Exactly,' she said, relieved. 'I tell him he's being too hard, on himself and on me.'

'Unless he's under the impression that you were going to fast and meditate with him, and he's trying to encourage you.'

'I did have a go, in the autumn,' she said, looking sheepish. 'But it was horrible. Look, I'm just too thin!' She pulled her t-shirt tight.

'Looks like you need to eat more puddings,' I said.

'Yes!' she said. 'But he says it's not really about the body; it's about training the mind.'

'Is your mind lacking in discipline?'

'No.' She sat back in the chair, looking thoroughly vindicated as to her reservations over fasting. 'I've decided that I need to have more of a life of my own in Greyston,' she concluded.

'And so you came for tea,' I said. 'And I'm glad.'

Her eyes softened and she looked suddenly somewhere near tears. 'Thank you, Juniper; it's been a lovely evening. What time is it?' It was midnight. She had an uphill cycle ride home, on the bike she'd borrowed from a housemate. I saw her off in the deserted, silent street. It was a clear, chilly night, with Orion hanging just over the horizon.

'See you Sunday, perhaps,' I said.

'Oh yes – what time?'

'At two. At the Aldgate Lane entrance to the salt marsh. That'll be easier for you to get to than if you came here. Will you be able to find it?'

'I've got a map,' she said. 'How do you think I found you tonight?'

She disappeared into the sleeping town, standing on her pedals to push like a boy.

on time and feelings

CHARLOTTE DIDN'T TURN UP on Sunday.

It was a fine spring day, and the sun glinted on the many pools and sodden gullies in the marsh as we walked along the earth dyke that kept the tides off reclaimed pastureland. Clumps of sheep nibbled the springy salt-tolerant grasses in the distance, near the muddy ribbon that was the estuarine river. It was low tide, so most of the wading birds were out on the far mud. Hawthorn glowed with fresh green tips along the field borders, and the bush-brambles along the dyke were already extending soft new fingers. Wrens belted out territorial warnings and a few larks rose singing.

Jim had persuaded Beth to come out walking. She had returned to work and had nearly regained her bonny disposition. She walked beside Jim on the path in front of me, her head at the level of his upper arm, looking up at him earnestly from time to time as they spoke.

'Are you and Beth looking to get together?' I asked Jim later on.

'Aye, and the world's a giant pancake,' he replied, laughing vigorously. 'But she's a fine lass, with a fine mind. She's been introducing me to the philosophy of Star Trek.'

I noticed his mention of her mind: it meant he definitely liked her.

'Star Trek!' I exclaimed, with mock disdain.

'It would no doubt be beneath you to spend time speculating on the physics of the warp drive, if you've even heard of it,' he said.

'No doubt,' I agreed. Jim laughed and slapped me affectionately on the back. I didn't know whether he was serious about Star Trek or seriously in love.

'I saw Ros last evening,' Beth said to me, when she and I happened to walk together. 'She sends her regards.'

'Was she staying with you?' I asked.

'She usually does on a Saturday night. It gives us a chance to catch up. She likes to watch TV.'

'I suppose she's become a Star Trek fan as well, has she?' I had an image of Albion Cottage, with a TV in the lounge, even a video recorder, concessions to the pitiful modern world, which Ros had installed now that I'd moved out.

'Ros? TV?' Beth exclaimed. 'She thought Baywatch was a local natural history programme. I can't ever imagine her actually having a TV. She just likes certain films, especially action ones in foreign countries. She says it expands her horizons.' I felt relief. I refrained from asking Beth what Baywatch was about. 'She's thinking of buying a small van, though,' Beth continued. 'To transport her pottery and make it easier for her to see people.'

'Is the pottery going well, then?' I asked.

'Have you not heard?' Beth said, looking at me with excited wide eyes. 'She's going to be exhibiting in the Pottery North West show in Carlisle. It was on a personal recommendation from her teacher. And that first batch of tableware she had in the craft shop in Silverthwaite has all sold, so the owner's ordered loads more, with a section of the shop just for her stuff.'

'Excellent,' I said, genuinely pleased, but also feeling the pain of being outside her success, and of Harry being in it.

'Do you not want to send your regards back?' Beth asked.

'No,' I said. 'Not like this, second-hand and polite.'

'Oh,' said Beth, pouting. 'I thought, you know, because it's been three months −'

'I'm really glad to know she's doing well, but it's painful too. We agreed to meet in the summer, after six months, and I don't want to try to sort anything out between us until then.' Beth seemed disappointed at my reticence.

'It's not that I don't care, Beth,' I said. 'But I find it hard, that's all.'

'OK,' she said, softening a little. 'Sorry.' We walked along in silence for a while.

'When exactly is the exhibition, then?'

'In the autumn,' Beth said, smiling. We both burst out laughing, not needing to say any more. The spring sunshine splashed on a larger pool on the marsh below the dyke. Children were running on the grass, leaping the wet gullies and pulling at the tangled driftwood and sea-debris that was heaped all along the base of the dyke, the high-tide mark.

'This is about where the hard shoulder of the bypass would be,' said Jim, rejoining us.

IN THE LAST WEEK of the spring term, on a Tuesday, I cycled to the campus through another bright morning, past the greening hedgerows and meadows shining with new colour. I felt − I had to admit it − happy, in the familiar, renewable way. It was more than three months since I had left Albion Cottage and last seen Ros, long enough for new emotions to happen, long enough for the awesome natural processes of frost-death, decomposition and regrowth from fat rhizome to occur.

Three months isn't so long in the calendar's perspective, but in human terms it's long enough to change the texture of the present.

While the clock ticks steadily on, each moment like the last, in the lived realm of human time events pile on events to form the sense of self through which the moments have meaning. Human time is no long linear trek through the void; in it, events link past and future in a lumpy tumult of flowing, eddying, speeding and slowing time. It takes twenty minutes to cycle to the Greyston campus, past the meadows and hedgerows, an experience characterised by rolling tar, cars, pumping legs and the push of breath. On the campus, the lecture is a new experience, with its mass of heads sloping down to Professor Merwin Bludgett and his droning voice; and the bike ride and the lecture are separate events, related not just by time but by the meaning of a life.

Events pile up in the laundry basket of the past, new experiences dropping on top of the old, odours mingling and ripening, until washday. How long does it take for any given experience to disappear under the mounting weight of piling events; how long until it is squeezed like glacier snow along the strange valleys of the mind into the mind's washing machine and system of neatly putting things away? About three months, after which some deep instinct switches on and the wash programme begins. But perhaps the past doesn't just get washed into memory. Maybe the laundry basket is more like a compost heap; old events retain their texture and smell for a while, though fading – for about three months – before disappearing into fine crumbly humus. In the mind's earth are bacteria and worms which eat into the textures of recent events, turning complex experience into loamy and friable humus, which we shovel back onto the gardens of our selves. Past becomes memory, still fragrant, but changed.

After three months away from Albion Cottage, my connection to my home had not been lost, but reduced to a tilth in which I could sow my own future. A new Juniper was sprouting, in his spring. The irrepressible human spirit was leaping in the sunshine and feeling happy. It is a blessing of nature, this susceptibility to redemption that shelters in our slowly dying bodies, that the workings of our minds have inherited from our vegetable past; in true human time there is always an instinctual belief in the possibility of renewal.

WALKING OUT OF THE LIBRARY later that day, I met Charlotte. It seemed like a sweet surprise at the end of a plain, industrious afternoon.

'I'm glad to see you,' she said. 'I wanted to apologise for Sunday.'

'I wondered what had happened.'

She smiled wanly. 'Nothing nice. Look, do you want to have a coffee? I just need to return some books and I'll join you.' She hurried through the swinging wooden doors, already digging into her weighty-looking bag. I waited, looking up at the pale sky with its ribs of clouds, enjoying the primrose and hyacinths in the concrete flower tubs in the square. Charlotte emerged, smiling, and we headed for the Nelson Mandela. There was an end-of-term feeling, students snatching rapid breaks from final coursework.

Charlotte drank black coffee and smoked. I rolled a thinner stimulant and drank tea. We talked about work. I looked at her face as we talked. It can take a little while to be able to look at someone closely and see the significance in what's observed; but then a body's ciphers crystallise into clear messages. I had a sense that she wanted to say something.

'So what happened on Sunday?' I asked, risking a refusal.

'Bad time,' she said. She took a few seconds of chewing her lips to decide if she would say any more. 'You remember what I told you about Toby and his fasting? And about how things were getting difficult between us? Well, things got worse.'

'Sorry to hear that,' I said.

'He's decided that he wants us to stop having sex. He says sex always involves a compromise of his spiritual endeavours.'

'Ah,' I said. The mention of sex sent a hot lump into a smooth conversation. 'I don't suppose you like that idea.'

She laughed. 'No. He told me on Saturday evening, and we talked about it until Sunday morning. I went home at lunchtime and I felt too upset to see anyone else.'

'Does that mean that your relationship with Toby is finished?'

'Not exactly,' she said, and I felt both disappointed and relieved. 'Oh, you don't want to know all this. It's horrible.'

'But you need to talk things over with someone.'

Charlotte started crying. 'My best old friend from school, Clare – she lives in London – thinks the whole relationship is mad.'

'Why?' I asked, but she waved the question away, sobbing.

'There's a girl in the house I live in called Julia, but, to be honest, she doesn't know much about sex or boyfriends, so there's no point saying anything to her. I have a friend here called Sue, but I don't know her very well yet. Then there's Paul. But I don't want to tell him this kind of stuff; he'll think I'm pitiful or stupid. I don't know anyone else in Greyston – Toby is quite solitary, and he was the reason I came up here. I've worked really hard on my MA for six months and made hardly any effort to make friends.' Her words ceased tumbling briefly. 'And Clare thinks the relationship is crazy because when she came up to visit after Christmas, he wouldn't come round because he had already seen me twice that week.'

'Already seen you – ?'

'At Christmas he decided that we should ration our contact, to make sure we weren't getting too attached to each other, so –'

'– you only see each other twice a week,' I said. She nodded. I couldn't help laughing. 'But what counts as 'seeing each other'? An evening together, or a ten-minute chat on the campus? And does he keep a little notebook?'

'Don't make fun of me,' she blazed out. 'It's not my rationing system.' She crossed her arms and looked out of the window.

'So don't take what I said personally, then,' I said, looking at the side of her face, hot and bright. 'I didn't mean to make fun of you, but I'm sorry if that's how it sounded. And you don't have to answer my questions.' There was a spiky silence, but then she relaxed.

'Oh shit; I'm sorry as well,' she said. 'The whole thing is so embarrassing.' She trailed off, the anger that followed her tears fading into sadness.

'Do you want another coffee?' I asked. She nodded, holding her head in her hands. By the time I came back with drinks she was gone, though her bag was still dangling off the back of her chair. Then she reappeared through the outside door, still moving with precision, but preoccupied, like a precise bedraggled stoat. She sat down heavily.

'Went to the loo,' she said. 'We were so close in India, just like they say – a meeting of souls. It was so – irrational.' She looked up at me, smiling weakly. 'There was a time in Rishikesh, in our hotel room – after walking by the river, then meditating together in the room – we just sat on the bed, holding hands, looking at each other. I've never felt so close to someone, so present. I hadn't been looking for a soul mate, or even a boyfriend. But it felt so right.'

Charlotte had been looking up and out of the window, towards a remnant of old hedging still left among the new moonscape of the campus. A blackthorn, white flowers among dark, tangled branches. She looked at me. 'So I don't care too much if we only see each other twice a week – that's two evenings, and meeting for coffee doesn't count – and I don't even care if we don't have sex, at least for a while, as long as I know that there's still that connection between us.'

Charlotte leant back, and lit another cigarette. 'Unfortunately, he says that sex involves a loss of vital energy, and in the long run he wants to be celibate. This was on Saturday night. I told him I was not OK with this.' She sat puffing, calming herself down.

'So that means he wants to finish with you,' I said.

'That's what we talked about on Sunday morning. I put it to him straight that we split up. I wanted to know if that was what he really wanted. It wasn't like that, he said. We could go forward on the spiritual path together, he said, transforming our carnal love into a spiritual bond–'

'Did he actually use the phrase "carnal love"?' It sounded so arcane, medieval.

She was quiet, looking into air. 'If I'm honest, what I want is the carnal love. I've just thought of that.' She looked at me. 'In India, I think he felt free. Back here, he gets himself tangled in knots.'

'Give me chastity, Lord, but not yet,' I said. 'St Augustine.'

Charlotte laughed. 'I'll tell him that. Oh shit, all this is so ingrown compared to issues in the real world, like this Greyston bypass plan; but I couldn't face anyone so soon after all this shit with Toby.'

'Fair enough,' I said.

'So tell me how it went on Sunday,' she said. 'Tell me about something real.'

I told her about the weather, the walkers, the photos in the local papers. But Charlotte was staring at someone behind me, whom I could hear pulling out a chair and sitting down.

'I know, Fiona,' a voice said. 'I asked him again, but he's as stubborn as a mule. Once these philosophers get an idea into their heads, they hang onto it till grim death.' The voice was painfully, startlingly controlled, clipped as if dipped in wax and squeezed through the teeth, words crunchily foreshortened. Just discernible were flattened Yorkshire vowels, as if a childhood lay lonely and abandoned somewhere within.

Charlotte and I turned slowly in our seats, until we could look at the mass of yellow-blonde hair tumbling over the collar of a long brown greatcoat, just behind us. Jackie turned to look at us briefly. I was amazed at the impression wrought by a combination of a large, slightly bent nose, those watery eyes and that powerful mouth. She turned back to Fiona.

'I'm sure he must have a new girlfriend, you know,' Jackie went on, oblivious to her rapt audience. 'He exchanged glances with a woman in a pub.' Charlotte looked at me enquiringly, and I nodded. She grinned.

'Oh Jackie, you're just speculating,' said Fiona. 'Paul has his own life, just like you.'

'But, Fiona – glances! The sub-audible dialogue of romantic discourse! He's trying to pull the patriarchal wool down by denial – the usual trick. But I know him too well. Something's changed. He's slipped back into traditional modes of domination; you know, hidden knowledges, male inscrutability. He used to be much more open with me – and more kind.' Fiona shrugged. Charlotte and I quickly left the coffee bar, unable to contain ourselves.

'What a battleship!' Charlotte exclaimed, excited, once we were outside.

'So Paul's told you about his struggle for independence?'

Charlotte shrugged, grinning at me as if a little embarrassed. 'He tells me all sorts. He told me you and Jim had helped him prepare for a showdown, but he didn't tell me how.' I was pleased to hear of Paul's discretion.

'Men's stuff,' I told her. 'It's time for me to go home now.' We were standing in the main university square. Charlotte took my hands, stood on tiptoe and kissed me on the cheek.

'Thanks for letting me talk, Juniper. I feel much better for it, whatever happens next with Toby and me.' She swung my hands from side to side, and I felt an awkward thrill at her affection.

'Anytime,' I said, meaning it.

'Oh yes,' she said, letting go of my hands. 'Something I meant to tell you. There's a talk on at the Buddhist Society tomorrow evening, by a monk. Last term he spoke about love; it was really good. That's why I thought you might be interested. And I'm going to it,' she added. I laughed. 'And if you come, you might get to meet Toby.'

'OK,' I said. 'I might see you there.'

'CAN SOMEONE TURN out the lights?' said the monk.

The room plunged into brown darkness. On a low table were two candles, a small wooden meditating figure and the red tip of a burning incense stick. We sat in a small circle of chairs. The room fell quiet. It didn't feel entirely comfortable; I certainly was not. Charlotte hadn't turned up and I felt out of place. When I had told Jim I was going to a Buddhist Society meeting, he had snorted, saying he knew my real reason. But I'd still gone. I sat in the silence, wanting to escape. The bald monk, dressed in dull brown robes, sat totally still, with eyes closed. Then he took a deep breath, swayed from side to side and adjusted his robes.

'I live in Silverthwaite,' he said, arriving out of his silence. My mind leapt to an interested attention. And then Charlotte and Toby crept in and took seats at the back. The Venerable Jagaro had lived in Silverthwaite for three months, in a rented house provided by supporters. He hoped to establish a monastery there. It was oddly painful to hear of developments in my own home village that I knew nothing about.

I caught Charlotte's eye as the monk talked, and we smiled. Toby was a handsome fellow, with a wide Teutonic jaw and high cheekbones. His blond hair was cut to stubble.

'I'd like to talk about feelings,' the monk said. 'Feelings, eh? Emotions are a problem, eh? That's what you might think. All those confusing conflicting urges moving around in you. They're a problem, aren't they?' The monk laughed.

I thought of Bosch. He says that it's the emotions that fool us in love. These deep promptings from the instinctual brain that nature has left in us to make sure we reproduce. But love, real love, is an act of will, not an emotion. The passions move us like puppets, but the mature personality weighs them with reason before acting.

'But here's a secret,' the monk said, leaning forward in his chair. Involuntarily I leant forward, as did several others. He scanned the circle. 'Emotions are OK. They're not a problem. In fact, they're all that we have to move us along, with which we can break out of our suffering, find a higher meaning in life. Don't hold back on emotions!' He laughed, leaned back, and adjusted his robes again. 'The problem's not emotions at all, it's the fixed sense of self that turns emotions and feelings into solid shapes. You need your emotions! But you need to hang loose and not judge them too much. Don't act right away. Be intelligent, and allow your heart to investigate – if I act on this emotion, will I find happiness? Or will I suffer? Say you're angry – the anger's fine, that's emotion, that's energy, that's not a problem. But if you act on that anger – will you be happy? Or will you suffer? So you need to be aware, be intelligent.'

He stopped and took a drink of water. 'I'm telling you all this because you lot are probably already too much up in the attic, full of ideas about religion and nirvana and all that. So instead, I'm letting you in on my secret – feel what you feel, stay in touch with your emotions. But use your mind to reflect. Sitting in silence like we were doing just now – that's a way to hang loose to how we feel, keep a sense of space around emotions. You should do that.'

He carried on in this vein, talking without notes, stopping for minutes at a time, then starting up again when something occurred to him. Some people were looking at the monk with mild interest; a few with what looked like a certain attention. An older man lolled forward with his eyes closed. A young student with curls kicked her feet together and stared at the ground. Why had Charlotte thought I'd be interested? Was she keen to see more of me? But with Toby there I couldn't see how we'd manage to have much of a conversation.

'All right, now you can ask me questions,' said the monk.

A man asked about reincarnation. I looked over at Charlotte and Toby. Toby was still sitting bolt upright and seemed deep in thought. Charlotte seemed engrossed in Jagaro's words. I caught her eye briefly without smiling.

'How do you regard asceticism?' I asked.

'Say more,' the monk replied, frowning.

'Would you say that there is any value in the discipline of abstaining from sensual pleasures, from sex and food?'

'Well, of course, it's quite traditional,' said Jagaro. 'But why on earth are you asking?'

'I've heard it's important for one's spiritual development,' I said.

'But not at all necessary,' he said impatiently. 'What was I just saying? The important thing is to learn to hang loose to your feelings, create some space around your experience. There's really no need to be starving yourself. In fact, I think that people in the west generally need to learn to be kinder to themselves. The only ascetic practise I recommend for you lot,' he said, looking at me, 'is getting an early night.' People laughed.

Someone asked another question. I glanced over at Toby; he was writing in a little notebook on his lap. Charlotte was rocking backwards and forwards on her hands, grinning at me while trying to hide her face from Toby. I nodded at her gravely.

When the talk was over, a woman student announced that all present were welcome to adjourn to the nearest students' bar. I picked up a leaflet about Jagaro's little monastery, and stood about. Toby approached the monk.

'I want to ask you some more about fasting,' I heard him say, before his voice dropped too low. I walked over to Charlotte.

'I'll buy you a drink,' she said, taking my hand, and leading me off into the dingy atmosphere of student drinking. As we stood waiting for the barman to pour our pints, she thumped me in the chest. 'That was so clever; how did you think of it?'

I basked in her attention. 'It was embarrassing,' I said.

'You might have saved us,' she said as we sat down.

Charlotte's friend, Sue, who ran the Buddhist Society, joined us. Toby appeared and sat next to Charlotte.

'Toby, this is Juniper,' Charlotte said, and we shook hands across her lap.

'I was really glad that you asked that question,' he said. 'Do you do much fasting yourself?'

'Not really,' I said.

'The monk gave me some really useful advice,' he said. 'So you're a philosopher?'

'That's right,' I said. 'Charlotte and I share a supervisor.'

'Paul Corbett, you remember,' Charlotte said, pushing Toby's arm.

'Yes,' Toby replied, unconvincingly.

We talked until closing time. Charlotte and Toby went off towards the bus stop together as I headed towards the bike park. The chilly night air cleaved the smokiness of the bar from my nose. I noticed the subtle tang of the daffodils in the night air as I sped down the hill to the main road, and the coughing sheep behind the hedges along the now-quiet wide tarmac. My heart sang quietly, I didn't know why.

in the garden

THE DAY AFTER the Buddhist Society meeting was a warm April day, and I didn't feel like putting my head into books. Beneath the newly sprouting weeds and the overgrown tangles at the back of Lyndhurst, I found the remnants of the previous owners' probably much-loved garden. There were strawberries, whose anarchic runners had strayed far and wide, and raspberries, choked on their own dead stems. I found a half-ton of well-rotted manure buried under jasmine in a midden of old doors, so I spread it around the gooseberries and blackcurrants in a corner that had been lost to invading brambles. I left the tit-box, hidden in bushy clematis, but cut the clumps of damp rye and dock back to a flat, liveable lawn. I left the thick bluebells, massing in a dense promise under the sycamore where a rose garden had once bloomed, and pruned back the over-needy roses.

Archie kept me company as I worked. He had been based at the house for years, swapping owners as they swapped their dwellings; a dogged old fighter who returned to sit in a cardboard box in the open back porch every three or four days, to lick his wounds and sleep, before disappearing again. Matt and Chris had taken him on as a fixture, giving him a blanket for his box and half a tin of cat food when he liked. He had agreed to his renewal of tenure in his own stolid way, once or twice making the rounds inside, doing his quick tail-up spurts of tomcat juice on the doorjambs.

But his masculinity had been his downfall. Although Matt and Chris had put up with his appalling, though impermanent, odours, the next-door-neighbours had complained. Their daughter had begun to toddle, and they wanted her to be able to explore the garden without running into a fallout-zone of Archie's bold effluent. When they had offered half the money for the operation, Matt and Chris had made the inevitable compromise. Archie went to the vet's, where his little bollocks were tugged until the tubes twanged free; he turned into a couch-cat within a week. Liberated from his hormones, he began to hang out with the people he lived with, forming relationships with all the emotional clumsiness of an old coal-miner forced by redundancy into housework and gossip. And he had soon made friends with Jim.

'I don't understand it,' Jim told me that evening, 'but me and this cat, we love each other. Somehow, there's a soul-connection between us, as happens only very occasionally with folk; that feeling that you were always part of each other's lives but that you'd been parted from each other until you met again.' He looked down at Archie, the cat's long, heavy body sprawled in an ungainly way over Jim's thick legs. Archie looked up at him upside down. I suspected that there was more than an element of cupboard-love in Archie's devotion, in that Jim was more willing than the rest of us to share the contents of his milk carton. But I kept such thoughts to myself.

We were waiting for Paul to arrive for tea. When he'd descended into the kitchen, he brought out a bottle of wine.

'It is a night to celebrate,' he announced. 'Let us drink tea and then I will requite your curiosity.' Jim made a pot of specially bought Assam.

'I have decisively ousted Jackie from my life,' Paul said, sitting at the table, still smiling.

'Aye, and about bloody time,' replied Jim.

I recalled Tuesday's sighting of the blonde beast, and my apprehension then of a possible showdown. 'Tell all,' I said.

A week after the previous occasion on which Jackie had stayed at Paul's, after which he'd undergone his ritual, she had rung up to ask whether he would do her a favour: check various books in the university library for references.

'Why can't Fiona or Alison do it?' Paul asked in return.

'Oh, Paul, they're busy, and I don't want to burden them, and I know I can ask you to do little things like this. It won't take five minutes.'

Paul had agreed grudgingly, feeling put upon, but also feeling that a refusal would be churlish. And then, weeks later, there had been the familiar message on the answering machine.

Hello, Paul, it's Jackie. I wonder if I can stay again tonight? We've had another meeting today, and it's taking longer than we planned, so we're going to carry on tomorrow. I'll turn up about six again – hope this is OK. See you later.

Again he felt that sinking feeling and again, madly, that joy in his belly, like he might get a little dose of love. Jackie arrived at seven. He felt calm, yet alert and determined.

'Hello, Paul – gosh, am I tired. All I want to do is have a bath and watch TV, so I can stay right out of your way if you have things to get on with.' Her eyes sparkled hugely as ever, and the hall light haloed through her hair. Her vivacious charm wafted through his habitual rooms like perfume. But he had made his decision.

'I'm sorry Jackie, but you can't stay.' The expression on her face collapsed.

'What? What do you mean?' She was genuinely confused, having never met resistance from him before.

95

'I'm afraid I've decided that you can't stay here anymore. You exploit my goodwill without there being the least parity in our expectations.'

'Paul!' said Jackie, laughing. 'I expect you're over-reacting because I told you about Ken. But it doesn't need to make any difference to you and me.'

'It makes all the difference because it tells me just how very different our attitudes to each other are. You enjoy the convenience of having me at your beck and call, while I continue to hope that there might be more.'

Jackie was evidently taken by surprise. The machinery of her energetic mind caught in its gears, tripped over its thoughtless abandon. An oil of irritation began leaking out.

'This is all very inconvenient right now. Where shall I stay tonight? If I'd known I wasn't welcome −' but she tailed off.

'Feel free to use the phone if you want to ring one of your colleagues or friends.'

Her large open face closed, and tears welled from her eyes. He couldn't remember the last time he'd seen her cry. The tears provoked a feeling of tenderness, a desire to comfort her, to apologise and heal; but his determination remained. He showed no emotion.

'So you can leave now.'

'Paul −' but the pleading look in her eyes was not enough to touch him, and she had run out of words. As she left the flat she was muttering, half angry, half embarrassed and shocked.

'Goodbye Jackie,' he said as he closed the door. He stood, shaking, in the firmness of his own hallway.

'AND THAT, GENTLEMEN, is the story of how I raised warrior-energy to good effect and made a decisive change in my life.' I served platefuls of that thick and tasty macaroni cheese; but before we dug in, Paul proposed a toast.

'To the firm counsel of friends,' he declared.

'To the force of truth,' Jim replied.

'To your growing freedom and joy,' I said. 'I saw Jackie on the campus the other day; it must have been just before she went to your place. Charlotte and I were drinking coffee in the Nelson Mandela when we heard her talking behind us.'

'You were with Charlotte?' Paul said, a sudden look of fear clouding the open joy in his face.

'We bumped into each other. Jackie has an extraordinary voice − and is it a broken nose?'

Paul laughed, recovering composure. 'A man-eating voice, someone once called it; and she broke her nose playing hockey at school.'

'You gave us the impression she was just a stunning blonde,' said Jim. 'I think we should drink a toast to the health of Ken Evans.'

Paul laughed loudly. 'Yes, yes; not just a stunning blonde. To Professor Evans! May the gods protect him!'

'May the gods protect you from the hidden fangs of *woman*!' shouted Jim.

'Never again!' Paul cried, downing his glass. 'So, here we are, three men, each defined apart from the female, stoutly single, and nevertheless fully alive and well.' He looked at Jim and me, seeking affirmation.

'Aye,' Jim replied, but elaborating nothing.

'You remember what you were saying last week,' I said to Paul, 'about conceiving those extraordinary affections towards your students? Well, I seem to have developed some of my own – towards your favourite, Charlotte Newby.'

'Really?' he said, taken aback. 'Well, well.' There was no guile in his voice, but neither a trace of light-heartedness. Rather, there was a twinge of pain. I felt a pang of regret that I had said anything, and tried to backtrack.

'Don't take me wrongly; I only thought you might appreciate the irony of it. I don't intend to act upon these curious little fires.'

'No, no, of course not,' said Paul. 'And of course she has her boyfriend, as I told you.'

'Yes, I met him last evening,' I added.

'Really?' said Paul again, and with another pang I felt I was somehow causing him to retreat into the emotional cave that he'd been emerging from with such gaiety just that evening. I didn't know what else to say. I freewheeled.

'A very curious man,' I said. 'Their relationship seems to go very deep, but in an unusual way.'

'Yes, yes,' said Paul curtly, not wishing to talk about it; with a slightly sick feeling I sensed that he felt I was alluding inappropriately to confidential matters.

'The lass came to tea,' said Jim. 'Smokes, drinks and argues like a man. Pretty too.' Paul and I both laughed at Jim's less subjective perspective. 'You're not falling for her, are you?' Jim said to me.

'No, no,' I replied. 'Just noticing certain appreciative emotions rippling along the bruised channels of my heart.'

'Oh shit,' said Jim, rolling his eyes. 'You are such a fool for women.' Paul laughed.

'What was it that Shaw said?' I rejoined. 'Love is "overestimating the difference between one woman and another." Let's toast the correct estimation of one's friends, shall we?'

Jim roared a cheery assent, Paul smiled, and Archie put a front paw up on the table while looking at the laughing humans around him, not wanting to be left out of the reckoning.

After sharing a spliff, I took myself to my room while Paul and Jim adjourned to the lounge to play chess. I lay down and felt my duvet settle in a soft cup beneath me, my head held in the feather hands of pillows. An image of Charlotte from the previous evening, looking up into my eyes in the beery light of the student bar, formed before me. 'Certain appreciative emotions rippling through the bruised channels of my heart.' This was true enough, but also signified a slight but crucial cognitive distance on my own feelings, the assumption that their meaning was incidental, limited, even amusing. But was it? Paul's response had jarred me from my cosy sense that these pleasant, delightful little feelings were harmless. To the extent that he had guessed them, his response had been a serious alarm, not laughter. I began to face up to a new conclusion. Under the influence of the soft drug, the ordinary habits of the heart slurred and released, and fat tears rolled from my eyes.

Brown eyes, a precise manner of moving, a mind whose sharpness seemed apiece with the immediacy of her emotions. Why this, why now? I thought, pointlessly.

Another image arose, of a yellow-robed monk, smiling at me. A voice said, very definitely, 'hang loose to what you feel.' There was laughter in that voice, but it was not mocking me. So, what did I feel? Feelings of love: light flakes breaking off the rising lava of joy, flakes each embossed with the name of the beloved. But I could also sense a resistance, a judgement – an ordered sky averse to the chaos of wild flakes – the feeling that it was all very inconvenient, unworkable, damned daft; I was in love but at the same time pushing the feelings away, categorising them as the irrational passions of the frail heart. After all, last time I'd felt this kind of tumult was with Renata, and that had been a disaster. But, my mind spliff-loosened, I began to remember the time before that – my first love.

I WAS SEVENTEEN, and my parents were having a party. The oily perfume of may blossom drifted over the lawn from the hedgerows, and swallows twisted in the warm air around the barn. My father was laughing in his embarrassingly jolly way, and mother was rushing about neurotically. I was sitting on the limestone wall next to the orchard, watching the robins fly to their nest in an apple tree.

'Heh, Roger!' came a voice behind me. Beth was smiling her chubby smile, and we kissed flamboyantly as we used to do. She was wearing a wide brown felt hat.

'You look great!' I said, and then reached a hand towards the friend she'd brought.

'I'm Kate,' the friend said quietly, and a thin, clear smile spread from her small mouth up to her clay-blue eyes. Her small grip contrasted with Beth's embrace. She had blonde hair in a bob.

'You look great too,' I said, exuberantly. She looked away.

Catherine Antonia Mitchell. I spent hours aching with interest and awkwardness around her, then, miraculously, we found ourselves alone together, in the hall.

'Can I show you around?' I said, without thinking.

'Show me the garden,' she replied. We walked out into the warm blue night.

She sat on the grey stone steps to the garden, with her arms around her knees. I no longer felt awkward because she seemed to like me too. I was amazed by new feelings happening in me, churnings in my belly and whirlings in my mind.

We talked of ourselves, in the open way of that age, with great leaps and inconsequential detail. She stretched out her thin arms and fingers, and I looked on the pale skin and fine hair of them with awe. My own young man's body seemed so awkwardly large, while hers was painfully thin porcelain.

We walked in the wet grass of the garden in bare feet, among the smells of flowering rosemary and oregano. I picked starlit bluebells and closed ox-eye daisies from the hedgerow near the orchard, and presented them to her.

'A memento.' The words sounded stupidly clichéd. She received them in silence, which I could not really read. She walked back towards the house, grabbing her shoes from the steps. I wasn't sorry to go back indoors; I felt nervous with Kate alone. But when our friends cheered as we entered the room, I felt both embarrassed and pleased.

'Shall I see you again?' she said, holding her flowers, as she left with Beth and Beth's parents in their car.

'I hope so,' I said coolly, but smiling inside. We exchanged phone numbers and she left.

She was a sudden new world, a pale, unexplored island in an unknown clay-blue sea, about which I knew nothing, towards which I felt strange, new, strong pangs of attraction. A clear moon rose inside me, casting its mysterious, wonderful light. Over the summer we fell in love. Except we didn't know what 'falling in love' might be: there were only the hundred little details in which we were completely absorbed. I learned the quick moves of her face and hands, the way feelings lived there, and thoughts came and went. We shared our lives, out on long walks; she met my family. Mother was somewhat put out with this new woman in my life, but Kate was approved of, even by sister Erica. While for me Kate was my first fascinating love, for them she was simply 'Roger's girlfriend'. Love is ever new, yet very old.

She went to school with Beth, and lived with her unmarried aunt and widowed grandmother in Silverthwaite; her mother had died when she was young, and her father hadn't been able to cope on his own. Kate saw him often, with his new wife and their young children, though her aunt and grandmother viewed him with ancient disapproval. She was riven with mixed feelings, living with the women who had brought her up, but loving the man they felt an old grudge towards. I listened to her various tales and conflicts patiently, but said little. Her aunt and gran were friendly enough to me, but didn't seem very keen in principle on men.

It was exam-time at school, but I didn't much care. I found that I could speak to Kate of things it hadn't occurred to me to share with boys: how I loved the colour of young oak leaves, and what I felt towards my parents; and she took it all in as if it were serious knowledge. We held hands; we kissed; we held each other for hours. There was a simplicity about the way I felt about Kate that I could not quite link to the little I knew about sex; still, the gravity of attraction took us gradually down the natural path.

I'd been making Albion Cottage into my own place. It turned out to be a great place to take Kate, and it was there, among the musty smells of old stone and peeling wallpaper, in a low-roofed room with a small dormer and a view filled with pear tree leaves, that we first made love, on a warm evening in July.

It was secret, of course. Our friendship melted into physical delight, and we quickly lost all fear of each other, or restraint. I would meet Kate, and we'd walk over to my place for the afternoon. She would throw herself at me, small, thin ball of desire, and we would disappear into each other for hours. Later, we would talk some more, in our bodies' quiet. It was new, this total intimacy, and through it we both gained some of the independence of adulthood. The summer took on a tranquil satisfaction, and I thought very little about anything other than Kate. In September, we started back to school again, but saw each other often. It was clear how much we'd both changed, learned through each other, as we met old schoolmates again. Perhaps there was some envy; rumours spread, which got back to Kate's aunt and grandmother.

On her seventeenth birthday, late October, I went to her house, but was met with grim glances. They had made Kate tell them all that we'd done, which of course sounded furtive heard by suspicious ears: an older boy, a secret cottage, her precious innocence. I wanted to tell them how she was a little squall of love, but for them she was their strange and childlike girl. I felt awkward, off-guard, even guilty, though I couldn't think of anything that we'd done wrong. Kate came downstairs, dishevelled with tears. She was too young to be able to argue with her guardians, too unconfident. The clear, thin charm that had captivated me, that disguised such a witchy passion, now became frailty, and pulled her back into a world of distrust.

'We think you a common, dirty boy; and you will not see Kate again.' Those rehearsed, insensitive words etched into my mind: I can still hear her grandmother's judgemental, dismissive tone. I wandered home dazed, not knowing what to think, hoping that Kate would manage to talk her family round. But I found that they had telephoned ahead; the grandmother told my mother she forbad me seeing Kate. Later, my father asked me what had happened, and I told him we'd been careful. He was sympathetic: 'healthy for a chap of your age.' I sent letters through Beth, but got no reply. Beth said Kate was subdued and not saying much.

The summer collapsed into memory, isolated in its privacy and secret joys. Autumn fell into winter, and the pear tree shed its leaves onto its own rotting fruit. I was sad, but somehow not heartbroken; by Christmas I was thinking about how Kate and I differed. She was so nervous, I was not; and, looking back, although I had been happy to hear her out, her woes were endless and my interest would have waned. I felt that my body had returned to me, settled back into my own power. first love died like the echo of a slamming door; closed cleanly like a lid on the honey we had relished, so that I did not miss the loss of it. My heart was whole.

I met her again at the next May party at the farm, and shook her familiar hand; her eyes, though, looked darker and more silent.

'I'm sorry I didn't write back to you,' she said. 'They watched me all the time, and there wasn't any point. I've moved to my father's now, up in Cumbria. I'm going out with a boy from school.'

'Yes, I'd heard,' I said.

'Are you going out with anyone?'

'No,' I said. 'But that's OK. That jacket suits you.'

'Oh, thanks; it's kind of – mature – isn't it?' She spread her arms and looked down at herself. That sparkle in her eyes – the genuine shock at a compliment, the simple directness. I felt a fondness as for an old record, something from childhood almost. We took our leave, and I hadn't seen her since.

ALL THAT OPENNESS and trust in what I'd felt. And now my heart, in a language I had forgotten how to use, was telling me, shouting across the dark courtyard to my ears and brain, that it had found something precious and beautiful, and asking me, please, just feel.

'But really do you zink zat zere can be love viz zis Charlotte?' said the Professor Bosch within.

'Probably not,' said my heart. 'It doesn't matter.' The point was to assent to my own heart's beckoning into greater life. Out in the garden, accompanied by a large ginger cat that watched me with ineffable composure, I raised an assent into the blank spring night. A few scents, blackcurrant blossoms and first-cut grass, witnessed it. Ros would be pleased, I thought. I'd decided it was better to feel than to live in books.

enchantment

DURING THE EASTER VACATION there was a bright quiet on the campus, a peacefulness into which the sycamores in the university square unfurled. I watched the vivid interplay of blues and greens from a seat in the nearly empty library: the sky a brightness that I'd forgotten through the winter, the greens as fresh as hot bread.

Why the overestimating of a particular woman? I called at Charlotte's house on the way home to try to answer my own question, but there was no one there. So I went into town to buy organic vegetables at the indoor market; and I met Charlotte buying a duvet cover at the textiles stall.

'I just called at your house to say hello,' I said.

'But you thought you'd say hello to me in the market instead?' she said. 'Nice to see you. Want to go for a coffee?'

Heart aglow, I followed Charlotte into the café that adjoined the market. I felt like I'd walked into heaven. The angels and saints were pasty-coloured teenage girls, heavy old ladies with blue coats and hairdos, and an old man with a shopping bag on wheels. St Peter looked like a fat unshaven Italian with balding black-grey hair and a white apron over his fried belly.

'Yeah?' he said.

'Two coffees,' I said, piously, 'one black; and two vanilla slices.'

'Siddown,' he said, taking my money. I sat.

'Guess what?' said Charlotte, devouring her vanilla slice. 'You'll love this. I've had a proposal of marriage.'

I smiled, somewhat hollowly.

'I have this cousin – I met him last summer in Delhi for the first time in years – and his father's written to my parents to ask if they could arrange a marriage between us.'

I relaxed. 'What's he like?'

She shrugged. 'He's quite good-looking really, but very serious, involved in local politics. He sent me a note, just to warm me up, I think. Look.' She pulled out a letter and spread it on the table.

Dear Charlotte,

I am recently finished BA Engineering and have now good job with our Uncle Krishnan, earning three lakh rupees per annum. I am living now again in

Delhi with family, in this large house that you visited. Do you remember? I think you were finding it very beautiful, isn't it? Certainly I am wheatish and prospects are good. Please thinking of me, and happy to have letter.

Yours,
Rohit.

'Wheatish?' I said.

'A light brown colour,' said Charlotte. 'The lighter the better for marriage prospects.'

'Ah,' I said, thinking that Charlotte didn't seem very wheatish.

'I know,' she said. 'My mother's family is from South India, where the people are much darker than in the north. But I'm still desirable because I'm Western educated; it's a status symbol. And before you ask, the name 'Newby' came from my father's father, some diplomat sowing wild oats among the natives. My granny was almost ostracised.'

'So is Rohit actually interested in you as a person at all? Or is it just your status?' I felt slightly aggressive towards him.

'No, no; it doesn't work like that. Let me explain. Most marriages are still arranged in India. Love-marriages are problematic because the two families haven't been consulted, so they might not accept the situation. The couple might have to live outside the normal society, which is why mum and dad didn't go back after they got married. So you see people have different perceptions in India: they see individuals as connected into family and caste. I think Rohit likes me; but he doesn't have the same perception of individuality as you, so he wouldn't be able to distinguish between loving me as a person and me as someone who comes with a certain status.'

'That's not very romantic,' I said. 'True love should always win out over social differences, and your soul mate is the person with whom you can finally be your true self. That's the Western story, anyway, if you can believe it.'

'They still fall in love though,' said Charlotte. 'After they've got married. The human heart is basically the same.'

'So what happens now?'

Charlotte shrugged. 'Nothing really. I'll send Rohit a note to be polite. Mum and dad will courteously refuse the offer of a husband for their daughter, saying that, although Rohit sounds like a suitable boy, Charlotte, having been brought up in England, will make her own decision when she wants to.'

'How do you know that's what they'll say?'

'Because that's what I've told them to!' said Charlotte, laughing.

Conversation moved on. It seemed that my question, or rather Jagaro's answer, at the Buddhist Society meeting had smoothed things between her and Toby. He had eased off the asceticism. He was even about to take a week out of his revising so that they could go camping together in the Lakes.

Why her? I asked myself, looking at her as she stood at the counter ordering more coffee. I watched the way she engaged St Peter with that wide-open intelligent face, the bright half-smile, the way she moved both restlessly and precisely on the spot. She brought back more coffee.

'How goes the study of the Great Kant?' I asked.

She immediately became serious. 'I'm investigating the consequences of his assumption of the truth of Euclidean geometry,' she said. 'Since his time, several consistent alternative geometries have been formulated, and the universe itself appears to be non-Euclidean.'

I had no idea what she was talking about. 'So what is it about his philosophy?' I asked, looking for the meaning of my beloved's love. She sat and thought for a while. I admired the way she considered her answer. She put out her cigarette before she began to speak.

'Here's how it started,' she said. 'There are some woods near my parents' house, where I used to walk, especially through the year I spent working in London. One time I was there, and something strange happened. The trees had been rustling in the breeze, and I'd been watching this bird with a yellow beak in the brambles −'

'A blackbird,' I said.

'− a blackbird poking about in the leaves. Then there was this huge rushing sound that came from everywhere, and everything started going dark. I was frightened. Then came a buzzing sound, again sounding like it was coming from everywhere. I looked up into the trees, but I couldn't see anything. Pretty soon it got light and quiet again. I'd stopped walking and was just standing still, listening. A fox suddenly appeared out of nowhere and trotted right up to me. It was just going about its business, head down, and didn't see me. Off it went again, into the trees. Is this making any sense?' Charlotte looked at me worriedly.

'Yes,' I said. 'So what happened?'

'That's the point − *nothing* happened.'

'Nothing?'

'Not to me anyway. It was though I wasn't there in the woods at all. All these dramatic events were happening there, the blackbird and the bees and the fox were living their lives, and I was suddenly aware that I wasn't really needed. All week I'd been up in London, absorbed in looking after these potty and drunken homeless people, and all the time the woods had been there, just like that.' She paused and lit another cigarette.

'I know what you mean about walking in the woods,' I said.

'Hang on, I haven't finished. The point is that there's this paradox. All the time – we can't help it – we're caught up with what's going on for us. We perceive things, we perceive ourselves as living our lives, as going about the world, and we get completely caught up in our own perspective on it all. It's like a spell is cast over us so that we feel that *I want this* or *I don't like that*. The whole way the world appears, the whole experience of instinct and emotion – everything that Jim thinks is the truth – is just a spell cast over our minds. When I was standing in the woods, the spell broke. Just briefly. I saw the world as the trees see it, as the fox sees it. They're even more spellbound than we are, of course. But for a while I wasn't; I saw things from outside, which included all these inside points of view. It was seeing the truth of things, the real nature of everything beyond anyone's interest or involvement. The point of philosophy is to break the spell.'

She stopped speaking and pulled on her cigarette. The hum of heaven around me washed in again, but didn't break the spell that I was under.

'That state can't last, of course. We have to get on with our lives, which means practical thinking in terms of our own perspectives and desires. But when I read Kant, at Cambridge, I found that he put words to what I'd seen. Space and time are like the spectacles through which we're obliged to perceive the world; we don't know what the world is really like; all we have is what we perceive. But our mind also imposes on our perception its categories of thought, like cause and effect, through which we can think about our experience. So we have an ordered and intelligible experience, which we call the world, but there's also the transcendental reality beyond appearances, that we can explore through reason, or religion I suppose, or art.' She looked up at me intently. 'Do you know what I'm talking about, Juniper?'

'I love walking among the trees,' I said.

'A Rousseau to my Kant,' said Charlotte playfully. 'Of course, Kant's system goes way beyond what I saw in the wood, but it started me off. And I still prefer the German idealist interpretation of Kant over the modern Anglo-American analytical approach, which ignores the metaphysical dimension of philosophy.' She was running intellectual rings around me, but I didn't mind because I felt that my love was confirmed. I felt, without being able to explain, that Charlotte and I had the same colour souls, and that that explained why I had fallen in love with her. It was as if my heart had smelled out a deep compatibility between us and thrown itself towards her, before my mind had learned what I was attracted to.

'We must bump into each other again,' Charlotte said later, as we parted.

'How about next week?' I suggested.

'Toby and I will be off camping then. I'll be in touch when we get back.'

I watched her walk off. Relaxed precision in the swing of her arms. I turned, appalled that the miraculous meeting was over. Feel what you feel, I reminded myself, and cycled home.

A WEEK LATER I was back in that café. I'd just overheard two older ladies in the indoor market, talking about how men's brains were only wired up on one side.

'I saw it on telly!' said one.

'That must be why they're like they are,' said the other.

Above the counter in the café was a row of coloured cordials in upside-down bottles; next to them a black pegboard with white plastic words and prices in wobbly rows. I ordered a milky coffee and watched the stainless-steel steam machine hoosh and belch inside its shine.

With Charlotte away camping with Toby, I was fighting the stupid feelings that I was dragging pointlessly around. I re-read Bosch on the reproductive urge. Falling in love as a hormonal and emotional change that disables higher thought, makes the business of raising a family attractive. Four guys came into the café, aged about eighteen; they bought cokes and chatted up the serving girl, then sat down and smoked. Lads with their brains half-wired perhaps, but hearts nevertheless full of life and lust. A bunch of girls came in and sat near the counter in a fleshy, made-up huddle. They hunched around the table with milkshakes, smoking Silk Cuts and glimpsing over at the lads. There was the same brightness about them, though a different kind of lust; female, both-sides-wired lust; desire on the other side of the mammalian divide. Soon the boys and girls were looking at each other, laughing among themselves. One of the lads sauntered over; someone was going to get asked out. Beneath his grin and the hair-oil coolness of his style, organic memories of earth-mother comfort, girl-flesh excitement, the stupendous mystery of the shadowy yoni, were moving him vaguely, powerfully, towards a pink-faced girl with hair sticking up like a fibre-optic lamp.

And if he had been a lion, he would have felt that way about a lioness, would have felt the same excitement about the way her neck was ruffless and her mane was thin; would have marvelled at the smooth curve of flesh beneath her tail that led to regions that he wanted to put his nose into. Mice, pigeons, ants and moths all fall for a particular sort of body that at the right time seems to them the most enchanting thing in the world. The girl was nodding; they'd made a date. She looked cool about it, but her friends were poking her and giggling.

If lions could speak, you can imagine a bunch of lionesses, gathered in the shady afternoon cool of a baobab tree, looking over at 'their' lion, the leader, who was lying behind a rock over yonder.

'Our Leo,' they'd whisper; 'he's wired up differently from us, you know. It's been proved now; poor thing, he only has one side of his brain hooked up.' They'd look over at Leo, who was licking his great paws, feeling a smug pity.

'Oh, but he's still lovely,' says a younger lioness, and the older ladies of the pride roll their eyes and tut. Leo looks over with a dull sleepy look in his big green eyes. He opens wide his enormous mouth in a huge yawn and smacks his lips, shakes his head, and his collar sprays out like rays of light around the sun. The young lioness stares, enchanted.

'Hiya, kiddo,' says Leo, then goes back to sleep. She shudders with a strange delight and puts her head down on her paws.

Was it simply the shadowy yoni that was beckoning me to my sweet brown beloved? Was it a hundred million years of animal mating instinct, calling irresistibly on the subconscious wavelengths of shape and smell? Was I crazy, trying to think my way through the forest of genes, trying to ape the eidetic angels? I looked at the lads and girls again. Would the two that had made the date fall in love at the cinema? Would there be a mystical valley of fascinating secrets between them, into which they would read the fulfilment of their deepest needs? Enchantment requires only objects good enough to bear our dreams.

An old man had walked into the café and was standing at the counter in old man's clothes. The skin on his face was drooping, and reddish flaps dangled down from his chin to his collar. He put his hat on the counter and rested his hand on the crown; he waved the other hand towards the chalked 'specials' board.

'Would you like chips or a baked potato?' said the girl.

'How much?' the old man replied.

'WOULD YOU LIKE –' she said, but St Peter, in the same dirty apron as the week before, came up.

'OK, Tracy, he has chips. WON'T YOU, STAN? YOU'LL HAVE CHIPS.' He had his hand on Tracy's shoulder and he leant towards the old fellow.

'That's two pound fifty for you. Siddown and the girl'll bring it over. Tracy, you take him some tea.'

Stan shuffled over to a far table. Perhaps he'd roared through his life like a lion with big bold male emotions, charged down cowering Germans in the desert in 1944, and cried with the other men in his platoon when a shell blew up their lieutenant. And when he got home, perhaps he'd made love to Ethel up on the moor, and dedicated his soul to her as she put her small hand in his and rocked her head against his chest. He might have been disappointed with Ethel, with all her fears, but stayed with her 'for the kids.' For the spellbound and enchanted, the paired off and bonded, there's ample scope for disappointed expectations.

Tracy brought over his cup of tea. There was a kindness about her, the way she said 'there you go.' One of young men went over to the counter and leant on it to chat her up. She flicked wit with her eyes as she made him a milkshake. Tracy could be a serving girl in a cheap café anywhere in northern England; there could be a thousand Tracies, and a thousand young men admiring their curves and chatting them up. I heard a rumbling from St Peter's cave. The boy took out some money to pay for his milkshake.

'I pay you to talk?' said the chef, bearing down on Tracy. She didn't speak but reached for a cloth. He came out from behind his counter and scanned the café. He walked towards me and reached for my empty cup.

'You wanna pay me some rent?' he said. I didn't understand. 'You gonna pay me some rent for that seat?' I caught his drift. 'You know what I mean?'

Tracy looked up at me sympathetically as I left the café. Outside it was raining the slow grey rain of the north. Down the grey-green paved pedestrian area of town, the young plane trees held new tongues out into the wet. It was just before Easter, and there weren't many people about. I wandered through the old market square, past the fountain hoisting its thick dribble into the rainy air, and up the steps of the town museum, its portico carved of local grey limestone in heavy neoclassical style, etched by acid rain and soot. I walked past the temporary exhibition of local watercolours and up the stairs, past large portraits of the town's industrialist benefactors.

I went on into the museum of the local regiment. I found a life-size first World War dugout; on one wall was pinned a postcard; at the top left was printed, *When the war is over, Maggie....* Beneath was a picture of soldiers in a trench, firing their rifles towards the right, the air full of grey smoke. A woman's head floated in a white cloud above. A verse appeared in small writing, bottom right.

> *Amidst a rain of shot and shell my comrades round me fell,*
> *Would you know why I was spared, dear? the secret I will tell:*
> *Your sweet face was the guiding star that led me through the fray,*
> *And your spirit hovered over me, and brought me safe away.*

Tommy loves Maggie, meaning a boy loves a girl – it doesn't really matter who; the passion is animal and true for all. But yet it isn't contrived; a particular Tommy really does love a particular Maggie; her love-letters find their way through the supply-lines to him in his trench. Love is an instinct, but is personal too; a transmutation of animal passion that creates meaning out of the body's blindest desire. The mind dreams a million reasons why it loves a particular girl.

hubris

BACK AT LYNDHURST, JIM was not entirely unsympathetic to my melancholy plight.

'She's a lovely lass,' he said, 'and if I were a sentimental romantic fool for love, I might have done the same as you.'

'Thanks.'

'Come on,' he said. 'Distract yourself by helping me canvas support against the bypass.'

We went out into the warm, still-light April evening, armed with leaflets and petitions. We had a rack of small streets allotted to us, long terraces without gardens next to a derelict industrial estate. We worked our way methodically along the rows, moving in a smooth overlapping motion from door to door. I enjoyed the sensation of confronting the unique front door, with its paintwork and fittings, in the midst of an apparently uniform street. The door would open, and I was briefly able to see into the private spaces of all these separate lives: a hallway, a sitting room, stairs, with their colours and carpets, ornaments and pictures; it was like touching briefly on a hundred hands.

'I'll sign that,' said a man in a tartan bathrobe. 'That bloody road would be right on the path where I walk the dog.'

'I'm sorry,' said an attractive middle-aged woman, holding her TV remote control. 'But I'm in favour of the plan. There would be less traffic coming down the Salt Marsh Road to the industrial estate.'

'They can build a new road if they want,' said another woman. 'What's wrong with it?'

We reached a short and run-down terrace. I passed Jim, having dispensed leaflets to a sympathetic young man who was in the middle of his beans on toast. Jim looked happy, talking animatedly to an equally animated woman. As I passed, I glimpsed Barry Driscoll coming down the stairs in the hallway behind. I stopped and we met on the now-crowded doorstep.

'Heh, Juniper! How are things?' Barry seemed bright. This was the Danish girlfriend, I assumed.

'So-so,' I said. 'Jim – this is Barry.'

'Hello,' said Jim, looking up and smiling, before returning to his exposition of the road's route to the woman, to which she was paying close attention. Barry and I struck up a separate conversation. But he kept glancing across at Jim and the girlfriend, who were laughing, heads leaning together over pieces of paper. Breaking off suddenly from me, he put his hand on her shoulder.

'Come on, Tina, time to go back in.'

'Not yet,' she said. 'We haven't finished.'

Barry hovered nervously. I gathered that Tina had been involved in road protest activities in Denmark, and that she and Jim were comparing notes. Jim didn't seem to have noticed Barry's agitated state. Barry's impatience suddenly grew too much for him to bear.

'That's enough!' he shouted. Jim and Tina looked up, shocked. 'Come on Tina; let's go in.' He put his hand on her shoulder and pulled. 'We're going out soon and we have to eat,' he said to Jim and me. Tina shook his hand off.

'You go and cook if you want,' she said. 'We're talking here.'

'Sod the road, Tina,' he hissed at her.

'The lady doesn't want to go inside,' said Jim. 'She wants to talk to me.' He looked at Barry squarely. Poor Tina found herself ignored. Barry bobbed around but drew closer to Jim.

'If you'd just go away, then she would come in,' he said.

'Look, mate, I'm not going to steal your girlfriend,' said Jim.

'Barry, just go inside,' Tina broke in. 'I'm just talking to this man; it's nothing else.' I liked her approach, but I thought it was the moment to walk away. Jim didn't. Ignoring Barry, he resumed pointing out to Tina aspects of the road's route on his map. Barry paced up and down inside, then came to the front door, grabbed the map and ripped it up, throwing the pieces outside.

'Barry, you idiot!' screamed Tina, but he pushed her inside the house.

'*Piss off!*' he shouted in Jim's face, and shoved him in the chest. Jim barely swayed, but stood looking amazed and disdaining at the crazed academic. 'Juniper,' said Barry, waving his finger around Jim's face, 'you should keep away from this guy. He's trouble.'

'I'd hate to see how you treat the Jehovah's Witnesses,' said Jim. 'OK, asshole, you can cook your tea now. I'll call round again,' he called over Barry's head to Tina. She looked ghastly in the background.

'You will not,' growled Barry, and launched a fist into Jim's chest. It bounced harmlessly off the barrel of bone and donkey jacket. But Jim, more through instinct than anger, punched back. The smaller man fell backwards, tripping over the doormat and banging his face into the door before crashing onto the floor. Blood leaked from his nose as he got up onto all fours on the bare tiles of the hall. Tina screamed. I stepped into the hall and helped Barry sit against a wall. Tina fetched warm water and a cloth to mop up the red mess dribbling down his face and across the floor. He moaned and gingerly touched his nose.

'You've broken my nose, you bastard,' he groaned. I looked at Tina.

'I can look after him,' she said. She looked up at Jim, who stood at the doorstep, staring amazed at his clutched fist. She shook her head. 'You men are so crazy,' she said, then burst into Danish to give more exact expression to her feeling. Barry ignored me when I left him. I took Jim's arm and shut the door behind me. We walked in silence back towards Lyndhurst.

In the kitchen I made tea; then we sat at the table and smoked. The atmosphere was like the time that Jim, Paul and I had come back from Peter's, but now there was no sense of triumph.

'What a wanker,' said Jim.

'I used to think he was a friend.'

'And the way he was treating his girlfriend!'

'She didn't seem very impressed by your hitting him though.'

'No,' said Jim. 'She must be in love with him or something to put up with all that shit.'

'But why did you have to hit him? You could have walked away, but you were too proud. Admit it.'

'That pride is a warrior's strength,' said Jim, pointing a thick finger towards me. 'Don't try to shame me.'

'Oh, what crap, Jim,' I said. 'Can you imagine Achilles even bothering to hit someone like Driscoll? It was schoolboy stuff.'

'I trust my instincts, Juniper, and you do not. That's a difference. Driscoll needed a lesson.'

'Now you're replacing our justice system with instinctive natural justice, just what we were talking about before we sorted out Peter.'

'Don't be such a nancy. There's a *principle* involved.'

'What principle?'

'The Principle of Non-Collusion with Untruth. I've been thinking about it since Peter was threatening Beth. You have to draw a line. If I'd walked away from Barry Driscoll tonight he would have thought that his reasons for acting like he did were true. But I did not collude. My knuckles hurt, though.'

We laughed, and I made another pot of tea while Jim rolled a large spliff.

The doorbell rang at eleven-thirty. It was late and we were stoned. Jim answered it, but I went up when I heard raised voices. There were two policemen at the door, with Barry Driscoll in the background, saying, 'that's him, Officer, that's him!' The second officer seemed to be employed in holding Barry back.

'So you admit that you struck this man at about eight o'clock this evening?' I heard the sergeant say, writing in his notebook, but finding it hard to concentrate because of Barry's noise. Jim bent his head down.

'I was a witness to the incident,' I said, and the sergeant looked up.

'I think we'd all better come along to the station where we can make our statements in peace,' he said, looking at the bobbing figure of Barry. It looked like he had a black eye coming, as well as a bruised nose. I was glad.

We all squeezed into the police car, with Barry in the front. The officer driving told him to be quiet, and we drove in silence. At the police station, the officer on duty took statements one at a time in a private room, starting with Barry. He went home after he'd spoken, striding out after a last scowl at Jim. Jim and I were asked to stay while one of the policemen who had stood in the doorway of Lyndhurst had a quiet word in the duty officer's ear.

'Please empty your pockets on the counter,' he said to Jim, who compliantly tipped out small change, and a lump of cannabis resin wrapped in cellophane. The keen officer must have caught a whiff of our spliff as he stood at the door.

No one seemed to mind him having bashed Barry, but he was charged for possession of cannabis. We walked home through the empty streets in the dismal silence of the early hours.

'About half an eighth,' Jim said, disgusted and frustrated. Now he was angry and I was shocked. 'Have those chaps nothing better to do than to bust me for a blim?' The only person we could blame was Barry Driscoll, and this time I felt like beating him up.

In the morning, the perverse scenario worsened. I met Jim in the kitchen, looking ragged and unslept, explaining his position to Matt and Chris, who both happened to be in.

'You stupid twat,' said Matt. 'I've got a kilo of dried mushrooms in my room, and a wardrobe full of drying grass.'

'The cops might come round and bust the place,' said Chris.

'You have to move out today.'

'But if the police want to search the house, they'll do it whether or not Jim's here,' I said.

'Look, he's fucked up,' said Matt. 'There's a price to be paid. It's seriously inconvenient for us to move all the shit. If they found it, the quantities would make us look like dealers, and you know what that means.'

Jim wasn't saying much. The world seemed full of friends turned tossers. Matt and Chris got him to agree to move out that day.

'I've got nowhere to put all my stuff,' said Jim, but they told him he could leave most of it temporarily as long as he got a new address.

Jim climbed up to his attic room and began packing up, though he owned very little. I stowed his notes and books in my room where they'd be safe.

'Where will you go?' I asked when we'd packed and were drinking a last mug of tea.

'Back to Leeds for a bit. I haven't seen my mum for a while, so I'll stay with her and sort out a new room from there.' He seemed quite happy, as if he was about to go on holiday. 'I don't mind getting out of town for a while. If I stayed here I might be tempted to go and have another conversation with Tina while Barry Driscoll was in the house.'

'Yeah,' I said, and we laughed a bit.

I walked with him to the station in the early afternoon, and waved him off as the old diesel multiple unit clanked away from a back platform towards the slow line to Leeds. I walked home sorrowful and alone. That evening I finished the half-smoked spliff of the night before, then sat in the back of the kitchen watching the wood stove burn. Archie sat on my lap. At ten, I realised that I hadn't thought of Charlotte once since the day before.

eros

CHARLOTTE DIDN'T GET in touch. I was abandoned to the lonely Easter vacation, dumped in an empty aftermath of absence. Moonlight spread on Jim's mattress at Lyndhurst, shining through the skylight of his empty attic room. I hadn't heard anything from him. I met with Paul a couple of times, but then he went away to a series of conferences. Even the library lost its safety; as I tried to revise, my brain kept flashing into a panic every time I saw, among the sad, studious faces of those who had not gone home for the holiday, a dark-looking woman gliding along the carpets or browsing between the dark walls of books. I escaped into the Nelson Mandela to smoke.

One day I had to endure a young couple canoodling at the table next to me. She was touching his hand, touching the edge of his jacket, touching the live, honed edges of the large and fresh slice of manhood she had acquired. He was grinning, all besotted with the bright little creature that he'd found, with what she was like and what she was doing to him. She ran her long fingernails along his huge pink paws, the paws of her bear, her tamed Adam.

He talked like a man made real, his words all reasons for her to smile or tease; he was so enamoured by her attention that he felt he could speak everything, anything. In return, she poured out a babbling stream; words seeking to form the fragile construction of reciprocated desire, to feed the unlikely fusion of these two young lives; words as the means by which two paper bags tried to get inside each other. She wasn't really listening to him, only to what she wanted to hear; he hardly saw what she was doing, the clever affirmation by which she made him her own. Each saw the other in terms of the meaning of love that a thousand films and adverts had made them think is their fate; each touch was a gateway into a passion they'd seen rehearsed, a divine performance they were blessed to repeat.

They stopped talking. He had a little moustache of frothed milk from his coffee, and she stretched her forefinger out to wipe it away. He was patient, passive, then made to bite her finger; a small mock-fight followed, ending with her head buried in his chest, a defeat, surrender. Then soft words; her voice, its tone rising and falling, had a soft quality of disclosure that flowed around him like soft, pale limbs, touching, embracing, dissolving. He was honoured with her intimacy, he was needed, was possibly the one man in the universe who could save her or at the least console her, who she wanted to be saved or consoled by.

He was delighted as the woman disclosed herself, seemed to give her soul over to his care; while for her this was the currency of her dreams that she was spending at last on the real thing, a man. He responded in monosyllables, little helpful comments from his small inheritance of wisdom. But what she took as his strong silence was untrained confusion. His worship mistook the gush of her feeling-talk for a bigger understanding. For him, at last, here was a woman who drew forth his soul. He enjoyed her sharp, witty humour that seemed to cut through to what mattered, prompting thoughts of which he had always considered himself capable but never quite attained. They loved the pact they formed in their heroic lives.

And this animal coupling raised to cultic refinement was spread across public space like a cake on a stand, or underwear on a line. It was so commonplace, this conducting of private passions in the midst of everyone else, yet, noticing it, I thought how strange it was, like a window on a room in which people danced and kissed, in which the lights were brightly shining, with no curtains; outside was dark, and I could see into their love with entire clarity. Meanwhile, they saw nothing in the windows but their own reflections; and a man sitting drinking his coffee, alone.

She pouted, and he laughed, stroking her cheek. She quickly turned her head away, and he had to regain her love. She looked out of the window. He whispered something to her, taking her hand, and her face broke open like a flower. She was a young woman only slightly aware of the total power she was wielding over this predictable male; he seemed only slightly conscious of the enslavement a smell, a touch, a glance, some confiding words had achieved. She, perhaps aware only of her small portion of female charm and her particular individual needs, gambled her whole self on a game which, miraculously, she always seemed to win. He, meanwhile, used to the feel of his bigger body, the way it swung and the confidence it gave him, was unaware of what it might mean to her; assumed, perhaps, that she shared his perception of uncertainty, the fear that, despite manly appearances, still accompanied most of his encounters with the real world.

I saw the two young people ride the rollercoaster of hormone, instinct, sex, pleasure and romance, race along tracks of stereotyped and predictable couple behaviours. But of course, they didn't notice; they were enjoying the thrill of the ride, the fresh wind in their hair. All happy couples falling in love think they are taking their rightful place in heaven; here on earth we watch them hold hands, close their eyes and leap, like countless brave and blinkered lovers before them.

'So you promise you'll remember?' she said, standing up, pulling down the skirt of her dress.

'Yeah, yeah, of course,' he replied, getting up, swinging his jacket over his shoulder. 'And you'll come with me Monday night?'

They walked out of the Nelson Mandela. They say you feel on top of the world when you're in love; it's a place where flying and standing still feel much the same.

I STAYED IN THE coffee bar, reading a book on Greek love, the way the upper-class men tended to go for pre-bearded youths. Even Socrates fell in love with boys, though dry old Aristotle was above it all. The passions were fierce and familiar, but what they found beautiful was not. Outside, warm spring sunshine flooded across the waterlogged lawns, and the wet grass shone back its love. I was missing being able to watch springtime among the woods of Silverthwaite, the succession of aconite, snowdrop, daffodil and bluebell, before the trees managed to rouse their larger machines to roll out leaves then drown the wood floor in dimness. I missed the colours of the sand on the bay and the night-sounds of owls. I missed all the beauty I was familiar with; this love for Charlotte was becoming another part of exile.

Then she walked into the Nelson Mandela, with Toby. I hid behind my book, suddenly brought up against the monster of my affection, but hiding was worse than meeting her. She looked as gorgeous as a boy without a beard. She saw me and came over. Toby looked over vaguely.

'Hello Juniper,' she said, smiling. 'Can we join you?'

'Please.' Polite ironies. I wished she wasn't there, or that Toby wasn't there, but would have felt annihilated if they hadn't joined me.

'Seems like ages since we last met,' said Charlotte, sliding onto the plastic chair next to me while Toby bought her drink.

You said you'd get in touch with me, I thought with a little bitterness, but didn't say anything. My hands were shaking. I tried to pick up my cup, but had to put it down again because the wobble might have given me away. Charlotte seemed oblivious to my physiological symptoms. I felt like my pupils were huge. My heart was knocking. It was ridiculous. Feel, feel, feel. Madness.

'So, how was the camping trip?' I asked blandly, my reliable adult voice something to hide behind.

'Yeah, the camping was good. We caught that spell of sunshine, so it was warm in the daytime. Then at night it froze. I had to wear all my clothes to keep warm.'

Why didn't you get Toby to wrap himself around you? I wanted to say. Toby sat down with drinks and Charlotte and I rolled cigarettes.

'A philosophy book?' asked Toby.

'What? No, not really.' I was surprised he was being friendly, assuming that he must have picked up that I fancied Charlotte. But there was no sign of it.

'So, where did you walk?' I asked. This talk was laboured, yet I wanted to avoid saying anything about myself, as it all led back to Charlotte.

She explained their route, and Toby added details. Her hand made deft, proportional gestures to indicate directions and distances; her face was alive with sensual memories. I wondered if Toby was in love with Charlotte. Was he also enthralled by her vivacity and attention? Looking at him now, the way he sipped his herbal tea and stared across the room, he was distracted from her, from us, returning only occasionally with a smile and a few polite words. But her hand, as she spoke, moved sideways to brush against him, or push a finger into his thigh, reminding him of a high tarn in which the snow-streaked peaks had been reflected. A thick smoke of jealousy seeped down through me. He didn't deserve her. It was a sick feeling, utterly pointless.

'I have to go now,' I said, looking at my watch. 'I'm seeing Professor Rampton, so I don't want to be late.' In fact, I had half an hour to go before the appointment.

'Oh,' said Charlotte, her face dropping. I felt gratified at her disappointment. 'I've missed seeing you after all those coincidental meetings.' I laughed lightly, but I was also pained, because only someone not in love could be so open and uncomplicated about liking me. Merely being liked by Charlotte was a mild form of torture. 'Call round to my house again if you like,' she said.

'OK,' I said, packing up my books. 'Bye Toby.'

'Goodbye,' he said affably.

I hurried to the footpath around the wooded edges of the campus fields. Bluebells hissed the dry ice of their peculiar blue under the budding beeches, and I gave myself to the mauve quiet, leaving the jealousy behind. Wrens and blackbirds sang the new season, reminding me of the brief, delicate, hand-woven garment of time that I wore, a human life, an utterly unrequested gift.

PROFESSOR RAMPTON HAD RUNG me up the day before. She was back in the country and had wanted to see how I'd got on with my project. It was supposed to be finished, but I'd arranged an extension. When I pushed open her office door, she was sitting in her big old armchair, fingers bridged. The curtains were closed, and the dim light that trickled through them lay quietly at the edges of the room, while two standard lamps burned in the corners to each side of her. A hidden spotlight illumined a bust of Socrates, and I noticed that on the plinth was a small bronze vase of freesias. She rose to greet me, pushing her ageing, somewhat spread bulk out of the chair.

'Good afternoon, Mr Johnson,' she said, shaking my hand, then holding it in both of hers. 'Aah,' she said quietly, then dropped my hand and, turning her back on me, returned to her chair. 'Would you draw the curtains, please?' Daylight washed in as I pulled back the thick woven pile. 'And switch off the lights? The switch is at the floor by the door.'

'You have a fine tan, Professor,' I said, drawing a chair towards her.

'California!' she exclaimed. 'Takes years off one, you know. Who needs plastic surgery, eh?' Her large bosom bounced at her own joke. 'I'm afraid I've been a forgetful master for your philosophical apprenticeship,' she continued. 'Though I think you will forgive me, in that I have made the time to complete my book, my life-work, the *magnum opus*.' She lifted her right hand from the arm of the chair and placed it on a thick pile of paper on a table beside her. I saw '*The Archetype of Wisdom* by Nicola Rampton' typed on the top sheet.

'Will it be published soon?' I asked reverently. The Professor's attitude changed, and she shuffled a little.

'Having problems,' she said, not meeting my eyes. 'These damned academics: with their post-modern, post-this-and-that, post-bloody-*metaphysical* – how the hell can you *not* be metaphysical? – Told me to rewrite. Damn them! I'll find someone else.'

I nodded sympathetically at her plight.

'So, Mr Johnson, how are you getting on?' It was an open, general question, and seemed to invite a completely honest answer.

'I'm struggling, Professor,' I said, and it was now my turn to shift uneasily. 'Events in my life have overtaken the flow of clear thinking.' The Professor raised her eyebrows, but said nothing, inviting me to continue. I gave her a potted history of events, from the split-up with Ros to my unrequited passion. I started to summarise my reflections on Bosch's book, but the Professor waved them aside.

'What,' she asked, 'have you learned about love from your recent experiences?'

I wanted to say how useful I'd found Bosch's critique of falling in love, but I knew that didn't answer the Professor's question.

'There is no trick,' she added, 'and I have no preconceptions regarding your answer.'

We sat in silence for some time, the Professor bridging her fingers again. I considered the question in a slightly panicky state. I took the plunge.

'I thought I knew what was love and what was an illusion, but everything's been turned upside down. The stable relationship with Ros has fallen apart, and I'm burning with feelings for Charlotte that feel as real as anything. But there's something else that I've learned – that the camaraderie and shared purpose between Jim and Paul and me is a kind of love too.'

'Which kind of love do you most value? The love between friends, which is rational and clear as well as warm and useful? The mad passion for someone you hardly know that's shot through with bodily urge? The long steady love of commitment that drags itself up, over and over again, through mistakes, lessons, disillusion, argument, that is in a real sense a self-surrender?'

'There's also a more basic sheer feeling of sympathy, like that between Jim and his cat.'

'All right,' said the Professor, smiling. 'Which of these four kinds of love?'

'How can I say?' I said. 'At the moment, I value friendship. But that steady committed love always used to seem the real thing; and that basic sympathy seems to underlie both of them in a way. I suppose I don't value the falling in love so much, because I don't trust it.'

'But you must value it in some sense because you're doing it, are you not? It isn't just happening to you, is it?'

I thought of my going to the Buddhist Society, and the conversation in the café.

'To be honest, it feels fantastic,' I said. 'But it's so painful too.'

'A purely philosophical question, Mr Johnson: is it sex you want from Charlotte?'

I considered. According to Bosch, the whole thing should end in us making babies together. But though I couldn't deny that I found her attractive, I hadn't begun to entertain sexual fantasies about her. They would have seemed somehow demeaning to us both.

'There's definitely a sexual element in the attraction,' I said; 'but I don't think that's the essence of what I feel.'

'So being in love isn't the same as sexual attraction?'

'No. It's much bigger, much more personal. It's *her* I want, which means her body too, which is maybe just a confused way of saying I want to obey the natural drive to mate with her.'

'Let's not leap so quickly to conclusions,' said Professor Rampton. 'From what you say sex and so on might be a *consequence* of your following your desire, but is not necessarily to be taken as the *motive* for falling in love.'

'Not at all. Charlotte was telling me that in India people fall in love *after* they're married, so for them a family can't be the motive for the experience. So what is it? What is it that we want when we fall in love?'

'Turn to your own experience, Mr Johnson. What is it that you want from being in love with Charlotte?'

'Maybe there's some lack or need that I'm not properly aware of that I suppose she'll fulfil. I've had a sense that there's something about Charlotte, her soul, which matches mine so precisely; don't we all crave meeting that other person who will complete us?'

The Professor laughed. 'It's true that many of us do. But how well do you know Charlotte? Well enough to know that she is your other half? I doubt it. I wonder if we ever know anyone so well. But somehow the experience of falling in love itself suggests the possibility of that completion.'

'So, falling in love itself suggests a possibility which makes us think that the other person is that special one – that makes sense.'

'It might be quite a dynamic psychological, even existential, process that Charlotte, or at least whatever you know about her, has triggered off in you. But it isn't simply happening, is it? It's not passive; you're involved in it.'

'Definitely; it's almost addictive. One surge of whatever 'it' is, and not only do I want Charlotte, but I want that surge again. Even now, when the force has gone all tangled and difficult inside, I want to try it again, see her again, because of the memory of how significant that desire once felt.'

'Deep down, falling in love feels like it is part of the meaning of life, does it not?'

'I've never consciously believed that.'

'But you act as if it's true.'

'I've tried not to.'

'But not very effectively, it seems.'

'No.'

'Reflect on your actual experience, Mr Johnson. Don't use thinking as a means to keep perceived dangers at bay. It doesn't work.'
We lapsed into a contemplative silence. I felt exhausted.

'Close the curtains again, please,' she said eventually. 'And switch on the lights.'

When the room was yellow once more, the Professor stood and looked up above her chair towards the plaster bust of Socrates, with his curly hair and snub nose, that had come into the light again. She reached up to the plinth and took down a thin book that had been lying invisibly on the flat surface.

'Here is something for you that should help you forward in your thinking,' she said. 'It discusses, in its own way, much of the ground we have traversed this afternoon, although Plato reaches his own very distinctive conclusions.' It was a thin hardbound book with no title on its cover. Inside, I read '*Symposium* by Plato, translated by Nicola Rampton. Privately printed in 1959, number 191 of 200.' And written in fresh blue ink, 'to Juniper Johnson, with my best wishes, Nicola.'

'Thank you, Professor,' I said, clutching the thin old book. 'I didn't know you were a Greek scholar.'

'I'm not,' she said. 'But this was my own offering to *eros*, a labour for love. You're not the first philosopher to fall in love, you know.'

'Thank you,' I said. She smiled at me.

'All the best for your work, Juniper,' she said. 'I look forward to reading your dissertation.'

I cycled home and read *Symposium* straight through, by the warm woodstove in the basement, till the early hours.

a trip to Leeds

NEXT MORNING, I READ *Symposium* again. A group of Greek men gathered for dinner and then spoke in turn in praise of *eros*, the god of passionate love, who impels men towards those beautiful youths. Socrates relates how the priestess Diotima had instructed him in the higher mysteries of love; he had learned to see true beauty beyond the attractive surfaces of bodies.

I imagined Professor Rampton, in love, in her twenties. Had she been beautiful? Whom had she loved? Perhaps it had been some philosophical divine, studying alongside her in the faculty at Cambridge. It would have been the 1950s, when porters at gates kept the forces of nature at bay. But Nicola and her beloved might have strolled through the college gardens, along the Cam shining in the spring sunlight, while linen-suited groups punted through the unscholarly afternoons; and Nicola might have savoured every nuance of desire, desired every nuance of feeling. It might have been some rich and confident young aristocrat, exquisitely groomed for a life in the highest circles, while her lowly background meant her feelings were impossibly above reality; I imagined her own amusement at the cliché. I imagined her pride, the rejection of any hint that her emotion might have some false, aggrandising motivation, and her consequent fierce focus on polite, intense Platonic friendship. What irony! – that 'Platonic love' should have become debased to mean something like a friendship between a man and a woman without a sexual component, where one might have been expected. What Plato describes, and brings to life in the literary persona of Socrates, is friendship actively brimming with instinctual life, the fecundity of sexual urge, the rapture of physical passion, yet a passionate attachment tamed and contained by a higher goal than mere sensual gratification. I imagined Nicola, tingling, talking, while her oblivious friend appreciated her witty intelligence and spark. And he looked among the sweet roses of the aristocracy for some suitable wife, and courted in the tea gardens of Sunday afternoons, while real love bloomed secretly in the riverside meadows, if not in the hot, wild jungles of the night.

Before lunch, Beth came round, clutching a grubby picture postcard of a new theatre complex in Leeds. I recognised Jim's small, neat handwriting on the back. It said:

Dear Beth,

Sorry I haven't been around, but I had to move back to Leeds to avoid the heat – ask Juniper what I mean if you don't know. In fact I've gone underground for various reasons, one of which was to think about things and make some decisions. Anyway, I just wanted to let you know as I've been thinking of you quite a bit. I don't yet know when I'll be back, and I don't have an address, but don't worry and I'll be in touch as soon as I return to Greyston. Could you tell Juniper I've intercalated.

Jim

'So, what's happened?' Beth demanded. I told her, ashamed that I hadn't done so before.

'And actually, a court summons arrived for him this morning,' I added.

'You bloody men can be so thoughtless,' she fumed. 'If you'd told me at the time Matt and Chris chucked him out, I would have put him up at my place. Why didn't he think of it, the stubborn idiot? And you're just as bad.'

Beth was more or less back on form.

'What the hell does "intercalate" mean anyway?'

'It means he's taken a year out of university. That's radical. It means he won't be taking his finals until next year now. Maybe he told the university that he's gone mad over a woman or something.'

'When you find him,' she said, 'tell him he can come and live with me. Tell him I'm pissed off he didn't think to ask. Tell him he's proud and stupid, but I owe him a favour. He'd have to do a lot worse than hit some misogynist and get done for a bit of dope for me to stop liking him.'

I cycled up to the university to see Paul. He looked at the court summons and the postcard blankly, shaking his head. There was a knock at the door, and Charlotte walked in.

'Are you coming for lunch with us?' she said to me, looking pleased. I shook my head, half-jealous and half-glum.

'We've encountered a difficulty,' said Paul, and showed Charlotte the postcard. I explained what had happened.

'We should go and find him,' said Charlotte.

'It would appear that a trip to Leeds is in order,' said Paul, frowning.

Charlotte smiled. 'We'll need somewhere to stay,' she said. I looked at Paul.

'I suppose I might ask Jackie if she could put us up,' he said. We burst into laughter.

We went to a sandwich counter together to eat, but finished quickly. We agreed to meet at the station at three.

STEPPING OUT OF THE STATION in Leeds at five-thirty, we saw into the pumping heart of the city: thousands of anonymous beings milled in cars, buses and on foot out of the huge buildings and towards their smaller huts. The sterile air was mildly acrid, despite the spring. We walked past closing shops and threaded through hurrying people. We caught a packed, rocking bus through miles of slow traffic, past the grand buildings of the university, on and on through the tedious grids of houses, until we reached a district with many small lawns like patches of blue in a showery sky. We stepped down into the foreign streets, following binary instructions – first left, second right – to reach an Edwardian semi that looked like a thousand others.

The house Jackie shared was cool and large, with polished wood floors and a ceramic fireplace. An Aga hissed very quietly in the kitchen. Jackie chattered on defensively, but started to relax once Molly arrived home from work. Molly told us of a woman she knew who had lived on the streets for four years, happier with privation and discomfort than with poll tax, rent, bills and needing to answer to the world. But homelessness had taken its toll on physical health, so she now had a council flat and was learning how to comport herself to the anxieties of civilisation.

'I think we should assume Jim's living somewhere on the streets,' said Charlotte; 'so we should start by asking around for him.'

'We'll be back late, I suppose,' Paul said to Jackie.

'I'll come with you,' Jackie said. 'I know my way around.'

'That would be splendid,' said Paul, looking pleased.

Molly gave us a lift to a homeless centre, where Charlotte talked to one of the staff. We hung around for a while, asking and looking. Had anyone seen a big man with dark, tousled curls? We received sidelong glances, gruff denials or mangled, hot-breathed non-answers. At ten, Charlotte divided us into two pairs, sending Paul and Jackie in one direction and taking me in another, to well-known sleeping haunts.

We walked down the night-quiet streets of the business sector. What is a city? A refuge from boars and enemies, a fortified den, that has become a world of its own; that starts producing its own beings from a womb of anonymous unnatural culture. Within it, some people go back to the wild. As we passed walls, corners, yards and patches of green, I saw all the myriad places to hide from wind and headlights and tax demands; yet still safe in the arms of the city.

We found a deserted multi-storey car park, built on a derelict Victorian industrial site, the unwashed armpit of a worked-out body. We entered the stairwell on a dark side street of locked fences and brick-heaped wastelands, through a dimly lit door marked 'P'. Voices echoed up, with shrill laughter. Our footsteps clattered around the concrete box; the laughter stopped. At the bottom of the first turn of the stairs three men and a woman stared up and scowled. Charlotte put her arm through mine. I felt a soft thrill go through me, of both love and fear.

'We're looking for a friend of ours called Jim,' I said. 'He's big, with curly hair, comes from Leeds. Have you seen him?' My voice scraped over the yellow gloss of the walls and died in piss-stained corners. It didn't seem to touch the ragged, staring crew. We had to walk through them to continue down the stairs. They parted, avoiding eye contact. We passed the double swing-doors marked 'Lower Ground', and kept descending.

'Where ya' gooin'?' the woman above shouted hysterically. We turned; I repeated my question, looking upward, back into the light. Bits of meaning seemed to stick uncomfortably in her eyes.

'Jim? Everyone's called Jim. Heh, Jimmy, heh?' She poked one of her friends, who had been staring down. A scrambled Glaswegian syntax dribbled over the floor.

'Jim is a very common name,' said a small man, in an impeccable accent. 'And I haven't seen anyone corresponding to your description. Now if you'd excuse us, we were having a private conversation.' He turned his back on us, and the thin man next to him looked at us sourly.

We kept going down. A pool of acidic-smelling vomit spread in front of the doors marked 'Upper Basement'. From above came the slamming sound of the doors to the street swung hard. People were coming down the stairs fast, yelling. One passed us as we pressed back into the wall, a small young man, closely followed by another. A stink of hot sweat and cigarettes wafted along behind. They both leapt over the chain across the stairs and disappeared on down. The cavern quieted again to the murmur of the conversation above. We climbed over the chain, past the sign that said 'floor Closed', and walked on down, into bulb-blown darkness. The stairs were strewn with rubbish in the corners: paper and bottles and cans. Charlotte kicked something that clattered down the steps, and we waited for the quiet to hide us again. We were at the bottom of the stairs, where the steps ended and a square corner sloped down under the ascending concrete. From its black recess came a rustling noise.

'Jim?' I whispered.

'Get lost!' answered a gruff male voice, not Jim's.

We could just read the 'Lower Basement' sign, and I slowly pushed open the door. Inside, we stopped, our eyes unadjusted to the dark, surrounded by movement and by low voices. Charlotte dragged the wheel of her lighter, and in the quick dragon-light we could see a pathway between bodies, blankets and boxes. A few faces turned malevolently towards us. She put the light out again.

'Come on,' she whispered, and pulled me onward, into the heart of the dark. Flame-light and shadows beckoned us around a corner. A crude brazier burned at a far wall, under a high-up grill that let in distant streetlight in long trapezium portions on the floor, through grey columns of oily smoke. Dark figures huddled there, or moved through the yellow light.

Silence spread through the crowd as we approached, and faces turned. I felt, not fear, but something close: disorientation. Charlotte held my arm with both hands. We could barely see faces, only old blankets around shoulders, unbrushed lank hair.

'We're looking for a friend of ours called Jim,' said Charlotte quickly. 'We don't know where he is.' We were ignored, and conversations started up again. I could feel Charlotte shudder as with tears, and I squeezed her hand. We stood by the fire. Small spots of red punctured the dark, described arcs, glowed at mouths, hovered quietly at hip level. The murmuring continued. Yelling began, in a distant dark corner of the cavernous space, then died away. No one took any notice.

'Have you a cigarette?' said a voice behind us, with its impeccable accent. We turned around. The little man, with his three friends, approached.

'Of course,' said Charlotte, disengaging my arm. She pulled out her packet and offered them around. We all stood and smoked. The three continued swigging on their cans, without interest in us.

'My friends are ill mannered,' the man continued, 'but they mean no harm. Now tell me again what you wanted: some burnt offering from the ragged underbelly of the night, perhaps?' He turned to the sour-looking man who raised his can in appreciation.

'Our friend, Jim Fletcher,' I responded. 'He's very big, tangled black hair, very clever. Got thrown out of his house, came over here.'

'Watch your language, young man,' he said sharply.

'Sorry,' I said. 'But –'

'Sentences require subjects, and subjects need stating, do they not?'

At that his friends cheered, and the man took a small bow. Charlotte giggled.

'We were wondering,' I said again, 'whether you might –'

'– know the whereabouts of your friend Jim? I'm no miracle worker, you know, despite having this thing in my head.' He pointed to his forehead and sighed. 'It's still in there. They can't get it out. It's always, always going. Always.'

'What?' said Charlotte, leaning in to look at the man.

'I believe it is known as a microchip. Enough of that.' He turned towards the fire. 'Lennie!' he called.

An enormous man wearing thick, oily blankets, his face creased like a Tibetan's and with hair sprouting like dandelions, approached from the shadow beyond the fire. He glared at the little man, then looked at us.

'Who the fuck – what the – what – fuck are you?' he spluttered. His eyes burned black. Charlotte cowered.

'Lennie, these are friends of Jim's. He's big, he's bad and he's brainy. Have you seen him?' Lennie thought to himself for a few seconds, with what looked like enormous effort.

'Would you like a cigarette?' Charlotte asked him. Lennie snatched the packet, and with his filthy, broken fingers pulled out a bent stick, then handed the packet back tenderly.

'Fuckin' thanks, Paki. Queer,' he said to me.

'These shadows against the wall,' the little man said, pointing at the black shapes against the breeze blocks and pillars, cast in waving dances by the smoky brazier, 'these mere phantoms of reality, debased illustrations, are all these people know of the world. Forgive them their ignorance.'

'The myth of the cave!' Charlotte said, amazed. 'From Plato's *Republic*. Have you read it?'

'I have – have – dabbled,' he said, with a wide, satisfied smile, head leant back and eyes closed, relishing attention. 'That is to say, before –' he tapped his forehead '– they put in the semiotic detector. I always preferred the Greeks.'

'Our friend Jim is a philosopher,' said Charlotte. 'You'd get on with him, I think.'

'Yes, yes,' said the man enthusiastically. 'I think I might. I think so. When you find him, send him down. I lack conversation here, don't I, Lennie?'

'This cunt talks like a fucking – fucking cunt!' said Lennie, putting his arm around the man affectionately. They both laughed. Charlotte discretely moved half-behind me and held onto my arm. 'Don't know no fucking big bastard Jim, neither.'

'I don't think Jim's here,' Charlotte whispered to me.

'We have to leave now,' I said 'to hopefully find Jim.'

The little man creased his face up, moaned and hit his head. 'Don't you split your infinitives here, young man,' he said. 'And "hopefully" is an adverbial form of "hopeful" appropriate to describing someone doing something in a manner full of hope, whereas you are looking hopefully, because you haven't yet found. I suggest "hoping to find".'

'Cunt,' said Lennie.

'Sorry,' I said.

But Charlotte's quiet, high voice piped up around my shoulder. 'I think you could regard "hopefully" as a sentence-phrase adverb in this case, like "frankly" or "understandably". They refer to the whole sentence, not just to the actor, as would an ordinary verb-phrase adverb, as in "politely depart".'

'Really? Really? No – no – surely not –' the little man said, looking down, looking up, holding his head in his hands. I wished Charlotte hadn't said anything. What if he took offence? What if Lennie thought we'd upset him? 'Lennie! Lennie! She's right!' The little man leapt up and down on the spot, waving his arms. Lennie whooped and slapped me on the back. Charlotte dodged away. We laughed, while the little man danced with small steps, chanting, 'sentence-phrase adverb, verb-phrase adverb.'

'Let us show our guests out,' he said to Lennie.

'What about big-fucking-brainy-fucker Jim?' Lennie said, concernedly.

'If you see him, tell him his friends were looking for him,' I said. 'I'm Juniper and this is Charlotte,' I said, as we reached the door to the stairwell. 'What's your name?'

'Name? Full name? Dr Arthur Freckles. To you.'

Arthur stayed at the bottom of the stairs as we started to wind up. Lennie burst through.

'Fucking lighter!' he shouted, waving Charlotte's lighter. 'Fuckin' hopefully yours, Paki.'

'Thanks Lennie,' she said, going back to collect it. She reached down from as far up as she could to pluck it from his extended thick fingers. He looked at her with a mournful, frowning desire.

'You shouldn't call people cunts or Pakis,' she said, speaking down at him, when she had reached my arm again. 'It's rude.'

He stared at her, open mouthed. As we climbed out of sight, we heard a man's voice shout 'get lost!'

Back in the open air, we hugged, the first time I'd put my arms around her. We caught a taxi back to Molly's house after midnight. Paul and Jackie were already home. There had been no sign of Jim, though in a way I was relieved not to have found him in among the people we'd met that evening. We drank tea together. I watched Jackie's fascinating face, capable of huge distortions of expression, amplifying emotion in a drama of masks.

Charlotte slept in one of the bedrooms vacated by Molly's fledged girls, and Paul and I slept in the other. It was one-thirty.

'How did it go with Jackie?' I asked, after we'd climbed under cloud-covered duvets.

'Extraordinary,' Paul said. 'She treated me at last as a separate individual. She said she has realised how much she has taken me for granted.'

'Excellent,' I said. 'Progress.'

'Indeed,' said Paul. 'Something I noticed,' he continued, rolling onto his side, 'is that I now feel more confident in my attitude towards her. That ritual has restored the correct order of things.'

'Do you think you'll be able to stay in touch?'

Paul paused. 'I suspect that I will conclude that we will need to go our separate ways more definitively. Although I am confident that I would be able to maintain my boundaries, I cannot deny that I still suffer from inappropriate and unhelpful habitual feelings of – not quite love – something more like a needy affection. They are there. Jackie and I talked about this, just before you returned this evening. For her part, though she can treat me with respect, as she demonstrated, she admits to having enjoyed the sense of power and domination over the little boy in me that wanted her blonde, strong comforts. Because of these feelings, ingrained into our relationship over years, I doubt we can maintain a healthy friendship. Besides, the stronger man in me would like an amicable parting and a proven independence.'

'That makes sense,' I said.

'And how about yourself?' Paul enquired. 'You have made mention of your attraction to the delightful Ms Newby, and this evening you spent an evening in the underworld in her divine company. I presume this evokes some beatitude.'

'Something like that,' I said, laughing. 'Though I've been practising Platonic containment of my passionate attraction.'

Paul laughed. 'You really are the practical philosopher. I am impressed.'

'How about you?' I asked. 'As I recall, you had a certain attraction to the unwheatish one yourself.'

'Yes, yes,' he said distantly, then rolled back onto his back. 'Juniper,' he said eventually. 'I am not confident enough to consider myself your rival for Charlotte's affections. She and I are friends – you know as much – but there has never been a hint of anything more.'

'Hang on there,' I protested. 'Let's not talk of rivalry. She's told me enough about her feelings for Toby to convince me I'm also just a friend.'

'Whatever,' said Paul. 'My point is simply that delicacy demands discretion. Let us no longer talk of my feelings for Charlotte. I would wish our friendship to remain established beyond a sharing of our feelings for women. On the other hand, and I have had it in mind to do so for some time, I would wish to convey to you, man to man, than I harbour no objection to your interest in Charlotte.'

Was Paul as potty as Arthur? What did he mean?

'Thanks,' I said eventually. 'So let me get it straight. You want us to be friends, me not to ask you how you feel about Charlotte, and you don't mind her and I getting together, should that unlikely possibility arise.'

'Indeed,' he said, unsmiling, still looking at the ceiling.

'OK,' I said, sensing old-fashioned rigidity combined with decency, even generosity. I was glad to know Paul. 'OK.'

'Good night,' he said, and switched out the light. I think we both lay awake for a quite a time, and it was almost certainly me who fell asleep first.

NEXT MORNING, PAUL returned to Greyston, and Molly and Jackie went to work. Charlotte and I stayed, though we didn't know where else to look. Then I had an idea. If Jim had intercalated, as his postcard had said, he wouldn't have got his student grant. So he was probably signing on for income support. And if he were signing on, he would need to have an address, even if he'd been unwilling to tell Beth what it was.

So we headed towards the DHSS offices in town, through the tall shops and roaring bus lanes of Leeds city centre. Inside, a constant stream of people of all ages and appearances came and went, doing things at various desks in an open-plan office. Youths bounced around on bored energy. Working men queued with an aloof, embarrassed air. An arrogant young man argued with a patient young woman at the enquiries desk. Canned music dribbled from ceiling grills. It was hard to see the difference between those who worked there and those who were signing on; people clutched papers and moved between desks. Only the long-term unemployed – drop-outs wangling their keep and thin depressed-looking slouchers – stood out as old doleys. We stood inside the door as on the threshold of a world.

'Jewellery and char-pot! June-a-lot and Chariper!' The impeccable little voice carried over the whole office, but only a few people looked up. Dr Freckles approached from the armchairs in the waiting area further down the room, swinging his arms and smiling.

'Arthur!' I said.

'Hello,' said Charlotte.

'9.30! 9.30!' he said, excitedly. 'F for Fletcher, F for Freckles; only half a chance he'd be on the same week as me; but bingo, Jimbo – big and curly and not at all – not at all – happy. I pick up these things. So there was no philosophical conversation today. I thought to myself, Arthur, you must wait.' Arthur shook his head sadly. It was midday.

'Have you been here since 9.30?' asked Charlotte, 'waiting for us?'
Arthur raised himself proudly.

'The lady of grand grammar speaks correctly.'

'That's very, very kind and lovely of you,' she said, and took his
hand. Arthur coloured deeply, pulled his hand back and looked away.
In daylight, out of the underworld, Arthur was a peculiar sight. He was
dressed much like an academic, but he was very run down. His face was
puffed and creased, and knitted with unnatural worries. His grey,
balding hair was hacked short but filled with dandruff. His cuffs and
collars were frayed, and his shoes had broken laces. He was about the
same height as Charlotte; Charlotte, ever elegant in her quiet way;
Arthur on the other side of youth, and on the wrong side of the line
between human successes and those who can't quite cope.

'The voices said, just you wait here, Freckles,' he explained,
tapping his head. 'Charlotte and Juniper will be along soon. It's always
like that. They suggest and instruct, and I can but listen; I think myself
akin to Socrates, in this respect. They have led me astray, though,
whereas his didn't. Perhaps he had a superior demon; I have a rabble of
malcontents and shoplifters. Come along!'

He strode off, out of the heavy plate-glass swing-doors, past the
large adverts featuring people of many ethnic backgrounds joyfully
seeking employment, and back into the cold air of the city. Charlotte
and I hurried after.

'Where are we going?' I asked Arthur, as we strode along.
Charlotte had to break into short runs to keep up. We crossed over a
busy road.

'I sent Cerberus after him. He will not have escaped.'

'Who's Cerberus?' I asked Charlotte.

'Guardian of the gates to the underworld,' she said, smiling. 'I
think it's Mr Get Lost.'

'Honey-cakes, money-cakes: what do you have?' said Arthur.

'Would he like us to buy him lunch?' Charlotte asked.

'You would like me to ask him if you'd like to buy him lunch, is
that what you would like me to ask him?' Arthur said crossly, still
hurrying along, through the busy hall of a bus station.

'Arthur, please, no!' she said. 'Of course we'll buy you lunch as
well. We'll take you out.' Arthur smiled again, another wide, self-
satisfied smile.

'Roast meat, roast potatoes, Yorkshire pudding, carrots, peas and
gravy, with bread and butter and a mug of hot tea,' he shouted with
relish. People waiting for buses looked at him sideways. 'And apple pie
and custard, and then, perhaps, a *second* mug of hot tea,' he said more
quietly, secretly.

We found ourselves hurried into a large Victorian church. Arthur smiled and helloed to people he met there, older parishioners who were around. There was a small café near the porch, and the lady behind the counter welcomed him in with a smile. We walked into the church and came to a stop in the middle of the nave. After the rush of the walk, there was a church-quiet and the sound of our breathing. Arthur gazed around him at the church interior, its dark oak panelling, large pulpit and balcony. It was cool and slightly musty.

'Is Cerberus here?' asked Charlotte. Arthur tutted.

'You should be admiring the renowned architecture,' he said. 'Consecrated in 1841, the church was rebuilt by the visionary vicar, Dr Walter Farquar Hook, who strove to make his ministry available to the industrial poor of the area.' He sighed with solemn reverence. We stood respectfully, allowing the good Doctor's church interior to settle into our minds.

Then we were off again, around the back of the church and towards a redbrick building associated with the parish. Arthur leaned over a railing to look into a sunken concrete yard. Two sheets of cardboard were folded with a grimy sleeping bag, next to a blue-painted drainpipe, tucked into a large recess that would have made a good shelter at night. An empty sherry bottle lay on the ground nearby.

'Not here,' said Arthur. 'I didn't think he would be, but I thought you would want to see the church.'

'Yes, thank you,' we agreed. And off we set again, past old warehouses in the process of conversion, on into the thronging heart of the shopping centre, following Arthur's brisk rush. We climbed steps into another churchyard, this one older. The path was made of gravestones. Inside the church, masses of pews and large wooden screens dominated.

'1634,' said Arthur, again pausing reverentially. 'By John Harrison, noted philanthropist and provider for the poor.' Charlotte and I also paused. We strode out of the church again and around the back.

'Aha!' said Arthur, pointing.

There was Cerberus, in the graveyard.

'Oh shit,' said Charlotte. He was an eye-watering mess, skin blotchy with eczema and dirt, clothed in a filthy conglomerate hide. He was sitting on a wooden bench overhung by a mass of elder. He didn't look up. A half-empty plastic bottle of cider leant against his side.

'Ahem and hello,' said Arthur politely. He sat on the bench beside the heap, and we heard a low mumble. Arthur nodded and hummed and hawed. Cerberus pulled something from within his folds and passed it to Arthur, who passed it to me. It was Jim's UB40, in its neat plastic wallet, address written in quick biro on an inside page.

'How did our man come by this?' I asked.

'Things they don't teach at universities these days!' said Arthur. 'It's hot-fingered, nicked, pilfered and pinched, that's what it is. Cerberus says your friend should be more careful.'

'Did he steal anything else from him?' asked Charlotte, sternly.

'Tra-la-la, la-la,' sang Arthur, looking up at the grey sky. Charlotte and I looked at each other.

'Perhaps Mr Cerberus would like us to buy him lunch,' I said. Mr Cerberus mumbled to Arthur.

'Due to my friend's dietary regime, derived from his study of both Pythagoras and Ayurveda, he is averse to prepared foods,' Arthur reported. 'However, he would appreciate such delicacies as ginger nuts, cigarettes, cider and tinned tuna.'

'How does tuna fit with Ayurveda?' asked Charlotte.

'Get lost!' growled Cerberus, low but unmistakable.

We bought the man his supplies from a corner shop nearby, and then took Arthur out to lunch, at an inexpensive local restaurant suggested by him. A group of bus drivers smoked and laughed on the other side of the room, clutching their shoulder bags. Some women with lank hair, wearing nylon miniskirts and shiny plastic jackets, laughed hysterically at another table. Arthur tucked a red paper napkin into his dirty collar and waited patiently for his meal to arrive, knife and fork clutched and at the ready. Charlotte smoked, looking around uneasily.

'Looks like Jim isn't homeless after all,' she said to me. Arthur was absorbed in anticipation.

'Thank goodness.'

'This is all reminding me how difficult it was working in that hostel. I used to crave my days off, when I could escape home and to the woods, but then I'd feel guilty about everything I had.'

I nodded, looking at a small man who had joined the hysterical women, wearing awkward glasses mended with sticking plaster. His unshaven, gaunt chin quivered continuously.

'Do you think I've run away from the problem, Juniper? Do you think philosophy – you know, academic life – is an escape?' Charlotte looked at me with searching eyes. She trusts me, I thought. That's worth more than a lot of what's called love.

'I don't know,' I said. 'How can you compare these things?' I knew too little of it all to say anything of worth. Charlotte looked away, nodding.

'Arthur,' I asked. 'Would you tell us how you came to live the life you do? Are we philosophers just indulgent academics, do you think?' I didn't necessarily expect a convincing answer; I just wanted to hear his point of view. Charlotte looked at me, frowning, and I suspected she thought I was making fun of our friend.

'I will tell all,' said Arthur, reassuring Charlotte that he didn't feel patronised. 'But after having eaten, if you don't mind.' Lunch soon arrived, steaming, on chipped plates. Charlotte and I ate greasy eggs and chips. Arthur ate his meat and veg platter heartily, with great sighs and exclamations of delight, completely absorbed in his task. During his second mug of tea, after pudding, he talked, sitting upright, both hands around the mug, eyes closed.

'After ritual satanic abuse and blah-blah-blah other such things that hover tantalisingly on the edge of memory like the ghosts of warriors in the halls of Beowulf —' he opened his eyes and smiled slyly at us.

'Nice opening,' I said.

'— Arthur Freckles emerged into conventional view the son of well-known Oxford academics who both doted on and despised their sweet little bag *de vomitus et excrementum*. Perhaps he only wanted ever to be loved, to be himself, to be able to run happily in the meadows of summer. Alas, only child, he was burdened with expectations of scholastic exactitude.'

'Boo,' said Charlotte.

'He went up to Cambridge in a time of free love and experiment that interested him greatly. Theology was dry as rabbit pellets, but the alleged ancestors demanded their tithe of mind. However, no free love occurred in his rooms, though he did imbibe lysergic acid diethyl amide on twenty-eight occasions and five times in the company of women.'

'You old hippie,' said Charlotte. He lifted his hand as if to dissuade us from comment.

'Through painful inability to garner sufficient gumption to rebel, he began theologico-philosophical postgraduate studies. But then came the surge of new memories, like flowers of bliss explaining everything, though dying quickly on the tongue. He wallowed helpless in mad thoughts until he, little man, wandered trouserless on the lawn chanting 'get it over with, hate me,' and the big men in silver-speckled blue took him away. It was then a relief for him to cut ties and notice that his former friends and peers had spurned him. Freedom! But much pain also.' Arthur produced a handkerchief and wiped his eyes, then dissolved into further sadness, small sobs.

Charlotte moved to sit beside him and put an arm around his shoulders. He sobbed into her chest. It was a performance, but a very good one. He recovered with dramatic timing, slurping his tea before continuing.

'And so my friends, to Leeds! — Where he discovered like-minded persons. He rose to his full stature and took on a profession of his own choice. Friends, I am a shaman!' He looked up at us with proud fire. 'I am a gnostic technician of the sacred, an enlisted vessel of spiritual communications, I am the wizard Rag-Nol-Kur!' His voice had risen to a room-wide boast. 'This is all very secret, of course,' he whispered, low across the table. 'I have become a kind of shamanic priest among the nomads. I bless newly weds, lead services of remembrance, and generally take care of my flock. I also commune with far spirits and discover what people need to know. Any contributions towards my work gratefully accepted.' He looked at us expectantly.

'So you aren't really a Dr?' asked Charlotte. He closed his eyes again, imperturbably disdainful.

'I was granted an honorary degree by a deity with whom no doubt you are not acquainted, and I sport my title with pride, and in honour of Dr W.F. Hook. Let me give you my card.' He dug into a pocket inside his jacket and produced a piece of card cut from a washing powder box. 'Incredible!' said one side, in comic lettering, within a burst of light. On the other side was written in neat black biro:

Dr Arthur Freckles
– shamanic pastor –
1a Gorton Street, Leeds
tel. 671536 (Tues & Thurs 6–7 PM)

'Where's your phone?' I asked. He tutted, crossly.

'At the end of the street. I attend during office hours only.'

'And you have a house?' Charlotte asked.

'I have a flat,' he said, still sounding cross. 'Also a social worker, a psychiatrist, a chemist and a regular supply of very special dietary supplements.' He pulled out two bottles of pills and a typed sheet of names and addresses to show us, spreading them on the table proudly. 'My unusual gifts require much care and, as you can see, attract generous government funding. And as for your second question regarding academic life, I would say this.'

He looked at us with an expression that was totally sane, totally present. Involuntarily, both Charlotte and I leant into the table to be nearer him, as his voice had dropped. He looked from face to face.

'Friends, we each have a vocation, if we have the ears to discern its true shape. As you have heard, I have found mine. Perhaps there is a philosophical vocation also, though academia is just a context for it. Philosophy does not help the homeless, but it feeds the questioning souls of the young.' Charlotte was nodding her head slowly, chewing a lock of hair. 'Friends,' Arthur continued, 'love is a movement of the whole soul towards that which we know is our true delight. When you know your soul's innermost desire, you will be able truly to love. And when you can love, there is no question of indulgence; your life becomes pleasure and play. For myself, I would not choose a different way. And now,' he said, putting pills and paper back in his pockets, 'I must go. A little voice tells me I must proceed to the public library, there to acquire certain information relevant to my task.'

I paid for our food, and we stood together outside the café, in the busy rush of the street.

'Thank you very much for helping us today, Dr Freckles,' said Charlotte. 'And I wish you well in your work.'

'It has been a great pleasure to meet you,' I said. Arthur beamed, rubbed his stomach and shook our hands warmly.

'Tell Jim Fletcher to give me a ring as soon as he can, and we can meet to discuss matters. He looked very unhappy.' Arthur strode off purposefully up the hill, with a hand raised over his shoulder in a gesture of goodbye. Charlotte turned to me.

'Amazing,' she said. I nodded.

A THIN, MIDDLE-AGED woman, apparently drunk, opened the door that afternoon at Jim's address. He wasn't in. We went back to Molly's to crash out for a while. When Jim answered his door in the evening, he didn't seem in the least pleased to see us.

He had a small attic room in a house full of bedsits. The dormer window faced north and looked over railway lines. There was a sink and a Baby Belling in the room, a fridge, a foam sofa with a torn cover, a table and chair, and a plywood chest of drawers. The walls were tarry magnolia and the carpet thin grey.

'I've brought some gear for making tea,' I said, pulling out loose leaf, strainer, teaspoon and milk. Jim smiled and put a pan of water on a ring.

'I've only two mugs, I'm afraid, but here's an empty jam jar.'

Charlotte told him the story of how we'd found him, and he relaxed.

'I wondered where my UB40 had gone,' he admitted. 'I gave that guy some change when he asked, and then he bumped into me like he was drunk.'

He almost always gave money to beggars; he had a Principle of Sharing Resources, which seemed to me rather close to socialism. He shrugged. One Principle had led him into obscurity and now another had led us back to him.

On the train over to Leeds, he'd decided that he couldn't tell his mother what he'd done, but he couldn't lie either. So he'd spent the night sleeping on a bench in a park. In the morning his rucksack had been stolen, leaving him only the money in his pocket. He'd had to pay £100 up front for the room, which he'd borrowed off an old school friend who'd put him up for a few days. He was taking stock, he said. That afternoon, when we'd first called, he'd been visiting his mother. She'd been more supportive than he'd thought, and given him the money to pay back his friend.

'How come you didn't get in touch with us?' I asked. Jim looked at the floor. 'Beth says you can live with her anytime, and she's pissed off you didn't ask before.' He tried not to show it, but I could tell he was pleased. 'We're missing you, Jim. And your court case is coming up.' I gave him the summons.

We ate dinner from the local chippy, sitting on a wall, and then went to a pub. It was run down, but quiet enough, and we drank beer and smoked and talked until eleven-thirty. Jim enjoyed our company, but he wasn't going to come back to Greyston. Not yet. He wasn't forthcoming about his reasons, but he said he needed time 'to stew a bit.' I didn't argue.

There was no bed in Jim's room, but the foam sofa folded out into a pad wide enough for three. Jim had two blankets, so Jim slept under one and Charlotte and I under the other, all of us more or less fully dressed. But as we relaxed, I felt the tension of Charlotte's presence next to me; my body yearned for the simplicity of an embrace. Jim fell asleep at my other side, and his breath wheezed in his big frame. I lay still, too close to my heart's desire to sleep, feeling what I felt: in my heart, a warm pouring; in the space next to my body, an electric presence beautifully humming. Small snores escaped from the little rounds of her nostrils.

'Juniper,' she whispered. I must have fallen asleep, though I was still lying on my back. 'I'm cold.' The night air in the uninsulated attic had cooled, and Charlotte was at the untucked edge of the bed. Jim wheezed heavily through his penitent dreams. She moved closer; I turned on my side and put my arm around her, drawing her into the warm aura of my chest. My other arm lay under her head. Where to end my enfolding embrace? Gently she took my hand and held it against her chest. I could feel the smaller beat of her heart, her firm young body against mine, and could smell cigarette smoke and shampoo in her thick black hair. My breath moved among the filaments of her crown. Nothing was said. She held onto my hand and I closed it around her fingers. I let no stray motion of desire escape the edges of my body, keeping lips and fingers still, their urges contained. There was nothing between my beloved and I except the invisible, intangible limit of my will. In the quiet of the cold night, my will softened to wonder. To love, and yet to hold back! Why did this human state demand these tender abstentions? Both Charlotte and I lay awake a long time, not speaking.

At last I felt the grip on my hand relax, and her breath move into sleeper's depths.

Alone, my thoughts were pure and enamoured. Is it love that reaches after a lover's body and follows it through the movements of the sexual dance? It can be done with affection, or with a hot, brutal lust. What is it makes love? The body follows its natural courses, and the mind thinks well of a lover for the knowledge given and released. Does love mean simply intimacy, the trust felt, the secrets shared, the tenderness unlocked, when lovers descend to flesh beneath public words? But there I was, in love, holding my beloved, and yet chastely, as if only glimpsing as pure, absent possibility all this affection, intimacy and tenderness that lovers call love. I remembered the conversation with Professor Rampton. What is love? What is there beyond the pure intensity I felt at that moment, lying with Charlotte in a sibling embrace? Of course, my feelings demanded onward motion, satisfaction, all the ecstasy singing in the suggestions of my nature. My resistance was an informed, visionary stance that heightened the very feelings into a more present intensity. I thought of Socrates and the ladder to true beauty. I saw no beckoning rungs, but enjoyed a clear sense of freedom within: that I could feel such intense, natural emotion, yet choose the way of non-action and restraint. I was unshackling bit by bit from the chains of compulsion, seeing my beloved not only with the hot eyes of the body, but also with the sad, wise eyes of the spirit. And Charlotte was lovelier for being wisely loved.

My unsleeping mind kept on its thinking. Love was the heart-quality brought to the free moment: not the actions of instinct nor the relief of intimate disclosure, but something quiet, that lies before these and makes them loving, if they can be made so. As the dawn gathered behind thin curtains, and milk floats hummed among the houses, a wonderful thought gambolled out of sleepless delirium: love – if there's love in raw passion – is friendliness; the gentle wish that the other be well. Even there, holding my beloved, I loved her to the extent that I sought her well being, wished what was good for her, for her happiness. Love is not the passion nor the relationship, not the talk nor the companionship; love, as a human virtue, ground of ethics, first rung on the ladder of spirit, is the quality of friendliness brought to all that is made through instinct or expectation or desire. That was why it was so much easier to see the love between Jim and me: in such friendship such well-wishing is the quiet concernful core. Between lovers passion eclipses subtleties, yet at the same core there is only a loving human bond to the extent that there is friendliness, mutual respect, regard and goodwill. This was diamond knowledge made within the pressure chamber of restrained desire.

After dawn the room warmed. My upper arm, stretched beneath Charlotte's head, was dead. Charlotte woke and gently lifted my hand from her breasts. She shifted away from me, rolled back and looked at me, quizzically. I smiled. She looked around the room, piecing together her life from suggestive impressions and inferences, then looked at me again and smiled. My arm was coming back to life with indignant pains. She rubbed it consolingly, and it lay back, numb and passive and redeemed. She went off to the shared bathroom in the hall, with a coin for the shower and her washbag and towel. I made tea while Jim gradually came around. He was slow in the mornings.

We went out for breakfast and ate more greasy, satisfying food, Charlotte putting it away like a lusty kid. We spent the morning being shown around town by Jim, three friendly spirits against the anonymous dull city, and winning; then Jim waved us off from the station at three. I had given him Arthur's card. On the train home, Charlotte seemed uncomfortable with me, and I hoped that she wasn't retreating from our new intimacy. But I felt giddy with tiredness and all our experience, and unable to engage with worried thoughts. At Greyston, we parted with awkward half-sentences.

'See you soon, then,' she said.

'Thanks again,' I said.

Back home, Matt and Chris had left a heap of washing-up in the sink. Archie wanted food. My room smelt damp. Weeds were springing up in the garden beds that I had cleared.

a surprise

I WAS LEFT ALONE in Greyston surrounded by mindless spring. It was hard to remember the joy I'd felt with Charlotte in Leeds, the amazing energy of contained desire. Now all the passion congealed once more to solitude diseased with pointless passion. I saw Paul to tell him about what had happened with Jim, but I didn't talk about my stumblings on the Socratic path. I couldn't get in touch with Charlotte as if we were merely friends; I just hoped that she'd get in touch with me, but she didn't. Gloom oppressed me, as the sense of possibility in falling in love collapsed into itself and left me more than ever alone in exile.

After a week I remembered to hang loose and leave space around all these feelings. The same day I found myself turning my bike quite spontaneously into Paradise Hill while cycling back from the university. A young woman with lank blonde hair and a pale complexion answered the bell. When I asked for Charlotte, the young woman looked worried, but showed me in. She left me standing in the hall while she went upstairs. The house was a once-grand Edwardian family dwelling, with curls of stained glass ornamenting the windows and a wide back-turning stairway that spoke of confident ascents. But now the paintwork was peeling and bicycles leant against the dado in the dusty hall.

Charlotte came down, her hair unbrushed, looking like she had been crying.

'Juniper!' she said. 'I wasn't expecting you.'

'I was passing, so I thought I'd call in.' I regretted it already.

'Would you like some tea?' she said quickly, trying not to look at me, but walking into the dining room. I followed her.

'If that's all right,' I said. The blonde-haired girl walked in, hurrying towards the kitchen.

'Julia, this is Juniper,' Charlotte said. Julia hovered and smiled nervously. 'Julia lives here,' said Charlotte, although it was obvious. Julia rapidly moved off. 'What do you think of the house?' Charlotte seemed distracted. Julia clattered back through with an armful of washing. 'Give me a hug,' said Charlotte, when Julia had gone upstairs. I put my arms around her, and she pulled into me. She wanted comfort; that was clear. I didn't mind that. She broke off and made a pot of tea.

'Let's sit in the lounge,' she said. The bay window looked out over the garden. A laburnum hung its masses of yellow flowers into a dark grove, the overgrown lawn. A horse chestnut lifted its candle-flames at the far end.

'Full-grown trees in your garden!' I said. 'There can't be many student houses like this.'

She laughed. 'In Cambridge I had a room that was four hundred years old that overlooked a garden almost the same age. But this is all right.'

I felt rather put down. She seemed to be flaunting her superior past.

'I suppose you must always compare houses with your country cottage; what was it called? – Albino –'

'Albion Cottage.' I didn't know whether she was making some sort of fun. It was certainly clumsy. We discussed what we'd been reading and thinking about. There was a thin, uncommitted feeling between us. We lapsed into silence after we'd drunk tea.

'Would you like some more?' asked Charlotte, jumping up.

'No, I think I'll go now,' I said. She looked blank.

'Juniper,' she said suddenly, as she showed me to the door. Her shoulders were hunched. 'Can I come down to your house sometime? Soon?'

'Whenever you want.'

'The day after tomorrow?'

'For supper?'

'Will that be all right?'

'Of course.'

'OK,' she said, looking like she was going to cry, then almost moving to hug me again, then changing her mind and moving indoors. 'Bye.'

I felt bitter as I cycled home. I didn't know what was going on for Charlotte, though I was happy to be there if she wanted. That was the least meaning of friendliness.

WHEN THE NEXT DAY came, I found that I was quietly looking forward to having Charlotte over for tea; but the day after that I was looking forward to Charlotte's arrival with an enthusiasm that was like new kindling catching on covered embers. The irrepressible hope of the heart. She arrived at eight, with wine, looking very smart. Such care betokened respect, and a small fear lifted from me. The kitchen was full of the smell of hot bread mixed with woodsmoke and mulled wine, and she smiled to be back in its belly. She looked much happier and more at ease. She sat and gave Archie some attention while I turned out the loaves, tapping their hollow backs.

'If I ever have a cat, I think I'll call it Arthur,' she said.

'Professor Rampton used to have a cocker spaniel called Cerberus,' I added.

'When I was a kid I had a guinea-pig called Hercules,' she said, sniffing at the mulled wine I'd poured into a jug. 'It escaped once and did a small amount of damage to mum's herbs.'

'The old myths,' I said, dishing up a thick, beany, dumpling-laden stew.

'I shall make a libation before we eat.' She swilled some wine around in her glass and splashed it into the ceramic sink. Drops flew off, and one landed on Archie's nose. He pawed and licked at it with interest.

She looked up at me. 'You've got libations splashed on your cheek.' She reached over to wipe it with a finger.

'Sorry about when you called,' she said after we'd eaten. 'I was pleased to see you, but I was having a horrible time. In a way you saved me, just by breaking in, but I was terrible company I'm sure. I wanted to see you again soon to say how much I appreciate you.'

'I wondered what was going on,' I said.

'I'd just had a very difficult conversation with Julia,' she said, then looked up at the ceiling. 'My crazy fucking love-life.'

'I thought things had got better with Toby?'

'Ha,' she laughed, bitterly. 'So Paul hasn't said anything to you?' I shook my head.

'Let's sit by the fire to talk,' I suggested. She sighed. I poured out big glasses of wine.

We settled and smoked, and Charlotte reflected. She shook her head.

'I just can't understand how men's minds work,' she said.

'I went out with a woman once,' I said, 'who was a mystery to me. It was because she was deceiving me, actually.'

'And what did you do to her then? Punish her?' Charlotte's tone was almost violent.

'No,' I said. 'I didn't know that she'd been two-timing me, and when I found out, she became violently argumentative, and that was more or less the end of the relationship.' Charlotte's hard expression crumbled.

'Shit, I feel defensive,' Charlotte hissed.

'Come on,' I chided. 'Something's happened with Toby, but you're taking it out on me, just because I'm male. That's hardly fair, when I don't even know what's gone on.'

She took a deep breath. 'When we were in the Lake District, we decided that we'd split up, at least for a while. You remember that I said he'd eased up on the asceticism?' I nodded. 'Not for long. He soon went back to his old views: sex is unspiritual and all that. He told me when we were camping. I was really straightforward, Juniper – I think it was the conversations with you – I just said, I can't go on with this. So we split up, just like that. We decided that our friendship was the really special thing, and that meeting in India had been a blessing, whatever happened in the future.'

'It was too cold anyway in the tent,' I added.

She smiled. 'Right. Anyway, it was an amicable split-up and a big relief. We had a lovely time walking about among the hills, and when we came back to Greyston we agreed we'd see each other soon.'

'When I saw you both, you still seemed like a couple,' I said.

'That's because I was trying to be reassuring for him. He was jealous of you.'

'Really?' I said. 'But he seemed affable enough.'

'Yeah, he's like that. It was me he didn't trust.'

'Ouch,' I said.

'Then, when you and I were in Leeds, the fucking idiot sleeps with that silly bimbo, Julia. In our house.'

'Why?' I asked.

'How the hell do I know?' she said. 'I came back – you know how exhausted we were – and there they were, a little reception committee. We thought we should tell you, all that shit. Why did you do that? I asked him. No point asking Julia, she's too dumb. I felt that I was free of obligation to you, he said, all neatly defended and rational like a politician who's sold missiles to a tyrant. I screamed. I really lost my cool. It was embarrassing. Julia stood there all righteous like an angel. She'd fancied him for years. Toby told me he thought that I'd been sleeping with either you or Paul, and I screamed some more. He couldn't work it out. Oh, it's been a horrible week.'

'So what was going on the other day with Julia?' I asked, after bringing over the bottle of wine Charlotte had brought along and pouring out two glasses.

'A charming little codicil,' she said, looking up at me with a hard smile. I saw again how strained she looked, compared to a week or so before. 'She says she forgives me for my outburst when I got back from Leeds.'

'Forgives you for what?'

'Honestly, I think she might be nuts,' said Charlotte. 'And Toby's got himself into a right mess. I'm sorry for him in a way. He's trying to do his exams.'

We sat in silence for a while. I sat with fingers bridged, thinking. On the face of it, Charlotte was coping pretty well. I stared into the fire, watching flames lick around a ten-year-old piece of ash-wood, thick as my forearm. The blue-grey bark blackened and peeled from the heartwood at the ends.

'Can I sit on your lap?' asked Charlotte.

'All right,' I said, sitting up a little. She came over and sat down gently, then curled her legs up and leant her weight into my chest. I put my arms around her waist and kissed her head. We sat by the crackling fire for a few minutes.

'You remember the part in *Symposium*,' she said eventually, 'after Socrates' speech, when the beautiful young Alcibiades comes into the dinner party, raucous and drunk?'

'Of course,' I said.

'And the way he speaks in praise of Socrates, for his wisdom and courage?'

'Alcibiades is praising Socrates in the same way as the other men were praising *eros*. Why do you ask?'

'And do you remember how Alcibiades tells everyone how he'd lain with Socrates all night, and how Socrates hadn't moved a muscle to seduce him?' She was still talking into my chest, but I understood what she was getting at, and a thrill ran through me.

'I don't expect Socrates slept all that well, though. He was very enamoured of the boy.'

Charlotte lifted her head up. 'Your voice booms amazingly in your chest,' she said. She held her face in front of mine. Her speech was slurred, her eyes vague. She looked tired. 'You're such a gentle man. I wouldn't have minded if you'd kissed me that night in Leeds, you know.'

'But maybe you were more impressed because I didn't kiss you,' I said.

'Maybe,' she said. 'Kiss me now.' I kissed her. She tasted of wine and cigarettes.

'Paul said you were in love with me,' she said later.

'Could you not tell?'

'Sort of,' she said.

'Did you tell him that you'd split up with Toby?' I asked, thinking of the conversation between Paul and me in Leeds, when he told me he didn't object to my interest in Charlotte.

'Yes,' she said, shrugging. 'I tell him most everything.'

'Why didn't you come and see me?' I asked. She shrugged.

'It was too much. But I was glad you came to me.'

The log in the fire fell apart with a burst of sparks.

'Come on,' she said, getting out of my lap, pulling on my hand. I closed the door of the fire and we went upstairs.

I WOKE WITH A WOMAN in my bed, with her back to me, softly snoring and having most of the duvet. We'd kissed and then gone to sleep; we'd both been drunk. I got up although it was still early. I needed fresh air and movement. I drank tea and walked in the garden, then read in the kitchen while Charlotte slept. She appeared at ten, looking bed-worn and strained.

'Good morning, Alcibiades,' I said, light-heartedly. She smiled. 'Would you like some breakfast?' She didn't know whether to come and kiss me or not.

'Just coffee please,' she said, sitting down opposite me at the table. She lit a cigarette when she had a mug. I joined her.

'Was it all right, me staying?' she asked.

'fine,' I said. 'I liked it.'

'Oh good,' she said.

'Were you surprised?'

She shrugged. 'I was hoping you'd ask me to stay; but also that you don't feel I only slept with you to get my own back on Toby. It was more than that.'

I didn't remember asking her to stay, but I didn't say that.
'The implication being that you slept with me to get your own back on Toby, at least to some degree.'

'Shit,' she said. 'I said that wrong. I slept with you because I wanted to.'

'Well, I'm glad you wanted to.' Her expression clouded. We smoked and drank in silence for a while.
'I meant what I said last night, though,' she said.

'What was that?' I asked, not sure what exactly she was referring to. Clumsiness hung in the kitchen air like cigarette smoke.

'About that night in Leeds —' she trailed off. 'Oh, is this a good idea, Juniper?' There was wavering doubt in her voice, a despair.

'Is what a good idea?' I asked, aware of vagueness, unwilling simply to guess at what she was talking about. More silence between us. She inhaled stiffly.

'Look, maybe it was a mistake me staying,' she began. 'Maybe I'm not ready for this.' She was shaking her head and looking into the ashtray, stubbing out her cigarette.

'Ready for what?' I asked.

'God, you're being unhelpful,' she said, looking away.

'What would be helpful?' I asked. 'I could guess that you're trying to check out that what you thought happened last night is the same as what I thought happened, and that you'd like some reassurance that there's now something happening between us, which right now doesn't seem to be happening. But I don't know how helpful all that would be. On the other hand, I could be friendly and make you some breakfast.' She looked at me, smiling.

'Oh, I'm sorry. And you're probably right; I mean, that I'm looking for reassurance. All that shit with Toby – it's so undermining.'

'Hardly surprising,' I said. 'So maybe last night was a one-off. And I meant what I said last night as well.'

Charlotte laughed. 'What was that?'

'That Socrates was very enamoured of the boy.'

'So this is friends having breakfast together, right?'

'Toast?' I asked.

'All right,' she said, laughing gently. We ate toast and drank more coffee together.

'I've been thinking,' I said, 'about how the initiation of a love affair can be a tremendously delicate thing; tiny gestures and implications have to be recognised and returned, in the right order, at the right time, for the sense of trust and mutuality of feelings to move forward. Lovers need to know that the beloved's feelings for them are like their feelings for their beloved; and this is a knowledge that is almost impossible without establishing the subtle means of communication that love itself is supposed to bring about. So how is this movement into knowledge ever made?'

'By making assumptions,' said Charlotte. 'About what the other person is thinking.'

'Also assumptions about how one should act on one's feelings; what comes next, what certain gestures and words are supposed to mean. Lovers capitulate to inauthentic modes of speech and behaviour in order to make an improbable leap into intimacy possible.'

'So that sleeping together often means that two people are "starting a relationship", even if they haven't actually talked about whether that's what each of them thinks that's what it means. Not that that means they're being inauthentic; it's just the social convention that they're working with.'

'I suppose the inauthenticity depends on intention,' I said. 'If you were following the social conventions even though you didn't really believe in them, in order to get a partner, because that's the only way to get one, that would be inauthentic.'

'Obviously,' said Charlotte. 'But the whole point of the conventions is that they're what people generally believe.'

'Have you ever thought about the "I love you"?' I asked. 'It's something lovers say that they really believe in, yet it doesn't really *mean* anything at all. It's something you say in order to elicit a response – to find out if the other person has the same interpretation of the situation as you. So I say "I love you," just at the right moment, and then the other person has to say "I love you, too," and then we can go on from there. The tiniest changes from this script will disrupt the formation of the relationship.'

'Shit, did I tell you I loved you?' asked Charlotte, shifting uncomfortably.

'I can't remember. I don't think so. But you invited me to kiss you – an irreducible cultural signal that initiated a sexual encounter, without need of any particular explanations.'

'The semiotics of sex!' she declared, and we laughed, kitchen-tension releasing into the intellectual banter we were more familiar with.

'How do you know all this stuff?' said Charlotte, through more smoke. We laughed together.
'It's not hard to notice the way love happens,' I said.

'These days,' she said, 'you can sleep with someone, and it should mean you like them, but it doesn't necessarily mean you want to spend the rest of your life with them. So, this morning, I needed to check out that we'd both understood the significance of what happened, because in the circumstances it wasn't clear.'

'This is quite recent, I think,' I added.

'If I'd seduced an innocent like you two hundred years ago,' said Charlotte brightly, 'it would have shown my dishonourable intentions and proved I didn't really love you.'

'Exactly. You would have been a callous, deceiving beast, taking advantage of my innate weakness and tendency to form helpless emotional attachments.'

She briefly quivered around the mouth, tried to smile, failed, quivered, and then burst into tears.

'What is it?' I said, reaching for her hand.

'What you just said – Toby used to say things like that,' she said.

'Ah,' I said.

'He used to say I could get him to do just what I wanted. Julia said to me the other day – that ridiculous conversation – that Toby had told her I was manipulative, that I used to seduce him and that the whole relationship just suited me.'

'What do you think of that?' I asked.

'What the hell could I do?' she said. 'Be some passive victim? Do what he wants? The fucking idiot was so half-hearted that I had to make all the decisions, persuade him to sleep with me, keep the relationship going. He would've just let it all slide by. And he tells me I was being manipulative!'

I thought of Ros and her exasperation with me, but it wasn't the same really.

'A lot of men are immature,' I said. 'Being unable to be clear and committed in relationships comes from not having properly become an independent individual. Without a proper grounding for their sense of identity, a lot of men look to women, but they also know that they won't really find what they need in their sexual relationship. So they're half-hearted like Toby, yet also confused. If they had mature, nourishing friendships with other properly grown-up men, they would be able to relate to women without so much confusion.'

Charlotte looked at me with a mixture of incomprehension and fear.

'At least you're positive about relationships,' she said.

I shrugged. We finished breakfast and washed up. Matt and Chris arrived, so I introduced them to Charlotte. She was charming.

'I've arranged to visit Jagaro at his monastery this afternoon,' I said, when we were alone in my room. 'But I think you should stay here rather than going back to your house.'

'That would be great,' said Charlotte, looking relieved. 'But won't I be interrupting your nourishing male friendships?'

nemesis

I WASN'T SURE WHY I wanted to visit Jagaro at his monastery. It was curiosity, partly, about what a Buddhist monk was doing in my home village. Beyond that, however, there had been a vigour about his teaching at the Buddhist Society meeting that I wanted to know more about. I'd rung him up and he'd been keen for me to visit. In the event, however, I was aware of leaving Charlotte sitting in my bedroom with her woes. I wanted to return to Lyndhurst as quickly as I could.

I arrived at the monastery at three, having walked from the station. It was in a terrace a bit away from the village, in the house of my old primary school teacher, Mrs Caldicott. She had moved to an old folk's home not far away, but the house was owned by a local farmer who had put it up for rent again. Jagaro and his supporters had repainted the interior in light browns. But I'd hardly been shown around before Jagaro had strapped on his sandals and told his dour monk-companion he was 'off for a long one, so don't misbehave.'

I found myself out for a walk along the familiar footpaths around the village. Jagaro was about five foot nine and wiry, but walked quite fast. We didn't say anything for a while, but he seemed quite happy about that.

'I wanted to tell you something,' I said.

'Speak,' he said, not looking over.

'Do you remember that question I asked, about asceticism?'

'Oh yes,' said Jagaro, brightly. 'It really got one young man going. He grilled me for ages afterwards.'

I told him why I'd asked about fasting, adding that Toby hadn't heeded his advice not to for very long.

'Oh well,' Jagaro shrugged. 'Some things we have to learn the hard way.' We were walking through a bluebell-filled woodland surrounding a shallow lake, with its verging alders pushing into leaf. We walked in silence again. A cuckoo called nearby, the first I'd heard that spring.

'Lovely part of the world, this,' he said. 'I'd be very happy to find a more permanent home for the monastery.'

I smiled. It was strange but welcome to be reintroduced to the beauties of Silverthwaite by an outsider. We soon arrived at the edges of a large bird reserve and could see a flat area of brown reeds stretching to wooded hills. Jagaro walked purposefully to a public bird hide. Inside there was a hushed concentration as the broken row of people aimed their binoculars and telescopes out at the lagoon. From beyond the window came the constant calling of gulls, fighting and circling over the water.

'It's like meditation,' whispered Jagaro, producing a small pair of binoculars from an orange shoulder bag. 'Their bodies are settled and their minds are focused. And there's a pleasure simply in observing the birds, in what they do and how beautiful some are.'

'Here come the marsh harriers,' said a grey-haired man sitting near us, pointing. 'Watch them sky-dancing.'

Jagaro and I sat on the wooden bench and looked out over the water and reeds. Two large, brownish birds were gliding in from the right, quartering the marshes. One, with black wing tips, the male, flew higher and began aerial acrobatics, swooping then tumbling and pulling out into a glide. It climbed and levelled. The other, the duller brown female, flew up from below; the male dropped; the female turned upside down, and briefly they flew together, talons touching, as if passing food from one to the other, before quickly gliding apart again. It was magnificent, and Jagaro passed me his binoculars after a minute to watch. After a while the harriers flew off towards the left and into the trees.

'I've never seen that before,' I said.

'Nor me,' said the monk. Just then a soft booming sound came drifting over the busy water. It was a male bittern, calling for a mate. Jagaro's face was lit up with pleasure at the deep and deeply hidden bird voice. I listened more, seeing Jagaro's calm enjoyment, but all I could think of was the way I'd spent weeks booming 'Charlotte', but that now she'd arrived I was having second thoughts about mating. After more time of gazing out at the birds, we left the hide.

'Why don't I show you my parents' farm?' I said. I had rung my mother earlier to say that I might call. Ros and I had an arrangement whereby I told my mother if I was going to visit, so she could let Ros know. Mother hated it.

'I don't know why you two can't just talk your problems through,' she would say. 'Your father and I stuck it out together.'

'We're not you,' I told her, and I could tell from her reaction that Ros had told her the same thing. Jagaro and I walked the couple of miles up to the farm, pointing out to each other various flowers and signs of spring.

Both my parents were in the kitchen.

'I've seen you about, in the village,' said father to the monk. 'Livens things up. Are you finding that people are interested in what you're doing?'

'Would you like a piece of cake?' my mother asked.

'No thanks,' said the monk. 'I don't eat after midday; but a cup of tea would be most welcome. And yes, some people are interested. In fact, we really need a bigger place.'

Later I showed Jagaro around the farm.

'A converted barn or smallish house in a corner of a field hereabouts – that's what we need,' he said. 'Somewhere more private, more isolated.'

'So you plan to stay in the area?' I asked.

'I wouldn't go anywhere else now if you paid me,' he said. 'Not that I handle money. But we need guest facilities, a retreat house, and somewhere separate for me as well. I spent five years more or less in solitude in Burma, you know,' he said, looking at me intently.

'I want to show you the house where I used to live, which I helped renovate,' I said on sudden impulse. Mother had said that Ros wasn't in. We said goodbye to my parents and walked down to Albion Cottage. The gardens looked tidy, though I knew I'd done a lot of the pruning and digging before I'd left. However, things looked curiously different around the back, as if in my absence I'd changed, and hence was looking at the familiar back step, the vegetable gardens and the path to the orchard and chickens with fresh eyes. I wanted to show Jagaro the kitchen, but when I tried my key in the lock on the back door, it wouldn't turn. I noticed that the lock had been changed.

'She's changed the lock,' I said. 'She's changed the lock.'

We walked back round to the front of the cottage. We'd never used the front door much, so the big old key hung inside. I stood on the front lawn and looked up at the house with a dismal impotence.

'Oh well, another time,' said Jagaro.

'Not much choice,' I said. We walked back towards the monastery by a route through more woodland. The clouds gathered and a fine drizzle began. Jagaro didn't seem much bothered, but in my new mood the rain was unwelcome.

'Sky-dancing,' said Jagaro. 'The sky-dancers of the Buddhist tradition are naked females, flushed red with fierce energy and dedicated to the truth.'

'All the booming and enchantment redirected to a higher beauty.'

'Yes! But not in some forced and unnatural way. They drink blood and dance in the Great Void.'

'Why female?'

Jagaro shrugged. 'There are male ones as well, I expect.'

'So they're like spiritual warriors?' I was thinking of Jim, and Charlotte too.

'Something like that,' said Jagaro, smiling.

By the time we said goodbye I was considerably cheered up. I hadn't forgotten about the lock to Albion Cottage, but I wasn't going to fight the unexplained, not yet anyway.

'Why don't you come back on Saturday morning? Come out for another walk and then share our meal?'

'OK,' I said, not sure why Jagaro was so interested in me, but keen enough.

BACK AT LYNDHURST, I found Charlotte crouched against the wall in the hallway just inside the door. She was crying dismally, a little sad thing crumpled against the pocked and gashed flower wallpaper.

'Heh, what's up?' I said. I extended a hand, and she grasped it. I pulled her up. She was still sobbing.

'Toby was here,' she said.

'What did he do?'

'Oh, nothing. It's just −' but she couldn't say anything else.

'Something must have happened.'

'We were talking through the letter box,' she said, suddenly brightening up. 'It was pretty mad.'

I laughed. 'You really don't want to speak to him.'

'Certainly not! I asked him if he was still seeing Julia, and he said he was.'

'Did you think he'd split up with her?'

'He says it's not a serious thing, and that he wants to get back together with me.'

'What do you think of that?'

'I asked him what Julia thought.' Charlotte shook her head. She was quickly regaining her composure. 'It's nice to see you again,' she said, putting her arms around my neck and kissing me.

'Hello,' I said. Her small, dark lips were slightly bitter.

We went down to the kitchen and I made some tea.

'He doesn't like me living here,' she said, smiling. 'He wants us to "work things out". I hate that phrase. It makes a relationship sound like something you're condemned to suffer.'

'What do you want to do?'

'I really don't think I have any choice. It would have been great if he weren't like he is. I love him, but he's such a prat. I don't think anything would change if we got back together. If it's OK with you, I'd like to stay here.'

'That's OK with me,' I said.

'Can I ask a favour?' she asked. 'He caught me by surprise that time. I really don't want to see him unexpectedly like that. If he calls again, and you answer, could you not let him in?'

'Why?' I asked. I didn't much want to become her bodyguard.

'I told you, I just don't want to see him like that. I've told Toby to leave me alone, but he's very tenacious when he wants something.'

Next day, Charlotte enlisted Paul and his car to help her move her stuff down from Paradise Hill, and she settled herself into Jim's old room. She and I talked a lot, went out to see a film, and relaxed together in the Red Cow with beer and cigarettes. But I didn't make any attempt to sleep with her again. I thought of Jagaro and sky-dancing, and slept on my own.

EARLY THE NEXT SATURDAY I caught the train back to Silverthwaite. As I walked over to the monastery I felt amused at how it was Jagaro who was bringing me home. While I had a mug of tea, a whole group of Sri Lankans arrived, armed with Sainsbury's bags and trifles. Jagaro came in and talked to them and everyone laughed a great deal; then he and I headed out for another walk.

'The thing is,' he said, as we strode straight into the woods, 'the lease on the house is only for a year, and I don't know what will happen once it expires.'

'It's owned by Farmer Talbot isn't it?' He was the mole-killer who'd pissed Ros off.

'I think his son has plans for the place.'

'Ah.'

'So now I know you're a local, I'm hoping you might keep an eye out for possibilities.'

I wanted to say that I didn't live in the area any more, but I was too flattered by Jagaro's interest in me. We strode about in the big area of old woodland quite near the monastery, and he got me to identify various plants and trees for him: wood anemones, honeysuckles, wild cherries and pears. But I found that I was on the look out for Ros, and once when I thought I'd seen her, among distant trees, I became quite shaky. I still felt angry with her for having changed the lock on the door. The person disappeared. The trees showed shades of delicate green, and I showed Jagaro how you could eat young beech leaves, when they were still tender and new.

We arrived back at the monastery at eleven, and the Sri Lankans were laying out cutlery and bowls on a cloth spread on the floor in the front room. Jagaro went upstairs, and I waited in a quiet room where there were books and chairs. I heard more people arrive and saw a small, neat, blonde-haired woman pass by, walking towards the kitchen. Then she came out again.

'Roger!' she said in surprise. China-blue eyes.

'Kate!' I said, smiling.

'You two know each other?' said Jagaro, coming down the stairs, now robed differently but barefoot, and holding a large steel bowl.

'He was my first boyfriend, Bhante,' said Kate. 'I haven't seen him for nearly ten years.'

'Why did she call you Roger?' asked Jagaro.

'I changed my name.'

'Cool,' said Kate.

'Cool!' said Jagaro, with the same wide-eyed surprise.

We ate in silence once the monks – there seemed to be four of them, including two dressed in white – had chanted a blessing in the ancient Buddhist language, hands folded, eyes closed. Then they leant over their bowls to eat, while the laypeople helped themselves to what the monks had left. Sunlight streamed into the room. There was no furniture, except a large shrine on which sat a bronze Buddha, with flowers, candles and ornaments. Birdsong and breeze came in through the open windows, the distant sound of laughter, the passing caw of a crow. The monks' life was lived in deliberate beauty. Kate and I kept looking at each other and grinning.

'I didn't know you still lived up here,' I said, after the meal. 'Have you seen Beth?'

'Is she around?' said Kate excitedly. 'You must give me her phone number. I moved back here with Geoff – he's my husband – and our twins six months ago. We were involved with setting up the monastery, so we wanted to live nearby. We were near London before that. Geoff programs computers.'

She hadn't changed much. She had filled out a lot and her face was lined, but her eyes were quite pristine.

'It must be nice for the kids to live up here,' I said.

'It's what I'd always wanted for them,' she said.

'I live in Greyston,' I said. 'It feels like exile.'

'Maybe you've been spoiled,' she said, smiling. Geoff and the two boys arrived, and Kate introduced them. Geoff was a slim, neat, relaxed man. There was a sense of significance in meeting Kate again at the monastery, so I invited her and Geoff to dinner.

'Come back soon,' Jagaro told me, when I headed back to Greyston at one.

ONE AFTERNOON THE FOLLOWING WEEK, Toby arrived and tried to persuade me to let him see Charlotte. I stood in the doorway, being firm.

'I'm afraid she's asked me not to let you in.'

'This isn't fair,' Toby said. 'You don't understand.'

'Fairness doesn't come into it,' I replied. 'Charlotte asked you not to visit, and we both understand that.' As we were talking, I observed Jim quietly approaching the house and then standing at the gate. 'Hello Jim,' I said. 'I don't think you've met Toby.'

Toby turned round and was confronted by a big raggy fellow with shoulder-length matted hair and a grimy face with furious little eyes, cloaked in a filthy donkey jacket and wearing enormous black leather boots.

'He-he-hello,' said Toby.

'Toby recently started sleeping with someone else, but now wants Charlotte back.'

Toby turned back to me. 'Don't say that,' he said. 'You don't know.'

'Jim's also a friend of Charlotte's,' I said, 'so he'll be as concerned for her as I am.' Toby stood sideways between Jim and I. 'Please can you leave now?' I said. 'Charlotte says she'll contact you when she feels ready.'

'Look here —' began Toby.

'RAARR!' shouted Jim, and pulled from within his jacket, with a rasping noise, a long sword, and lifted it above his head. Toby panicked and jumped over the low fence into the neighbours' front yard, then tripped and crashed into their hedge. As he got up, Jim leant over the fence and slapped him on the buttocks with the yellow blade; the plastic bent harmlessly. 'RARR-RARR!' shouted Jim. Toby ran away.

Jim followed me into the hallway, and we closed the door.

'Nice weapon.'

'A leaving present from Lennie,' said Jim, slipping it back into its blue scabbard. 'He probably stole it.'

'I hope you aren't going to take it to court tomorrow,' I said. Charlotte peeked down the stairs, having been sitting at the top, listening to the doorstep conversation. She cheered to see Jim again and ran down, arms outstretched, but stopped before she reached him.

'Phew!' she said. 'You stink. Do you think we're mean to Toby?'

'People deserve mercy, I'm sure, but justice too,' said Jim. 'It doesn't sound like he was very nice to you.'

He had a bath while his clothes were washed. Then Charlotte cut his hair while I cooked tea. We heard out Jim's tale. He'd taken up with Arthur, met the lower basement community, and discovered that Cerberus had once been a neighbour of his. He felt he'd done what he needed to do back in Leeds, which mainly consisted of learning about the lives of Arthur and his friends. It had been a sort of moral duty for him, it seemed, but he'd felt ready to come back.

'I'm afraid you've lost your old room,' I said, and Charlotte smiled at him nervously.

'I didn't think Matt and Chris would want me back,' said Jim. 'Anyway, I've rung Beth, and she's expecting me round.'

'Would you mind,' I asked Charlotte, 'if I took this fellow out for a pint?'

'Of course not,' she replied. 'A man must have his shredded wheat. And anyway, I might be going out myself tonight.'

THERE WAS NO FIRE lit in the Red Cow, and the curtains were still open, letting in the evening light. Jim was quiet as he rolled a cigarette and drank his beer.

'I didn't know what I was doing in Leeds to start with,' he said after a while. 'Then I realised that I was there partly to get away from you.'

'From me?'

'I realised that I blamed you for what had happened. It was you who persuaded me into joining the Green Party, and it was on your account that I was out on the streets talking to people about the bloody bypass.'

'Rubbish,' I said. 'It was you that persuaded me to go out door-knocking.'

'But it was you who got me involved in it all to begin with; I was an innocent anarchist. Once I got to Leeds, I started thinking about why I didn't want to go back, even though I'd had my stuff nicked. I was in Leeds to be on my own, to take stock.'

I leant back in my seat and folded my arms.

'So it was nothing to do with fear of getting involved with Beth, then?'

'Ha,' he said dismissively.

'You weren't right pleased to see us when Charlotte and I found you.'

'No, sorry. I warmed up after a bit, though, didn't I? In fact, I was touched. Though by the look of it you were happy enough to be wandering about with your new lass.'

I shrugged. 'Why did you want to get away from me then?'

'I realised that I'd become dependent on you. After hitting that Driscoll bloke, and after Matt and Chris chucking me out, I felt vulnerable, as if unless you were supporting me I'd not know which way to turn. I didn't like that. So I stayed in Leeds and I went back to some of my own roots.' He paused. 'Arthur and I talked for hours about what it's like, this modern life. About the way most people aren't really alive but just surviving. He said, look at me; I'm a worst-case scenario. That's why I have to follow my heart; because if I didn't, what would there be? The look in his eyes when he said this: you knew he was talking from the edge, that he could see down into the darkness, that he'd been there.'

'So now you've come back to Greyston,' I said.

'Arthur talked about his vocation and how important it was to him, and after that I realised that philosophy is what matters to me. I've got a lot to do, so I came back to continue with it.'

I nodded my head, remembering the conversation Charlotte and I had had with Arthur. Jim and I sat in silence together, while around us the pub filled with talk. He looked up at me before taking a swig on his beer.

'And I've given up the bloody local food diet,' he said. 'I went out and bought bananas and chocolate, and Antarctic penguin sausages.'

He laughed at his own joke, his laughter booming out into the room. I shook my head in mock disapproval.

'I missed you a lot,' I said. He looked at me and smiled.

'All right,' he said. 'So what's the story with your new lover?'

'She's not really my lover,' I said.

'Pah,' he said, rolling another bulging cigarette and taking a great gulp of his second pint of beer.

'What?' I said.

'A fuck is just a fuck,' he said, looking at me with his hard little eyes. 'You've spent so long all tangled up with – *women* – that you forget it's not such a very personal thing.'

'Yes it is,' I retorted. 'I would say it's one of the most intimate things you can do.'

'Aye,' he said. 'Very bloody intimate. And, when our friend Lennie cleaned up the mess Cerberus got into after he got so pissed he shit himself – that was very bloody intimate too. Tell me exactly what the difference between fucking one woman and fucking another is.'

'I can tell you're a philosopher,' I said, smiling, but thinking of Ros too, her unfaithful fuck and what that had meant.

'If Archie – when he was *whole* – had gone out and wondered to himself if this one was little-miss-moggy-right, or whether this one might be a bit of a handful if they got into a cat-thing, then he would've got his bollocks in a right twist,' said Jim.

'I'm trying to avoid getting my bollocks in a twist,' I said. 'Charlotte's still tangled up with Toby, and I'm in love with her, and don't tell me you don't know what I mean.'

Jim smiled at me and didn't say any more.

AT ELEVEN THE NEXT MORNING, Paul arrived, then Jim and Beth. Jim was wearing a slightly tight suit and tie.

'From Beth's new neighbour, a policeman,' he said. 'Not bad, huh?'

'You look like a crook,' said Beth.

'Nice haircut,' said Paul.

'Salon de Newby,' said Charlotte, with a dry smile. Beth and Charlotte were introduced, tea was drunk, and we set off on foot for the twelve o'clock court hearing. The magistrates fined Jim £40, which was the least possible. Paul and Charlotte each immediately gave him £20, and he paid his fine on the spot.

We all went out for lunch, not so much to console Jim for the fine as to celebrate his return. Paul was the odd one out among the quasi-couples, but he didn't seem to mind. Charlotte poked and prodded me as she had done Toby. Beth felt free to be rude to Jim. After lunch I travelled with Paul back to the campus and worked in the library.

Walking back to the bus stop, I met Barry Driscoll. I was pissed off just to see him, but he addressed me as if we were still the best of friends. I told him about the morning's court hearing and its outcome.

'That bastard!' exclaimed Barry. 'He really bruised my nose, he did. You should stay away from him, Juniper; he's dangerous!' Anger prickled through me.

'If I may say so, Barry,' I began, 'you deserve –' but just then Jane, the ES department secretary, walked up and broke in.

'Excuse me, Juniper, I must speak to this man.' Her voice was quivering, her fists clenched. Right at that moment, I realised I was sexually attracted to her without feeling the least bit in love. It wasn't personal. She turned to Barry.

'Dr Driscoll, is it true that you've been knocking off Alyson Cox since your Scandinavian girlfriend dumped you?' Barry looked at Jane blankly. She turned back to me. 'Alyson is a nineteen-year-old who's had a bit of a crush on him. She came into my office crying this morning, saying that he'd persuaded her to sleep with him, but that now she regrets it, because her friends are telling her that it wasn't right.'

'It's none of your business,' Barry said to Jane. He turned to me. 'Women can be so touchy when they're jealous.'

Jane took him by the shoulders. 'Now *that's* what I call touchy,' she said, and kneed him hard in the balls. He yelped, then doubled over with a sharp exhalation. 'We went out together a few times, years ago,' she told me. 'It didn't last very long, though he said he loved me, and since then I've had to put up with hearing about his affairs. Bonking a first year is just the last straw.' She kneed him again, in the thigh, and he collapsed onto the ground. She walked off. I helped Barry onto a nearby bench, where he sat, clutching his groin. He couldn't speak, could only make constricted noises. I opened his briefcase, I didn't know why.

Inside were a couple of porn mags among the papers and pens. I ripped out photos of naked girls and stuffed them down his collar, in his pockets, between his legs, then left him sitting there, groaning, clutching his balls, covered in pictures of tits and bums. I walked away, pretty sure he'd recover in a while. When I looked back, a crowd was gathering, and a couple of university security men were hurrying over.

When I told Charlotte back home what had happened on the campus, she looked shocked. I thought that perhaps she was appalled by violence.

'Barry Driscoll is the guy that hit Jim?' she said weakly.

'He used to be my friend,' I said. 'You'd hate him. He's deeply irrational.'

'I think I met him recently.'

'He was pretty charming, probably.'

She nodded, but without looking at me.

the dark horse of appetite

I INTRODUCED KATE to Charlotte somewhat vaguely as 'someone who lives here', and they shook hands politely. They were about the same height and build. It was a Saturday evening, two days after Barry's demise. Geoff looked smart but casual, his face scrubbed pinkish. Charlotte, in new company, showed off her breeding by being bright, courteous and engaged.

Geoff, Kate and their boys lived on a new estate in Kendal, where Geoff worked. They had a car and a cat. They'd been married seven years. Geoff, it turned out, was the boy from her school she'd gone out with after me. They'd moved to the southeast for the sake of his career, and it was there that they had begun visiting a Buddhist monastery. They'd been instrumental in establishing the monastery in Silverthwaite. They had both wanted to move back north.

'Can't be many jobs in computing in Kendal,' I observed.

'More than you think,' said Geoff; 'though I seem to have got several of them.' The main thing had been to settle where they'd like the boys to grow up.

'Your plates!' exclaimed Kate, as I took them from the oven. 'We bought some made by the same potter. Aren't they great!'

We all duly looked at Ros's lovely plates, with their dark gold leaf patterns against a metallic blue glaze.

'They're so distinctive,' Kate continued. 'She's called Ros Trevelyan, and – do you know – she lives in that cottage where we – that you used to stay in!'

'Actually, she's my ex,' I said, wondering at Kate's powers of deduction.

'Really?' she said, clearly unsure whether to believe me.

'He's in exile,' said Charlotte. 'Though he's making the most of nourishing male friendships.' She poked me in the arm.

'She's to have an exhibition of her work up in Carlisle, I've heard,' I said.

'Oh yes, she told me about that. You're the bloke she was talking about, then,' said Kate, having decided she wasn't being deceived. 'I thought it was someone else because of the name.'

'So, what did she –' said Charlotte and I together, then laughed.

'What a nice woman,' Kate continued. 'I met her at the monastery a month or two ago; she was with that guy from the village who's been cutting the grass – what's his name, Geoff?'

'Harry,' said Geoff, looking over at me. 'Tread carefully, K.'

'What?' she said. 'Oh, all right. I mean, he's nice too. He does all that work for the monastery, doesn't he Geoff? For nothing. He grows a lot of vegetables, in the back garden of the cottage, I think he said. Is that right?' she said, asking me.

I shrugged. She was probably right.

'So, what did she say about Juniper?' asked Charlotte.

'Juniper, that was it,' said Kate. 'It's a tree, yeah?'

'That's right,' I said.

'Nice,' she said, nodding. 'Cool.'

I dished up a cheese and potato bake, with boiled spinach. Charlotte poured some wine. We talked about Kate and Geoff's boys, whom they obviously doted on.

'What she said,' said Kate, out of the blue, 'was that she was having a break from her partner, who was a philosopher or something. I've just remembered. I thought it all sounded rather romantic, what with her in what seemed like an open relationship, you know, with the nice gardening man.' She looked over at Geoff at this point, but he wasn't looking at her. 'And then it turns out she was talking about you!'

'Kate's romanticism excludes people she knows,' said Geoff drily.

'What? I –' said Kate, retreating into a fluster of gestures.

'Goodbye darling!' exclaimed Charlotte, dramatically waving to a leaving lover. 'It's hard to say farewell, but what is love without distance, without imagination, without a break?'

'Dull, dull, dull,' I said, shaking my head.

Geoff smiled and clapped. Charlotte took a bow. Kate stared, wide eyed. Had Kate always been so clumsy? All I remembered was passion and nerves. Geoff went to the toilet after the meal.

'I never told him about what we got up to in your cottage, you know,' she said, looking up out of her big eyes. She had obviously taken me exactly at my word when I'd said that Charlotte was just the other lodger. 'I didn't know what to say, and then the time went on. It was very nice,' she said, then turned bright red, 'though of course I'm a married woman now.'

As Kate spoke, Charlotte politely sipped her wine and nodded, while grinding her heel into my foot beneath the table. Kate was chaos. If Geoff had this little squall in thrall, it was a miracle of co-dependency that I was in awe of. They left at ten to pick up their boys from Kate's aunt in Kentside. Her granny had died two years before. She had never really accepted Geoff, it seemed.

CHARLOTTE AND I SAT ON her bed with hot chocolate later on.

'So, what happened in your little cottage with Kate?' she asked, kicking my shin with inquisitive ardour.

'It was intimate and personal,' I said, smiling.

'I gathered that!' she said. I too had never told anyone about Kate's and my pioneering explorations. But then, no one had ever asked about them before.

'It was good clean teenage fun,' I said.

'So you drank pop and played cards?'

'Never!' I said.

'So,' said Charlotte, taking my mug and putting it and hers on the floor, then pushing me onto my back on the mattress, 'what exactly did you do?' She pinned my arms, and her hair fell in my face.

I looked up at her face, lit sideways by a bedside light. It twitched with avidity, almost voracity, which excited me. I still felt unsure. She looked down, waiting. Does thinking make any difference at these moments? Instinct takes charge: either the sense of interest in following the body's enthusiasm, or the belly-felt reluctance in the consequence. Charlotte's breath fell upon me with its alien odour, and I surrendered into its sensual presence.

'She kissed me,' I suggested. Not drunk this time, we fell upon each other with unpent appetite. There's a glory about the first time that lovers give their bodies to each other, like the way a birch tree gives itself to the breeze on a hot summer's day. Charlotte shivered as I stroked her breasts.

'Then,' I said, slowly learning the contours of her thin, long back, 'I suppose there came a point where we both stopped trying and went into a sort of trance of arousal.' She pulled me down onto the bed, her hair flicked sideways off her face, unsmiling.

'So this is different,' she whispered urgently. 'I want you alive and conscious.' I switched off the light and we slipped naked beneath her duvet. She looked into my eyes as our bodies fused smoothly, though her attention gradually moved elsewhere, to our bodies' surgings. Then slowly she relaxed, her hair splashed out on the pillow, her face releasing its nerves. Her arms lay out on each side of her trunk; her legs, bent at the knees, leant outwards, toppled wands. She became quite passive beneath me. Puzzled, I slowed until we lay hot and still together. Ordinary desire, I thought, takes lovers beyond intimacy into something that knows only its blind and impersonal goal of pleasure; but we'd turned back from this excitement and were resting in the strangeness of sexual intimacy. I felt her breathing pushing me slightly up and down.

'I am flesh beneath you,' she whispered. I kissed her flaccid lips.

'Flesh bundled with nerve endings,' I whispered, withdrawing from her, avoiding her eyes by moving my kisses down to her breasts. But she pulled on my hair and hauled my face back up to hers.

'No,' she said. 'It's Sartre's philosophy. In sex, the beloved is incarnated as flesh beneath you, her subjectivity spread across her body, made plain and ready to be captured, made yours.'

'Well, if you're flesh beneath me, what are you doing telling me about Sartre?'

'Maybe you're not trying hard enough to capture my attention.'

'Maybe you'd captured mine.'

Charlotte laughed and reached for my penis.

'OK,' she said. 'Now try and escape from this.'

I didn't try. Through orgasm, we disappear into ourselves briefly, dipping into that warm well in which the whole self briefly dissolves. Later I watched her come, and it looked like it was painful to fall apart from the self so far. But lovers come back together, in the warm nest of the night, and reconstitute themselves in each other's arms. I don't know what Sartre used to do.

When Charlotte rose to go down to the toilet, my eyes were adjusted to the grey dark, and I watched her silhouette wind over the floor. I saw the inner working of her precise machine, the skin-picture. Her hands turned behind her, her fingers curved down. Her slim legs were light motions. When she returned, we lay facing each other, entwined.

'The colour of cherries,' I said, sweeping the hair from her face. 'You in the dark.'

'Moonlit limestone,' she said. 'You didn't mind me philosophising mid-screw, did you?'

'You call that philosophising? It was more like oral sex.'

'Toby would hardly speak, you know,' she said, rubbing my cheek. 'That was OK, but I like it better when I can speak.'

It was not late. I made more hot chocolate, padding around the empty, quiet house in delicious cold nudity. Charlotte came down to the kitchen wrapped in the duvet with a lit candle for the table.

'Come inside,' she said, and we sat enwrapped on the bench. 'Heh, guess what?' she said, looking at me conspiratorially. She lit a cigarette. 'You remember that night when you were out with Jim? I went out to meet my Buddhist friend Sue. We met this chap in a pub, and we got talking, and he asked me back to his place. Guess who it was?'

I shook my head.

'Barry Driscoll.'

'Oh yeah, you said.' I remembered her reaction after I'd told her about his demise. 'You didn't —' I couldn't believe it.

'Didn't what?'

'You got off with him?' I said, feeling suddenly anxious. 'And you tell me now?'

'I didn't say that,' she retorted. 'And anyway, what's it to you?'

'What's it to me? Don't be stupid. The guy's a shit, and –'

'And you're jealous,' she said, tipping her head up and exhaling smoke.

'I had to put up with Ros sleeping with Harry, and I wasn't thinking of venturing into that kind of territory again.'

Charlotte shrugged, stubbing out her cigarette.

'Of course I didn't sleep with him. If I had, you'd have noticed I wasn't here, wouldn't you? So don't take out your shit on me.'

'So what did you do with him?' I'd started feeling quite angry by now.

'Oh, piss off, Juniper. I only mentioned him because I thought this was another one-off, you know, a bit of a fling, so we could be straightforward –'

'But you actually did something with him.'

Charlotte was staring at me with a distinctly unfriendly expression. 'Fuck *off!*' she said finally, and went upstairs, trailing her duvet.

The way the energy tingled in my chest was like the messy play of light on broken glass, with mud and blood mixed into it. I didn't know what had come over me; I had definitely felt angry with Charlotte, and it wasn't her fault. She'd been prickly of course, but I hadn't been pricked by it before.

I went up to my room and dressed, came back down to the kitchen, made a pot of tea, and smoked intensely. Postcoital exhaustion, anger and shame made a rich compost of emotion. As it rotted down in the midnight quiet, I began to feel sorry. Then Charlotte came downstairs in her pyjamas. She'd been crying.

'Tea?' I asked. She nodded and sat down.

'Sue and I talked to him in the pub, because he was looking miserable,' she began. 'It was obvious that he fancied me, so when Sue went home, I went back to his place for a coffee. He'd said he was called Barry, I knew that his surname was Driscoll because of things in his house, but I just didn't connect him with the guy you'd told me about. Like you said, he was so charming.... Anyway, we snogged a bit, and he wanted me to stay, but I went home. I just knew I'd regret it if I stayed. Juniper, I'm really grateful to you for being so kind to me, you know, keeping Toby away and everything, but I don't think I did anything wrong, and I don't want to spoil things between us.'

I poured her some tea.

'Thanks for telling me that. I'm sorry I got angry with you. It was definitely my shit.'

'So you don't mind that I snogged him?'

I had to swallow hard.

'No. I mean, as long as you don't do it again.'

She shrugged. 'No, Juniper, that still sounds like jealousy. I'll do what the hell I like actually.'

I sighed. 'All right, all right, I give in. Just don't expect me to be sympathetic if Barry charms his way into your knickers then locks you in his house.'

We laughed.

'The thing is, Juniper, Toby really let me down, sleeping with Julia. I just want revenge. Nothing much seemed to be happening with you, so I went along with Barry to see what he was like. Obviously, I'm not going to sleep with him now I know who he is; I'd much rather sleep with you, if you really want to know.'

'Sweeter revenge,' I said.

'Exactly. Come on,' Charlotte said. 'Time to get your own back on Ros.'

IN THE MORNING, we had some more sex, then talked. It was a Sunday.

'How many boyfriends have you had, then?'

'Toby was my first proper one, actually.'

'Really? Your first? What happened?'

'I've had lots of *lovers*,' she said. 'I suppose I've slept around a lot, to be honest. I think I wanted to feel like I was in control, and the whole boyfriend/girlfriend thing seemed like a joke, you know, all that holding hands and saying I love you, when you're nineteen or something, and the boys fall in love with anything with tits. I don't really think you can say that sexual attraction is anything else than a matter of inclination; it's not really to do with love. I mean, I found it quite easy to get men into bed, and invariably they then go all gooey over you.'

'You're quite attractive,' I suggested.

'Thanks,' she said. 'But the point is that love has to be about something more intelligent, something more like a volition, or even a duty, not just an attraction.'

'Friendship,' I said.

'Well, maybe,' she said. 'But we usually make friends in the same sort of way: you meet someone fairly randomly, you find you have something in common, and on you go.'

'So who do you love?'

'Toby, obviously. He was the first person I actually felt inclined to sleep with and willing to love. And the crazy bastard screwed it up.'

'So, how many men have you slept with?'

Charlotte waved her hand vaguely. 'Like I said, lots.'

'How many is that?'

'Seventeen, not including you.'

'Not bad,' I said, thinking of my four, including Charlotte.

'That includes a girl,' she said. 'A cellist in my college. I was in love with her, actually, or I thought I was. I decided I must be a lesbian, and that explained why I didn't seem to fall in love with men. One night we were in my room, and we ended up kissing, and so on. But she freaked and wouldn't speak to me after that. It was only ever her, though; I didn't fancy any other girls.'

'Toby's a fool,' I said.

'Really an idiot,' Charlotte said, not looking at me.

'You've obviously been unfortunate with him. But I'm sure that you'll meet someone whom you can trust and who loves you.'

Charlotte looked at me directly, with a hard expression, which I was realising was part of who she was, but that had only started happening once we'd got quite close. She smoked, holding her cigarette by her temple like a protective charm, other hand at her elbow. The skin of her shoulders and arms shone gently. She still looked at me, then nodded, without sharing her thoughts. She nodded some more, then looked down at the ashtray while stubbing her cigarette.

'And Ros must be kicking herself for chucking you,' she said.

'Our splitting up seemed quite mutual at the time.'

Charlotte suddenly flashed a smile. 'From what you've told me, Juniper, she really has done well for herself.'

I shrugged. 'What do you mean?'

'The cottage is actually yours, right? She was demanding that you have a family, which you weren't sure about, so she shakes things up by sleeping with another guy, in response to which you move out so you feel like you're in exile. Meanwhile, she has the house, her new lover, everything.'

'Technically, we're joint tenants of my parents' property.'

'But still, you've been so *nice*, Juniper. And Ros obviously hasn't given you up yet.'

'Why on earth do you think that?' I was thinking of the changed locks.

'Did you not notice that Kate said that Ros told her she was having a "break" from her partner?'

'Oh yes, and she even described me as a philosopher.'

'And what does the term "break" imply, as opposed to a "split"?'

'That there will be something after as well as before.'

'So obviously she hopes there's an after.'

It was quiet in the bedroom. Church bells drifted down from Greyston's old hill-top church.

'So what do you want?' Charlotte asked.

I had to laugh. I was in bed with the woman I'd been in love with for months, and she was asking me what I wanted. I knew she was fishing for her own sake, and it was tempting to say what would have been most endearing.

'I want a big fry-up for breakfast. How about you?'

'With fried bread and beans,' she said.

'And what do *you* want?' I asked Charlotte, as we were digging into eggs, mushrooms and beans on toast.

She grinned. 'This is great, being straight with you. We do have these honest breakfast conversations, don't we? Do you know, right now I'm happy to be here with you, even though I'm only just out of a big thing with Toby.'

'Two exiles in love, then.'

'Am I in love with you?' she asked me, looking up suddenly. 'Oh shit, maybe that was too honest. I mean, I don't know, not really.'

'OK, one exile in love, the other not sure, but probably liking the first one.'

She laughed. 'Probably.'

This, I thought, as I placed my last forkful of yolky toast into my mouth, might not be regarded as the most auspicious start to a relationship. It was as though I'd fallen off Plato's ladder of love, right back to the bottom, to the dross, the comedy and the mess of sexual love; and yet I didn't mind; I had my love.

CHARLOTTE STOOD OUTSIDE, in the dark of the garden. It was midnight in late May. I watched her from the window of my room. Her cigarette hovered around her face and shoulder. I walked barefoot through the cold grass to stand behind her. She leant back into me and I put my arms around her waist.

'Listen,' she whispered. The night was very still. There was an intermittent rustling from the bottom of the wall to our right. Small shrieks pierced the cool air from the end of the garden. A goods train rattled slowly along the mainline. Beneath these sounds an ongoing, gentle chomping, rough jaws on green leaves, a hundred eating mouths on the ground around us.

'Hedgehog, shrews, train, slugs,' I whispered into her hair. Cigarette smoke drifted through the pristine night air. She turned in my arms, dropping the cigarette, which hissed briefly in the dew. The bitter taste on her mouth and on her breath was like smearing ashes on my chest. Her hands moved on my torso and unbuttoned my jeans. Clothing dropped into the wet darkness; we sank to the ground. The damp long grass was full of the smell of earth, and I rubbed my wet hands over her face and body, and she rubbed hers over my back. As later we lay together breathing, shivering in the cold, the hedgehog appeared and sniffed at our wet, filthy faces, then snuffled off towards the neighbour's hedge. Its hot, unwashable stench remained briefly. As our breathing calmed, the sound of eating crept back into our ears.

WEARING AN IVY-GREEN, plum-bordered polished cotton sari, with a lighter, lichen-lime short blouse, she entered my room. I was sitting in bed, reading.

'Namaste,' she said, hands joined in front of her. 'A present from granny.' She moved about the room with the grace required to bear her attire, opening my curtains and window. Her slim midriff stretched and folded. If her parents had met in India, if they had not decided to stay in Britain, if she had been brought up in the East, this clothing would be what she was used to, along with the language, customs, expectations and thoughts that go with an upbringing in a different culture. Would she have been this same Charlotte?

She unwound the sari, forming a green heap on the floor, until she stood in her lime-coloured undergarments. Beneath these, her tight white department store underwear shone against shoe-polish skin. She ran her fingers through the black hairs on my chest, against the pasty white flesh. Her dark hand rose to my neck and her fingers tightened around it. She moved her face closer.

'She says, be careful of those white men. They do not know how to love, only to conquer.' She increased her grip and pulled on my hair, which had grown back almost to my shoulders. With one hand I pushed on her chest and with the other on her face. She bit my middle finger but could no longer reach my neck. With both hands on my wrist she twisted my arm until I lay sideways on the bed, then repositioned herself to sit straddled on my chest. Her thighs gripped my ribs. She grasped my big white ears with her two hands, her dark body leaning over me, breasts curved in bright-white cups.

'Surrender,' she hissed through clenched teeth, and pulled on my ears, moving her knees to pin down my shoulders. She moved her face closer until, with a flash of white teeth, she pushed her tongue into one of my nostrils. The smooth, wet muscle slid into the space while her wet mouth closed over my nose. Shocked, I shook my head sideways, and with a surge pushed her up and back. I wiped my nose with my hand. She slid a hand up to my face and ran her fingers around the edges of my nostrils.

'Big nose,' she said. She reached sideways and pulled over the end of the heaped sari, and sat up. Facing me, she began to wrap the long, light cloth around us. I held the sides of her head and closed my mouth on her small, wide nose, exploring the snotty-tasting cavities with my tongue. She gripped my ears again.

'DO YOU MIND ME seeing Paul?' Charlotte asked, rhetorically, as she stood in the kitchen. It was nearly three weeks after we'd begun sleeping together, a Friday morning. She had her bag over her shoulder and her suede jacket over her arm. She was about to leave for campus. The previous evening I had been telling Charlotte what the thought of her many previous lovers made me feel like.

'It's like an instinctual sense of my woman not quite being "mine",' I'd said. 'I don't mean that personally; it's quite bodily really.'

'Every man wants to marry a virgin,' she said, 'though it's highly undesirable that he should be one himself. And how the hell can I *not* take it personally?'

We were sitting outside a pub on the canal in Greyston, while the sky glowed with a huge fading blue. The swifts were back, and tore through the slender air like paper knives opening up memories of old summers.

I shrugged. 'I mean, there's nothing you can do. It's my stuff.'

'It's like one of those factoids you hear,' she said, 'that more men have affairs than women. The logical correlate of this is that there must be a few unmarried mistresses screwing with an awful lot of men, while most of the wives continue in faithful obedience.'

'Though in real life, for every wayward male there must be a harlot cuckolding her mate.'

'I think you have to consider a sort of biological critique of pure reason,' she said. 'Natural selection, a cunning mistress, endows us with minds capable of the highest, clearest thinking, but also smuggles in really warped perceptions that keep her own need for effective reproductive strategies fulfilled. So men think of themselves as getting about and notching up conquests, but perceive women as naturally more "innocent" and incapable of that kind of thinking.'

'But, biologically, it's not at all advantageous for women just to stay at home, waiting for brave males.'

'Nope,' said Charlotte, putting down her pint glass abutting the wet ring left by mine on the thick wooden table. I held my glass in the air. 'But it's advantageous for nature that men feel that women are passive and faithful. It makes men feel protective.'

'Although men have to think their women faithful to be persuaded to protect them.'

'The point is that what we *think* about love, or our lovers, is only a function of the terrifying truth that nature has us by the goolies.'

'But women don't have goolies.'

'Exactly!' said Charlotte. 'Despite the fact that women have a truer perspective on sexual love, the peculiarly warped male perspective is regarded as generally true, so that in some patriarchal ethical codes, men are expected to want to sleep around, but women can be stoned for doing so.'

'Sounds like you've got the truth by the goolies,' I said. 'But did you know that there's a tribe in South India in which marriage is just a formal matter. The women take lovers, up to twelve at a time, but they only visit at night. The marriage is recognised as having ended if the man doesn't give his wife a present at a certain annual festival.'

'Didn't I tell you that my mum's from a South Indian family?'

'You can't inherit a cultural practice through your genes,' I said.

'I've often thought,' said Charlotte, well into her stride, 'that romantic love is a man's invention. The fantasy of a soul mate isn't half as convincing to women, I'm sure. We see how impersonal sexual attraction really is, and how much you need realism in emotional life. Men don't really understand much about us, generally, and have this habit of getting into very charming fantasies about what we're like.'

'OK,' I said, having had enough of all this feminist rationalism. 'So, if falling in love is just some kind of con trick that men fall for so much more easily than women, how come it's women who read Mills & Boon, while men read Wilbur Smith?'

'Who reads romantic fiction? Intelligent, independent women? Or housewives who've bought into the whole patriarchal game? And why do you think men read adventure novels, if not to escape for a while from their own lack of emotions?'

'You told me you were in love with Toby,' I said. 'And in a romantic relationship with him.'

'I *was*,' she said. 'I *was*. And what a dismal failure that little experiment in conventionality turned out to be.'

'You didn't exactly choose a representative example of manhood, did you?'

'But you don't choose who you fall in love with.'

'I bet at the time you felt you knew why he was the one.'

'And I bet that now I'm seeing it all in a different light.'

'Do you know why I fell in love with you?' I said.

'You mean, you want to tell me what occurred to you as the reason for your strong desire to mate with me?'

'It was just this,' I said. 'All this. You're a thinker.'

'You're a fucking pervert,' she retorted, then tipped the rest of her beer back rapidly. 'Talking of nature,' she said. 'I keep thinking of that species of spider of which the male, preparing to mate with the female, scrapes out the semen of the last one in. Horrible, isn't it?'

'I was watching the swans on the canal the other day,' I said. 'They do these lovely dances before and after they've mated. They rub and twine their necks so elegantly. But I was also reading about chimpanzees. They're our nearest neighbours genetically, and they're entirely promiscuous. The males sometimes queue up to get their ends away. What is it about that spider?'

She shrugged. 'I don't know.'

I HEARD THE DOOR SLAM as Charlotte left for her lunch date with Paul. They saw each other regularly, mainly for lunch. I didn't mind at all; I had complete trust in Paul. I got back to studying Plato's *Phaedrus*. In it he describes love's divine madness as a route to blessedness. Again, the key is a restraint of the sexual urge towards one's beloved. The soul is like a chariot, he says; reason its charioteer, spirit and appetite the horses. The soul, in love and attracted to a lover, is remembering true beauty and regrowing the feathers that would fly it thence. But appetite, the dark horse, wants physical love, and reason has to control it with the bridle and bit. Harmony of soul, says Plato, is attained through a brutal repression of appetite's gross urge.

I began to smell something amiss in all this, a sense reinforced by discovering that Plato himself was for a long time the unrequited lover of one Dion and, for that reason one supposes, needed to resolve within himself the incompatible strands of his desire. It seemed to me that Socrates' taming of his desires was the more believable achievement, since he remained married, with sons, all the while. This makes a difference to how one considers his restraint towards youths. It was not chastity like that of Jagaro, but more like a clear ethical orientation towards wisdom and away from lust.

I had certainly slipped from the heavens of chaste Platonic love. And, as Plato remarks concerning the lover who has given in to the promptings of the appetite's black beast, I had acceded to desire, but not with the whole of my mind. I was still in love, but I had no illusions about the permanence of the relationship Charlotte and I were enjoying; and what I was enjoying was sex.

in the south-west

THE EXAMS WERE OVER. Paul was going down to Bristol to give a paper at an academic conference on the theme of friendship. I decided to go with him; Hans Bosch was going to be there, and I could give him my dissertation on his book.

Paul and I set off after lunch on Charlotte's birthday. We took her out to the best restaurant on campus, and she was in fine fettle, poking me in the arm and ribs and being attentive to Paul. She saw us to his car and then left us, striding briskly back towards the library.

His old hatchback was hot and smelt of plastic. There was a feeling of adventure as we sped down the motorway, windows down, past cow-parsley lacing verdant hedges and pink flecks of campion beneath them. I pointed out a hovering kestrel along a steep verge, seemingly suspended on the pole of its laser-beam gaze, and Paul declaimed Hopkins' 'The Windhover' at sixty-five miles an hour.

'I was recently confronted with a truth about myself,' Paul mused after a small pause. 'I took a walk early in the morning, at about six-thirty, from my flat to the playing fields two streets away. I walked around the hedges, all bursting with their early summer life. I walked along a stream flanked with nettles, bearing flag iris. And I realised that none of it any longer touched me; and even poetry has become thin, mere words. Years ago, I would walk thus in the morning and the trees, the sky, the grass, would all speak – even sing – to me; I can now barely remember about what. It seems that I have become so comported to the life of the mind that I have unwittingly removed myself from intimacy with nature. I've become a philosopher in his tower.'

'How can you lose touch with nature?' I demanded. 'You're part of nature; you have a body, you experience weather and the seasons; you're surrounded by living beings.'

Paul sighed. 'I mention it as a mystery, my friend. I am saddened.'

We sat without speaking for a time.

'I have an idea,' I said. 'Tim and I are organising a men's gathering, for friends. We're going somewhere remote, to spend time together, for games, rituals, whatever. Are you interested in coming? It might help you reconnect.'

'I would very much appreciate the opportunity to participate,' said Paul immediately.

'The Sunday after the solstice. Two or three days.'

IN BRISTOL, WE FOUND our way through tree-lined streets to the building where the conference was being held. Paul, in shirt and tie, greeted colleagues old and new, engaging with the event in a business-like way. I hung back, feeling much less of a piece with proceedings than he. Ladies in white aprons served cups of coffee and tea, their backs to the paintings of past Chancellors and Deans, their hands on the handles of their urns. I fell into conversation with a young American, whose green sweatshirt said 'Ohio State'. Had I read Foucault and Derrida on friendship? Levinas on the eroticisation of philosophy? I was afraid not. I wished Jim were there. He knew about this new stuff. Was he, I asked, familiar with Plato's views on love? He smiled at me sideways. You like that paedophile stuff?

After dinner we got straight down to business. Gathered in a large seminar room, the first speaker presented his paper, took questions and was followed by the second. In the bar later, conversation pushed into themes opened up. I came out of my initial dismay and found that most of the academics were friendly and willing to explain what I hadn't studied or read or ever thought of before.

'This is great,' I said to Paul, as we retired to our rooms.

'It's something of a holiday for some and an opportunity to gossip for the rest,' he said. 'Fortunately, our conference has such an unfashionable theme we've not attracted the careerists and high-flying argumentative types.'

'Is that good or bad?'

'I would say good,' said Paul. 'Unless of course you had wanted to puff yourself up for theorising the repositioning of the post-modern masculine in the democratisation of love.'

After lunch, Paul took me for a walk above Clifton Gorge, and we sat on the very bench where he had first read Spinoza. The view was spectacular, the far cliff wild and green.

'I used to bring Rosemary here, and we'd read Shelley to each other.'

'Who's Rosemary?' I asked.

'Do you remember, some months past, when I mentioned I had indeed once fallen in love with a student, though I elaborated not at all?'

'Not really,' I replied.

'She was a young woman I met while I was here. She was, of course, betrothed to another,' Paul smiled, 'and we never spoke of my passion. A friendship nevertheless sprung up, though we failed to stay in touch once I moved to Greyston.'

'So you weren't really in love, then.'

'Hmm,' said Paul, crossing his arms. 'What do you mean?'

'If you forgot about her so quickly, you couldn't have been very in love.'

'I was *too much* in love,' Paul said, turning to face me. 'I couldn't stop thinking of her; it would have been too painful to stay in touch. I still regularly dream about her.'

'Ah,' I said.

'There's a current of emotion still flowing in me, under the surface. It feels like it's been blocked in over the years, but it can't quite be stifled.'

'Just like your feeling for Spinoza,' I said.

'Yes, I suppose so,' said Paul, smiling. 'Rosemary, Spinoza; it's all mixed together; wonderful student passions.'

'Where's Rosemary now?' I asked.

Paul shrugged. 'Living in her home village I expect.'

'Let's go and visit her.'

'Don't be ridiculous,' scoffed Paul. 'She won't want to see me. What would I say? It's all too long ago.'

'So you want to stay blocked and intellectual, up in your tower?'

Paul looked at me angrily. But I wasn't sorry to prod him a bit; his preciousness about the grind of years, or the loss of youth, was sometimes as wankerish as his arrogance.

'A man's *gift* is his passion,' I said. 'What else have you got? Habits, a bit of discipline, a sense of duty, your job.'

'I have the counsel of my friends, evidently,' said Paul.

'So let's visit her. Have you got her phone number?'

Paul got up suddenly and walked away, along the side of the gorge. I stayed where I was. He came back after a few minutes and sat down.

'What on earth would be the point?' he said.

'You tell me.'

'Would it make any difference? Perhaps I might feel a little – *released*.'

'Let's see.'

Paul allowed himself to express a little excitement.

'It would be an unutterable blessing to see her again,' he said. 'And you'll accompany me?'

I smiled. 'OK.'

PAUL READ HIS PAPER that evening, on the concept of philosophical friendship, and it went down well. And then Hans Bosch gave his talk, more a collection of his ideas than a scholarly presentation. He was a small, energetic man, well into his seventies, and seemed delighted to have been invited to the conference. He talked about the quality of love in friendship, the way that in cultures other than our own – in which romantic love has taken on the mantle of passionate love – it is love for friends that is regarded as the highest affection.

His manner burst with glee. I approached him in the bar that evening, inserting myself between the suited elders who orbited his fame.

'They have even said,' he was saying to someone, 'that Achilles's love for Patroclus is homosexual, reading into it the later tradition of Greek love. But this is not said in the *Iliad*, it is not written there. It was friendship! It was love!'

'Professor Bosch, I have something to give you,' I said.

'What is this?' he said, grasping the proffered dissertation.

'It's my critical reading of *Love Without Illusions*,' I said. 'It's just an undergraduate thing, but I thought you might be interested.'

'Interested? Yes! Come, come, let us talk!' Professor Bosch led me by the arm, away from the satellites to an empty table and, sipping his lager, made me tell him exactly what I had written.

'Yes! This is good, very good!' he said, as I told him how my reading of Plato had led me to doubt that falling in love was in fact an illusion, and could be experienced as a route to a kind of blessedness. 'But what is your experience? Have you known this route?'

'A bit,' I said, and then told him how, once Charlotte and I had got together, that sense of blessedness had faded away. 'It's as if the reality of getting to know someone makes it less possible to experience them as a window onto the divine.'

'Yes!' exclaimed Herr Bosch. 'Let us not think that the illusions are useful for being in a real relationship.'

'But falling in love isn't just an illusion, that's what Plato meant,' I said.

'To think that sexual love will make you happy, that is an illusion.'

'But that's so black and white!'

'I am a black and white person!' he said. 'I want to help people to be happy and to avoid being unhappy. So I tell them what I think about love! But love is not so simple, eh? There are some grey areas, you are thinking.'

'It's more that falling in love isn't only an illusion.'

'No! The illusion is thinking falling in love will make you happy.'

'But it's only an illusion if you think it's about sexual love.'

'So you do not think when you are in love that you would like sexual love?'

'No, but –'

'There is passion for sexual love, yes?'

'Of course, but it is possible to choose not simply to follow one's passion.'

'Good!' said Bosch. 'You did not stupidly follow your passions as if to do so would make you happy.'

'Well, in the end I did, but I didn't think that would make me happy.'

'But this was doubly stupid!' exclaimed Bosch. 'To have the illusion of being in love, and then to follow the passion but not in order to make you happy! If you acted stupidly, that is why you are unhappy!'

'I am not unhappy!'

'Yes, yes. But you are stupid. You forget what I have written. The act of will! There must be love as an act! Not a passion. A passion is what moves us, like a tree blown in the wind. But what is the wind? It is the body, it is the mind. There is always the wind of the passions, blowing. If there is no understanding, there is the stupidity of believing in these passions. If there is some understanding, then there is love as an act of will, there are decisions made by the intelligence. Happiness comes from creating our own destiny, despite these winds of fate and passion.'

'But happiness can't come from repressing your emotions, or from not following your feelings just because you're scared of what might happen.'

'STUPID!' shouted Bosch. 'Nothing good comes from repression! Nothing good comes from cowardly fear! But if you expect that happiness will come from believing in your emotions, you will have to come to me for expensive therapy many times!'

By this point Bosch was almost spilling his lager.

'What is this, Hans?' said an attractive woman in her forties, approaching him from behind, holding a wine glass. 'Are you lecturing people again?'

'No, Matilda, this young man and I were simply discussing some fine points regarding my book on love. She is my wife,' Bosch explained.

I stood to greet her. 'No,' said Matilda; 'please carry on with your discussion.'

'He and I were addressing whether there must be passion for there to be love,' said Bosch benignly.

'There must be love for the passion to be loving,' said Matilda, placing a hand on her husband's shoulder.

'Yes!' Bosch said, but quite gently. 'Love as directed benevolent concern. When there is concern, the passions and emotions are very beautiful.'

'But still illusions, I suppose,' I said.

'Not so much illusions,' he said. 'There is understanding. There is the correct seeing of passions.'

'The leaves of the tree rustling in the soft breezes,' said Matilda, stroking Hans's bald head.

'Professor Bosch,' said a suited elder, breaking in. 'May I introduce you to Clara Fitzsimmons? She has been working on a feminist philosophy of friendship.'

Bosch's attention moved on, and I slipped away from the table as new talk swirled around above my head.

PAUL AND I SET OFF south next day. Rosemary had been delighted to hear from him, and invited us to her home in a North Somerset village. We drove twenty miles, for the last five twisting and turning on small lanes, examining cast-iron road signs at ash-straddled intersections. We reached Chilcombe at three. Pond Cottage was a long, red sandstone house with a sign saying '1692'. The front porch was arched with yellow roses. We walked a flagged path between lawns strewn with balls, a plastic tractor and nets. The door was opened by a woman with short hair, pale skin and near-black eyes; her straight nose and thin lips setting off a beaming oval face. She seemed both young and old, still youthful, yet lined with motherhood and life.

'Paul!' she said, delighted, arms outstretched. She kissed both his cheeks. He smiled, speechless, clogged. I knew everything would be well. We followed her through the dark, cool hallway to a kitchen at the back, a light, open new extension. She wore a cream and red cotton dress, pleated, buttoned, home sewn. Her figure was womanly; I thought of Beth.

'Rosemary, this is my friend Juniper,' Paul said.

'Nice to meet you,' she said, shaking my hand. 'And how was your conference?'

'A great success,' I said.

A man came in the back and took off his wellies.

'Afternoon,' he said. He looked us up and down, nodding. 'Kids is up Borden's,' he said to his wife; 'ferretin'.' He walked past us and into the house.

'Damned ferrets,' she said, when he'd gone. 'Are you ready for tea, gentlemen?' She produced hot scones, with butter, fresh strawberry jam and clotted cream. She poured tea into bone china cups of great age. I felt glad we'd come. Paul was looking around him, taking everything in. The place had the busy look of children at home.

'How many children have you?' he asked.

'Just the two,' she said. 'Ben's seven and Kelly's six.'

'And Fred's the man to whom you were engaged through your degree?'

'The same,' she said, in a soft, singsong voice both a little sad and quite content. 'He was a farmhand along the road; I was brought up on a farm in the next village, and I met him when he came to help with the baling. Childhood sweethearts. I teach at the school here now, part-time.'

'These scones are fantastic,' I said. 'And did you make the jam?'

'Thank you, and yes,' she said. Fred came back in, capless.

'Would you show me your garden?' I asked him. I'd glimpsed it through the window.

'You'm a gardener?'

'My father's a farmer,' I said. 'I work a kind of smallholding.' I enjoyed saying that, even though it wasn't true any more.

'Come on,' he said, and we pottered out the back door. The garden was long, extending down a south-facing slope towards a spring-fed pond in a field.

'Do you come from round here?' I asked him.

'My mother were born in this 'ouse,' he said blandly. ''Er mother were born 'ere an' all. I were born in 'ospital, but I ain't gone far since. Here's what I wanted to show 'ee.' He pointed to a chaotic-looking vegetable garden, where green shoots and bushy leaves tumbled all together amid fruit trees. 'It's a forest garden. You've heard o' "permaculture" I s'pose?'

'No,' I said. 'Tell me about it.'

'There's no diggin', no weedin'; it's all about watchin' and usin' yer noodle. You'm been at university, eh? So you must 'ave a gert noodle on 'ee,' he said, smiling slightly.

I nodded. He showed me his whole garden. The family was self-sufficient in vegetables for six months of the year, and a whole system of intelligent design elements meant that little work was needed now the garden was set up. I'd been looking for this kind of integrated approach for years. I felt myself filling with excitement as we talked.

'I'll give 'ee a book,' he said, as we headed indoors. In the kitchen, Paul and Rosemary were sitting together, holding hands on the thick elm table. Paul looked awkward and happy, like a boy, and glanced nervously at Fred.

'Look at they lovebirds!' he said to me. 'Doan you listen to all o' what she says of I!' he growled at Paul.

'Get on, Fred,' she said. 'He knows I love you.'

Paul grinned sheepishly. Fred and I went into the room on the left of the front door. Afternoon sunshine fell on the three-foot-wide windowsill and bathed the low room in sparkling quietude. There was a small oak desk with a Captain's chair, a glass-fronted oak cupboard full of books and a horsehair sofa opposite. A rug covered the uneven floor.

'We don't let no kids in 'ere,' he said. I saw a collected edition of Thomas Hardy bound in blue and many books of poetry. 'All they's Rosie's. An' 'ere's the one I were tellin' you 'bout.' He pulled down an introduction to permaculture from a shelf of well-read gardening books. 'It's a gift from I. Pass it on to one of your mates when you've read it.'

Fred and I sat in the study and talked farming. He was no longer a farmhand; he was now an agricultural contract worker, moving between farms as needed. It was an ill-paid, precarious existence, and he wanted to buy a farm of his own to convert to organic methods. It was exciting talk, until the children arrived home in a rush of noise. They hadn't managed to catch any rabbits. We joined them and Rosie and Paul in the kitchen. Paul and I left at six. We had a long drive north ahead.

'I WAS IN LOVE WITH YOU for years, I told her. I know, she said.' Paul and I were at a service station just north of Birmingham. I poured tea into chunky, functional cups, from a steel pot that dripped onto the plastic tray. 'Juniper, I was able to say something significant, and it was received; I feel returned to myself!'

'Congratulations,' I said, passing him a cup and a rolled cigarette.

'Why are we so afraid of our emotions?' he went on. 'Why so bent on the contortions of pretence? She said, it was written all over you; but all the time I convinced myself it was an irrational passion that was best kept safely suppressed.'

'Perhaps that was all you could do at the time,' I said.

'No!' he said vehemently. 'She said, I missed you terribly when you didn't stay in touch. She had no choice but to marry and live in Chilcombe with Fred, but she says she was in love also with me. We could have been friends. Those wasted years!'

'What do you mean, she had no choice?'

'She had promised herself to Fred and she meant to keep her word,' said Paul. 'Besides, her heart is in that corner of Somerset. You'd have to know her better to know quite what I mean. She never pretended to be an ordinary student, from a socially mobile middle class.'

'I know exactly what she means,' I retorted.

'Perhaps you do,' he laughed, and then paused. 'Yet there was an adventuring part of her that was in love with me. And when we lost touch, that broader view was hard pressed.'

'But wouldn't Fred have minded if you'd stayed so close?'

'You heard him this afternoon. One cannot make assumptions about such people. Besides, our love was never quite sexually charged. It was sexual, of course, but in a Platonic sense. And yet, the point is not so much to side with one's tendency to suppress emotion, but to expand awareness, even sensibility, to hold all that one feels.'

'That sounds familiar,' I said.

'By choosing,' he continued, 'to ignore rather than to hold those feelings for Rosemary – through naivety, conditioning, lack of support – I lost the capacity to feel very much at all. Juniper, we walked in the garden. She showed me her spiral of herbs. She took up sprigs and pressed them into my hands and face, and I began to cry, to cry; I haven't cried for years! She held my head against her shoulder. The current of feeling reconnected once more. I feel alive! The wrens in the back hedges – did you hear them?'

'I did.'

'They shouted – we are alive, we have a place in the world!'

'And have you?'

'I have regained a certain faith.'

We sat in silence, smoking and drinking our tea. Around us tired businessmen in shirts, jackets over the backs of their plastic chairs, ate dinner; children ran back and forth to the flashing lights of the games machines; an emaciated teenager cleared tables; and from outside came the continuous roar of the M6.

'I suspect,' I said, having poured more tea, 'that realistically it would have been difficult for you and her to have stayed in contact when you were a mass of mutual adoration.'

He laughed. 'I expect you're right. Today's release illuminates so much lost opportunity that I speak without clear thought. And you are right in that the sexual element would have been impossibly difficult to manage. It takes some experience to know quite how to ride one's body's waves.'

For the rest of the journey north we barely talked. I dozed, and a certain thought unwound itself in my mind, in the light of Paul's opening-out of feeling.

'How do things go with Charlotte?' asked Paul, as if reading my mind, as we approached the Greyston junction. We hadn't spoken directly about her during the trip.

'It's difficult to say,' I said. 'It's pretty clear to both of us that we're in a relationship on the rebound from each of our own disappointments, which is not exactly a brilliant start to a lifelong intimacy.'

'Which, however, you'd still like, presumably.'

'I don't even know that.' I looked across at Paul, who had creased his forehead, as if frustrated by what I'd said. 'Have you still got feelings towards her in that way?'

'Yes,' he said, directly; I looked over again, and his face wore a determined expression.

I didn't think for a minute that Paul was going to persuade Charlotte from me; but, still, I found myself slightly regretting having expressed to him my mixed feelings about her.

IF I HAD NOT SUCCUMBED to physical desire, would I have preserved a passionate adoration for Charlotte? On one side of this purely speculative question lay Toby's asceticism, on the other, Paul's long repressive restraint. In between those extremes, Charlotte and I didn't cease sleeping together, while continuing to fail to become a couple.

When I got back to Lyndhurst, Charlotte had stayed up to welcome me back, and then we went to bed, holding each other in the spring night. But over the following few days of living together, the situation rekindled my ambivalence. When I sat in my room to read, she seemed to feel obliged to come in and sit with me; when she stayed in her own room, she felt that I was ignoring her. Living with Ros hadn't been like this.

'I've never lived with a boyfriend; it's really hard,' she said one day as we greeted each other a bit stiffly in the kitchen, in the midst of our working days.

'Just be yourself,' I suggested.

'The thing is,' she said, 'I'm here because you're here, right? It's not because of a conscious decision to live together as a couple; it's more like we started sleeping together once I'd moved in.'

'That's right,' I said. 'So it's no big deal.'

'It's just not working,' she said and, over tea and cigarettes, we went on banging words into walls until the feelings dropped out. I had to admit that I found our relationship strange, half-lovely but half like a marriage that I wasn't interested in. She admitted that she found herself making demands on my time and space that she didn't necessarily want, but which she felt impelled to make, to test my interest in her.

'And it's not long until you see Ros again, and I don't know what'll happen.'

'And nor do I,' I said, impatiently. 'So let's not speculate.'

'That's all right for you, but it'll be me who's left high and dry if you leave.'

'Look, it won't happen like that,' I said, but I couldn't prove it, and she didn't believe me.

'I've decided I'm going to leave,' she said, a couple of days later.

'OK,' I said.

'You don't really care, do you?'

This was an entirely rhetorical question, and I hated that, the way that I was supposed vehemently to disagree. In a flash, I saw how, woman-wise, she was trying to keep a frail roof over her head called 'boyfriend'. Something burst in me, that holding back that a man feels when relating to a woman, the gentleness that he doesn't have to have with his male friends. It reminded me of my ritual on the men's weekend, the feeling of holding up that notched old sword.

'Just tell me your fucking plan.'

'I'm going to India,' she said, apparently unaware of the shift in my attitude. 'I'm going back to the house in Delhi for the summer, to write my dissertation and have a break.'

'But what about me?' I said.

183

'You can sod off,' she replied, and we laughed together for a minute, then she cried. I felt sad.

'When will you go?'

'I don't know,' she shrugged. 'But soon. It's out of season, so it should be easy enough to get a flight.'

Her plan had the obvious effect of making it less relevant what happened when I saw Ros, and with that there seemed no need for us to curtail any physical enthusiasm.

'What about Paul?' I asked her once, leaning on my elbow after we'd made love.

'What about him?' she said, lifting her eyebrows, still stroking my face. 'He's my friend; we talk about philosophy.' She looked at me for some time, thinking.

'I think he'd be quite into having a relationship with you.'

'Really?' she said, holding my cheek, her leg on mine. Her eyes had widened as if caught by surprise.

'I wondered what you thought.'

She laughed. 'Well, thanks for telling me, but I don't think so.'

'Why did you look so interested when I mentioned it, then?'

We both smiled. Those weeks were an exquisite time; this, I thought, this peculiar passion, this on-the-rebound, sex-and-friendship affair with a sweet little avid-eyed tough-nut philosopher: maybe this is a mature and human love.

at the solstice

MATT AND CHRIS HELD A PARTY at the solstice. They didn't have many mates, so they'd encouraged Charlotte and me to invite our friends. Tim and Brian came up from London before the party; the next day we planned to drive north for our men's weekend. They arrived in the afternoon, and then Tim went up to Silverthwaite to visit Ros.

Brian, Charlotte and I helped Matt and Chris with their preparations. Brian and I went down to the salt marsh to collect driftwood from along the sea defence, loading up rucksacks and walking back with high, unsteady loads of faggots, bent over like medieval peasants. Back at Lyndhurst, we cracked and sawed the wood ready for a bonfire in a pit I'd dug in the middle of the lawn. Charlotte, meanwhile, was in charge of the mulled wine, and helped Matt and Chris clear out the kitchen to make a drinks and dancing spot.

At seven-thirty Jim and Beth arrived, walking through the back gate and into the garden without bothering to announce themselves at the front door. I hadn't seen Jim for a while; maybe he was still keeping his distance, or perhaps he was just absorbed in Beth. I was surprised he'd come, given how he'd been treated by Matt and Chris.

'I'd best go and say hello to them,' he said, and went upstairs.

Beth and I hugged, and I kissed her on one bonny cheek. Beth's face was a little lined, but she looked happy. Charlotte gave her a paper cup of mulled wine.

'So, how's it going with your philosopher-knight?' Charlotte asked.

'Well enough,' said Beth.

'Enough for what?' I asked.

'Enough for your big nose,' she retorted.

'Oh, come on,' I said. 'Until recently, Jim was a well-known bachelor and doubter of the virtues of intimacy with women, so we have a reasonable curiosity about how it's going between you.'

'I'm working on him,' said Beth. 'The first night he came he said, I don't want you trying to get me to father your babies, you hear? That was after our first snog. So I said, OK, you can sleep on the sofa. And he did – for a week. It's a horrible sofa too.'

'I gave you that,' I said.

'It was out of a bloody skip,' said Beth. 'But I went back on the pill and told him, all right, you can sleep in the bed.'

'You call that working on him?' said Charlotte.

'Hang on,' said Beth. 'I got my own back. I left the MOT certificate for my car out, accidentally like, with a cheque for the garage for £150. He took one look at that and said, you're not going to pay that for an oil change and filter replacement, are you? I said, well, what choice do I – a *woman* – have? And he said, look, I'll do it for you for the price of the parts. And I said, oh would you? And he went all manly and decisive and said, piece of cake.'

'One-all then,' I said.

'I'm feeling cold and my cardigan's upstairs,' said Charlotte, wrapping her arms around her shoulders and looking up at me.

'In your room?' I asked, ready to go and fetch it.

'It's so easy, isn't it?' she said to Beth, relaxing, and they laughed. I put my arm around Charlotte and squeezed her. Jim came downstairs, brandishing a long white spliff.

'Beth's been telling us that you make her iron your underpants,' I said.

'And I've been servicing her bloody car,' he said, looking at Beth, but she was looking at the floor.

'Let's leave these old bores together, shall we?' Beth said to Charlotte, and escorted her out into the garden.

'So Matt and Chris and I are back on speaking terms,' Jim mused, twirling the spliff between his fingers. 'They gave me this as thanks for clearing out so quickly when I'd been busted.'

'And you've forgiven them because you've ended up with a buxom lass who seems to care for you a lot.'

'Who also happens to be your cousin. Seems like I can't get away from you.'

'Give me a hug, you unsociable bastard. It's good to see you here.'

We talked while I did the mulled wine duty, which Charlotte appeared to have abandoned. Jim had been hard at work on writing a paper on ethics, which argued that power and goodness were not incompatible; that strength and the exercise of mastery can be informed by the desire for truth.

'Once Ashoka, an emperor of ancient India, had conquered a neighbouring country, he became disgusted with the carnage and suffering he'd caused,' he said. 'He converted to Buddhism, and reorganised his empire in accordance with the principles of non-violence and tolerance. It was very successful.'

'So maybe his conversion was just a way to consolidate his power and doesn't indicate real goodness at all.'

'That's just what I thought you'd say,' Jim scoffed. 'But is goodness any more than what goodness does? Your objection is the classic cynicism of your rationalist nihilism: you can't believe in something without hearing *reasons*, even when reasons can only be given after the event. If you'd asked Ashoka why he'd stopped wanting to kill his enemies or eat so much meat at his banquets, he'd give you his reasons, but they don't explain the change at all.'

'And you've become a husband,' I said.

'Don't talk like a bloody fool,' said Jim.

OUT IN THE GARDEN, Brian was sitting cross-legged near the bonfire, tending it and telling people to be careful. Jim took him a cup of mulled wine, while I joined Beth and Charlotte. Kate arrived with her boys, who ran up to Beth, shouting. Beth picked up the smaller one and held him fondly at her waist. Kate kissed me on the cheek and shook hands with Charlotte. The boys ran shouting around the fire, thoroughly excited, until Brian told them to stop. They ran back to their mother, who gathered them into her legs.

'Good evening,' said Jim to Kate, having walked over from the fire to stand behind Beth. His hands rested on her shoulders, and she lifted her hands up to hold his.

'Hello, I'm Kate. I suppose you're Beth's Jim?'

'Aye. And are these your two lads?'

'Yes,' said Kate, lining them up in front of her and fussing over their hair. They looked way up at Jim. 'This is Wilfred and this is Bede. Say hello, boys.'

'Hello, Beth's Jim,' they chorused.

'Sounds like they've got you sussed out,' sniggered Beth, putting her arms behind her and squeezing him.

Perhaps the sight of Jim and Beth apparently having so comfortably paired off had an effect on Charlotte also; she put her arm around my waist, and as we talked with Kate, Jim and Beth, she and I attached ourselves to each other in that public physical way which couples have. Kate looked at Charlotte and me.

'Are you –' she said, extending her finger towards us and moving it rapidly from each to each, 'together?'

Charlotte looked up at me. She said 'not really' at the same time as I said 'sort of,' after which she said 'well, sort of,' at the same time as I said 'for the moment.' Kate looked at us perplexedly.

'Yeah, what's going on, then?' asked Beth. Jim looked at me intently, with a slight smile.

'We –' began Charlotte, then looked up at me again.

'We're just fucking,' I said.

There was a silence. Beth started to snigger, but Jim pressed his hands on her shoulders to stop her. Kate's face was trying to figure out what I had said.

'Yes, that's it,' said Charlotte. 'We're just fucking. I like that.'

'They're talking in terms of a philosophical relationship,' added Jim, and this time Beth turned her head quizzically to look at him. 'Their minds meet at one level, characterised by intellectual objectivity, while their bodies meet at the bodily level of spontaneous lust.'

'Yes, I see,' said Kate, nodding interestedly, and glancing at me.

'Bollocks,' said Beth.

'And brains,' said Jim, still maintaining a straight face. 'Bollocks and brains, in their respective places.'

Charlotte started laughing first, and then we all started. Kate looked bemused, but smiled. Charlotte let go of me, but we kept on laughing.

IT MUST HAVE MADE a pretty scene: Jim and Beth, Kate, myself and Charlotte, laughing together, with Wilfred and Bede scampering around Kate's feet, with the bonfire to one side and, behind us, the evening sunshine coming out from beneath a northern cloud. And this was how Ros saw us as she came out into the garden with Tim. I happened to look over as we laughed. Tim was smiling; Ros looked grim. I didn't recognise her at first; she'd also cut her hair short. She wore tennis shoes and a cream sleeveless cotton dress with small orange flowers. It was one of her smart dresses, and I knew that it had a bronze-coloured plastic zip at the back, running down from the plain collar.

What struck me, at first sight of her after six months, was her height. She was of course taller than Charlotte, but also taller than Beth or Kate – about five-nine. Somehow I'd forgotten that. Tim's attention had been diverted to Brian, towards whom he was now walking, so Ros was alone, walking slowly towards a close group of friends who were laughing together. Beth made some comment towards Jim, and Charlotte made a general one that made everyone laugh again. I was feeling an intense awareness of Ros, slowly walking towards us. Charlotte put her arm around me again, and Ros watched while she kept walking. Our eyes met and I smiled, awkwardly aware of Charlotte's arm. My first response at seeing her was pleasure. She lifted her eyebrows, her sandy-coloured, thick eyebrows, slightly, and then looked away. She walked around Jim and broke into our group between Beth and Kate.

'Hello Ros!' said Beth, moving her weight forward and away from Jim. 'I didn't expect you to be here.'

'Nor did I,' she said, looking at me briefly. 'But Tim persuaded me.'

'Hello again,' said Kate to Ros, nodding. 'I met you at the monastery, remember?'

'Yes,' said Ros. 'Hello Jim.'

'Good evening,' he said, soberly.

'I'm Charlotte,' said Charlotte, smiling and reaching out her hand. She hadn't realised who Ros was.

'Hmm,' she said, shaking Charlotte's hand briefly.

'So are you two going to get back together again now?' asked Kate, looking between Ros and me, and smiling. I think this was supposed to be funny.

'Oh shit,' said Beth, turning away and hiding in Jim's stomach.

'It's *that* Ros,' said Charlotte, looking up at me, then back at Ros. 'I really like your teapot and plates. Can I get you some mulled wine?'

'That would be kind,' Ros replied.

Charlotte detached herself from me and headed off inside. Tim came over to our group.

'I thought Ros might like to come to the party, so I invited her,' he said, in my direction. I nodded. 'I hope you don't mind,' said Tim to me, quietly. Ros was determinedly talking to Beth.

'Was this really your idea?' I asked him.

'Yes,' he said, grinning. 'It's exactly six months since the winter solstice, so technically you're allowed to speak to each other again.'

'You could have warned me.'

'What difference would it have made?'

'We need to be able to speak privately, not like this.'

'There'll be a chance.'

'Did she want to come?'

'No, she was terrified.'

'Why did she come, then?'

'Well, talk to her and find out.'

Charlotte was taking a long time fetching the drinks. Tim turned to Jim, and Ros slipped around Kate to stand near me.

'Hello,' she said.

'You cut all your hair off,' I said, remembering the green of her eyes.

'You look *so* different with short hair, Juniper.'

'I think my nose sticks out more.'

'Is this your new girlfriend, then?' Charlotte was walking towards us, looking down at three cups of drink.

'Sort of,' I said.

'Meaning what exactly?'

I didn't want to say any more because Charlotte had reached us. Ros and I took a cup each.

'Are you a student?' asked Ros.

'Another philosopher,' said Charlotte, looking up at me. 'It's been very stimulating meeting these two.' She gestured towards Jim.

'Don't you find all that heady stuff a bit – uh – *male*?' said Ros, half-smiling.

'Not in essence, no,' said Charlotte, examining Ros's expression. 'You can't be suggesting that only men can think.'

'No, of course not. But the philosophers are all *men*; they're all so *out of it*,' said Ros.

'It doesn't bother me,' said Charlotte. 'Philosophy's about the search for the truth, which isn't the prerogative of men.'

Ros shrugged.

'But there are a lot of patriarchal assumptions in the philosophical tradition, just because most of the philosophers have been men,' I offered.

'Define them,' said Charlotte.

'You know, the whole way that a disembodied concept of reason, which is, like Ros said, a bit male, is taken to be the most important human capacity.'

'Disembodied, that's the word,' said Ros. 'Not *lived*.'

'But that's just so vague,' said Charlotte scathingly. 'And even if some concepts of reason – don't you just mean Cartesian dualism? – are disembodied, that doesn't mean they're patriarchal.'

'No, but –' I said, but my thinking wandered.

'What's the alternative, then?' Ros asked me.

'To disembodied rationality? Well, I suppose a thinking that starts from the realities of the body and its desires, for a start.'

'That sounds interesting,' said Ros.

'Interesting? It sounds like the philosophy of Foucault, which is really up it's own ass,' retorted Charlotte.

'Well, it sounds more interesting to me,' Ros said firmly.

'You'd probably find it just as heady, Ros,' I said. 'You just aren't into philosophy.'

'I don't know; I've been reading some environmental philosophy recently,' she said. 'It doesn't strike me as being up in the head, like the stuff you read. It's *about* something, it's practical.'

There was a weird sense of everything that was unsaid and shifting beneath the conversation as we talked; we must all have been aware of it. But it was like that first time that Paul and I talked, when politeness and civility controlled the deeper instinctual forces we felt. Charlotte put her arm around me again, leaving Ros looking on uncomfortably. It had been obvious that, although Ros had been sizing her up, Charlotte didn't have anything she needed to prove. She was about to say something, but instead suddenly tightened her arm.

'*Shit*,' she hissed. 'Toby!' Ros looked at her, then over towards the back door of the house. We saw an anxious-looking Toby walking into the garden, followed by Paul. Paul waved at us all. As Toby looked over and saw Jim, he froze. Paul put his arm around Toby's shoulders and propelled him towards us, still smiling.

'Good evening, all,' he said. 'I happened to meet young Toby in town as I was making my way here. So I brought him along.' The lack of a causal relationship between these statements precluded a reply, and I wondered at Paul's mischievousness.

'He-he-hello,' said Toby, generally. Charlotte was hiding herself behind me. Of course, Toby had come to talk to Charlotte, and Paul was in some sense helping him. I trusted Paul, so I stepped away from Charlotte, leaving her exposed. She dashed over to Jim and hid behind him.

'*Tell him to go away!*' she said.

'What's happening?' asked Kate.

'It's her ex,' I said.

'He looks harmless enough to me,' said Ros.

'You don't know what he's like,' said Charlotte.

'Don't be ridiculous, Charlotte,' said Toby. 'You can't just hide. It's insane.'

'If she doesn't want to speak to you, she doesn't have to,' said Beth. 'You should leave her alone.'

'But that isn't what it's like,' said Toby. 'You ask Paul.'

'Come on, Charlotte,' said Paul. 'You know you have to face up to things.'

'No, I don't,' she wailed.

'Why not?' said Paul.

'I don't want to!'

'Oh, stop it, Charlotte,' said Toby. 'There's no need for all this. Just look at me.'

Jim looked at Paul, and Paul nodded. Jim stepped aside, leaving Charlotte nowhere to hide, so she rushed behind Kate and Beth. Beth looked appalled.

Toby stepped towards Charlotte, but she pushed Beth and Kate between them. Toby reached out, Charlotte ducked down, holding onto clothing, Kate tripped up, and then the women all fell down, with Charlotte underneath Beth. Toby, eager to get hold of Charlotte, moved forward and stepped on Beth's hand, and she cried out.

'Heh,' said Jim, stepping forward and picking Toby up by the arms. Toby, taking Jim to be the old enemy, lashed out. Jim put him down and, keeping his hands around his face, just let Toby hit him, but now Charlotte stepped in, shouting 'Stop it! Stop it!' and flailing out towards Toby.

By this time, everyone in the garden had stopped talking and was watching. Charlotte and Toby, becoming aware of the attention focused on them, calmed down and stood panting together.

'Are you all right?' Jim asked Beth, who was nursing her hand.

'Yeah,' she said.

'And are you OK, Toby?' said Jim, concernedly.

'Oh yes, fine. Sorry,' he said.

'Now tell her, tell us all,' said Paul.

'She stabbed me,' said Toby. 'Here, in my arm. And in my leg. With scissors.' He pulled up his sleeve and showed us little wounds. Then he pulled out a small pair of chromed steel paper scissors and held them up. 'I wasn't hurt badly, but it was horrible. I don't want to tell the police, I just want to talk to her about what happened.' He gave the scissors to Charlotte, and then burst into tears. Paul stepped over and put his arm around him.

'It's done,' he said. 'You did it.'

Charlotte looked around, her face contorted with fear, and ran into the house.

Jim limped over to me. 'You remember when we frightened him away?' he said. 'But we both felt somehow that we'd acted like Charlotte's bullies?'

'This was what we didn't know.'

'Interesting new woman, Juniper,' added Ros.

'Who are you to take the moral high ground?' asked Jim.

Ros looked angry, but then looked down at the ground, her eyes closed. I felt a lot of gratitude to Jim in that moment; he'd opened up the wound just where it needed proper healing.

'Ros,' I said. 'I'd better go and check what Charlotte's doing with those scissors. But don't go; we can talk later.'

'All right,' she said.

I left the garden for the kitchen, now candlelit and pulsing with talk and music. I made my way around people and through the sweet smoke, towards the stairs.

CHARLOTTE WAS SITTING cross-legged in the middle of her bed, her hair falling down around her face.

'That was *not* pleasant,' she said. I sat down on the end of the bed.

'Public humiliation,' I said.

'How could Paul have done that to me?'

'Because he regards you very highly and because he feels let down. You know how high his standards are.'

'And do you?'

'I do feel surprised.'

'I'm sorry. I'm really, really sorry.'

'Look, it's Toby you should say that to.'

'No, for asking you to keep him away from me.'

'Were you scared you'd try to kill him?'

'No, of course not. I just didn't want to face what had happened.'

'Was it after we came back from Leeds?'

'Yes. Yes.' She leaned over, put her arms around me and cried, the strong, racking tears of pent-up feelings releasing. I just held her and developed an eager erection. Nothing like a beautiful, highly vulnerable woman in one's arms to stimulate the worst in a man, I thought.

'I got back to Paradise Hill,' said Charlotte miserably; 'and he and Julia told me what they'd been up to, but a week later he and I actually slept together. He was already having second thoughts, I suppose, and the situation made me act out of desperation. Then he got up in the night, to go to the loo I expect, but he didn't come back, so I went to find him. And I looked in Julia's room, and he was in her bed. I lost my cool completely. I grabbed a pair of scissors and started attacking him. Julia was screaming, and there was blood all over the bed. I stopped when I saw how frightened he looked. What do you think of that?' She looked up at me suddenly. It was hard to take it all seriously.

'Toby's a man of extremes.'

'That was all that happened really. In the morning, he went to the doctor's and got bandaged and had a tetanus.'

'What did he tell them?'

'I don't know. He said they didn't ask. So then you arrived that day, once he'd gone home.'

'Why does he want so much to talk to you then?'

'Because he feels bad about how he acted, I expect.'

'Why don't you want to talk to him?'

'Don't you see, Juniper? I still love him, that's the problem. But he drives me mad and makes me hate myself. That's why I ran away.'

'From your irrational passions.'

'I know, I know. It's so embarrassing; no wonder Paul's disappointed.'

'You have to get to grips with your feelings, though, even if they're crazy. You could have killed Toby.'

'Fuck,' said Charlotte. 'All I want to do is get on with my work.'

'You have to learn to deal with things,' I said. 'I have to deal with Ros being here.'

'Oh yes, you'd better. I'll go down and talk to Toby then.'

I admired her courage. Together, Charlotte and I walked slowly down to the stairs towards the garden, me helping her along. Before we went outside, she kissed me.

'Thanks, Juniper,' she said. I felt that erection again.

IT WAS MIDNIGHT before Ros and I sat down together by the fire. The driftwood that Brian and I had collected burned well. Brian had been tending the flames assiduously, so that there was now a heap of embers that would glow for hours. The evening was cool and dry, and the wind had died away. Kate and the boys had gone home an hour before, and Beth and Jim had just left. The party was thinning out, leaving a core of talking and dancing that I suspected would last a long time yet.

Ros sat on her heels and had her hands between her knees. Across the fire, Paul sat between Charlotte and Toby. Charlotte was talking, but I couldn't hear her words above the fire's crackle and the background music and voices. Toby was throwing small twigs into the fire, but listening.

'So that's your supervisor, is it?' asked Ros.

'Yes,' I said. 'It was impressive, wasn't it, how he acted with Toby?'

Ros shrugged. 'I'd wondered what he was like.'

'How's the pottery going?'

'I expect you've heard that it's got very busy. In fact, I've hardly had a *minute* to think about children and all that.'

'No? That's a surprise. And where are you at with Harry?'

'Oh, Harry. He still helps in the garden. But we weren't, you know, *together*, for long.'

'So why have you changed the lock on the back door?'

'What?' said Ros. 'How do you know about that?'

'I wanted to show Jagaro the house. Mother said that you were out. But I couldn't.'

'You were going to show someone around without asking me?'

'It's not your house.'

'It's my *home*, Juniper.'

'I didn't think you'd mind. I know you've met Jagaro.'

'I'm *shocked*,' said Ros, shaking her head.

'You shouldn't have changed the lock without telling me, that's all.'

'Well I didn't know you would want to come round, did I?'

'That's true,' I said. 'But why are you keeping me out of the house? What if I want to come back?'

'I don't like your tone, Juniper; it's brutal. It's my home, you were happy about me staying there. I'm not keeping you out, I just didn't expect you to come round. Look, I've even brought a key for you.' She fished in the pocket of the turquoise fleece jacket that she was now wearing and passed me a key. 'There you are, so I *wasn't* trying to keep you out. Oh, you're *spoiling* everything, Juniper. I was going to give it you.'

'I didn't know what was going on,' I retorted. 'For all I knew, you could have changed the lock so you could shack up with Harry permanently.'

Ros turned her head away from me. I knew she was crying. We sat there for a while, not saying anything. Across the fire, Charlotte and

Toby were talking across Paul. My eyes met Paul's briefly. He looked a little strained.

'It didn't go very well with Harry,' said Ros, quietly.

'No?' I said.

'He got weirdly possessive after a while, so we finished, and he moved back into his flat in the village.'

'Was he, you know, bad to you?'

'No, not really. But he wanted to know where I was going and who I was seeing. Being with you was much more easy going.'

'Yes, I had a bit of that with Charlotte.'

'He knew you and I had agreed to be apart for six months, and he kept going on about what might happen after that. So I split up with him, to put him out of his misery.'

'I had that too. But do you still see him?'

'We're still friends, sort of. He's *fixated* on me, Juniper. That was why I changed the lock, just in case.'

I remembered that time when Jim had proved to Tim that I was dependent on Ros in a dog-like way. Well, I wasn't any more, but it seemed that Harry had stepped in. Perhaps something in Ros provoked it.

'So, are you going to come back to me?' said Ros, softly.

'A big question.' I decided it was the moment to roll a cigarette, fairly slowly. I took a piece of driftwood that was sticking out of the fire and lit my roll-up from the burning end. The cigarette smoke drifted between Ros and me before rushing into the fire.

'Juniper, if you don't come back, I've decided I'm going to move south again. So I need to know.'

I sucked on my cigarette. There was a coolness within that I knew was false and proud, but I didn't know what I wanted to feel. Feelings came slowly, like a stream rising during heavy rain. Fast, brown, frothy water, rushing along the wet banks.

'What do you mean, move south?'

Ros sighed. 'If you don't come back, I don't want to live at Albion Cottage any more. It's too near your parents and, as you've just made so *very* clear, it's your house too. And if I don't live there, well, I might as well move back to Totnes. There are a *lot* more potters working in Devon – there's the whole Dartington thing just outside town.'

'That's so typical. You did this when we split up. A completely safe defensive position, so there's no risk. If I don't come back, you'll do something else; you can't lose. Before, it was, if I can't promise I'll want to have children, you don't want to stay with me. No risk to *you*. But it was so fucking irritating. In fact, you'd slept with Harry, and our relationship was a mess, so it just wasn't the moment to ask whether I wanted to have kids with you. And anyway, it turns out you aren't so bothered by children –'

'That's so unfair, Juniper. I've been *busy*, which is good. And I didn't want to have a baby with just anyone; it was about *you*.'

'– and now you say I come back or you move house, but that completely ignores the fact that it was you sleeping with someone else that caused all the trouble in the first place, and even if I wanted to come back, I have to know at least that you won't do that again, that I can trust you.'

'*Rubbish*, Juniper. You know very well that you were part of it, because of your bloody ritual, and because your guru Jim told you that you were tied up with me.'

'How do you know what Jim said to me?'

'Beth told me, of course.'

'Why don't you ask *me* what I think rather than believing gossip?'

'And even if I *am* being defensive, what do you expect? That I should be all apologetic and passive, saying, oh Juniper, come back to me, I'll do anything you want?'

'No, of course not, don't be so dramatic. But there has to be room for discussion.'

'And what does that mean, apart from you being able to get things on your terms?'

'It means you not being so controlling, that's what.'

'I'm *not* being controlling, Juniper; I'm not trying to tell you what to do. All I've said is that if you *don't* come back, I'm going.'

'And that ignores the fact that before I can even think about moving back, we have to talk. Ros, you betrayed me, sleeping around like you did. You know that.'

'Look, I'm *sorry* about that, I know it was wrong, but you were so up in your head and everything. We've *talked* about all this, and you know you were as much responsible –'

'You've told me what *you* think, and I disagree. You betrayed me, Ros, and it's up to you to prove that I should want to move back with you. So don't give me your ultimatums. If you want me back, you have to be prepared to give.'

'And if I'm not?'

I shrugged, and threw the stub of my cigarette into the fire. 'I take back Albion Cottage and you do what the hell you like.'

'This is stupid. This is just stupid,' said Ros, getting up stiffly. She stood by the fire with her arms crossed. 'I've had enough; I'm going.' She turned round and walked towards the back door. I continued sitting by the fire, the spate of feelings rushing inside. I didn't feel bad. I'd said what I needed to say. What was love to do with anything? Charlotte? Ros? Even friendliness has its conditions, like truthfulness, and we were only just beginning to manage some of that. I looked over the fire, but Paul was gone. Toby and Charlotte both sat looking into the flames. Charlotte met my eyes, but didn't smile. She was wrapped up in her own drama, which was also nothing to do with love, only with pride.

Paul, Tim, Brian and Ros came back out of the back door, each holding a mug. Ros was holding two, and passed one to me.

'Tea,' she said.

'Thanks.'

The men sat down together by the fire, leaving Ros and me to talk again. I watched Charlotte watch Paul. A mist of sadness brushed coldly through my heart.

'Do you love her?' said Ros.

'I was in love with her,' I said. 'But not so much any more.'

'Good,' said Ros. 'I've missed you *so much*, Juniper. I've got something for you.' She pulled something from a pocket and passed it to me. It looked like soil wrapped in cellophane.

'What is it?'

'Our composted shit. Something to plant your thoughts in.' We laughed, and she very briefly touched my leg, then leant back on her arms.

'I want to move back to Silverthwaite, back to the lifestyle,' I said. 'I was talking with someone the other week about organic farming, and that's what I want to do.'

'What about philosophy?'

'I miss Albion Cottage. I miss living with you there.'

'Your father told me he's thinking of retiring soon. Farmer Allott from the Tower has already made him an offer on the farm, but he's told me he's going to talk to you first. Juniper, you could end up with the whole farm!'

'That's news,' I said. Excitement flashed through me, then alarm. The whole farm was a big project. Thoughts started tumbling. Fred was looking for somewhere to farm. Jagaro wanted somewhere to put his monastery, and there would be plenty of space for that. I could make a living with the caravans while I worked out what I wanted to do. I could do a course in permaculture. 'There would be room for you to have a larger studio,' I said.

'There certainly would.'

'If I moved back in with you, things wouldn't be the same,' I said. 'I still stand by my ritual at the men's weekend. I mean, I wouldn't want my roots to be so tangled up with yours.'

'But our roots would be in the same pot again, Juniper.'

'It would be different. Would you want that?'

'I don't know what you mean. We could have a go. Will you forgive me for sleeping with Harry? I know it was wrong; it goes without saying.'

'I'm going away for a few days tomorrow, with the guys. I'll think about it all while I'm away.'

'OK. I mean it, though, about moving south. I need to know.'

'All right.'

AT THREE-THIRTY, as light broke, Charlotte came to my bed. On his way home, Paul had walked Ros to Beth and Jim's place, where she'd arranged to sleep. The party wound gently down; Tim and Brian went to bed in Charlotte's room. She and I both knew that this would be the last night together. While I was up in Scotland, she would be going south to stay with her parents before flying to Delhi. In the tired early light, the moment had passed for final kisses, though nothing was said. It was like the swifts at the end of the summer, which do not stay to say goodbye.

'Will you go back to her, then?' she asked.

'Maybe,' I said. 'But we've got a lot to sort out.'

'Toby wants to fly to India to be with me there.'

'Do you want him to?'

'Yes,' she said. 'It's worth a go.'

'All the best,' I said.

'Thanks. And you. Goodnight,' she whispered, kissing my head and curling up behind me, in her shirt.

in Scotland

PAUL STOOD IN THE MIDDLE of the room on an ancient, frayed rug with his arm outstretched.

'Go on,' he was saying, 'see if you can cause it to bend.' Jim, with one hand on Paul's bicep and the other gripping his wrist, gradually increased the force of his effort.

'Look, I'm going to hurt you soon,' Jim protested.

'Please don't worry about that,' Paul said. 'Your task is simply to try to bend my arm.' Jim increased his effort, grunting. But the arm did not bend beyond a certain point. Paul's eyes were closed and his face relaxed. Jim gave up.

'You see? There is strength in the *chi*,' said Paul. 'Now you try. Stretch out your arm and hold it there, through muscle power. Now, Juniper, bend it.' I pulled on the big limb until it bent. Jim was more big than strong. 'Now, stretch it out again, but without tensing any muscles. Imagine a flow of energy along the arm – feel it. Don't tense up; just let the energy flow along your arm, right into your fingers. Now, this time, when Juniper tries to bend your arm, just concentrate your attention on the energy flow that's keeping it straight. Don't use any force; just concentrate. Juniper, don't go too quickly; increase your force slowly; give him a chance.' Jim closed his eyes. His arm buckled slightly, and then stopped. It refused to bend any more, like a thick bough of wood, no matter how hard I pulled. I let go.

'Aaee-HA!' said Jim, hand-chopping at me and grinning inanely.

It was mid-afternoon of the day after we arrived in Eskdale. We had left in the afternoon of the day before, in two cars, still tired after the solstice party. The cottage was in the middle of a short terrace and belonged to scouting friends of Brian's. I had shared a room with Jim and Paul, and slept in a soft double bed with Jim, who snored. The cottage was unrenovated, damp and cold. But in the evening we'd lit a fire in the grate with coal from the shed and spent the evening playing board games and drinking beer. We went to bed early and slept through the long Scottish dawn. In the morning, soft dew soaked the long grass and sedge in the fields outside the window.

'COME ON,' SAID BRIAN, after we had got in touch with our chi. 'Let's get over to the island.' We packed up what we needed in rucksacks and then walked. The island was wooded, about fifty yards long and twenty wide, in the middle of the fast-flowing Esk. It was reached by an inexplicable cast-iron Victorian bridge.

Brian had suggested that we stay up all night for private contemplation and ritual, something he'd done before. We could do whatever we pleased and meet again at dawn. Before night fell, though, we built a fire in a clearing, pitched a tent and unpacked drums, pans and food. Tim supervised cooking. The river rushed by all around us the whole time. We ate burgers, mash and beans, washed up, and then settled around the fire.

'What might one do?' asked Paul.

'Perhaps not talk too much,' suggested Brian. 'Follow your own inner promptings. Learn your own way.'

'All right,' said Paul, looking slightly worried nonetheless. Jim, meanwhile, rolled a large joint, and he, Paul and I smoked it while the fire settled into a hot heap. Brian scowled; he and Tim were abstaining from any kind of drug, and he didn't think it was a good idea to mix ritual and intoxication.

'Suit yourself,' said Jim. Tim had long been strict about what he put into his body, but he didn't mind what his friends did. I suspected Brian was still a rather tight kind of man. I felt slightly irritated by his presence, so went for a walk. I picked my way slowly on a path of dark brown mulch that weaved through the oak, sycamore and sprawling rhododendron, the constant rush of the river confusing my ears. At the front of the island, facing upstream, was a wall in the shape of a ship's prow. I sat and watched all that water piling towards me, hitting rocks, foaming, twirling, shouting and leaping as it made its way down. On my own on the wall, my mind fell back to the previous day, when I had said goodbye to Charlotte. It had been in a way quite perfunctory; we had both been prepared to leave.

'It'll be different not living with you,' she said, touching my hand, my arm and cheek.

'Well, come back safe and sound,' I said. She hugged me, more intimately than you would a friend, but not with the personal investment you would a lover. We kissed on the lips. Sitting by that river, I was suddenly glad about everything that we'd done, glad for every minute of our ambiguous passion, and now glad it was over; glad I'd been in love and glad I'd fallen out again – for I had fallen out of love, as earth in water slowly settles as the flood slows and drains, spreading fine silt over the landscape. Sediments of Charlotte – joys, pleasures, frustrations and a great deal of good conversation – lay on me comfortably, though the living flow of it all had ebbed away.

'I'm not sure what it'll be like with Toby now,' said Charlotte. She was holding my arms and crying a little. 'You've been –'

I held up my hand, not wanting her to continue. It was she who'd decided to leave me and go to India, and I did not now want to hear about her doubts. Adding Toby to the situation made me even less inclined to listen.

'Goodbye,' I'd said, climbing into Brian's car. She waved as we drove away, and then I saw her walk purposefully, precisely back into the house. My heart had been full of sadness on the journey up to Scotland. Some beauty was leaving my life; it was as simple as that, and it would be hard to replace it.

The light on the Esk fell slowly, but when it was so dim that the river had turned to grey and white, I turned back to the woods. I felt ready to take on this night, this ritual, these men, ready for this new, more bracing moment. I picked my way through the dimming undergrowth, following the sound of drumming back to the fire. Tim, Jim and Brian were gently beating a slow rhythm, with Paul not to be seen. I put my arms on Jim's shoulders and kissed his head. He grunted.

'I love you,' I said softly. He laughed, losing the beat. I pinched him on the chest, and he winced, tickled, and put the drum down. I pushed him backwards into the dry soft mulch of the clearing, and we wrestled, stuffing old leaves down each other's shirts, rubbing earth over faces, punching and pushing until we lay still, panting heavily, heads towards the fire.

AS DARKNESS FELL, we divided into our separate nights. I walked around the island, and then saw Brian squatting, silhouetted against the silvery running water and watched him awhile. He had a handful of pine cones and threw them one by one into the current, watching each one splash and disappear. I thought how easy it is to feel irritated by someone, or to put him into a box – tight man – and how much harder to sense the mystery of what he is, even to himself. And it is the same for every person in the world: each is the same mysterious portal into the void, each is conscious and questing, needing to know what lies out beyond the known and believed. Brian turned and, not seeing me, picked his way across the pebble river-beach and climbed back up onto the bank. He turned once and looked at the river, then walked away from me, down the path, pensive and alone.

Jim was lying on the wooden planks of the footbridge. I lay next to him. We looked up at the stars. I showed him Cassiopeia.

'What happened to Orion?' he said.

'It's a winter constellation.'

'No,' he said. 'The warrior dedicated to the truth. I'm living with a woman and enjoying it. Am I in love?'

'You'd know if you were, Jim,' I said.

'I'm afeared, Juniper. She wants me, she wants sex, she wants kids. I feel like such a bloody beginner.'

'But you wanted to live with her.'

'I want a base to work from, a home. Something more than friends' houses. I want somewhere to go out into the world from with a sense of confidence.'

'Do you think Beth loves you? Does she give you something you want?'

'Aye,' he said. 'I think so. No, I feel so. I like her nearly as much as I like you, and she's much more attractive. What scares me is the thought that I've nothing to give her.'

'Oh, Jim,' I said, laughing. 'Can't you see that, after the business with Peter, she's just pleased to find a reliable, trustworthy man? I don't think she has any more demands than that. She's pretty straightforward, always has been. Maybe that was the problem with Peter – she couldn't work out why he should be so unfaithful and perverse. She's got such a big heart, Jim; all you have to do is be yourself and stand by her. And you can always service her car if you feel like being useful.'

We lay in silence for a while. Then Jim rolled over and on top of me, grabbing me by my coat. His little eyes bored down at me from the dark of his face.

'I want you to know,' he hissed, 'that the Principle still stands.'

'It's you that hasn't wanted to see me,' I retorted.

'You've been so busy shagging I'm surprised you've noticed.'

'I'm a new man, Jim. A fuck's just a fuck. Intellectual friendship is something else.'

'Good,' he said, rolling off me and staring up at the stars again.

I left him, deep-breathing and pondering his fate. Back at the fire, I propped the kettle on fresh logs. The wavering base of the flames was murky with heat, the red so thick, so strong, that it seemed hallucinatory. Perhaps live embers are like the heart: another world at the centre of a blaze, a heat so strong its light need not shine bright, need not flicker nor flame. It radiates, without great show, sufficient to itself for meaning. I might have fallen out of love with Charlotte, but all the passion had recoiled into the heart and was waiting. It was like fire. If the night is still, if the wind in the trees has died down and you move close, you hear it: a mass of sounds like clinks and rattles, impossible sounds in the liquid red heat, like ghost-coinage, the true, invisible currency of the heart.

Sitting there, alone in the night, among friends, I knew that through Charlotte I'd learned quite a lot about fire: how to allow it to burn, how to contain its heat, how to let it warm someone. But I hadn't completely abandoned myself to its burning allure; I'd kept enough of a distance to learn a little about handling the flames. And being more informed about the heart and its fires, I had acquired a little more human freedom, a freedom from the passions that can hijack a life, a freedom to live from one's decisions, one's best thoughts.

As I pondered, the kettle came to the boil and I made a pot of tea. Paul emerged from the undergrowth with moss and dirt in his hair and quietly joined me at the fire. We drank tea together and smoked. The rough companionship of tobacco is best by a campfire, where the smoke drifts into oblivion and the little fire in your fingers is brother to the warming blaze.

'She loves me,' he whispered. 'The earth; have you smelt the ground, its perfume, the passionate odour of herbage leaking from the dark and wet of the night?'

I shook my head.

'She loves me and I have kissed her. I have drawn my hands over her mulchy, fertile body, lifted her brown clothing and outstretched myself upon her naked belly – and it is singing! My heart, like a cracked drum, is singing, wailing, railing against all the stiff silences of years. This is redemption!'

'Sounds good.'

'I am rent open, Juniper, a soft unknown song of myself. The strange feeling of wet wings in this delicate night, the breeze on new limbs trembling to touch air, every pore and nerve of me opened, the baggage of concepts shed, dumped in this kind, huge old river; I am renewed, refurbished, made whole.'

He burst into tears and wailed into the night, finally laughing, bubbling with nervous outpouring, subsiding into sighs and groans. His mind was a crazy dog's.

'Will you go back to Ros?' he said suddenly.

'I don't know yet,' I said. 'But I think Charlotte and I have finished. Is that the impression she gave at the party?'

'Yes,' he said. He burst into tears again. 'Nine years, the boy in the heart, living on water and biscuits. Suddenly, he's let out, and the world is so changed.'

'Just keep feeling,' I said. 'Did you never love Jackie at all?'

'What?' he said, looking shocked. 'Love her?'

'You know, feel strong feelings of appreciation, attraction, desire to –'

'Yes, to start with, of course,' he said. 'But after a while, well, not all that long really, I was caught in a cycle of looking for attention, getting a bit, chasing after scraps, crawling around on my knees. Love's a bit beside the point when you're with a tiger who keeps you on a lead.'

'Charlotte's got claws too, eh?'

He sighed, returning to his normal mind. 'Yes, it seems so. I dropped her in it by bringing Toby to the party, didn't I? But when I met him, and he told me his side of the story, I was so reminded of what I had felt at the hands of Jackie that I felt obliged to help him.'

'Charlotte told me that she stabbed him after she'd found him in bed with Julia.'

'Which is not untrue. But it appears that, from his perspective, she had split up with him while they were on their camping trip – to their mutual relief – so that he was free to start something with Julia should he so want. Charlotte had persuaded him against his will to go to bed with her when she returned from Leeds, and his shifting over to Julia was his way of making a statement.'

'A bit of a raw statement.'

'Certainly, though nevertheless hardly deserving of Charlotte's reward for it.'

'She said to me she regrets it.'

'One should hope so. Unfortunately, by refusing to speak to Toby about it and by not telling her friends, she has forfeited a great deal of sympathy.'

'I feel sympathetic,' I said.

'But not to her attempted denial, surely? The point is, Juniper, and I warned her of this, she is in danger of making a tyrant of reason, when she is in fact insufficiently mature thereby not to make a stronger tyrant of her desires.'

'What do you make of how Toby was with her, then? All the fasting and abstinence?'

'I believe he was considerably milder in his dedication than she was to having her own way.'

'So why on earth are they still pursuing each other?'

'Lovers live in hope, Juniper; you know that.'

'Does all this temper your affection for her, then?'

He looked at me with a pained expression, as if I had overstepped a certain limit. 'My affection has always been entirely tempered,' he said, with dignity. After a few moments he added: 'Falling in love is such a curious fire.' We both stared into the flames. 'But the essence of love is simply friendliness.' We didn't need to speak. We both contemplated the heart of the fire.

Paul wandered off again after some time, leaving me to consider what I could do with the night. I remembered my ritual from the previous men's weekend, and the way Ros and I had referred to it at the solstice party. Was Ros right? If we lived together again, would we necessarily find our roots clumped together in one pot? I left the fire and walked the path right around the island. There was Jim, doing something on the footbridge, and there were Tim and Brian, talking softly at the prow. Paul I couldn't see; perhaps he was back on his belly in the mulch. I was looking for clues. I found two trees, growing together at the back of the island, a sycamore and a beech. They were close enough to be interlocked; they must have started growing at the same time, or else one would have shaded out the other. But they weren't trapped inside the same pot; their roots were free to spread out, away from each other. I sat with those trees, getting a feel for their lives.

As first light spoiled the clean dark in the east, threatening us with bold, overpowering daylight, we moved the stones that had been baking in the fire into a flat area of clearing, then set down the dome tent over them. We sat on the ground under the nylon, naked, the zip closed. The hot stones radiated four hours of heat. I couldn't help glancing at Brian's dick, but it looked fine. Jim's hairy belly sagged down, and Paul's lean hairless torso began to sweat. Tim grinned, his brown body easily the most handsome of us all. He tipped water on the stones and hot steam surged up, scalding briefly the skin and then deep-healing us with heat. Perspiration burst out and dripped. Cold air slipped up from the ground at the base of the tent and grabbed our buttocks but got no further. finally the stones had lost their stored heat, and the water dribbled over them instead of hissing off.

'To the river!' said Tim, opening the zip and leading us through first light to the ever-rushing silver-grey. We plunged into whirling pools, whooping with cold and shock, then basking in the strong current pushing us back onto the rocks. It was dangerous and exhilarating. Even Brian, tentative at first, yelled and then sang to welcome a bright summer's day.

return

I WAS THE ONLY PERSON to step off the train at Silverthwaite station, and when the two carriages pulled away, I was alone in the quiet. Greenfinches droned in the drowsy overcast afternoon, and swathes of fireweed were beginning to burn in the scrubby woodland on the other side of the platform. I walked the two miles to Albion Cottage slowly.

Summer was draped over my home landscape like a well-worn, comfortable gown. I wandered into the garden of Albion Cottage, enjoying the click and swing of the gate. Ros's little van stood on the gravelled drive. I walked around the house and put down my rucksack. The back door was open, though there was no one in the kitchen. I found Ros in her studio. She smiled, switched off the power to the wheel, and waited for the sound and motion to calm.

'Are you visiting or home?' she asked.

'Home,' I said, looking at the racks of drying fired and glazed pottery around me.

'Hooray,' she said, putting her arms on my shoulders, her clay-grey hands stretched out behind my head. She pulled off her smock, washed her hands, and led me back to the house. The tea leaves by the sink were piled in a well-glazed but wonky bowl. On the table was a square slab vase holding white campion. We hugged for a while, saying nothing. It felt all right. I hadn't known what it would feel like.

'Did you have a good time in Scotland?' she asked, as we sat at the table.

'Yeah,' I said. 'How are things here?' I looked around at the neat kitchen.

'I cleaned up, hoping that you'd come back.'

Then Harry walked in through the back door, but stopped, shocked, when he saw me. I smiled.

'Hello, Harry,' I said. 'I'm home.' He stood, struggling for words, but then found some, as if they were on a piece of a paper in his pocket.

'After all this time, you think you can just walk in like you still belong here? You've got a nerve. What's going on, Ros?' She shrugged. I raised my hand so that she would not speak.

'Harry, could you come and visit another time? Ros and I haven't spoken for a while, and I've just arrived.'

'You must be joking,' he said, stoking up some anger. 'You think you can spend months away, while I do your work here, and then breeze back in like this?'

'I think you should shut up, Harry.'

'I think there are some things that need to be said, actually.' Harry squared up in the doorway, in wellies. I still had my walking boots on.

'I've just got back, Harry, so just piss off, will you?'

'What?' he said, his face contorting into a mask of disbelief.

'Or I'll kick you out.'

'Now hang on,' started Ros.

'Do you want me back?' I said. Harry looked at Ros. 'You said you did. Now I'm back, it's my place and I'm the man here. Harry, it's finished, so *piss off.*'

Ros tutted and looked away. There was a tense silence in the kitchen; then full-grown lambs in the fields bleating. Harry was waiting for Ros, who wouldn't meet his eye. He eventually turned and walked away. We heard the gate click shut.

'He won't go mad and try to kill me or burn down the house, will he?' I asked.

'I don't think so,' said Ros, leaning back in her chair and crossing her arms. 'But you weren't exactly diplomatic.'

'I had to make things clear.'

'But he's spent such a lot of time helping here.'

'He was wearing my wellies.'

Ros laughed. 'Shit, you're right. He never asked.'

I looked around the kitchen, at the low-beamed ceiling, the range, the quarry-tiled floor, and the view out of the back door and over fields down to the bay. This place had been mine for nearing ten years, but now it gave itself back more strongly than ever, offering the feeling of belonging. There was a chicken-coop light over the bay, a pollen sky.

'You can have a shower if you want,' said Ros. 'The smell of woodsmoke is very manly, but it's a bit intense in this small space.'

The solar-heated water was warm enough to wash me. I came out towel-wrapped, having no unsmoked clothes, and wandered around the upstairs of Albion Cottage. My small room had a vase of flowers placed on the desk. My books and clothes were in storage at Lyndhurst.

'Did you see what's on the bed?' said Ros, having joined me upstairs. We wandered into her large room. The light spilled in from the south-facing window. On the bed was a quilt of tessellating patches, in autumn colours, radiating out in circles to larger apples, pears and leaves in the corners. 'Beth made that,' she said. 'Isn't it wonderful? She said that it's for good luck. Is it right that they're moving from her little place to a big house owned by a charity for the homeless? – to be wardens, to look after people who get sent over from the homeless centre for the night?'

'Jim didn't tell me that.'

'Maybe it was supposed to be a secret. Beth said he hasn't said yes yet, but she thinks he will.'

'It sounds like Jim.'

'He's such a *caring* man, Juniper; and I used to think he was just a fat bloke.'

I lay on the bed that I'd made myself.

'Were you really going to leave?'

'I still might,' she said, though she was smiling slightly.

We sat in the kitchen and drank more tea once she'd found some clothing I could squeeze into. Then there was knock at the locked back door. I answered it, thinking it might be Harry.

'Juniper!' said Venerable Jagaro. 'Welcome home.'

Author photograph by Maitridevi

acknowledgements

My grateful thanks go first to my parents, Barbara and Richard, who supported me financially and welcomed me home again for a while in 1998-9 when I was writing the first draft.

Thanks to Miranda Potter for copy-editing, and for the gift of Robert Bringhurst's *The Elements of Typographic Style.*

Thanks also to the many friends whose support, inspiration and critical comments have helped the novel on its journey into print, especially Ananda and Manjusvara, Maitridevi, Diane Hopkins, Robert Clark, Rachel Ingrams, George Green, Ajahn Munindo, Ajahn Puñño, Abbot David Charlesworth and Akasadeva.

Printed in the United Kingdom
by Lightning Source UK Ltd.
135170UK00001B/290/P